Praise For
GREG BEAR
and
Anvil of Stars

"Whether he's tinkering with human genetic material or prying apart planets, Bear goes at the task with intelligence and a powerful imagination."

—Locus

"The sequel to his splendid *The Forge of God* . . . displays all of Bear's superior literary gifts."

—Chicago Sun-Times

"Compelling. . . . A major work of the imagination. . . . Transcends the science-fiction genre, making [Bear] a writer for anyone concerned with the human condition."

—Seattle Times/Post-Intelligencer

"A moving and insightful portrait of an emerging society aboard the starship . . . a substantial, inventive, and satisfying coming-of-age novel."

—Locus

more . . .

"This is powerful, well-thought-out science fiction, with believable characters and fascinating science. *Anvil* ponders in new ways some of literature's oldest themes of justice, conscience and even love. . . . *Anvil of Stars* is only the most recent proof of the permanent niche [Bear] has carved for himself in the field."
—*Flint Journal*

"Succeeds because of Bear's ability to create characters the reader can care about . . . a top-notch space war novel."
—*Kansas City Star*

"[A] riveting tale of interplanetary revenge."
—*The Bookwatch*

"An incredible adventure. It's a sequel, but easily stands on its own. It's thought-provoking and maintains an extremely high interest level throughout. What a frantic pace!"
—*Rave Reviews*

"This is a powerful work that is going to make you sit and think for a while, and hopefully disturb you just a little. A powerful hard SF novel from one of the top writers in the field."
—*Amazing Stories*

"Provocative and entertaining . . . an action-packed and often thrilling plot. . . . Bear draws on the full range of his gifts here, seamlessly pulling together action and characterization to create a gripping story."

—Publishers Weekly

"A satisfying sequel to a terrific novel."

—Eastsideweek, **Seattle**

"If, like me, you relish a neutronium-dense blend of Edmond Hamilton and Freeman Dyson, A. E. Van Vogt and Richard Feynmann, you'll risk super-deceleration under volumetric stasis to lay your hands on the latest Bear."

—Washington Post Book World

"*Anvil of Stars* shows him at the top of his form and poses a number of fascinating questions about the true nature of vengeance and what seeking it can do to the human heart. Don't miss it!"

—West Coast Review of Books

"Bear writes with a heady brilliance that communicates a sense of immediacy and credibility."

—Library Journal

GREG BEAR

ANVIL OF STARS

WARNER BOOKS

A Time Warner Company

For Dan Garrett, cousin and friend

WARNER BOOKS EDITION

Questar® is a registered trademark of Warner Books, Inc.

Cover design by Donald Puckey
Cover illustration by Bob Eggleton

Warner Books, Inc.
1271 Avenue of the Americas
New York, NY 10020

W A Time Warner Company

Printed in the United States of America

Originally published in hardcover by Warner Books.
First Printed in Paperback: February, 1993

10 9 8 7 6 5 4 3 2 1

Prolog

AT THE END OF THE FORGE OF GOD, *the Earth is dead, murdered by self-replicating spacefaring machines. A few thousand humans have been saved by other robots, machines sent by the Benefactors to defend primitive worlds and civilizations from the depredations of planet-killing probes. The Benefactor machines have succeeded in wiping out these probes within the solar system, but not before Earth's total destruction.*

Kept aboard a huge Central Ark while Mars is made ready for their habitation, the humans are informed of the Law, a galactic code that governs the behavior of civilizations. The Law demands that civilizations which make self-replicating killer machines be punished—with extinction. Humans must carry out this punishment, with the help of the Benefactors. Younger occupants of the Central Ark volunteer, and their journey begins.

This is how the balance is kept.

PART
ONE

MARTY SITS IN THE FRONT SEAT OF HIS FATHER'S BUICK, RIDING along a freeway in Oregon at midsummer twilight. The highway is thick with cars and rain glazes the road. Gray-blue sky, tail-lights brilliant red, streamers of reflection in wet dark blue road-ways, road reflectors gold, big trucks with running lights and turn signals flashing, windshield wipers streaking all into dazzles and sparks, raindrops reflecting microcosms.

He feels the smooth fur and warmth of his dog, Gauge, pressed between the front seats, paw and jaw resting on Marty's curled knee. "Father," he asks, "is space empty?"

Arthur does not reply. There are no more highways, no more Earth. His father is off the Ark and on Mars by now, far centuries away.

Martin Gordon stirred and tried to wake up. He floated in his net, opened his eyes and unclenched his fists. A single salty tear, sucked into his mouth from the still, cool air, caught in his throat and he coughed, thrashing to complete awareness. In the large, high-ceilinged cabin, beads and snakes of yellow and white light curled along the walls like lanes of cars.

He rolled over in the suddenly strange place. A woman floated in the net beside him, hair dark brown almost black, face pixy with fresh sleep, upturned eyes opening, wide lips always half-smiling. "Are you all right?" she asked.

"I think so," he said. "Dreaming." Martin had been dream-

3

ing a great deal lately, much more since joining with Theresa.
He had been dreaming of Earth; dreams both pleasant and disturbing, four or five each sleep.

"Of what?"

"Earth. My father."

Eight years after Earth's death, the children had left the Central Ark, in orbit around the Sun, and begun their journey on the
Ship of the Law.

Two years after the children's departure, measuring by the
Ark's reference frame, the survivors of Earth who stayed behind
had entered suspended animation, the long sleep.

Two years for the Central Ark had occupied only a year for
the children as the Ship of the Law accelerated to relativistic
speed. Now, cruising at more than ninety-nine percent of the
speed of light, time advanced even more slowly, relative to the
outside universe; six and a half days for every year. Years were
an archaic measure anyway, counted against the revolution of a
world that no longer existed.

If still alive, Martin's mother and father and all the remaining
survivors on the Ark had settled on Mars by now, after almost
three centuries of long sleep.

For Martin and the children, only five years had passed.

Theresa drew closer to him in the single net, curled her arms
around him, made a warm sound in the back of her throat.
"Always the thread," she murmured. She slept again, could fall
asleep so easily.

Martin looked at her, still disoriented. Dissonance between
that past inconceivably far away in all dimensions, and this
woman with her chest moving in and out, eyes flickering in
dreamstate.

The thread, umbilicus of all the children, cut only in death.

"Dark, please," he said, and the ribbon lights dimmed. He
turned away from Theresa, coughed again, seeing behind closed
eyes bright red tail-lights and mystic blue highways.

If the drivers had known how beautiful that traffic jam was,
how lovely that rain, and how few twilight evenings remained.

The Ship of the Law was made of Earth, smelted and assembled
from the fragments of Earth's corpse, a world in itself, cruising

massively close to the speed of light, hundreds of years from the dust and rubble of home.

Christened *Dawn Treader* by the children at the outset of their voyage, the ship resembled a snake that had swallowed three eggs, five hundred meters from nose to tail. Each egg, called a homeball, was one hundred meters in diameter. Between the homeballs, hung around the connecting necks like fruit in baskets, storage tanks held the ship's reserves of volatiles: hydrogen, lithium, helium, nitrogen, oxygen, carbon. Food and fuel.

The first two homeballs belonged to the children, vast spaces divided into a variety of chambers flexible in design and even in size.

Dawn Treader reminded Martin of a large plastic habitat his mother had pieced together in their house in Oregon; two hamsters in a maze of yellow plastic pipes, clear boxes lined with wood shavings, a feeding box and sleeping box and exercise wheel, even what his father had called a "remote excursion module," a plastic ball in which a single hamster could roll outside the habitat, across the floors, carpet, into corners.

The eighty-two children had even more room in proportion to their numbers. There was sufficient space for every Wendy or Lost Boy to have dozens of quarters in the homeballs. Most chose one primary residence, and used two or three others as occasion suited.

The third egg, farthest aft, held training centers and weapons stores. The spaces between the homeballs, the necks, were filled with huge conduits and pipes. The second neck was cramped by protrusions that Martin had long since decided must be part of the ship's engine. How the engine worked, or its location on the ship, had not been explained.

There were a lot of mysteries. Huge but light, most of the *Dawn Treader*'s bulk consisted of what the robot moms called fake matter. Fake matter had the properties of size and resistance to pressure, but no mass. *Dawn Treader* massed little more than twenty-five hundred tons unfueled.

The children trained with weapons whose inner workings they knew next to nothing about. What they did not specifically need to know, they were not told.

The necks—dubbed wormspaces because of the twisty

pipes—were ideal for gymnastics and games, and thirty Lost Boys and Wendys, two cats, and three parrots even now skirmished, using wads of wet clothing as missiles. Sheets of water crawled along the outer wall beneath a transparent field. Shadows lay deep and black everywhere in the wormspaces, offering even more places to hide.

Martin watched his fellows. They might have been part of a street gang in a city robbed of up and down. He breathed in their beauty and harmony, focused on a select few: Hans Eagle of the Raptors, a year older than Martin—oldest on the ship—pug-nosed, broad-shouldered, short-legged, with powerful arms, blond hair cut close and bristly, skin glistening pale; Paola Birdsong, small and graceful, flowing black hair tied up in a waggling long braid; Stephanie Wing Feather, with gentle, intelligent gray eyes, hair wrapped in a compact bun; Rosa Sequoia, large, red-haired, with her characteristic look of puzzled concentration.

The children screamed, hissed, yelled instructions to fellow team-mates, tossed wads of wet clothes, kicked back and forth among the pipes, all but Rosa, who kept apart.

They had been weightless for over four years now. Ladder fields allowed them to get around where it was inconvenient to echo—bounce from the walls and surfaces—or fly, or climb on physical objects. Whenever possible, the children tried to avoid using them. That was part of the game.

Cats bounded between the children, or hid in the shadows. Birds squawked and pretended to be upset; but birds and cats always followed the children, scrambling along ladder fields or gliding free in the air.

Martin puckered his lips and whistled shrilly. Play broke off in a clatter of shouts and jeers and the children gathered, grumpy at being interrupted. The air between the pipes filled with ribbons and sheets of faint light, ladder fields intersecting, like curling thin paper floating in water.

The children formed a ball around Martin. Most were only half-dressed. Four retrieved the wet, wadded clothes.

"Time for pre-watch drill," he said. "The rest can carry on."

Martin had been elected Pan six months before. Pan was in charge of all strategic functions, the most important now being drill planning and crew training. Five previous Pans had commanded the children, beginning with Stephanie Wing Feather.

Rex Live Oak, Stephanie Wing Feather, Nguyen Mountain Lily, Jeanette Snap Dragon, Carl Phoenix, Giacomo Sicilia, David Aurora, Michael Vineyard, Hu East Wind, Kirsten Two Bites, Jacob Dead Sea, Attila Carpathia, Terry Loblolly, Alexis Baikal, Drusilla Norway, Thorkild Lax, Leo Parsifal, Nancy Flying Crow, Yueh Yellow River. These made up the Pan's drill group today; each day, he drilled with a different group. There were five groups. Once a year, the groups reshuffled. Some members with well-honed skills moved from group to group depending on the drills.

The children's skins, yellow and white, brown and black, shone with sweat. Slender and stocky, tall and short, manner not obeisant, not insolent, within the observed forms, they were family and team, forged by five long years into something his mother and father would not have recognized as a useful society, but it worked . . . So far.

The twenty rotated and bounced in mid-air, sliding into damp overalls, Wendys in blue, Lost Boys in red. Dressed, they followed Martin aft through the second neck, toward the third homeball. Behind them, Hans Eagle urged the others to continue the game.

Most of the children wore painted designs, chiefly on their faces and bare arms and legs, patterned after things found on Earth. The designs revealed ship family associations, also reflected in their names: Cats, Places, Birds, Gifts, Plants, Foods, twenty-one families in all. Some chose not to associate, or freelanced, as Hans did, though originally he had belonged to the Birds.

A Pan was required to be more circumspect than other children. Martin came by it naturally; he wore no designs, and had never worn paint, though he belonged in a semi-formal way to the Trees family. Behind him, bulky, strong Rex Live Oak followed with an oak leaf on each cheek; Stephanie Wing Feather carried parrot feathers in her hair; and so on, back through the ranks, climbing through the dim, close spaces of the second neck, dipping hands and toes into ladder fields. They used ladders in the neck to keep discipline before drill. The bunched-up colors of twenty ladders—personally selected shades of red, green, blue and yellow—made a dim rainbow down the neck's clear center aisle, smearing like paint poured down a gutter.

Each child carried a wand, a cylinder of steel and glass about nine inches long and two inches wide, with no buttons or visible moving parts. The wands served as monitors and communicators and gave them access to the ship's mind, the libraries, and to the moms. Nobody knew where the ship's mind or the libraries resided—nobody knew where the moms went when they were not among the children, or even how many moms there actually were.

The wormspaces this far to the rear smelled of water and exercise, but that cleared with the push of air to the ship's aft homeball. Around them, dark protrusions—round-edged cubes, lines of hemispheres, undulating conduits—reflected the light of their passage and their murmurs of conversation. There was always a steady breeze in the wormspaces, cooling and fresh.

The children's sense of smell was acute, and even slight differences in odor were apparent. They knew each other by smell as well as by sight. The children had not known colds since the first few weeks on the Ark; there was nothing in the *Dawn Treader* to cause allergic reactions, except the cats and birds, and for one reason or another they did not.

Their physical health was perfect. They did not suffer ill effects from weightlessness. Minor wounds healed quickly. Wendys did not get pregnant.

For five years the children had been training and drilling, at first under the steady tutelage of the moms, then, as their social structure became solid, under their own leaders and appointed teachers. At the start of the voyage, the children had been divided into four teams: navigation, planning, crew maintenance, and search. Martin had been placed in charge of navigation and had learned the techniques of controlling ship motion.

After the first few months, however, navigation became unnecessary or routine. The *Dawn Treader* was largely self-directed, and the children all knew that much of the work was for their own benefit. Emphasis had then been switched to drill and study; Martin had become more interested in crew maintenance and the search team.

The Job they trained for was at once simple to express and almost too large to understand: if and when they located the civilization that had made the machines that destroyed Earth—the Killers—they would pass judgment and carry out the Law. The core of the Law had been translated for the children at the beginning of their training: "All intelligences responsible for or associated with the manufacture of self-replicating and destructive devices will be destroyed." The message had dug deep, expressing in stiff, cold words the hatred and need they all felt. The Law was administrated by an alliance of civilizations, the Benefactors, that built machines to search out the Killers' machines, to thwart them and destroy them, and to track down their makers.

The Law required that some of Earth's survivors partake in the hunt and the destruction. *To those who killed the Earth: beware her children!*

Destroying an advanced civilization was a daunting task, even with the weapons contained within the Ship of the Law. Still, it was possible for the small and relatively simple to destroy the large, the powerful, and the complex. The moms had taught them tactics and general strategies; how to use the weapons, and how to avoid direct encounters with superior defenses.

But the moms had not told them everything they wanted to know, and as time progressed, the lack of trust or confidence or whatever it might be called rankled many of the children.

Martin tried not to question. He tried not to think too deeply; to lose himself in the drills and the training, and to concentrate on being a good Pan.

Still, the dreams came, and memories of Theodore Dawn. Theodore had been a good friend to Martin, practically his only friend in the beginning. Witty, learned, Theodore had spent hours alone with Martin, talking. Martin had helped Theodore study vats of terrestrial pond water, the little micro-organisms and crustaceans and insect larvae supplied from the ship's biological records.

But two years into the journey, Theodore had used a ladder

field to hang himself and the moms had not tried to stop him. Freedom of choice.

The moms did not discipline the children or issue direct orders; nor did they protect the children from themselves.

If we all tried to kill ourselves, would they intervene? What if we went to war with each other?

Three children had committed suicide since the journey began. Once they had numbered eighty-five.

Martin in the lead, thoughtful and quiet, they emerged into the center of the third homeball. Here the lighting was bright as a sunny day, lines and spots of warm luminosity varying in angles and brightness as they progressed toward the weapons stores.

For the last three years, they had been training in the actual vessels they would use in a real encounter. They had not yet ventured outside the ship for external flight and were confined to the hemisphere of the weapons stores, training with simulations. The simulations were convincing, but the children were beginning to grumble. Martin felt their frustration acutely. How long must they wait to actually fly?

"Fall to," Martin said. The group broke line to form a hemisphere behind him. "Here's today." He slaved their wands to his and each child saw what he had planned a few hours earlier. "We'll be dealing with an offense, kinetic weapons with passive tracking, ambush near-planet. The planet is a gas giant, and we're taking the *Dawn Treader* into a graze to refuel."

Graphics projected by his wand illustrated the procedures. They had performed this drill before; it used maneuvers necessary to other scenarios and was good general exercise.

"Let's do it. Four hours' training today, triple squeeze."

The children groaned; triple squeeze condensed drill time by two thirds. It was exhausting; it also got them out sooner, and Martin needed to make his tenday report to the moms before the communal dinnertime.

The weapons locker was a broad blister on the port side of the third homeball. Martin led his group to the wide bulkhead separating the locker from the rest of the homeball. He drifted to a smooth, unmarked, curved wall and the wall opened to a circle, exhaling a sigh of colder air. Stephanie smiled at Martin and swept her arm forward magnanimously. "You first, Pan," she said. Martin laddered into the cavernous space beyond.

All piloted weapons were stored here, and all the smaller remotes and other mobile equipment. Martin glanced up at the interior. When weightless, "up" was pointing forward or away from a door in all directions; "down" the direction of a door or neck, or pointing aft. One came up into a room, down out of a room, up into the ship's nose, or down to the third homeball.

Inside the locker, smaller bubbles of gray spotted the pale gray and brown walls like sporangia on fern leaves. The comparison was apt; these held millions of tiny robots, makers and doers, some the size of microbes, some a meter wide, most no larger than a human fingernail. Makers could burrow deep into a moon or planetary surface and create weapons of mass destruction out of the raw materials available. Doers could insinuate themselves into many kinds of machinery and break them down.

At the end of pylons or snared in pale fields hung matte gray tubes three meters thick and ten to twenty meters long. Gray ovoids, saucers and sausage-packed spiked cylinders five to twenty-five meters across were stacked double and triple, gripped by fields wrapped around pylons.

Entering the locker, Martin always felt as if he had walked into a sculpture hall dedicated to geometric abstractions, or onto a microscope slide of plankton and bacteria magnified huge. The style—if one could think of a style with regard to such simple shapes—was the same as the style Martin had come to associate with the moms, the Central Ark, and the general design of the *Dawn Treader*: utilitarian, muted basic colors, a subdued raw metal appearance for all surfaces.

Martin counted the piloted weapons stored here: not including those hidden in the blisters, there were ninety separate pieces.

"Let's study," Stephanie said, swinging down from the middle of the ranked weapons. They gathered at their craft.

The bombships and rifles opened their sides with soft hisses. The children deftly kicked themselves into the cockpits. Ladders vanished once the hatches smoothed shut. Martin entered his rifle last, feeling the soft interior conform to his shape.

"This craft belongs to Martin Spruce," the rifle told him. The children knew the voice of the moms, warmly impersonal, craft voices cool and technical, and ship's voice, rarely heard, soft and pleasant, not quite feminine. Martin believed they were actually all the same, but that was one of the questions not answered.

"All wands slaved to your wand, simulation drill," the craft voice told him. "May we draw the simulation plan from your wand?"

"Yes," Martin said.

The simulation began. The craft did not move from their docked positions. The children became enmeshed in the drill, and time passed.

They skimmed the cloud tops of a gas giant planet three times larger than Jupiter, while the Ship of the Law grazed the atmosphere ahead of them, wrapped in plasma friction fire. The *Dawn Treader*'s wing-like scooping fields dragged huge gouts of atmospheric hydrogen and methane and ammonia from the thick atmosphere, slowing the ship at dozens of g's, torquing it tail over nose, and the smaller weapons sped ahead of the ship, encountering enemy craft, setting up a circuit of protection, drawing the attention of kinetic weapons designed to smash into them at high speed, using the roiling energies of the fireball created by the *Dawn Treader*'s passage to deflect energy beams . . .

As usual, they did well.

They had done well at this sort of drill for years now. It was second nature to them. It had also become a kind of game, difficult to connect to reality, to the actual performance of the Job itself. However convincing the simulations—and they were very convincing—they no longer expanded the children's skills.

Still, they drilled tenday after tenday, year after year . . .

Growing older. Martin could feel their impatience, and it worried him.

He was responsible. He had been Pan for six months.

Martin laddered deep past the pipes and conduits in the long first neck of the Ship of the Law, going to the forward homeball and the schoolroom to meet with a mom and report for the tenday.

Aboard the *Dawn Treader* there were twenty-eight hours to each day, three tendays in a month, twelve months in a year.

Once each tenday, it was Martin's duty as Pan to report to the mom. To tell what the children had been up to, and listen if the mom had anything to say.

He completed his climb through the neck, into the homeball and down a long cylindrical corridor to the homeball's center. His ladder field stopped at a wide hatch; he kicked away and grabbed a metal pole within, swinging gracefully until the friction of his hand stopped him.

The schoolroom periphery was cool and dark. Light from the corridor cut at an angle and made a spot on the opposite curved wall.

Martin had arrived fifteen minutes early. He was alone.

Under weightless conditions, the schoolroom took a shape like the empty interiors of two wheels run through each other, sharing a common center, axes perpendicular. Twenty meters below, at the hub of the schoolroom, the homeball's center, hung a spherical blackness filled with stars, a window to what lay outside the ship—but not directly viewed; like so much else in their life, a simulation.

At the ship's present speed, the universe outside the *Dawn Treader* did not much resemble this pretty simulation. Outside the true stars were gnarled and twisted, rotated and compressed into a scintillating ring that flexed around the ship like a loose bracelet, blue on one side—the direction in which they flew— and red on the other, with a muddy and narrow mix of colors between. Ahead lay a pit empty to the unaided eye but in fact filled with hard radiation; behind, another pit, touched with weird sparkles of red-shifted X-ray sources, distant galaxies dying or being reshaped, dead stars ghoulishly eating their young.

The starry sky in the sphere appeared little different than it had on Earth, unless Martin looked for familiar constellations. None were visible; the *Dawn Treader* had traveled too far. Associations of the brightest stars had changed radically.

He took his wand from a pocket and let it hang in the air, floating beside him in the warm twilight. Martin and the wand precessed slowly, blown by idle air currents. Martin reached out with a finger and wrote two names large in the air: *Theresa, William*. The names glowed pink and electric blue, respectively.

Under *Theresa*, Martin used his index finger to write *I've*

*lived with or near you for five years, but only in the past tenday
have I known what I feel for you. What you feel for me. Odd
how we haven't come together until now! I think of you always.
I miss you when I am not near, even just a few minutes away.
It's not just physical wanting, though there is that, and it is
almighty powerful, but a kinship, a matching like two molecules
meeting in just the right way, and that is strange, because that
is how I have often thought of God. I hope you don't think this
is all too intense; but perhaps it is through you, our love, that I
really feel God. Don't be afraid. I haven't lost it. But can you
tell me why we have not felt this before, have not known it until
now? So fast!*

The glowing message beneath *Theresa* shimmered slightly:
the wand querying whether he wished to continue or quit and
send. He lifted his finger again and wrote more:

*I've told William, and he approves, or at least he does not
tell me he objects. I know that you do not detract from our
friendship, though I feel less free with him now, but he knows
or intuits what there is between us, you and me, and that makes
him wiser than I. He is a noble spirit. I realize your reluctance
to break up a dyad that seems so stable, but you cannot take
away from us what is most important. William and I are brothers,
as I never had a brother. You cannot break that, and you cannot
replace it.*

*I send you this, because I miss you even when I am on duty,
and there is a short time here before I report to the mom.*

*I feel so naïve but my love for you is more intense than any
positive emotion I have felt until now, and I want you to know
that.*

He read the message through several times and winced at its
awkwardness, its revelation. Even among the children Martin
was reluctant to open himself so. He felt like a boy again, though
at twenty-two he was one of the oldest on the *Dawn Treader*.
Theresa was three years younger; William, a year younger.

"Send," he said, and the message and Theresa's name vanished, leaving *William* hanging alone. The name flickered. "I'm
thinking," Martin told the wand. Could he really remain involved with William, when he focused so much attention on
Theresa?

Irony here. Throughout the voyage he had tried to keep above the play of emotions, to maintain his dignity, finally joining in a dyad with William because he could not resist the pressure to make some tie, and William seemed safest, and they did match.

Because of his aloofness, Martin had gained both respect and isolation; he had been voted sixth Pan of the Watch, an important position, and then (it seemed inevitable now, understanding the venery associated with position and power) the Wendys had courted him, and he had dallied; that was expected. William did not object, in fact fantasized of what *he* would do when he became Pan.

Martin had lost his shield; and flirting with Theresa—initially innocent sex—had plunged him deep into what he had avoided for so long. It had to happen.

Still in him lingered fear of loving and losing, not just through separation, but through death. All of them had known the same losses—Earth itself, great Mother of all they knew and were; then separation from family and friends on the Ark.

They were more than children sent on a time-bent crusade; they were avenging angels, soldiers trained but not yet tested, given access to incredible power they did not completely understand. Eventually they would use that power if they were to fulfill their mission, and some of them would not survive.

As for William, Martin had nothing to say to him that he could not say better in person. "Fade," he instructed. The name vanished. He raised his arms and crooked a finger and a thin ladder of green light crossed the periphery. He pointed his finger and the light flowed, broke up, and reformed, spanning one wheel of the schoolroom and intersecting the star sphere.

Martin poked his hands and feet into the plane and pushed himself ahead, drifted lazily around the sphere, viewing the stars from many angles. Folded his arms and drew up his long, thin legs to wait for the mom.

Martin had inherited his father's physique and his father's long, grim face; he also had his father's sweetness of temper and sharpness of mind. But his almond eyes and his sensuous, full lips over protruding front teeth were his mother's.

A mom entered from below and moved up silently beside him, a squat flattened cylinder about a meter tall, copper and tarnished brass, with a head-like bump but no features, no arms, and no legs.

"I am ready for your report," the mom said. The mom's voice was authoritative but not shrill or insistent. It never demanded, never ordered, merely instructed and guided. A mom always referred to itself in the first person, as did the ship's mind on the rare occasions it was heard from. The children had no evidence, other than tone of voice, that ship and moms were any different.

"We're doing okay," Martin said. "The children all seem healthy, physically." He looked away. "There's some tension with four or five individuals who aren't getting along with the rest. Rex Live Oak has troubles now and then. A few others. I'm keeping track and trying to work them back into the group. Rosa Sequoia's the worst. She attends the meetings, does her drills, hangs around when we play games, but she has few friends now. She doesn't even talk with the Wendys much.

"Exercises are going well. We've been simulating small-craft navigation in planetary space, orbits and evasive maneuvers, ship's defense, shepherding makers and doers. I guess you know that."

"Yes," the mom said.

His neck grew stiff. Here it came. "I'd like to see some outside exercise. The real thing. I think we're ready."

This was the third time he had made such a suggestion in his six months as Pan. All the children were anxious to get outside the *Dawn Treader* in the craft they had been training to use. "Five and a half years is a long time. We've come a long way. We know it might take much longer, but . . . We're impatient."

"Understood," the mom said. "Continue."

"I suppose we're growing up, more mature. There's less upset . . . not as much squabbling about sexual stuff. Fewer arguments and noise. I talked about this last tenday."

"These are all expected events."

"Well, they're still significant," Martin said, irritated by the mom's attitude, or non-attitude. "I'm trying to use this . . . calmness, whatever, to help us focus on the training. It's working, a little, anyway. We're doing better in the trials. But there's still grumbling about how well informed we are. I'd like to suggest fuller participation. I've suggested that before."

"Yes," the mom said.

"That's about it. Nothing spectacular."

"I see no signs of major trouble. You are doing well."

With a characteristic lack of the minutiae of social grace, the mom glided from the schoolroom along its own unseen ladder field.

Martin puffed his cheeks, blew out a breath, and turned to leave, then spotted Hakim Hadj in the doorway below.

Hakim moved aside for the mom's passage and spread his ladder to where Martin waited by the star sphere.

"Hello, Pan Martin," Hakim said. He climbed to within a couple of meters of Martin and assumed a floating lotus. "How are you today?"

"As usual," Martin said. He bit his lower lip and gestured at the door with an unenthused hand. "The usual friendly brick wall."

"Ah yes." Leader of the search team, Hakim was shorter than Martin by seven or eight centimeters, with smooth brown skin, a thin sharp nose, and large confident eyes black as onyx. He spoke English with a strong hint of Oxford, where his father had gone to school.

To see Hakim blink was a wonder; his face conveyed centuries of equanimity in the midst of strife, his lips composed a genial and unjudging line. "I am glad to hear it."

He had taught Martin Arabic a few years before, enough for him to read Arabic children's books from the libraries, but the lingua franca of the *Dawn Treader* was English, as it had been aboard the Central Ark, Earth's death having frozen the American moment in history.

"The search team may have a suspect," Hakim said. "I would like to present the evidence to you, and then to the moms. If you do not agree, we will keep our thoughts from the moms until better evidence comes along." Hakim was usually cautious and taciturn to a fault about the search team's work.

Martin arranged himself in a less graceful lotus before him. "I just gave my tenday report . . ."

Hakim apologized. "We cannot be certain enough to render final judgment—but there is sufficient evidence that we believe the ship should send out remotes . . ." He caught himself, apologized again, and said, "But that is your decision, Martin."

Martin said, "No offense taken, Hakim."

"I am glad. We have found a stellar group of three stars less than a light-year from our present position. The spectra of the two contain a mix of trace radioactive elements and rare earths in proportions similar to those in the remains of the captured killer machines."

Hakim presented the facts for Martin with his wand; they appeared to float before him, or he among them, words and images and icons and charts, a visual language created by the moms. Martin had become used to this method of teaching on the Ark; now he took it in stride.

At the center of the displays hung diagrams of three stellar systems. Figures surrounding the diagrams told him that these stars were no more than a trillion kilometers from each other.

The moms used stellar classifications based on mass, diameter, luminosity, age, and percentages of "metals," elements heavier than hydrogen and helium. Martin was more used to this scale than the one that would have been familiar to his father. The children had converted some of the moms' technical terms to more informal language: Thus, the closest star was a Buttercup Seven, about nine tenths the mass and diameter of Sol, bright yellow, relatively high in metals. The second closest was a Cornflower Two, one and a half times Sol's mass, with a lower percentage of metals. The third star in the group was an aging Firestorm Three, a brilliant bloated red giant. The Buttercup Seven had four planets, two of them peculiar, diminished gas giants.

Hakim noticed his interest in these worlds. "They are substantially smaller than might be expected—evidence of gas mining, perhaps," he said.

Martin frowned. Tough to refuel the Ship of the Law in a system that had already been tapped out by an old civilization.

Two rocky planets hugged close to the Buttercup Seven. In addition, there were several—perhaps as many as five—invisible bodies close to the star. Together, they might have added up to the mass of Earth's moon.

The Cornflower Two, a pale yellow giant, had ten planets, two of them apparent gas giants. The Firestorm Three was surrounded only by small rubble; at some ninety million kilometers in diameter, it could have swallowed several planets when it ballooned.

Numbers flickered in and out of his awareness; his eyes shifted around the display, picking out what he needed to know.

Martin examined the intrinsic spectra of the stars. There were intriguing diffraction patterns, unnatural ratios of infra-red versus other frequencies. A technological civilization had been at work around at least two of the stars, the Buttercup and the Cornflower.

"How long ago did the Firestorm balloon?" he asked.

"We estimate five thousand years," Hakim said.

"Did they armor?"

"The civilization around the Buttercup apparently armored. We have no direct evidence yet for the Cornflower."

"But they haven't built an all-absorbing envelope . . ."

"No," Hakim agreed. An envelope around each star—a Dyson construct of multiple orbiting structures surrounding the star in many layers—would have reduced the stellar images to heat-waste, dull infra-red only. Martin checked the information available on the interstellar particle fluxes surrounding the stars—the stellar winds—and felt a tickle of apprehension.

The Ship of the Law was one point eight trillion kilometers from the nearest, the Buttercup. Martin reached out to touch a glowing geometric shape pulsing slowly next to the star images. The shape unfolded like a flower into a series of pentagonal petals. He touched the petals in sequence until he had the information he desired. "The Buttercup may have large structures in orbit, besides these five dark masses. You think that's sign of armoring?"

Hakim nodded. Martin summoned and inspected occultations, spectrum variability, brightness fluctuations. He called up absorption spectra for the stellar atmosphere, outer stellar envelope and "wind" of particles, and planetary atmospheres.

The Ship of the Law had not sent out its remotes, and the

information he received obviously came from angles and distances not their own.

"I have obtained this additional information from the moms, three months ago," Hakim said, as if reading his thoughts. "They've kept watch on this group for a long time. Perhaps thousands of years."

The Benefactor machines that had destroyed the Killers around Sol had collected a fragment of a killer probe and analyzed its composition, checking for minute traces of radioactive elements and proportions of other elements. Martin thought it likely the Benefactor machines knew the characteristics of populations of stars for thousands of light years around Sol, and had sent the *Dawn Treader* in a direction likely to encounter stars matching the suspected origins of the killer probes. *Perhaps the moms know even more . . .*

Martin suddenly didn't like being alone with Hakim in the schoolroom, talking about such things. He wanted the others to share his responsibility and back his conclusions. He wanted a mom present. "How about the assay?" he asked, swallowing too noisily.

"You can refer to it."

He flushed, touched another shape marked with a spinning atom symbol, and it blossomed. The comparison between the probe's composition and the Buttercup's stellar spectra and estimated planetary makeup was close. The killer machines *could* have been manufactured in this system.

Additional information came up beneath his questing fingers. Four other inhabited worlds within two hundred and ninety light years of the group had been attacked and transformed by killer probes, all within the past thousand years. There were one million three hundred thousand stars within this radius, or roughly one star for every seventy-eight and a half cubic light years. Four civilizations had been murdered, five including the Earth; only two besides the Earth had left any survivors.

And where are those survivors? On other Ships of the Law?

The four victim stars lay within a hypothetical sphere determined by the density of stars within the possible paths of killer probes, and complex analyses of how often those probes would reproduce, and how quickly they would saturate such a sphere.

The center of the sphere was within two light years of this group of three, Buttercup, Cornflower, Firestorm.

Hakim had been through this material already, and with growing excitement, embellished details he thought might not be obvious.

"All right," Martin said. His hand shook. He controlled it. "It seems . . . interesting."

Hakim smiled and nodded once, then watched intently while Martin perused the data again.

On Earth, Martin's father had compared the attempt to destroy killer probes to the murder of Captain Cook by distrustful Hawaiians. To the islanders, Cook had been the powerful representative of a more technologically advanced civilization.

If Earth's Killers lived around one or more of these stars, the Ship of the Law would be up against a civilization so advanced that it controlled two or perhaps even three star systems, commanding the flux of an entire star, perhaps even capable of armoring that star against the expansion of a red giant.

If this was the home of Earth's Killers, the children's task would be much more difficult than just killing Captain Cook.

Such adversaries could be as far beyond human intellect as Martin had been beyond his dog Gauge, long dead, powder and ashes around distant Sol.

"The assay match is . . . I won't say unique," Hakim said softly as Martin's thoughtful silence lengthened. "Other stars in this portion of the spiral arm might share it, having come from the same segment of old supernova cloud. But it's very close. Did you see the potassium-argon ratios? The iridium concentrations?"

Martin nodded, then lifted his head and said, "It does look good, Hakim. Fine work."

"Tough decision, first time," Hakim said, awaiting his reaction.

"I know," Martin said. "We'll take it to the children first, then to the moms."

Hakim sighed and smiled. "So it is."

The call went out to all the wands, and the children gathered in clusters, a full meeting, the first in Martin's six months as Pan.

A few glued on to Martin's trail as he laddered forward to the first homeball. Three cats and four parrots joined as well, using the children's ladders to scramble after them into the schoolroom.

George Dempsey, a plump boy of nineteen from the Athletes family, came close to Martin and beamed a smile. Dempsey read muscles and expressions better than most of his fellows. "Good news?"

"We may have a candidate," Martin said.

"Something new and startling, not a drill?" asked small, mouse-like Ginny Chocolate, of the Food family. She spoke twenty Earth languages and claimed she understood the moms better than any of them. Ginny cradled a tabby in her arms. It watched Martin with beautiful jade eyes and meowed silently.

"A high-tech civ," Martin said. "Search team has a presentation." Ginny spun on her tummy axis and kicked from a conduit, flying ahead of him, towing the relaxed cat by its tail. She did not make much speed, deliberately choosing a low-traction ladder field, and the rest quickly caught up, dancing, bouncing, climbing, putting on overalls and stuffing other clothes into knapsacks.

"We're the lucky ones, hm?" Hans Eagle asked him as they matched course in the first neck. Hans served as Christopher Robin, second in command. Martin had chosen Hans because the children responded well to his instructions. Hans was strong, well liked, and kept a reserve Martin found intriguing.

"We'll see," Martin said.

By the specified time, there were eighty in the schoolroom, two missing. Martin summoned faces quickly and sorted through names, then spoke into his wand, to connect with their wands and remind them of the summons: "William Arrow Feather, Erin Eire." He had seen neither of them in the wormspaces. He felt a pang of guilt and wondered what William was doing, ignoring his wand summons; that was uncharacteristic. *Because of me?*

Rosa was present, bulky, red hair in tangles, large arms and fists. She was almost as tall as Hans.

Theresa was there, as well, hiding in the middle ranks, short black hair and small, strong frame immediately drawing Martin's eye. The sight of her made him feel hollow in his chest.

How long had it been since he last saw her? Barely seven hours . . . Yet she was discreet, expressionless but for a slight widening of the eyes when he looked directly at her. She did not show any sign of the passion they had shared.

Others in the crowd Martin hadn't seen in weeks.

Each carried the brand of dead Earth in memory; all had seen Earth die, that hours-long agony of incandescence and orbiting debris. Some had been only four or five years old; their memories were expressed more often in nightmares than in conscious remembrance. Marty had been nine.

This was the Job and they all took it seriously.

Martin called Hakim forward. Hakim used his wand to display the group of three close stars and what information they had. He concluded with the analysis of planet deaths near the group.

"We have to make a decision to launch remotes," Martin said. "We can gather a lot more information with a wide baseline. We also become a little more conspicuous. Our first decision is whether to take the risk now . . ."

"The moms should let us know what they think," Ariel Hawthorn said from across the schoolroom. "We're still not being told everything. We can't make final decisions before we know . . ." Ariel Hawthorn did not appear to like Martin; Martin assumed she did not like any of the Lost Boys, but he knew very little about her sexual tastes. She was irritable and opinionated; she was also smart.

"We shouldn't waste time on that now," Martin said.

"If we're going to make a decision that involves risk, we can't afford to be wrong," Ariel pursued.

Martin hid his exasperation. "Let's not—"

"You're only going to be Pan this watch," Ariel said sharply. "The next Pan should have a say, as well."

"If we make the judging on this watch, Martin will be Pan until we finish the Job," Hans reminded her.

Ariel shot a withering look at Hans. "We should select a new Pan to lead us into the Job," she said. "That should be our right."

"That's not procedure. We're wasting time," Hans said softly.

"Fuck you, Farley!" Ariel exploded.

"Out," Martin said. "Need a Wendy to second the motion."

"Second," said Paola Birdsong, lifting large calm eyes.

"One hour in the wormspaces," Martin said.

Ariel shrugged, stretched with a staccato popping of joints, and climbed out of the schoolroom.

"You'll talk with her after, won't you?" Paola asked softly, not pushing.

Martin did not answer for a moment, ashamed. *Pans should be calm, should never discipline out of anger*. "I'll tell her what we decide," he said.

"She has to decide, too. If it's a close vote, you'll ask her for her opinion, won't you?"

"Of course," Martin said. He did not think it was going to be a close vote. They were all impatient; this was a strong suspect.

"You'll work out your differences, won't you?" Paola pursued. "Because you're Pan now. You can't be out with her. That cuts."

"I'll talk," Martin said. He lifted the wand again. "We know enough to decide whether to release remotes. We can do the figuring ourselves. And I think we should all do it now."

The math was complex and did not guarantee an absolute answer. The possibility of detection when they issued the remotes—very slight at this distance—had to be weighed against the probability that this group contained the star or stars they were looking for.

Martin closed his eyes and ran through the figures yet again, using the techniques the moms had taught him, harnessing their inborn ability to judge distances and speeds, algorithms normally not accessible to the intellect, but far more powerful than higher, conscious calculation. The children had decided to call the new techniques momerath, suggested by Lewis Carroll and, some claimed, short for *Mom's Arithmetic Math*.

Martin blanked all thoughts and fell into contemplation of a convergence of spaces and planes, saddles and hills, balls rolling across territories and joining in colored pools.

What Martin visualized when he had finished his momerath, almost as clearly as if his wand projected it, was the group of three stars and a synoptic of the most important local stars. Systems that had been exploited by outside visitors flashed bright red; systems that had probably been explored, but not altered, flashed hot pink; systems showing no signs of external interference flashed green. Ships of the Law did not show up in the mental picture. They never did; the moms could not know where they were.

The children finished their momerath within minutes of each other. Jennifer Hyacinth and Giacomo Sicilia opened their eyes and glanced at Martin first. They were the sharpest at momerath, or any kinds of math and physics theory. They were followed by Stephanie Wing Feather, Harpal Timechaser, Cham Shark, Hans Eagle, and then the others. The last was Rosa Sequoia, but she did complete the work.

Five had difficulty and said, "Not clear." That was normal; they would not participate in the voting.

Hans as Christopher Robin did the counting as each raised two hands or none. He made a quick recount, and everyone lowered their hands.

"Fifty-two aye, twenty-two nay, five outs, three not present," Hans reported. "Pan calls it now."

"This is our first decision," Martin said. "I'll ask the moms to release the remotes. If the stars still look suspect, our next decision will be whether to go in closer, whether to enter the systems . . ." Some children stretched and groaned. They saw a long, boring process, rather than quick action. "We have to be sure. If we go into a —"

"We know," Paola Birdsong said. They knew it all by heart. *If we go into a civilized stellar system, we are in danger. All sufficiently advanced civilizations arm themselves. Not all systems subscribe to the Law. Not all know about the Law.*

The occupants of this group of stars did not know about or subscribe to the Law.

"But for now, the decision is to release the remotes. That's a start."

Martin looked around the assembled faces in the schoolroom. All solemn; the impatience and irritation had been replaced by anticipation and barely hidden anxiety. They had been traveling for five and a half years. This was the first time they had actually made a decision, the first time the search team had come up with a likely prospect.

"This is no drill, Martin? You're sure?" Ginny Chocolate asked with a quaver.

"No drill," Martin confirmed.

"What do we do now?"

"We wait and we practice," Hans said.

Most of the group raised both arms. Others sat in stunned silence.

"Time to grow up," Paola said, patting Martin's arm. Martin wrapped one arm around her and squeezed her. Theresa shot him a glance. No jealousy—he was being Pan, reassuring them all.

Martin released Paola, touched Theresa gently in passing— she smiled, caressed his shoulder—and they parted to go aft. He wanted more than anything to be with her, to get away from this responsibility, but they wouldn't get together for hours yet.

About ten went with Hans to exercise in the wormspaces. The rest vanished into their private places in the expansive maze of halls, spaces and chambers. Two birds stayed behind, preening themselves, floating with claws curled on nothing.

Martin had three errands now: speaking to Ariel to bring her back into the group as best he could, and then finding and speaking with William and Erin Eire.

By the time he had finished with them, Theresa would be attending a Wendys party in the first homeball, and that would keep them apart for additional hours.

In the farthest depths of the ship, where the *Dawn Treader*'s tail tapered to a point, among the great dark smooth shapes that had never been explained, Martin found Ariel floating in a loosely curled ball, seemingly asleep.

"You and I aren't getting along too well," he said. She opened her eyes and blinked coldly.

"You're a moms freak," she said. "You swim in it, don't you?"

Martin tried not to react to her anger. Still, he wondered why she had ever been chosen from the Central Ark volunteers, years past; she was the least cooperative, the most stubborn, and often the most assertive.

"I'm sorry. You know our group rules. I'll be just as glad as you when I'm not Pan. Maybe you should try—"

"I'm sick of it," she interrupted, curling her legs into a lotus. "We're nothing but puppets. Why did they bring us out here in the first place? They could do everything by themselves. How can we help them? *Don't you see that it sucks?*"

Martin felt her words like a slap. Still, he was Pan; he had to keep his calm or at least not let her see how angry he was. "It's not easy. We all volunteered."

"I volunteered without being told what I was in for," Ariel said.

"You were told," Martin said dubiously.

"We were *children*. We were playing glory games. Out for quick revenge. They're asking us to get serious now, and we don't even know why . . . Because they won't tell us everything."

"They haven't asked us to do anything yet. Hakim's team found the group—"

"The moms have been watching those stars for thousands of years. Don't you *know* that?"

Martin swallowed and looked away. "They're telling us all we need to know."

Ariel smiled bitterly and shook her head. "They sent us out this way deliberately, to track these stars. Now they're going to use us to kill somebody, or get ourselves killed," she said. "I'm not alone. Others think this is shit, too."

"But you're the only one with the guts to come forward," he said. He felt he had to leave soon or lose his temper completely.

She regarded him with nothing quite so strong as hate; more like pity, as if he were a mindless demagogue not responsible for his actions.

"I'm not alone," she said. "You remember that. We have our . . . doubts about all this. The moms had damn well better do something about it."

"Or what, Ariel? You'll leave?"

"No," she said. "Don't be an ass, Martin. I'll opt out for good. I'll kill myself."

His eyes widened. She turned away from his shock and pushed

out from a curved cylinder mounted to an interior conduit. "Don't worry about blood on your watch. I'm giving them time. I still hope we can do what we came out here to do. But my hope is fading fast. They have to tell us all, Martin."

"You know that they won't," Martin said.

"I don't know that, and why shouldn't they?" She turned around and echoed back, coming on like a slow tiger, extending her ladder field and hooking to a stop just seconds before they collided.

Martin did not flinch. "The Benefactors have a home, too. They come from somewhere."

"No shit," Ariel said.

"Hear me out, please. You asked."

She nodded. "All right."

"If the whole galaxy is full of wolves, no bird peeps, not even eagles. The moms need to protect their makers. If we knew all about the Benefactors, in a few hundred years, a few thousand years, we might become wolves, too. Then we'd know where they were, and we'd come and get them."

"That is so . . . cynical," Ariel said. "If they are so worried about us, why did they save us at all?"

This was a question with many answers, none of them completely convincing. They had all debated the point, and Martin had never been satisfied with any of the answers, but he tried to put his best theories into words.

"They believe in a balance," he said. "Whoever they are, they made the Ships of the Law to keep single civilizations from scouring the galaxy and having it all to themselves. Maybe it started out as self-defense—"

"Maybe that's all it is now," Ariel said.

"But they must believe that we'll contribute something eventually, when we're grown up."

Ariel blew out her breath.

"The moms tell us all that they can. They tell us what we need to know. We could never avenge the Earth without them. You know that. There's no reason to hate the moms."

"I don't hate them," Ariel said.

"We have work to do, a lot of decisions and thinking. I'd like us all to be together."

"I won't disappoint anybody," Ariel said.

"Please don't talk about killing yourself. It's stupid."

She looked at him with narrowed eyes. "It's the only thing that's really mine, out here. Leave me that much."

"I'm not taking anything from you," Martin said softly. His anger had flown, replaced by a cavernous awareness of what they were heading toward, what they were planning to do. "I ask nothing of you that you didn't volunteer to do."

"How could we know what we'd lose?"

Martin shook his head. "We've never had a chance to be people, much less to be *children*. We're a long way from a home that doesn't exist any more. We won't grow much older until after we do the Job. If we go back to the solar system, thousands of years will have passed for them. We'll be strangers. That's not just true of you, it's true of all of us. We need to stick together."

She seemed startled.

What kind of blind, unfeeling monster does she think I am? "We never will be children," he concluded. "Come on, Ariel. We don't need to lose any more, and I don't need threats."

"Why didn't the moms stop them?" she asked plaintively.

Martin shook his head. "They don't want us to be cattle, or zoo animals. Maybe that's it. I don't know. We have as much freedom as they can give us, even the freedom to die."

"We're getting so sad," Ariel said, looking away from him. "It's been so long."

Martin swallowed hard. "I . . ."

"Go, please," she said.

He pushed away abruptly and bounced from wall to conduit to wall, then summoned a field and climbed up the length of the neck toward the second homeball, where William kept his quarters.

"Why weren't you in the meeting?" Martin worked to keep his voice level. William Arrow Feather twisted within his corner net, pulled himself out, and nudged his head against a climbing field summoned with a mudra-like hand signal.

"I didn't want to make things tougher for you."

"You're supposed to be present for Job discussions," Martin said. "And you didn't vote."

William smiled and shrugged. "No harm. I got the info. I can make my decision for the big one." His expression shifted slightly. "Have you made yours?"

"We're going to investigate—"

"Not that," William said. "*That* was a foregone conclusion. I mean, have you decided who you are, what you are?"

"I don't understand," Martin said.

"It's important for you." William looked away. "And for Theresa."

"I thought you approved."

"I said I approved, but then we made love again, for the first time since you started this thing with Theresa—and I saw things a little differently."

Martin settled grimly in an opposite corner, as if he were about to be forced to take medicine. "Explain."

"Your heart wasn't in it."

"I've always enjoyed you."

"Martin, how many lovers have you had?"

Martin looked away. "I'm not a fruitpicker," he said.

"Right. You're not shy, you're just a little afraid . . . of hurting somebody, of being hurt."

"Wise William," Martin said.

"Slick that," William said, not unkindly. "You picture me as some sort of brotherly saint, Saint Francis maybe. I'm not. I'm a fruitpicker. Most of us are. You . . . and Theresa . . . are not."

"She's had and been had," Martin said, eyes rolling.

"Right. But nowhere near the average."

"More than I," Martin said. Weak defense.

"So how many have you had?"

William had never asked before; such things were seldom mentioned, being almost common knowledge in a group so small and tightly knit. "It's not important."

"Some say you're a bad choice for Pan because you lack connections. That you have to slick with somebody to understand them, and you haven't made love to enough of us to know who we are."

Martin frowned. "Nobody's said it to my face."

"They wouldn't, because they're gossips and cowards, like all the *humans* on this ship."

"I'm not human?"

"You try not to make mistakes."

"Oh, Christ, William. What are you talking about?"

William spread out his muscular brown arms and legs. Martin noted the play of muscles, the ripple of skin on strong arms, the beautiful sheen of upper thigh—and felt nothing physical—a mental admiration, a brotherly recognition and approval of William's health and supple vigor. "I'm homosexual, most of the time," William said, "one of eight males and seven females among the children. You're a crosser. You can slick or fall in love or whatever you want with so many more people . . . But I know something about you, Martin—you're probably more passionate than I am. I've crossed, and found the experience enjoyable but not fulfilling—so I've slicked with maybe twelve of the children. You've had five or six, I'd guess. What are you afraid of?"

Martin pushed from the corner, angry again.

"You hate the idea of rejection. You really don't like understanding people, accepting them for what they are. Why?"

Martin's face muscles worked. "You're not in a good mood," he said, kicking off the opposite wall, rolling past William.

William laughed. "*I'm* not?"

"You've never been cruel before." He put out a hand and stopped himself on the edge of William's door.

William's face contorted. "I'm not being cruel," he said sadly. "I just know what's going to happen, and I hate for you not to know, when it affects you so much . . . and Theresa. You're one of our best." William's expression warmed, as it always did when he praised Martin. "At least *I* think so, and the children voted you Pan."

"You'll be next," Martin said, avoiding his eyes.

"No, I won't," William said, very subdued. "Hans maybe. He wants it. I fantasize about it, that maybe it'll make more Lost Boys willing to cross . . . But it won't be me. I'm a soldier, not a general. You're a general. You don't believe it, though, do you?"

Martin shook his head. "I never wanted to be Pan."

"You didn't turn it down. You know what a general does? Contrary to the gossips' wisdom on this ship, he doesn't slick with all the troops. He watches them from outside, and he learns how to use them. How to keep them safe. And how to sacrifice some of them to save the rest, or sacrifice all to get the Job done. Any child who reads history knows that. You read history, Martin. Do you agree?"

Instinctively, Martin did not agree, but he had never voiced his instinct.

"Do you agree?" William asked again.

"One for all, and all for one," Martin said, knowing that was not quite the same thing. William seemed to think it was.

"Good. You need someone to stand beside you."

"William, this is so much drift, I can't be isolated and be any good . . ."

"Not isolated. Just outside a little bit. With a partner who can trim your sails now and then. I approve of Theresa, but you can't—I suppose I'm getting around to what I really want to say, finally—you can't be what you were with me, and have something even stronger with Theresa."

"I don't want to lose you, or hurt you."

"You don't want to lose *anything* or hurt *anybody*," William said. He floated forward with an ankle kick against corner pads and took Martin's shoulders. "But you're still a general, and you've got to do both.

"Listen to wise old William. Here's your fault, Martin. You think that if you slick with someone, you must fall in love with them, and they *must* fall in love with you. You think that if you lead someone, you must be gentle, and never hurt them, or make them angry."

"Bolsh," Martin said sharply, jerking his head back.

"And if they don't love you, you feel rejected and hurt. You want to love everybody, but you don't, and that's hypocrisy. You want too much, I think. You want your lovers' souls."

"Not so wise, William," Martin said. He pushed him back with an ungentle hand. "You've completely misunderstood me."

"Theresa's perfect for you," William said. "She's a little

smarter than you and a little looser, and she sees something in you that I see as well. But I'll stand aside. I don't want to be second with you; it's a losing game."

Martin saw the tears in William's eyes and reacted with his own. "I'm sorry," he said, floating closer. He stroked William's cheek. "You're a brother to me."

"Brothers we'll be, but don't give me charity slicks," William said. "Respect me enough to believe I can get along without you."

"You still don't make sense, but if that's what you want . . ."

"That's the way it already is," William said. "We're going to be soldiers and generals, and we have a Job to do, and I think it's going to be tougher on all of us than we imagine or fear. So no nonsense, no drift. We're not *really* our own masters, Martin, whatever we like to believe, whatever the moms do or don't do, except in whom we love and whom we call brother and sister."

Martin opened the door, rotated in the frame, and said, "Please don't avoid any more meetings."

"I won't."

Erin Eire was a puzzle to Martin; intelligent, reasonable in conversation, clear-eyed, agreeable for the most part, but with a strong and sometimes arrogant streak of independence. Martin found her in the swimming hall, filter mask strapped over her mouth against the spray. He had to call her twice to get her attention.

"Sorry," she said. She paddled out of an oblong of water and across the green ladder field that kept water and spray from the anteroom. The water rebounded through the spherical space; one swam in air sometimes, in water most of the time, the rest of the time in spray and fine mist like clouds.

Martin didn't particularly enjoy swimming. He had almost drowned in the river beside his family home in Oregon when he was four; that memory tainted any enjoyment of the swimming hall.

"I should have been at the meeting, right?" Her smell was brisk, clean and tangy. Though she was naked, her manner removed any ambiguity about sexual arousal. She was straightforward, natural, not in the least coy with him. The thought

simply did not cross her mind. Martin compared her quickly to
Theresa; with Theresa his instincts were clear. Though Erin was
well-formed, he simply did not feel much sexual attraction to
her.

"Right," Martin said. He hated being stern. "Why weren't
you?"

"I trust your judgment, Martin."

"That's no excuse, Erin."

She shrugged that off, smiled again. "Theresa's very nice. I
hope she takes the sting out of working with people like me."

Martin was exhausted from the strain of the day. His face
reddened. "Erin, why are you so bloody obtuse?"

Eyes level, she said, "Maybe because I'm afraid." She
wrapped herself in a towel, took an end of the towel and dried
her short hair. Most of the Wendys kept their hair short but Erin's
was little more than bushy fuzz. Her startling green eyes emerged
from behind the folds of towel, anything but nervous or afraid.
Whatever she felt, her appearance betrayed nothing. "I'm not
questioning your authority. I *don't* side with Ariel. Not many of
us do."

"I count my small blessings," Martin said.

"Did she agree with the others? About the decision? I'm
curious."

"She's withholding judgment. Did you listen to the meeting
on your wand?"

"Of course. I'm not a shirker. I just didn't feel like being
there. I hate formalities."

"It's important all the same," Martin said. "We do the Job
together. I need your input like I need everybody else's."

"I appreciate that, even if I don't believe it." She folded the
towel and let it float while she put on her shorts and shirt and
tied the tails below her sternum. Over these she slipped the
obligatory overalls. Then she looked away. "I won't make things
any tougher on you."

Martin started to add something but decided enough was
enough. With a nod, he left the anteroom, glad to get away.

The Wendys' party had gone on longer than expected, and Martin, fresh love exaggerated to a peak during the past few hours,

worked alone in his quarters, digging through the training and resource materials available in the ship's libraries.

Unable to wait any longer, he went in search of Theresa, and found her where she had said she would be. His relief was balanced by his chagrin at being so driven, by impatience and longing and an unspecified worry that something, anything, could go wrong.

The Wendys were making garments from materials supplied by the moms. Thirty had gathered in Paola Birdsong's quarters; the door was open, and he entered. Theresa kneeled at the periphery of four women. Kimberly Quartz projected patterns from a wand onto a wide, bunched sheet of cloth on the floor. Theresa held one corner of the cloth, smoothing it as Paola drew on it with a blue marker. A few of the women noticed him, smiled politely. Paola glanced up, and then Theresa saw him. For a moment, he was afraid she would be angry, but she gave her corner of the billowing fabric to Kimberly Quartz and came to hug him.

"Time passes," she said. "Sorry I was late."

"No problem. I've been hitting brick walls."

"Can you wait just a few more minutes?"

He took a seat near the door and looked over Paola's quarters, which he had never been in before. She had covered her walls with paintings of jungles, wide green leaves, flowers, insects. A parrot flapped around the room, delighted by the view.

Only two children not at the meeting. It could have been much worse.

Martin shook out of his musings and saw the cutout pieces of cloth suspended in a translucent, colorless field for inspection. Other Wendys talking or singing or working on quilts started to break up and wander out now, nodding cordially to Martin as they passed.

"Come see," Theresa said. She manipulated the projected images of the pattern, assembling them in the air. Paola Birdsong and Donna Emerald Sea smiled as they watched their design take shape. Donna's cockatoo preened itself on a rack that held samples of cloth the moms could manufacture.

"It's a gown. This is what it will look like, when it's cut and sewn together," Paola told him, smoothing the sheet of fabric.

He had never paid much attention to her, but in Theresa's presence, he felt a sudden affection for her, and by extension for all the Wendys, and he regretted not having that kind of loose, undemanding, insightful affection.

"Paola and I designed it," Donna said. She was quick and nervous, with generous eyes and a small mouth and short blond hair.

The final design showed a long white gown covered with tiny glass beads, glittering magnificently in a rotating light unseen beyond the projection. "A ceremonial gown," Theresa said. She stepped into the projection.

"My turn," Paola said. Theresa adjusted it for the smaller woman.

"It's for when we find our new Earth, after we do the Job," Paola said. "The first Wendy to step on the planet will wear this. The wedding of the children to the new Earth."

Martin had heard nothing of these plans and he found himself suddenly filled with emotion. "It's beautiful."

"Glad you like it," Theresa said. "Do you think the Lost Boys would like an outfit for their first step?"

"I don't know," he said. He had never given much thought to that time. Then, "We'd love them. Will everybody wear them?"

Donna looked at Theresa. "We were only making one . . ."

"Martin's right. Everybody will want them," Theresa said.

"Then we'd better plan more," Donna said. "A good excuse for more parties."

They tried a few more fittings, then Theresa made her farewells.

Martin escorted Theresa down a shadowed hall. They passed Rosa. She edged around them with a furtive nod. Martin wondered when he would have to talk with her, deal with her; she had few friends and no lovers. She was slowly opting out of their tight-knit society.

Theresa said, "It would be nice to make a gown for her," looking back at Rosa. "She needs something, Martin."

"I know."

Theresa took his earlobes in her fingers, pulling him lightly down to kiss her. "We're alone here," she said. "You've been very patient. Talking to everybody . . . It must have been difficult. Ariel can be tough.''

Martin looked up and down the corridor. "Let's go . . . to my quarters," he said between her kisses.

"Why?" she asked, teasing with her hips.

"Because I'm shy. You know that."

"Somebody will see us?"

"Come on." He tugged her hand gently as he led the way.

"It's because you're Pan, isn't it?"

"Theresa . . ."

"All right," she said wistfully. "Nothing adventurous for a Pan's lover."

He frowned, then pulled her toward him and unsnapped her overalls. "You'll make me do anything, won't you? Shameless," he said into her ear.

"Somebody in this dyad has to be adventurous."

He kissed her while mulling over that word, *dyad*. They certainly were that; he had not called their relationship such, reserving the word for what he and William had had, but what he felt for Theresa deserved it more.

"Wedding dress," he said, holding her high to suckle.

"For all of us," Theresa said, eyes closed, grinding her hips against his stomach. "Lower me."

"Not yet. Not until you say I'm adventurous."

"You're adventurous."

Martin heard something, a breath or a rustle of cloth, and turned to see Rosa coming back. Her quarters were somewhere near here; they were in her path. She looked both sad and embarrassed, reversed, laddered back around the curve.

"Sorry," Theresa called after her. "It's your hall, too, Rosa."

But she was gone. Martin lowered Theresa and made a face.

"You were right," Theresa said, chagrined. "She's so shy . . . she didn't need to see us. But it's nothing to do with your being Pan." She pulled up her overalls. "Your quarters," she said.

He lay beside Theresa in the darkness, awash in an abandonment he had not known in some time. He was free of care, loose in body luxury, all demands satisfied or put aside where they would not nag. Theresa lay still, breathing shallow, but she was not asleep. He heard her eyelids opening and closing. Long, languid blinks. *Such sated animals.*

"Thank you," he said.

She caressed his leg with hers. "You're so quiet. Where are you?"

"I'm home," he said.

"Thinking about Earth?"

"No," he said. "I'm home. Here with you."

And it was true. For the first time in thirteen years, here in the darkness, he felt at home. Home was a few minutes between extreme worries and challenges; home was a suspension outside any place or time.

"That's sweet," Theresa said.

"I love you."

"I love you, Martin. But I'm not home. Not yet."

He pulled her to him. The moment was fleeting and he wanted to grab it but could not. Temporary, ineffable. Not home. No home.

Martin entered the nose dressed in exercise shorts, neck wrapped in a sweat towel. He had just worked out with Hans Eagle and Stephanie Wing Feather in the second homeball gym when Hakim signaled that they might have enough information to make the next decision.

The *Dawn Treader*'s long nose extended a hundred meters from the first homeball, a slender needle only three meters wide at the point. Hakim Hadj and three of the search team—Li Mountain, Thomas Orchard, and Luis Estevez Saguaro—kept station in the tip of the nose, surrounded by projections.

Transparent to visible light, the tip of the nose revealed a superabundant darkness, like an unctuous dye that could stain their souls.

The remotes, four thousand tiny sensors, had departed from the third homeball two days before, returning their signals to the *Dawn Treader* using the same point-to-point "no-channel" transmission their weapons and craft would use when outside the ship. Within a distance of ten billion kilometers, information simply "appeared" in a receiver, and could not be intercepted between; hence, no channel. The effective rate of transmission was almost instantaneous. The children called the no-channel transmissions noach.

Moms, ship's mind, and libraries were unresponsive to inquiries on the subject of noach; it was one of the tools bequeathed without explanation.

With the remotes, the "eye" of the *Dawn Treader* had expanded enormously, and was now nine billion kilometers in diameter, nearly two thirds as wide as the solar systems they studied.

Hakim pushed through the haze of projections and glided toward Martin. Li Mountain and Luis Estevez Saguaro watched, fidgeting with their wands, but controlling their enthusiasm enough to let Hakim take charge.

"It's even better," Hakim said. "It's very good indeed. We have resolution down to a thousand kilometers, and estimates of energy budgets. The nearest system is inhabited, but it's not consuming energy like a thriving high-tech civ should. Still, it's the most active, and it's where we might expect it to be."

Hakim's wand projected graphics and figures for Martin. Assay fit very closely indeed. "We've been looking through the stellar envelopes and we've put together a picture of the birthing cloud in this region. Shock-wave passage from a supernova initiated starbirth about nine billion years ago, and the supernova remnants seeded heavy elements along these gradients . . ." Hakim's finger traced a projected purple line through numbers describing metals densities, "metals" meaning elements heavier than hydrogen and helium. He jabbed at a clustering of numbers. "The Buttercup is right in this gradient, right in this magnetic pool, to receive the only dose of exactly these proportions." Red numbers bunched within a dip in the galaxy's magnetic field, where gases might collect, waiting to be condensed into stars. "No other star system within a hundred light years matches the Buttercup's assay."

Martin felt numb, not yet realizing with all of his faculties how significant this was.

"Time for another gathering," he said thoughtfully.

"I'll report to the moms," Hakim said.

* * *

They had never before seen more than three moms together, although they had suspected there could be many more. Several times the children had kept track of their whereabouts in the *Dawn Treader* and tried to count them, as a kind of game, but they could never be *sure* how many there were. Now, all eighty-two children—Lost Boys and Wendys—gathered in the school-room to make the final decision, and there were six identical moms, all with the same patient, neutral voices.

More than anything that had happened before, this gave Martin chills. He had personally estimated there were no more than four moms in the entire ship. It seemed likely to him now that the *Dawn Treader* could manufacture the robots at will; but that meant the ship itself was a kind of giant mom.

Putting six into the schoolroom was a symbolic action, surely . . . And it communicated to Martin, at least, with full force.

Four moms hovered at the periphery of the schoolroom, silent and unmoving, like sentinels. Two moms floated in the center of the schoolroom, beside the star sphere. They waited patiently until the children were quiet, which took less than a minute. Martin saw Ariel enter with William and Erin just as the first mom began to speak.

The mom at stage left advanced and said, "The information on the candidate stellar group has increased. If the ship alters its course now, and begins deceleration, you are less than three months from this system, ship's time. Deceleration will use most of our reserves, and we will need to refuel within one of the stellar systems, the Buttercup or the Cornflower. There are unlikely to be sufficient volatiles available in the Firestorm system."

A diagram of their orbital path and velocities spread before the children. Deceleration for three tendays at one g, ship's reference, which would drop their speed to about ninety percent c and increase their *tau* considerably, bringing them into a position to enter the Buttercup system. Then deceleration of two g's for twenty-three days. They would enter the system at just over three fourths the speed of light, crossing the system's diameter of eleven point two billion kilometers in just under fourteen hours.

Martin noted that their trajectory would take them through the dark haloes of pre-birth material, through the plane of the ecliptic, and then under the Buttercup's south pole, considerably below the plane of the ecliptic. They would pass within two hundred million kilometers of one rocky world, and a hundred million kilometers of the second, directly between them, when both were nearly aligned on one side of the system.

"The remotes have given your search team more information. You will now be provided with the expanded figures to make your next decision."

Ariel watched Martin from across the room. Her expression said nothing, but he could feel her disapproval.

Hakim Hadj pushed forward from the search team. "The information is wonderful . . . Very provocative." He raised his wand, and the wand of each sang in tune, and projected images into their eyes.

They saw:

That the two yellow stars had altered stellar envelopes—that the streams of particles flowing outward from the stars' surfaces were being gathered and twisted like hair in braids, forming streamers above and below the poles. The magnetic fields of the stars were being altered to control their surface activity, and to allow fine tuning of their radiation output. None of the planets were swept by particle storms any more, nor were they subjected to the vagaries of stellar interiors. This helped explain the altered stellar signature—spectrum versus size and brightness—that had first pointed to the presence of an advanced civilization.

Other details could be discerned around the nearest yellow star, the Buttercup: altered planetary orbits, with a single gas giant world pushed in closer to the Buttercup, perhaps to allow easier mining of volatiles. The gas giants were even more depleted of volatiles than they had first estimated; refueling would be difficult around this star.

Between the Buttercup's outermost rocky world and the nearest depleted gas giant orbited a million-kilometer-thick halo of flimsy structures largely made of silicates. One or more rocky worlds, or perhaps an entire asteroid belt, might have been sacrificed to make the halo; what purpose it served could not be known yet. Hakim speculated they might have been enormous mirrors to refocus energy on the inner planets, or perhaps to deflect radiation from the red giant in its more violent phase.

The farther yellow star showed no high-tech activity. "Someone might be hiding," Hakim said, "but we have no way of knowing that."

He saved the most impressive displays for last.

"Some of the information we're about to show you was gathered by the Benefactors long before Earth was destroyed," Hakim said. "Several thousand years ago . . . The moms have given this to us."

In simulation, they saw dim flares around the two yellow stars, as viewed from hundreds or even thousands of light years away: the expenditure of vast energies necessary to move the planets and alter the stars. The flares had lasted only for a matter of decades—a mere instant on the time-scale of the galaxy, but obviously, eager eyes and ears had caught the flicker.

The transformation of the two solar systems had taken place simultaneously, about a hundred years before the Firestorm— twice the mass of Sol—went through helium flash to become a red giant, a hideous lively bloating that swallowed five planets. They watched in silence as the red giant cast away immense cloaks of gas, its face becoming pocked and ragged like a burning, decaying skull.

Hans Eagle spoke out. "If the Killers live here, did they send out machines before or after they made these changes?"

"Probably before," the first mom said. "In our experience—"

"Nobody knows how much experience you've had, or how long," Ariel said, voice chilly.

"Please, Ariel," Hakim said, infinitely patient.

"In our experience," the mom continued, "beings who build killer probes usually do so before they have mastered the techniques necessary to perform large-scale stellar reconstruction."

"Then it's been thousands of years since the probes were launched," Hans continued.

"Very likely."

Hans nodded, satisfied.

The last display traced the paths of intercepted killer machines, but covered a thousand light years rather than a dozen;

their known and postulated victims were marked by red dots, and the systems they had merely passed through glowed green. Approximate dates relative to Earth's death and distances of these events from the three-star group were given in flashing white.

Martin was astonished by the wealth of data; a partial answer to Ariel's doubts. His mind raced to gather the implications: sometimes the Ships of the Law *did* break silence, to transmit the locations of killer machines, to broadcast their captures and triumphs. *The transmissions would not have been hidden; the distances are too vast for the noach . . . They would have risked revealing themselves . . .*

Hakim concluded by placing all the displays around the star sphere for their contemplation. "That is all we have for now," he said.

Again, the children did their momerath, and the schoolroom fell silent.

Martin visualized the spaces of probability behind tight-closed eyes, hands opening and closing, seeing the numbers and the paths, making them converge and diverge. Each time he repeated the momerath he concluded there was a high probability—perhaps ninety-five percent—that the Killers came from this stellar group. The probes had probably been manufactured in the system of the Buttercup, the near yellow star.

After sufficient time had passed—perhaps two hours of steady concentration, in complete silence—the moms gathered at the center of the schoolroom, and the first mom said, "What is your judgment?"

"Comments first," Paola Birdsong insisted.

The comments were more expressions of personal involvement and emotion than substantive questions or objections; this much Martin had expected. He had watched the group reach consensus on other matters far less important than this, and this was how they worked: speaking out, finding individual roles.

Mei-li Wu-Hsiang Gemini, a small, quiet woman with the Starsigns family, asked whether there were other civilizations within the close vicinity of this group. Hakim called up a display already shown: all stars that might have harbored planets with life, within twenty-five light years of the group. None had shown even the most subtle signs of civilized development. That was not conclusive evidence one way or another; left alone, the planets might not have developed intelligent life—though the chances were two in five, for so many stars, that at least one civilization would have evolved.

There was always the possibility that the intelligences might have been smarter than humanity, keeping silent even in their technological youth.

But added to the other evidence, the lack was significant.

"What are the chances that civilizations would die off or abort themselves, in so many planetary systems?" George Dempsey asked.

The first mom said, "Given the number of systems with planets, and the probability of life arising, and the probability of that life developing technological ability—" The figures flashed before them again. Martin did not bother doing the momerath; he had done it already, the first time around. Chances were, so had Dempsey. This was socialization, not serious cross-examination.

Time of accepting what they all knew must come next . . .

More questions, for yet another hour, until Martin's eyes and tense muscles burned. He could sense the group's fatigue. He glanced at the remaining children in his mental queue, decided they would not have anything substantive to add, and said, "All right. Let's get down to it."

"You're prepared to make a decision?" the first mom asked.

"We are," Martin said.

Grumbling and rustling, the children rearranged themselves into their families and drill groups. They felt much more comfortable among their chosen peers; this was not an easy thing and none was happy to be hurried along.

"You are deciding whether to decelerate, at substantial fuel cost, and direct this Ship of the Law into the stellar group we have observed, to investigate the intelligent beings there, and to judge whether they built the machines that destroyed your world," the first mom said. "Pan will count your votes."

One by one, they voted, and Martin tallied. There could be no more than ten abstentions in the entire group, or the process would begin again. Seven abstained, including Ariel. Sixty-one voted to go in and investigate. Fourteen voted to pass the group by, to search for something more definite.

"We need an opposition Pan," Ariel insisted. Paola Birdsong, who had voted to investigate, disagreed.

"We've followed procedures," she said. "It's done."

"We've followed the *moms'* procedures," Ariel said.

"They train us and instruct us," Ginny Chocolate said. "I don't see what you're after."

"Are we puppets?" Ariel asked, glaring around the groups.

The other children seemed confused. The grumbling increased. Martin felt his stomach twist.

Jorge Rabbit intervened. Olive skinned, with thick black hair, quick with jokes, Jorge was popular in the group. "This is enough, poor children, Martin is right. We are here to do this work. We are not puppets; we are students."

Ariel tightened her jaw and said no more. Martin felt a sudden perverse tug for her.

"It's done," he said. "The children have voted. We go."

Martin ate in the cafeteria with the day's drill group when the maneuvers began.

The children felt it first as a deeper vibration through the ship, singing in their muscles and bones.

"Oh, man," Harpal Timechaser said. He brought out his wand and let it drift in the air. Slowly, precessing this way, then that, as the ship maneuvered to bring its drives to bear, the wand spun slowly, drawing their complete attention.

The vibration increased. The *Dawn Treader*'s hull made a melodic singing noise, deep and masculine, as all the stresses of the drive pushed through its fabric. The wand began to settle, first toward one wall. They felt themselves "pushed" with it, and they yelled with excitement, then groaned as the room oriented within the ship, as if spun on gimbals, one flat wall becoming a floor, the other a ceiling.

A gentle ten percent g as the drives came alive, stretched, clearing their throats.

"I'm going to be sick," Paola Birdsong said. "Why don't they smooth it for us?"

"Because we hate that more than this," Martin reminded her.

Half an hour later, the ship sang again, on an even deeper note. Martin saw the ship in momerath, felt its load of fuel decreasing steadily, flare of particles and radiation disappearing into the bottomless darkness of the ship's external sump, a way to conceal their wastes by scattering them across the surrounding light years as an increase in the energy of the vacuum.

They were going where fuel would be difficult to find.

Full gravity returned. The halls and quarters filled with complaints, more excitement; painted, half-dressed children running, stumbling, cursing, grimacing, trying to leap; falling, cursing again.

Two children broke bones in the first few hours. Their casts, applied by a mom in the dispensary after bone-knitting therapy, served as warning notice for the rest. Martin called a general meeting in the full-gravity schoolroom and the injured showed off their trophies.

The injured would be well within two days . . . The moms' medicine was potent. But until the casts were off, they could not participate in most of the drills.

The ship transformed itself subtly like a living thing, usually when no one was watching. Throughout, rooms oriented to the end of weightless coasting.

Once past their initial excitement, the children did not find the change disturbing. Psychologically, it was a return to the old patterns of the Ark, and to their year-long acceleration to near light speed away from the Sun. Not to mention their years on Earth . . .

More changes would come soon—two g's, a heavy burden— and if they decided to go for orbital insertion into the Buttercup system, the action would be spectacular.

They had never before experienced the Ship of the Law demonstrating its full power and sophistication . . .

The *Dawn Treader* was a single virus about to enter a highly protected and extremely powerful host, with unknown capabilities. Martin would report to the moms every day now, and a mom would be constantly available in the schoolroom; the same mom, with an identifying mark painted on it by Martin, at the suggestion of Jorge Rabbit and Stephanie Wing Feather, who thought it would boost morale.

The marking ceremony was attended by all the children. Just before his suicide, Theodore Dawn had written of this expected time: "We'll get dressed up in war paint and war uniforms, and we'll swear an oath, like mythic pirates or the Three Musketeers, and it won't be all nonsense, all childsplay. It *will mean something*. Just wait and see." The search for a meaningful ceremony had come too late for Theodore, Martin thought.

But now that moment had come for the rest of them.

The children gathered on the tiers of an amphitheater that had risen from the floor of the schoolroom at Martin's command. They wore black and white paint on their faces and forearms, "To eliminate the gray feelings, the neutralities, the indecisions." Even Martin wore the paint.

A mom floated near the middle of the schoolroom. Within the star sphere, a red circle blinked around the white point of the Buttercup star. Martin approached the mom with small pots of black and white paint in one hand, and a brush in the other.

"To show our resolve, to show our change of state, to strengthen our minds and our courage, we appoint this mom a War Mother. The War Mother will be here to speak with any of us, at any time.

"Now is *our* time."

Martin applied the brush thick with white paint to one side of the mom's stubby, featureless head. The other half he carefully painted black. Then, to complete the effect—something he had thought of himself—he painted a divided circle where the "face" might have been, reversing the colors, black within white, white within black. No grays, but cautious judgment of alternatives.

Painting completed, the War Mother decorated, Martin turned to the children on the risers. They stood quietly, no coughing, breathing hardly audible in the stillness, strong and beautiful and grim-faced with thoughts and memories. He stood before them, looking into their faces.

"Luis Estevez Saguaro and Li Mountain of the search team have suggested names for the star systems. They think the Buttercup star should be called Wormwood, the Cornflower Leviathan, and the Firestorm, Behemoth. Any other suggestions?"

"They're good names," Joe Flatworm said, scratching his sandy growth of beard.

No one objected.

"We've been training for years, but we've never exercised outside, in real conditions. I'm making a formal request of the moms, right now, that we begin external exercises as soon as possible, before this day is out if we can."

The moms had always turned that request down. Martin had not conferred with them; by asking them now, in front of the children, he was taking a real risk, operating only on a hunch.

"You may begin three days of external drill," the War Mother replied. "You may conduct a full-level exercise in the region around the ship."

Hans' face lit up and he raised his fist in a cheer, then turned to the children behind him. All but Ariel cheered, even Erin Eire. Ariel kept her face blank.

"We're in it now," Hans said to Martin as the group broke up. He smiled broadly and rubbed his hands together. "We're really in it!"

"What kind of drill are you planning?" Martin asked the War Mother when the room was almost empty.

"That must be determined at the time of the exercise," the War Mother said. Martin backed away, confused.

"No warning?"

"No warning," said the mom.

During the coasting, Martin's primary quarters—once shared with Theodore—had been spherical, nets at one end filled with the goods manufactured by the moms to give the children a feeling of place and purpose: paper books, jewelry. Since the deceleration began, Martin had redesigned the quarters to have several flat ledges he could sit on or brace against. His sleeping net had been swapped for a bag and sling hung between two pillars.

Theresa came to him in his primary quarters in the second homeball after a ten-hour period of self-imposed isolation. She stood at his closed hatch, inquiring discreetly through his wand whether he was available. With a groan, conflicting emotions making him ball up his fists and pound the yielding floor, he swung down from a ledge and opened the door.

"I didn't want to bother you . . ." she said, her face tight, hair in disarray, skin glistening. "We've been exercising. Harpal and Stephanie told me you were here . . ."

He reached out for her and hugged her fiercely. "I need you. I need someone to balance me."

"I'm glad," she said, burying her face in her shoulder. She wore workout cutoffs, blue shorts and loose-fitting top. "The exercises are good," she said. "We're really into them."

"I'm in the boneyard," he said, sweeping his free arm at electronic slate and books piled into his sleep corner. What they called boneyard was everything human stored in the *Dawn Treader*'s libraries.

"Tactics?" she asked.

He grimaced. "Call it that."

She hugged him again before moving away to riffle through the stack and pick up the slate. He didn't mind her curiosity; she seemed interested in everything about him, and he was flattered. "Marshal Saxe," she said, scrolling through the slate displays. She lifted a book. "Bourcet and Gilbert. Clausewitz, Caemerrer, Moltke, Goltz." She lifted an eyebrow.

"Their armies could see each other, make sorties against each other," Martin said. "We don't even fight with armies."

"These are the people T. E. Lawrence studied when he was young," Theresa said, surprising him yet again. "You've been reading Liddell Hart."

He smiled in chagrin. "You, too."

"Me and about twenty others. I asked for crew access records."

Martin grinned ruefully. "I should have thought of that. To see what they're . . . thinking, preparing for."

"Most are just doing your exercises. They respect you. They think you know what you're doing. Hans is doing a lot of extra research. Erin Eire. Ariel."

"I'm glad they're keeping me on my toes."

"We can't afford to take chances, even with you, Martin."

Theresa had never spoken to him in such a tone before; was

she implying lack of confidence? She smiled, but the question was raised, and she looked away, aware she had raised it.

"I'm not criticizing you, Martin, but you—we—won't find many answers in Earth strategy books."

"Right," Martin said.

"We can't keep looking back."

"It's all we have," Martin said.

"Not so."

Martin nodded. "I mean, it's all we have that's our own."

Theresa put the books back and returned the slate to the text he had been reading. "I'm sorry," she said, shaking her head. "I didn't come here to talk about this."

"I'm not just looking at Earth histories and texts," Martin said. "I've been going over everything the moms taught us. They haven't made up a drill for the external exercise—they seem to want to surprise us. I don't like that, but I see their point—"

"Martin. You need a break."

"There's no time!" he shouted, fists clenching again.

"Are you thinking clearly?"

He paused, shook his head, squeezed his palms against his temples. "Not very."

"I'm here."

He closed the entrance, reached for her, put the wand into quiet mode, kicked the books and slate aside as they moved against each other. "I don't want to be away from you for a second, not an instant," he said. "That's the bad part. I want to be someplace else with you."

She looked at him intently, face showing none of the insinuation of her undulating body, lower lip under her teeth; hips moving with graceful need. He felt the motion of her stomach against his, the press of her curly hair, the flexing wet warmth startling, her small breasts hard against his chest; sought her neck behind her ear, knew she had closed her eyes, face still blank but for the bitten lip.

The experience was more effort, less ethereal, with up and down reestablished. It was also more familiar to his inner mind, flesh and bones; somehow more real.

They rolled from the ledge with half-purpose, falling into a glowing ladder, and were lowered gently to tumble down a slope into a pile of Martin's clothes.

"I want to live with you always," Martin said.

"I didn't mean to make you think I . . ." Tears came to her eyes. "I'm so clumsy sometimes. I trust you. It's pretty amazing how *they* trust you. The past Pans—Harpal, Stephanie, Sig, Cham . . . Joe— They're right behind you." She smiled. "Hans is just doing his job, I think. I can't read Hans all the time. He seems to hide everything important. Ariel seems either angry or sad all the time."

"Is that why you're with me, because I'm trusted?" he asked quietly. *That's a stupid, stupid thing to ask.*

"Not at all," she said. "I don't slick for status."

"I know you don't," he said. "I'm sorry." He stroked her face. "I wouldn't call this slicking."

"Oh, it *is*," she said. "The very best. Don't be afraid of it."

"Of course not," Martin whispered, edging closer, careful not to let the slight weight of his body oppress her. "I want you to live with me."

"Dyad?" she asked.

"I want more than that," he said. "I want to eat you up."

"Ah ha."

"I want you so much it hurts not to have you near me."

"Oh." She looked away, pretending embarrassment even as they moved against each other.

"I want to marry you."

She stopped their rolling and lay quiet beside him, breasts moving up and down, eyes flicking over his features. "We don't marry," she said.

"Nothing stops us."

"We're Lost Boys and Wendys. Pans don't get married."

"We could get married in a new way. No priests or churches or licenses."

"Married is something different. It's for Earth, or back on the Ark. People got married on the Ark."

"I doubt we'll ever go back," Martin said.

"I know," she said softly.

"We're our own Ark. We have all the information here. All the living things in memory. They'll make every living thing we need, once we do our Job. We'll be like war dogs."

"War dogs?"

"Too vicious to be taken back. Because of what we do. We have to rely on ourselves alone. That means we can get married, whatever being married means out here."

"We've only been lovers for a few tendays."

"That's enough for me," Martin said.

Theresa drew back to him. "Slicking is so much simpler."

"We make love," Martin insisted.

Theresa suddenly put on an innocent look. "Do you remember," she said, pushing tongue behind her lower lip, pushing it out, gazing at him intently, "how serious this would be on Earth? How *fraught* with meaning, making love or slicking?"

"It isn't serious here?"

She put fingers to her lips, holding something: a cigarette, he remembered. Lowered her lashes, looked at him seductively, deep sensual meaning, smiling, drew back, flung back her hair. "I could be a temptress," she said.

"Harlot," he said.

"We would spend ever so much time worrying, once we were married, on Earth, about whether we were doing it right, whether we were in style."

"We have styles here," Martin said.

She made a bitter face, tossed the ghost cigarette away. "I read about it. In some places, we could have been arrested for . . ." She touched his limp tip with a finger, brought a drop of wheyish moisture to her mouth. "We could have been arrested for . . ." She reached into his mouth with the finger, and he obligingly tongued it. She moved the finger up her thigh, touched herself, moved without effort into a melodramatic vamping posture. "How can we be married without thousands knowing and approving or disapproving? Looking at us in our little home, approving or disapproving." She whispered the words again, but there was a strain in her face. "All those people. But it's okay." She looked at him directly, struggling to hold back more tears. "And we know we can make children. That's serious."

Martin smiled. His eyes focused not on her now, but on far

dead Earth. He had never thought or imagined such adult concerns on Earth. He had been a child when Earth died. So had she.

"Knowing you can make children if you want. That's *really* making love," she concluded, words catching in her throat. She closed her eyes and like a dark-headed bird laid her cheek and palm on his chest.

"We make love," he persisted. "The moms will let us have children after we've done the Job."

She wept in shaking silence in his arms.

If the children decided Wormwood was a source of killer probes, the Ship of the Law would break in two. Stephanie Wing Feather suggested the separate ships should be called *Hare* and *Tortoise*.

The two ships would decelerate at different rates. *Tortoise*, the smaller, would begin super deceleration—one thousand g's—days before reaching the system, and would enter at maneuvering speed. The larger, *Hare*, would shoot through the system at three quarters c, conduct reconnaissance while passing between the two inner rocky planets, relay the information to *Tortoise*, then escape the system and wait for results. It would decelerate more gradually, reaching maneuvering speed some hundreds of billions of kilometers on the other side of Wormwood.

If *Tortoise* was severely damaged or destroyed, *Hare* could continue, hunting for fuel around the other stars in the group.

Before then, the Ship of the Law would pass through a section of Wormwood's outlying haloes of pre-birth material: what around the Sun had been called the Oort and Kuiper clouds. It was possible that Wormwood's inhabitants had mined even these outer reaches of the pre-birth material, probably in the youth of their civilization, when comets were used by "hitch-hikers" to ride far beyond the orbits of the outer planets. It was also possible that the clouds had never been rich with volatiles; even the rocky pickings were slim by comparison to the Sun's cloud.

The *Dawn Treader* would release makers and doers into these diffuse haloes to manufacture weapons of mass destruction. If the judgment was guilty, the makers and doers would push these weapons inward toward the planets. The weapons would take

time to accomplish their backup mission of destruction, should
Hare and *Tortoise* fail, and at a net energy loss.

The energy required to make and move the weapons would
come from conversion of carbon and silicon to anti-matter—
what the children called anti em. Elements heavier than silicon
did not convert with any energy gain. Elements between lithium
and silicon converted with a marginal energy gain.

To make up for the clouds' paucity, they would have to give
the makers and doers substantial portions of the *Dawn Treader*'s
fuel.

They desperately needed to find more fuel within the system.

They would enter as black as the Benefactors' technologies
allowed. Entry would be an extremely dangerous time; dangerous
even should the children decide Earth's Killers did not live here.
How would the defenders of these stars know they had been
judged innocent or guilty, or whether the *Dawn Treader* was
itself a killer, a wolf between the stars?

The children filed into the weapons store, apprehensive. Martin
led the way, and the children went to their craft in a welter of
voices, calling names, moving on ladders to their vessels in the
up and downness. Paola Birdsong lost her grasp and almost fell;
Harpal Timechaser caught her halfway to the fore side of the
hemisphere. Seeing her safe, the children hooted at her lack of
attention. Paola crawled red-faced to her ovoid bombship and
hooked both elbows in the ladder's softly glowing field.

Martin stood beside his ship, watching his brothers and sisters
find theirs, watching Theresa climb to her rifle, watching William
join with Umberto Umbra in their cylinder cluster, called an
Oscar Meyer by some, and a cigar box by others.

Fifty children stood apart. They would remain in the Ship of
the Law. Hans would stay with them.

Martin moved forward along his ladder and hung next to his
assigned craft, a rifle.

"The moms have promised a target and we'll match ourselves
against it. I don't know what the target is, or how we'll fight
it."

"We don't have a set drill?" Erin Eire asked. Hans looked
at Martin; they had discussed this already, and Hans had ex-

pressed real reservations. Going outside without a plan the first time did not seem wise to either of them; going outside with no known adversaries, no expressed situations, seemed foolhardy at best.

"The War Mother won't tell us what it is," Martin said.

"That's stupid," Erin Eire said. The children shook their heads.

"What are they trying to do to us?" Rex Live Oak asked.

"Make us less dependent, I assume. At any rate, I haven't designed a plan; we'll see what they're up to, and see how well we react. They assume we're well trained."

Kimberly Quartz and her craftmate, Ginny Chocolate, hooted loudly. "Pan must be *confident!*" Kimberly called out. Martin smiled and lifted both thumbs.

Kai Khosrau, diminutive, with long head and long arms and muscular legs, began to sing the song and a few dozen joined in. The song was a rambling medley of tunes remembered from their youth on Earth and in the Ark, with new words.

Martin let them sing, watching Theresa in her accustomed place outside the cluster, at the rear. *Just to be alone with her, nothing else.*

Song finished, they climbed into their craft and the hatches smoothed shut. Martin took a seat in the rifle's black interior, felt the surface of the couch wrap around his legs, the crawl of transparent membrane around his clothes and skin. The membrane connected with air supply intakes and waste removal ducts.

He closed his eyes and took a deep breath. Cool fresh air filled his lungs. A faint green field surrounded his body, leaving arms and head free. Between the membrane and the field, water poured in, making a five-centimeter cushion around his legs and torso. A faint moisture fog rose up briefly around his face, covering the outer surface of the membrane, and almost immediately cleared. The membrane, water, and field protected him from accelerations up to fifty g's. Anything beyond fifty g's would require a volumetric field. He had experienced the volumetric fields in training; they were bearable, but not comfortable. At very high acceleration, they controlled motion down to the level of individual molecules.

Those not in ships departed from the hemispheric chamber. Deep bass pounding: air being rapidly pumped from the chamber.

A hatch opened to darkness and oily streamers of light.

They had not been outside the *Dawn Treader* since leaving the Ark. The interior of the Ship of the Law had been their home, their only solid universe; all else had been projection, simulation, memory and imagination.

Ten craft broke free of their pylons, wobbling as the maneuvering drives adjusted, pale yellow glows pulsing white opposite the direction of travel like captured fireflies. The pylons withdrew to the walls. Sporangia broke loose from the walls and ladder fields reached out from their escorts to lace them tightly to craft hulls.

The craft exited *Dawn Treader* in close formation, almost touching.

Martin rode his rifle. Through the membrane and a port close to his face, he saw the exterior universe—not in simulation, but in actual far-traveling photons.

The reality was not appreciably different from the high-level simulations; still, he *knew* it was real, could feel it in the twists and accelerations deep inside his gut as the craft swung about the *Dawn Treader*'s third homeball.

From within, the *Dawn Treader* was an all-encompassing universe, with no psychologically real exterior. Seen from outside, close up, it was simply immense. The scale confused Martin, confined for so long in spaces without infinite views.

The immensity of the Ship of the Law was enhanced by the strangeness of its environment. They still traveled at close to the speed of light; the universe "outside" was still twisted and distorted, with a lateral belt of blue and red stellar luminosity that followed him wherever he flew.

When his bombship rotated, the entire exterior universe seemed to tumble and reform, as if viewed through a madman's lens. But the children had been trained to recognize these distortions, to orient themselves along axes relative to the *Dawn Treader* by comparing the distorted frames of reference.

Now, two twenty-eight-hour days after deceleration began, they were still traveling at greater than ninety-nine percent of the speed of light. Day by day, as the Ship of the Law slowed, as its *tau* increased, the stars would correct themselves, the luminous belt would expand to normality, the tunneling effects fore and aft would end.

Martin was eager for that time; to see stars again, as he had seen them from Earth, though not all the same stars, not the same sky.

The small craft aligned themselves. Their pilots saw others as silhouettes against the distorted sky, and communicated by noach.

Martin remembered the lectures of years past, watching his fellows practice different formations, warming up for the exercise itself, which would be like nothing they had experienced before. The defenses could be ancient and straightforward; orbiting sentinels, kinetic energy projectiles, or . . .

The defenses may be sophisticated beyond anything you have trained for. Advanced civilizations are infinitely surprising in the varieties of their accomplishments, in the expansion of their knowledge, puzzling in their expertise in one area, and their lack in another. Civilizations have personalities, if we may call them such; weaknesses and strengths, talents and blindness. Even a technologically superior civilization has weak points.

That much he had learned during training; it came back with crystal clarity, as if spoken in his ear.

Killing Captain Cook. Guerrilla warfare; South-East Asians against B-52s. But theirs would not be a long-term guerrilla action. They would lay the seeds of weapons that could not be removed without performing the very actions the weapons themselves were intended for: planet killers.

He saw Theresa's rifle glinting in the weird light of blue stars emerging from behind the Ship of the Law. Theresa was to take picket duty with five others, reaching out thirty thousand kilometers beyond the Ship of the Law. He watched the rifle dwindle. Flies buzzing around a battleship; powerful flies, but no one could know how well-matched they might be against what was coming.

That was the unanswerable question. There was a very good chance they would encounter a civilization so far advanced that the power within the Ship of the Law would be insignificant.

Martin had had nightmares about what might happen then:

would they be captured like animalcules plucked by an eyedropper out of pond water? If the superior intelligence swallows the animalcules, they might cause disease, still might kill; but if the intended victim refuses to swallow, the fighters are isolated, the Ship of the Law is frozen and sectioned and examined, the children are pulled apart cell by cell and studied; harmless, defeated.

Martin banished those thoughts. The exercise was all that mattered for the moment. He strained against the membrane, the layer of water, and the surrounding field. In the actual offensive, as they performed the Job, they would be aided by makers and doers and robot craft not limited by human physiology. But one or more of the children would pull the trigger. The execution would be performed by the survivors of Earth. That was the Law—while any of the crew remained . . .

Paola Birdsong and Bonita Imperial Valley escorted a torus of sporangia; in actual offensive action, such a torus could carry a million makers and doers. It was their duty to guard the torus until it was ready to broadcast its contents.

"Defenses have been sighted using statistical scintillation matching," the mom's voice announced in his ear. He saw and felt through the rifle's sensors radiation pulses directed at their position: crude methods but effective. The pulses were absorbed in the *Dawn Treader*'s skin, but observers beyond the Ship of the Law could see its absorption shadow.

Judgment: the technology was more primitive than theirs, but possibly equal in destructive force, as a crossbow may equal a rifle in killing power.

The formation changed immediately to a protective envelope around the *Dawn Treader*. Picket craft had made it out to only twenty thousand kilometers, leaving faint trails of reaction mass, particles and radiation that dissipated quickly, but not quickly enough. Small craft like rifles, bombships, and pickets could not use sumps to hide their drives. The Ship of the Law, in effect, was pinpointed at the center of a star of ion traces.

The picket craft veered and the *Dawn Treader* changed its course abruptly and abandoned the formation. One instant, the *Dawn Treader* was clearly visible within the formation; the next, it was gone.

There would be hell to pay within the ship; volumetric fields would keep the children still aboard from being smashed to jelly, but the side-effects would be nausea and disorientation.

A weapon was being used against the remaining craft. It was quickly described to him: a hail of anti em needles, visible only through their attrition as they encountered stray hydrogen atoms: sparkles of gamma rays and brilliant white light. Five rifles jaunted into a screen formation, but that was not effective. The five craft—William's among them—were deactivated, destroyed, to all intents and purposes, for this exercise . . . And Martin was next.

He felt the voices move into his head. His neurological states accelerated, something he had long since learned to hate; but he was thinking a thousand, ten thousand times faster, as fields created virtual neurons that mimicked his thought patterns. His personality split; he left the old self behind like a shed pupa case.

It seemed entirely too real when light filled all his senses: needles striking chaff. He ejected his chaff and retreated in the direction of the *Dawn Treader*. Volumetric fields divided him into portions as small as molecules and kept each particle in place; the rifle accelerating at maximum power, five, ten, one hundred, a thousand g's, darting like a hellborn flea on an undisguised pillar of light, bouncing in and out of the flowers of dying anti em needles.

Paola Birdsong still shepherded the sporangia torus. Bonita Imperial Valley had been deactivated. Through his rifle's senses he saw three bombships on Paola's tail, spreading chaff to intersect the needles. They would be destroyed; Paola and the torus might survive. The needles hit the spread chaff. A vicious wash of radiation deactivated the three bombships and damaged Paola's; crippled, she tried to keep up with the torus. He saw the torus accelerating madly, leaving Paola behind, needles outstripped.

Delivered, the torus was on its own now. He thought of using the Ship of the Law itself, directing it to convert its mass to a neutronium gravity-fuse bomb and head for the likeliest inhabited world, to supplement the torus' destruction—but the situation was not yet desperate enough for such a suicide . . .

More needles coming in, floods of them. He was alone,

thoughts going over every possibility; out of command, out of touch, simply alone. *Just an exercise. Hell of an exercise.* Each surviving craft had instructions to make its way to the nearest inhabited bodies and inflict maximum damage.

Kamikazes. He hated the thought of such waste to so little potential effect. The more dangerous choice was to locate the Ship of the Law again, but his craft could not match *Dawn Treader* for speed. That meant he would have to decide where the ship would go, in its mad course to evade the needles. All the other children would be making similar decisions; most, he suspected, would decide to hunt for the ship, and failing that, to kamikaze.

Effectively, he was no longer Pan—no longer a leader.

He would hunt.

The residue of radiations from intercepted needles left a crazy tangle throughout a billion cubic kilometers of space, the center of the battle. How many other needles—in how many other orbital tracks—were set up for this exercise?

None of the needles are real. None of this is real. It is simulation projected for our eyes only against a real background.

No matter. To lose this exercise so completely would be a disgrace, and he could not stand to see the children disgraced before the moms, with so little time until the real Job began. Martin could not feel his body. His accelerated thought gave him long hours for every breath or pound of heart. The body was separate from him now; his present self existed as a virtual simulacrum, which would re-connect with the physical mind at the end of the exercise.

At this rate, the craft he controlled seemed positively slow and balky. And that was perhaps part of the problem; he was not matched with his capabilities, but outmatched them. He was too high powered in his head for the weapon he used. He did not need the extra acceleration to contemplate strategy for all the small craft.

He slowed, brought himself to one third and then one quarter his highest rate, adjusted the flow of sensory to match, watching the information integrate again like blocks tumbling to form a conceptual castle, and moved at moderate speed through the debris of battle. No more needles presented themselves; everything was spooky, at peace, but for the aftermath—clouds of debris.

Simulated. Only an exercise. He felt a quick moment of panic, blind fear, *not an exercise they caught us while we were out* but that made no sense at all.

They were still tendays away from the outer limits of Wormwood. Needles would not orbit in ranked shells out here; the sheer volume of anti-neutronium necessary for such a defense would consume hundreds of suns of mass. He pulled away from the fear.

A feeling of indignation. The children had not known what to expect; no preparation, no battle planning, and that was very unlikely. They had been set up artificially and artificially defeated.

He spotted an active picket: Erin Eire. He pulled up beside her rifle and sent a noach message to her.

"We've lost it," she said. "I'm just waiting for the call to go back."

"We have other options," he said.

"I know. Kamikaze."

"I mean other options besides that."

"Name them, *Pan.*" Her voice was only mildly sarcastic, but it still cut.

He raced through the scenarios they had trained for. "The Killers know we're here. We've exhausted their means of defense right now—no more needles. So we broadcast a noach call and pick a rendezvous."

She thought about that for a long time. He realized she was not accelerating her mind at all. That angered him.

"All right," she said.

"Go to speed five on your thoughts," he instructed.

"I don't—"

"Go *now* or I'll pull you from the exercise. You can ride free."

Riding free was something he had never threatened before.

"You can't do that—"

"Try me. Pull up, Erin."

She said nothing. Then he received a rapid burst of chatter from her. She had complied.

"All right. I'll send the message."

He broadcast the code signal. In tenths of a second, eleven active craft replied. Seven of the dead tried to signal, but he ignored them. The active craft met at an assigned point and regrouped.

"It's jaunted," Paola said, referring to the *Dawn Treader*.

A chorus of confused comment followed. Martin ordered cut-off and suggested they all think and offer plans, one by one. "And quickly. We can't afford to wait minutes out here."

Only thirteen craft. No fake matter in the craft—total mass: barely fifty tons. Complete conversion to neutronium, converting body mass to neutronium and anti-matter fuel to anti-neutronium, yields a total explosive force barely enough to sear a continent on a small world. It would be something, but . . .

In another channel of thought, Martin considered *long-term guerrilla action*, but that was quite outside the scope of the exercise. *What do the moms want us to do? What will they approve of?*

He realized that wasn't the point. It was easy to forget the moms were not there to be pleased or displeased; they were not human. In one way—the human way—they did not care, had no cares at all. They were simply goal-oriented. He should emulate them; they should all.

He heard Ariel's voice saying, *And then we become the moms, don't we?*

Out of the twelve others, four offered ideas, and eight kept silent. Three of the four ideas echoed what he had already rejected: searching for the *Dawn Treader*'s energy sumps. Sumps could not be detected from millions of kilometers away, unless one could monitor the local energy of the vacuum, and any number of high-tech processes caused that to fluctuate wildly; a sump *could* be located if one was right on top of it, within a thousand kilometers or so.

But at that range, energy sumps were dangerous. A hastily made, newly formed sump could leak bursts of radiation across a light hour of space sufficiently powerful to blind or even take out small craft.

Surprisingly, the fourth idea—a usable one, if not a scorcher—came from Erin Eire. *We scatter and conduct recon-*

naissance around the planet. The Dawn Treader *comes looking for us eventually, and we might have information to offer.*

That was probably outside the scope of the exercise, but then, so be it. No planet was postulated, none projected either within the craft or by the Ship of the Law, wherever it was; but they could conduct their part of the exercise, and at the very least earn marks for innovation.

"All right," Martin said. "We go down to the planet."

"There is no planet!" others chorused.

"Then we make one up. Paola, Erin, it's a rocky planet without an atmosphere—"

"Heavily defended by radiation and kinetic weapons," Erin suggested.

"Good . . ."

"And Paola's torus is nowhere to be seen," suggested Jack Sand, usually silent in such interactions.

"All right. So what do we do?"

"We search the entire planet, note *their* weapon positions . . ."

"How many do we lose?" Martin asked with a touch of irony.

"It's my idea," Erin said. "I'll volunteer."

Two others volunteered.

"That should be enough," Martin said, feeling light-headed. The whole exercise was turning into something crazy; what could he do?

They swept out to take up formations around a theoretical planet, positioning themselves in a sphere roughly ten thousand kilometers in diameter, sweeping in crude arcs to imitate orbits. Martin thought of youthful playtime, now made earnest; this dance of craft that would have dismayed his fifth-grade teachers on Earth, watching the ring-o and dodge-ball games on the playground.

Their wands made pictures of the hypothetical planet, projecting images into the areas usually reserved for their sensor reports. The effect was crude—no real artistry—but in their shame and fervor, somehow convincing.

Martin contributed weapons emplacements, dotting the mottled planet floating before him with finger-painted notations of defense and danger. Paola created a geology to match the airless ruined surface, and in quick noach updates, her sketches appeared on the sphere, cold ancient continents, internal heat fled, cracks in crust diving deep to solid cool core.

They played their game for several hours, caught in the raw high-speed spaces between the stars, between engagements.

They were growing weary when the *Dawn Treader* finally returned to retrieve them. Martin felt at first a neck prickle, before the ship alerted them to its presence; their sensors could not otherwise detect the great dark larval form hiding; then he felt a flood of giddy relief, apprehension, and finally a resurgence of shame.

They joined all their deactivated comrades and returned to the third homeball, flew to the outer hatch, connected to the pylons, pulled into the weapons store.

Their water drained, fields switched off, and membranes withdrew. Martin left his craft with an erection from the membrane's intimacy. They laddered to the hatch and walked out bleary-eyed. Silent, they parted to get cleaned up, to rest for a few minutes before meeting in the schoolroom to receive Martin's evaluation, to meet with Hans, who had been in charge of the *Dawn Treader*, and then to receive the War Mother's critique.

Hans met with Martin alone in the second neck.

"That was a royal slickup," Hans commented dryly. "Your outside teams were obliterated. We barely had time to get the ship to safety . . . We weren't prepared at all."

"First time out," Martin said. "Not that it's any excuse. We'll have to do better."

"Obviously," Hans said.

The children gathered in the schoolroom, subdued, to receive the critique. The War Mother waited while Hans and Martin went first, taking questions from the children, actually more confessions than questions. Some were close to tears. Those who had been deactivated in the early stages of the drill were particularly somber. They had been shut out, and Martin could feel their resentment and brooding anger.

Ariel, who had stayed aboard the *Dawn Treader* in charge of the team responsible for tracking radiation, was sharply critical. "You were doing nothing but slicking it out," she said, looking at Martin sidewise, lips downturned. "You could have been

detected! Your acceleration flares were too damned bright—
what are we doing, letting an *exercise* give us away?"

"The acceleration flares were too small to be detected by any
known or postulated methods from the distance of Wormwood,"
the War Mother said. Hakim agreed. Ariel fell silent.

Martin swallowed but said nothing. All voices must be heard.
The string of confessions continued. William took his turn after
the last craft pilot had spoken, and said, "It was our first time
out. We shouldn't be so hard on ourselves. The moms gave us
a blank deck and we played it." He glanced at Martin in the
center of the formation, winked one eye as if with a slight tic,
folded his arms and legs and stepped to one side.

"These evaluations are useful," the War Mother said when
the silence had stretched for fifteen seconds. "There was no
detailed structure to this exercise. The external team showed
initiative in providing a structure, but they were ineffective in
the opening moments of the engagement. What is the Pan's
evaluation?"

Martin's anger leaped to several sharp answers but he held
them back. "The exercise shows us what we need to learn. We
did badly. The simulation was confusing, but reality will be even
more confusing."

"And if we learn how to die before we accomplish anything,
what good is that?" Ariel asked. She leaned her head to one
side, eyes distant.

"We learn all we can on our own," Martin said, voice be-
traying his exhaustion. "The moms have told us that repeatedly.
That way, when we pull the trigger, it's our act as much as
possible, not theirs."

"When do we go out again?" Erin Eire asked, wrinkling her
face as if puzzled.

"As soon as possible," Martin said, suddenly aware he had
not conferred with the War Mother. He glanced at the robot.

"In nine hours," the mom said. "Time for sleep and food
and independent study."

Martin nodded. "Everybody out," he said. "Private time
with the War Mother. Ex-Pans, I'll need to confer with you after
I'm done here. Please wait for me outside."

"It was our first exercise," Martin said to the War Mother

when all the children had left. "We thought there would be some structure to it . . . We didn't expect to be stranded and have something completely random thrown at us. That's why we did so badly."

"We are no longer your teachers."

Martin stared at the divided circle where the War Mother's face might have been. "Beg pardon?"

"We are no longer your teachers. You are in charge of carrying out the Law. You tell us what to do. Now you train yourselves, and we help, but we do not lead."

Martin's astonishment was a painful black pit, and it took him a while to cross over it. "Who decided we're ready?"

"There have been five years of training. You are ready."

"I know you want us to carry out the Law of our own free will, but you can't abandon us now, leave us all on our own . . ."

"You are not abandoned. We provide the necessary information. We provide the tools. You use them. That is the Law."

"Slick the Law!" Martin shouted. "You can't just jerk everything out from under us!"

"You have been informed from the beginning what would be required of you. We have now entered a situation where you must be in control, not us."

"You warn us by letting us slick up on our first drill?"

"We do not make these choices. They are dictated by circumstance."

"So we take over from here . . . all the way?"

"It is the end of our role as teachers."

"There should have been warning," Martin said.

The War Mother said nothing.

"This will be a shock . . . it's a shock to me."

Still silence.

Martin fumbled for a means of explaining to the children what he had just heard, a rationale. "You're trying to knock us into action, break us out of our lethargy? You think that's psychologically appropriate?"

"It is necessary. We can lead you no further."

For the first time in his life, Martin became so furious with a mom that he felt he might lose control. He turned and ran from the schoolroom.

* * *

There had been five previous Pans, one for each year of their voyage. They had finished their year-long terms and returned to their groups and families, equal with all the children, but Martin always felt their eyes upon him: Stephanie Wing Feather, the first Pan, and her successors, Harpal Timechaser, Joe Flatworm, Sig Butterfly, Cham Shark.

All five followed Martin from the schoolroom to his quarters in the second homeball, saying little as they laddered and walked. This gave him time to calm down and frantically think. *Everything's skewed now, all our frames bent. How do we lead in this mess? How do I lead?*

In Martin's quarters, the ex-Pans took up positions in the center, in a cubicle of flexible tubes that Martin had made several years before. In zero g, the cage was for floating in while awake or exercising, or for guests to be close without being jammed together. Now that up and down had settled, the cage was just large enough to seat six.

"I'm going to need more help," Martin said.

"Why?" Stephanie asked. She was a year younger than Martin, a muscular gray-eyed woman of medium height with fine black hair tightcurled in a single ball that when liberated stretched a meter and a half. She was proud of the hair and took scrupulous care of it; Theresa would have said it was her thread.

"The moms expected something from us and I didn't provide it; they wanted us to design the exercise before we went out, to test our own skills and find our own weaknesses. That's why the drill was such a mess. They aren't going to make up any more tests for us."

"They should have told us earlier," Harpal said.

Martin shrugged. "I should have guessed. They want us to be more independent. Hell, I'm sorry. I'm not stating this exactly. I still can't believe it. *They're not going to be teachers any more.* We're on our own. We design strategies based on what they've taught us, and we control the *Dawn Treader* and all the weapons. They say they'll answer questions, give us information, but . . ."

"We've had trouble with their stinginess already," Harpal said. He was of medium build, black, with a long, sympathetic face. He wore wraparounds rather than overalls, and within his wraparounds he had hidden pockets that constantly carried surprises. Now he pulled out an orange and peeled it. They hadn't been fed oranges for fistfuls of tendays. He must have put several away in personal storage.

Stephanie shook her head in wonder. "They could have pushed us into this more gracefully," she said.

Sig Butterfly was less constrained. "God damn it all to hell," he said slowly, softly. Sig, dark skinned, with generous features and long hands that wrestled with each other as he spoke, continued, "I thought they understood human psychology. This is devastating. We screwed up thoroughly, and now they tell us we should have . . ." He shook his head and closed his eyes as if in pain.

"Maybe they *do* understand our psychology," Joe Flatworm said. Joe reminded Martin of California surfers, minus the tan. He kept his light brown hair shaggy above a friendly face that simply inspired friendship and confidence. When Stephanie groaned, Joe cocked his head to one side and smiled. "I mean it . . . playing Devil's advocate."

"I feel like I've dropped it all," Martin said. "I should have seen this coming."

"Nobody saw it," Harpal said. "Ariel's not too far wrong. The moms are starting to get on my nerves."

Martin frowned. "They're doing what they should be doing—getting us prepared."

Stephanie spoke again, but her words collided with Cham's. Cham Shark, coffee colored, long jawed, hair cut close to his head, had been a tough Pan, not very popular. During his time the children had been tense and unhappy and now he seldom said anything. He looked at Stephanie, but she waved him to continue, surprised he was speaking at all.

"They're making us prepare ourselves," he said. "They've given us the tools but we have to use them ourselves, and that means we make up our own large-scale strategies . . . Our games have always been weak on general strategy."

"So you said when you were Pan," Joe Flatworm pointed out.

Cham blinked, nodded, and folded his arms.

"If Cham is right, they won't let us in on any more strategies for the same reason they don't tell us everything about their machines . . ." Stephanie paused. "They may *say* it's because the Law requires we do the dirty work . . . But why not take multiple advantage? I've been speaking with Ariel. I don't want to second-guess you, Martin, but she's sharp and you haven't brought her into the fold enough. I see why she's frustrated."

"She's a pain," Martin said with uncharacteristic bluntness.

"You're spending too much time slicking between William and Theresa," Stephanie said, with typical candor. "Pull your wire in and open your eyes. She told me what you'd said about the moms' knowledge being too sensitive for them to explain everything. She thinks you're probably right, but she doesn't feel as complacent about it as you do."

"I'm not complacent," Martin said. "I just don't know what we can do about it. Fighting among ourselves, or fighting the moms, won't help."

"They want us to finish the Job as much as we do. They must," Joe said.

"Then they should trust us more," Cham said. "Our ignorance has been a constant frustration." He blinked again, looked around at the others, who regarded him with more surprise. "I'm no brick. I care about all this, too."

"Martin," Stephanie said, "if we're on our own, we should be equal partners. We should have a council of the children and take a vote. If we don't get what we want, what we think we need, we stand down on drills."

Martin closed his eyes and took a deep breath. "I . . . we can't just stand down after voting to go in. They must have reasons for doing what they're doing."

"Maybe," Cham said, "but the moms are robots. Maybe they just can't care, or can't understand us well enough to give us what we need." His reticence shattered, Cham had become voluble.

"Ariel is a rebel," Martin said, hating the thought that the children might support her over him. "She's sharp, but she's not wise. We can't just defy them. Who else do we have out here but the moms?"

"We have to get this resolved," Stephanie said.

"Agreed," Harpal said. "Martin, I concur with you about

Ariel. She's all mouth and not much common sense. I even agree
that the moms might know what they're doing. But we're alive
and they're not. We have the most to lose." He leaned over and
took Martin's shoulder in one hand. "My sympathies. It's a
tough watch."

"You want me to confront the moms, threaten to stand
down?"

"We need full disclosure," Stephanie said. "Especially now."

Martin made a small shiver. "After what they've done for us,
threatening something so drastic . . . seems like sacrilege."

"We have to be equal partners, not just trigger-pullers,"
Cham said.

"I hope you don't think we're ganging up on you," Harpal
said. "You asked for our advice. Consult with Hans."

Martin lowered his head, his misery evident. Stephanie
touched his chin with a finger, then stroked his cheek. "I'll go
in with you," she offered.

"No, thanks," he said stiffly. "Something has to be done.
We need to know what's required of us . . ."

"*Martin*," Stephanie said, irritated.

"Damn it, I'll do it! I'm just thinking out loud . . . We've
always assumed . . . or rather, our parents always assumed the
Benefactors were infallible, so much more powerful, our saviors,
and not human. Like gods."

"Gods aren't made of metal," Harpal said.

"How do *you* know?" Joe said, again playing Devil's advocate. That had been *his* flaw when he had been Pan—an inability
to settle on one course of action, to see all sides yet still concentrate on one plan. Martin saw that Joe sympathized with him,
and double-saw himself through Joe's eyes, and felt a puff of
annoyance.

He was being pushed by forces he could not resist to take
actions he had not thought through and might not agree with . . .
The fate of a Pan. The fate of all leaders. The group never
tolerates completely individual planning and initiative, not even
in dictators, if his readings in human history were any guide.

Human history. What sort of history had the Benefactors lived
through?

Know your enemy. Know your Benefactors.

"I'll go to the War Mother," Martin said.

"Talk with Hans first," Stephanie suggested again. "Never take full responsibility."

All but Cham nodded agreement.

"Somebody who's never been a Pan can't understand what it's like," Harpal said.

"Somebody's going to scream at you that you questioned the moms," Cham said.

"They'll find some reason to scream, no matter what," Joe said.

Theresa stood with arms outstretched under revolving spheres of sunbright light. She kept her room small and tidy, a scholar's room she had once called it, and Martin liked the style, although it differed completely from his large, messy sprawl. He stood in the open hatch before announcing himself, pleased just to be near her.

"Hello," she said. She came forward and he hugged her, nuzzling her neck. His response was not immediate; he felt a sour burn in the deep of his stomach.

"It wasn't so bad," she said. He lowered himself to his knees and she combed his hair with her fingers while he kissed her navel and belly. "The first drill, I mean."

"It was awful," Martin said. He pressed his cheek against the warmth of her stomach, chin nuzzling curled hair. "I'm going to speak with Hans now, and then I'm going to the moms." He stood, head bowed, and she wrapped her arms around his waist.

"No time?" she asked, teasing him with her fingers, rubbing the overalled cleft between his buttocks. She pressed his coccyx. "I'm sorry," she said, still touching him. "Not making it any easier."

"No," he said, sighing. "Are you going to a Wendy party this evening?"

"There is one," she said. "I'd like to. I'll stay for you."

"I won't be done until then, I think," Martin said. "But we've been together so much, I don't want to wear you out."

"Do I act worn out?" she asked, lip-tugging the tip of his nose.

Martin bowed awkwardly and curled his face into her breasts and felt for the nipples. Lip-tugged and suckled. Her breasts were small and firm looking, yet still soft to his touch. He thought about other Lost Boys touching her, felt vaguely neutral for an instant, realized he did not like that thought, bit her gently to emphasize his presence. "I don't want to bore you," he said.

"Do I act bored?"

She held on to his shoulders, wrapped her legs around his hips and moved her pubis against him. His erection was quick despite the distractions and he pushed her back to the pad.

"Don't ruin me," he said.

"Touch touch," she said, "then you can go." He touched each thigh with two fingers of his left hand, lifted her easily to his lips, tongued her lightly. Then he let her go and Theresa slid to the floor.

"Delicious," he said. "After the party?"

"Sleep here."

"Pans sleep in quarters where they can be found."

"Set their wands. They'll know."

Martin had always been shy of announcing the obvious. "Maybe," he said.

Theresa turned back to the revolving lights. For a moment he thought she might have completely forgotten him, so swift and decisive was her motion; as if he were easily dismissed. But she smiled and said, "Go now. Come back when we both have time."

Martin hesitated by the door, then passed through, walked down the hall, found a main shaft and laddered outward to the level where he would meet with Hans.

Hans was seldom in his quarters. He slept where exhaustion took him; he slept rarely, some said, exercising or researching for several days before finally collapsing in a corridor in a make-shift bed he carried in the backpack that was always with him.

Martin found him in the swim room. The water lay slowly rippling on the floor now. Hans lay back in the water up to his neck, pushing it toward one wall with broad sweeps of both arms. The water bounced from the wall and washed over his head, bounced from the rear wall and bobbed him up gently as he swam toward the edge of the pool.

Martin watched the water's behavior for a moment as if it were completely unfamiliar. Hans stepped out and toweled off. He finished by tousling his short blond hair. It stood up in insolent spikes.

"The past Pans think we should confront the moms and ask for full disclosure," Martin told him.

"Do what Ariel wants?" Hans asked.

"I suppose."

"Poor Martin," Hans said, chuckling. "What a grind."

"Don't worry about Ariel," Martin said, irritated.

Hans pasted the towel on the wall to dry, flinging it up so that it spun flat and its wetness made it stick, and when it started to slip down, deftly pinned it with a ladder field. Even in full g, Hans was incredibly skillful in subtle physical acts; he had the best control of any of the children. On Earth, he might have become an acrobat.

"Any suggestions how I go about it?" Martin asked.

"Spring it on the moms at a tenday conference," Hans said. "Unless they're listening and already know. In which case, they ignore us, or they do something."

"The moms don't eavesdrop."

Hans made a face but did not accuse Martin of naïveté.

"God damn it, they *don't*," Martin said. "They have no reason to."

Hans put on his overalls, his face slightly pink at Martin's tone. "If you say so, brother," he said tightly. "I just think they'd want to keep track of everything we do. Zookeepers and all that. They're responsible for us—or at least responsible for seeing that we get our Job done, according to the Law, and if I were them, dealing with a bunch of Wendys and Lost Boys, I'd sure as hell want to keep tabs on us."

Martin stood back as Hans walked by. Hans lifted his arms, shook his head. "But you believe them, that's okay."

Martin was speechless. "Has everybody on this ship gone flat cynical?" he asked.

Hans turned on him swiftly, pointing a finger. "Everybody feels bad and confused. What if we slick this whole Job? Who's to blame? You're Pan."

Martin said, without hesitation, "I am."

Hans stared, then grinned. "We are the leaders, brother. You and me. Maybe they'll cook us and eat us. The children, I mean, not the moms. But hell, I think it's a good idea we ask for . . . full disclosure, is it? I call it full partnership. My father was a businessman. Sold cars. I remember him talking about confidence and trust. He said he had to believe what he was doing was good for the customer, that they were actually partners, or he couldn't convince them. Even if he didn't tell the truth, he had to *think* he was while he was selling . . . I was ten. The Benefactors didn't think he deserved to . . ." He lifted his eyes and didn't finish. "Let's go for it."

Martin put a finger to his cheek and rubbed gently at the light bristle there. He hadn't shaved in two days; still not much of a beard.

"Together," Hans said. "More impact that way."

"Not together," Martin said.

"Why not?" Hans appeared puzzled.

"Because I'm Pan," Martin said, looking away from him.

Hans rubbed his nose. "Better you than me, brother."

Martin sat alone in his cubicle within the darkened quarters, wand in hand, concentrating. What *were* their limits? How much had they been told, and how much had they simply neglected to ask? It was time to find out, before he went to the moms and made a fool of himself.

"Strategy discussions," Martin told the wand. A list of possible topics floated in the air before his face and he picked two: *Armor and Deception in Deep Space Warfare*, and *Galactic Ecology and Galactic Defense Strategy*. He had studied both topics before; nearly all the children had. Theodore had recorded some useful glosses. But no one, to his knowledge, had actively pursued the question of where these literary and visual productions had originated.

Martin asked, "Authors and sources, please."

The wand projected: *Authors and sources not relevant.*

"I'd like to know anyway. As Pan. As leader for the children."

Authors and sources: Translations and reinterpretations of materials devised by civilizations signatory to the Law.

"More details, please. Which civilizations? When?"

Not relevant.

"I'm demanding the answer, not asking for it," Martin said, still calm, but understanding even more Ariel's frustration. He had never tried this before; in his ignorance he had been content not to upset his preconceptions.

The basic texts and corresponding sensory additions were created three thousand four hundred years ago. A single civilization was responsible for the primary sources; other civilizations added to them, and adapted them. Names of the actual authors of the primal texts are not known.

"What was the first civilization like?"

Martin had asked for details about a good many civilizations, and had always been curious about the general nature of the answers, but not so curious as to seem disrespectful. Now it had been made his duty.

The originating civilization was severely damaged in a conflict involving offshoot spacefaring relations.

"Offshoots? You mean, its own colonies? Detail, please." Martin tensed his jaw muscles as he waited for a reply.

Yes, its own colonies. Further details are not known to this source.

He had never pushed so far, and therefore, never received such an answer.

"Open another source, then," Martin said, taking a wild chance. "Another library or whatever."

Please refer to the moms.

"I'm asking now," Martin said. "These facts are important to us. We need psychological insight."

Details of civilizations participating in the Law are not relevant to your Job.

"I say they are," Martin pursued, his voice rising. "I am Pan."

Please refer to the moms.

There it was, then. The wall Ariel and others had doubtless hit. Martin could see why the moms were secretive about some things; the civilizations signatory to the Law could easily imagine another round of death and destruction if their whereabouts and the details of their defenses were known.

Earth had been an easy target because of innocent radiation
of energy into space, its baby-bird cheeping in the unprotected
tree branch of the solar system.

Martin felt a weary sadness, an echo of all the sadness he had
known since Earth's death. Was there ever a point in the scale
of galactic civilizations when strangers could trust each other?
Did civilizations ever develop sufficient scruples that not one of
them would think of creating machines of mass destruction?

Perhaps; but humans were certainly not on that level.

Martin's reading of human history easily led him to imagine
planet-destroying probes created by his people, and turned
against others. And if *he* could imagine it, the moms could
imagine it as well.

What sort of equality could exist between children and Benefactors under those circumstances?

Martin waited in the empty schoolroom, uneasy, a tic in his left
eye, simple nerves. He stood near the sphere. The stars appeared
normal now, and the sphere was offering an unaltered view in
the direction of Wormwood, which he could make out even
without help as a slightly brighter spot of light among the myri-
ads. Brighter still was the red burn of Behemoth. Leviathan was
not visible from this angle.

The War Mother entered.

"Hello, Martin," it said. "How are the children?"

"Fine, physically. A few social problems. Some aren't mesh-
ing perfectly." He always seemed to optimize the situation,
making it sound better than he actually thought it was. Was this
part of what Ariel might have called *toadying* to the moms?

"Have you developed plans for further training?"

He swallowed. "No," he said. "We feel stymied."

"Why?"

"We can't do the Job without knowing what might be waiting
for us down there."

"All the information you need is being provided as we
receive it."

"I mean background," Martin said. "Information about other
civilizations, other incidents—how the strategies were created,
how we can adapt them to suit our needs . . . I mean, to adapt

them, we have to . . ." He swallowed again. For a Pan, he was not showing much fortitude. "You have to trust us with all your information. We're calling for full disclosure."

To Martin's surprise and concern, the War Mother did not speak for several long seconds. "The information provided should be adequate," it finally answered.

"We're being asked to show independent thought, to devise our own strategies . . . and the libraries aren't detailed. How did others fight against the planet-wreckers? How did *your* builders fight them?"

More seconds of silence. Surely it did not need so much time to compute or think of an answer.

"Your requests cannot be met," the War Mother said. "The information you require is dangerous."

Martin was astonished by the word "dangerous." That doesn't make sense," he said.

"Cooperation was required to build the Ships of the Law. To encourage the cooperation of many civilizations and beings, certain precautions were necessary, among them, that security would be maintained. Ships of the Law might be captured, and their information used to seek out and harm those who built the ships."

Martin had never thought of being *captured*; it had seemed, from the very beginning, that at least the children were safe, traveling in a Ship of the Law, the ultimate power, the belated victor of the war that had destroyed Earth. *But of course that was not a war—just a battle. Probably an unimportant battle, at that.*

Martin was not about to budge. "We need to have all your information shared with us."

"Surely you hope to survive this mission," the War Mother said.

"Of course."

"Martin, if your brothers and sisters survive, you, too, could be dangerous. If you are given such information, you also might seek the builders of these instruments."

Martin swallowed hard. "We cannot create strategies out of nothing. I've asked questions that *need* to be answered, and received no answers."

"You have worked with the best information available. There are simply no clues to where the Benefactors might be found. The information you need is available. Use it."

"I've been told——"

"You are Pan," the mom said.

He swallowed harder, and his tongue seemed to grow thick. "We'll stand down."

"What is 'stand down'?" the mom asked.

"We'll refuse to enact the Law."

"If that is your choice, the ship will change from its present course."

Martin relaxed his clenched fists. He was not angry with the moms; he was not angry with the children. With regard to himself he felt nothing. He looked away from the copper-bronze robot, seeing too clearly how naïve they all were.

"We're just asking to be trusted," Martin said, working to keep his voice level.

"We are not empowered to trust or not to trust. Nor can we give you information that this ship does not carry. We cannot do the impossible, Martin."

He felt ill and exhausted. Why had he let the children put him up to this? Because he was Pan, and represented them? That didn't seem at all sufficient to explain his predicament and his misery.

"Why were we sent on this mission when we don't have the information we need to complete it?" He sounded petulant and petty, and he hated it.

"What you lack is information that our builders think you will not need."

Martin's mind worked furiously to find a chink in this thick armor of logic. *I would have designed the ship the same way! We all would have!*

"But the ship carries information about Earth. If it's captured, they could——the Killers could——"

"This Job would be impossible if you did not have access to your culture, your history and planetary memories."

"You'd risk our solar system, but you will not risk your . . . makers? Your planet, or planets?"

"That is the way it must be."

Another wall, huge and unyielding; two walls actually, closing with him between. "We feel inadequate to do the Job," he said softly, eyes turned away.

"Go back to the others and tell them they are not inadequate. They have the resources they need.

"There is, in this ship, something that goes beyond knowledge, that is hidden in its structure and the way it operates, which allows this ship to judge with high accuracy the chances of a mission's success. Call it a mechanical instinct. Your people are very capable. Tell them."

Martin lifted his head and stepped back. "I'll try," he said.

His face was red as he left the schoolroom. He had been maneuvered into presenting a case without believing it himself. That showed his weakness as a leader. Failing to get what he had been sent to get would make him seem weak in the eyes of some children—Ariel in particular. But he did not care what she thought.

What would Theresa think? And William?

What would Rosa Sequoia think? Rosa, who needed a strong leader to draw her back into the group?

Sitting on the edge of a table, Martin finished his crew report, the most difficult few minutes in recent memory. Most of the children—seventy-two of them—sat in the main cafeteria, the only space besides the schoolroom large enough to hold them all at once.

The ship's deceleration had hastened and they now faced a steady two g's. They were tired and they listened to his report quietly.

"That's it," he concluded, looking from face to face to keep direct visual contact with as many as he could. Then he gave that up; it might make him seem nervous. Instead, he focused on four or five in the front ranks.

Hans Eagle and Erin Eire sat in the front row. Hans' expression was quizzical. Erin cradled her cat, a fat gray thing with exhausted, bored eyes and matted fur.

"Did you argue with them?" someone asked from the middle. Martin looked up quickly and tried to spot the face, but answered before he had identified Terence Sahara.

"I did my best to present our case," he said. "Either we believe them, or we don't. And if we don't believe them . . ." He let the question hang.

Theresa sat on a bench to his right. He glanced at her; she smiled support. William, on the opposite side, about one third back into the crowd, sat with hands behind his head, elbows like stubby wings, eyes closed.

No one stood against the oppressive force; no one exerted themselves more than they absolutely had to.

"It's frightening," Erin Eire said. She swallowed; even speaking seemed tiring. "We thought they were all-wise, all-knowing. If the Ship of the Law doesn't know, then the machines that saved us probably didn't know, either . . . don't know."

"What *do* the Benefactors know? Anything?" Jack Sand asked.

Felicity Tigertail, in the front row—Martin's first lover, back on the Central Ark, during a brief two-day tryst—raised her hand as if she were in school. Martin nodded to her. Her arm was bruised, he noted; they all had bruises from such casual actions as letting arms drop. She lowered her arm cautiously.

"We're lost if we don't believe them," she said. "We have to believe them. That should be obvious."

"We don't have to believe anything," Ariel said from the rear, voice loud to rise above the murmuring. She sounded harsh, angry. Martin wondered where she got her energy to stay angry. "We have to ask questions. We should continue to ask questions! I think this is bullshit. They can defend themselves against the kind of machines that destroyed Earth! Why worry about what information they carry? The moms—the Benefactors—are simply afraid of *us*. They don't want *us* to know anything about them or their makers."

Martin started to speak, but Paola Birdsong, in the middle of the group, shouted out first, "Hold it! Does anybody here have enough imagination to see what the moms are *really* saying? Martin, do *you* know what they're telling us?"

"They're not all-powerful," Jack Sand said.

"I'm asking Martin!" Paola insisted.

Martin looked out over the group from his seat on the table top, then with great effort stood up, holding his hands behind his back. The table seemed very high. If he fell, he could break a leg. Or his neck. "They seem to say there are hunter-killers out there from civilizations much more technologically advanced than the one—or ones—that built the Ships of the Law."

"It never ends! Nobody ever learns!" Erin Eire cried out. Her cat tried to crawl away in distaste. "Nobody ever grows old enough to be kind or wise!"

"Hold it," Martin said, raising his hand. Noise rippled through the children, words of shock and dismay. "Hold it! Quiet!" he shouted hoarsely.

"Quiet!" Hans repeated, his voice like a bear's growl in the cafeteria space.

The children quieted. Ariel stood and lumbered from the room, followed by two others whose faces Martin didn't catch in the rear gloom.

"To get agreement to build these machines, the Benefactors have to guarantee security. Safety. They need to know that sending the ships and machines out won't backfire and lead bigger wolves down on them. That's just caution. Maybe there aren't really any bigger wolves out there. But they have to be cautious. And of course, in time, maybe we will become dangerous, like a lion turning on its keeper." He looked at Felicity and smiled. Felicity nodded.

"We shouldn't be cynical," Martin said. "The moms tell us we're good, and that we have what we need. We just have to work extra hard with what we have. We have to drill. We have to make up our own exercises based on what we've already been taught. They took risks by teaching us what they have. We're powerful, given the weapons we're taught to use. That shows some kind of trust, doesn't it?"

"We have what we need," Hans repeated. "We have work to do."

"Vote on it!" Ariel had returned and looked at Martin from the shadows at the rear.

Martin's face flushed. "No," he said. "We don't do everything by some sort of silly consensus. If you don't like the way things are being done, you elect another Pan. You can do that now if you want. The moms say we'll be diverted if we stand down. Who wants to lose this chance, after five years?"

Silence.

"God damn it, we have the right to vote!" Ariel said, tears obvious in her voice.

"One vote only," Martin insisted. "Whether I stay Pan." He swung his arms and folded them in front of his chest, aware that this was a silly and classic pose of blustering leadership, and waited for a response, half-hoping for a swell of dissent to take the weight from his back.

Silence.

"God damn you all!" Ariel cried out. The children hunched their shoulders and looked back at her resentfully, but she stayed in the room.

Martin gingerly lowered himself, feeling a moment of vertigo. "We already voted to go in," he said, voice softer. "This doesn't change anything. We just have to work harder."

"Time is short," Hans said. "We work up a drill schedule now, and we drill by our own designs. We workshop what we might expect to find in this system, and we *plan* for it, and we take whatever help the moms offer!"

Martin's heart went out again in a perverse way to Ariel, standing in the back of the room, face shiny with tears. He had done his performance and they had agreed, tacitly at least, to continue; he had exerted leadership and had molded consensus of a sort. How long would it last, though, and how strong was their resolve?

In that sick moment, he knew he was wrong to agree with the moms, not demanding a stand-down, not calling their bluff— and that Ariel was right.

He stood on the floor and took a deep breath. Hans came up to one side. Behind him, Stephanie Wing Feather and Harpal Timechaser sat on benches, not looking at him. Finally Stephanie turned.

"Way to go," she said.

"Ignore them," Hans said.

"You've got them dedicated now," Stephanie said without sincerity as Martin turned to walk away. His entire head felt warm. He turned back suddenly, back muscles twinging. "What would you have done, God damn it?"

Stephanie kept her seat as he approached.

"What would you have done?" Martin repeated, less loudly. The other children had filed out now, leaving only Stephanie, Harpal, Hans and Martin in the cafeteria.

"I don't know," Stephanie said, swallowing. "I might have tried harder."

"No," Martin said, wiping his eyes and straightening. "No. You wouldn't have."

Stephanie got up from the bench and ran her hands down the sides of her overalls, smoothing the fabric. "It's the weight, Martin," she said. "I didn't mean to be sarcastic. Sorry."

Martin's anger wouldn't go so easily. He backed away, glanced at Hans, who pursed his lips and shook his head. "I'm sorry, too," he murmured, and left the room, Hans following three steps behind.

In five days, as they flew through the pre-birth cloud surrounding Wormwood, the children would reach the next point of decision—to judge whether the system had been the source of the Earth-killing machines, and decide whether to split *Dawn Treader* into *Hare* and *Tortoise*.

Through the tendays of oppressive weight, the children drilled endlessly. Martin actually looked forward to time in the craft, to the relief of volumetric fields. Hakim pushed the search team patiently, trying to absorb as much information as possible about Wormwood before they pulled in the remotes.

Hakim could shed little light on the unresolved problem of the five dark masses close in to the star, orbiting in nearly perfect circles.

Martin pondered all this alone, preparing the preliminary order of battle in his quarters. He had not seen Theresa for eighteen hours; had not slept for thirty. Love-making was out of the question.

The children engaged in routine drills without him. He had to finish his work soon—in a few hours at most—to give time for final practice and one final external drill before they entered the pre-birth cloud.

They had flown for five and a half years, and yet there was the inevitable urgency and panic now, something that proved their humanity. He half-suspected the external drill had been

deliberately arranged to be disastrous, that the moms in their
subtle way were shocking the children, guiding them into battle-
readiness . . .

But he could not assume that. The moms might be as coolly
unconcerned as they seemed in conversation, relying entirely on
the passion of the children to carry out the Law. Do the Job.

He rubbed his sweat-matted hair. Sometimes he could hardly
think; he would curl up on the floor, eyes tight shut, trying to
ignore exhaustion, frustrated desire for Theresa, and concentrate.

Despite these distractions, he was coming to a conclusion
about the plan of battle.

Pan was in charge of general planning. No votes would be
taken after the judgment had been made by all the children;
Pan and Christopher Robin would have complete control, acting
through the division leaders, the five former Pans. Each division
leader would oversee a team of fifteen or sixteen children; each
team would be assigned a task. Two teams would stay with the
Hare. Three teams would fly *Tortoise*.

Tortoise would accomplish the main objective. Makers cast
into the pre-birth cloud would use the available raw materials to
manufacture weapons, gravity- or proximity-fuse neutronium
bombs that would comprise a second automatic assault, in case
the initial assault failed.

Tortoise would launch small craft. Their task would be to
divert and/or destroy any defenses and accomplish reconnaissance. Two ex-Pans would lead these small craft teams.

Martin suffered a deep conflict when studying strategy and
tactics. Too many possibilities occurred to him; he could not see
his way through to a clear line of attack. With some chagrin,
he knew the reason for his conflict: he regarded the massive
destruction of space war, the necessary total vanquishing of an
enemy, as an essentially immoral act. Yet he desired justice for
the Earth's murder as much as any of the children.

Clear thinking on the matter was very difficult; he simply did
not trust his own instincts.

Many children had created and filed theoretical tactics over
the years; Martin had consulted nearly all of them, particularly
those created by Theodore Dawn.

Theodore had been a kind of brilliant child, wise in some respects, but supremely strong willed and irresponsible in others, a complement to Martin's indecision and second-guessing. More effectively than Martin ever could, blithely ignoring questions of morality, Theodore had created a mathematics of space war tactics that used nearly all the features of the momerath to great advantage. His schemes covered many contingencies, all suggested by the principles taught by the moms. Basics of space warfare, as taught by the moms, had flowered in Theodore's mind into a graceful dance devoid of consequences.

In Theodore's plans, concealment was the only armor. Concealment, what Theodore called "silence," was a fine art among high-technology civilizations. Silence meant complete damping of radiation; invisibility meant unaberrated replication of incident radiation. Advantages over an adversary could be measured mathematically by how silent each was. Silent delivery of weapons—and the silence of the weapons themselves—was next in importance.

Theodore had studied manuals of submarine warfare on Earth. But space was far more dangerous than a deep sea, because it was vast, transparent to all radiations, and a perfect medium for weapons delivery. Yet space had many advantages over ocean; it was three-dimensional without limit, travel paths were limited to orbits, and even the largest unconcealed weapons platform, given sufficient distance, was tiny compared to the background.

Interstellar space had no weather, and rarely changed its character during a period of confrontation. Interplanetary space—the region most likely to be assaulted and defended—was subject to the vagaries of stellar atmospheres and stellar particle streams, but advanced spacefaring civilizations were not bothered by them.

Interplanetary space was extremely difficult to guard. When assault could come undetected from almost any angle, the best defense lay in deceit—either camouflage or outright disguise. What did not attract attention was not attacked.

The libraries told them that only primitive civilizations, such as Earth's, blatantly announced their existence.

If deceit and camouflage failed, space warfare was comparatively clean and dependent on initial conditions. Knowing the differences in technology suggested probable outcomes for most confrontations even before battle began.

For an invader, this could be turned into an advantage. If an invasion force was discovered within a system, it could "pigeon puff": provide misleading evidence of overwhelming superiority, thus forcing its adversary into ineffective and energy-wasting tactics accompanied by a sense of certain defeat. Psychological weapons were difficult to design because the psychology of an adversary might be unknown or, when facing machines, virtually nonexistent. Even the methods of perception of an adversary might be problematic.

More effective sometimes, Theodore postulated, was an appearance of weakness, of lesser technological ability. One part of an assault could perform deception while other parts deployed silently. If the adversary were deceived by this "lapwing," it might exert its forces prematurely, inappropriately, or not at all.

These were solid but not brilliant reflections of what the moms had taught them. Where Theodore Dawn's genius truly shined was in describing an adversary's course of actions under the imagined circumstances of confrontation. Theodore seemed to have an aptitude for creating alien psychologies, and applying them to space warfare.

He created four categories of adversary: inferior, equal, superior, and unknowable. Unknowable could encompass any of the other categories; for example, a weak, low-technology adversary might have stumbled onto effective methods of maintaining silence, or of deceiving.

Inferior was easily enough defined, and even dealt with, given due caution; but it was unlikely the Killers were inferior to the Benefactors. Theodore outlined a few simple instances, warned of dangers, and went on to equality and superiority.

Equality was most difficult to plan for, simply because it *could* be planned for. Martin, choosing the most likely scenario, studied Theodore's writing and displays on the tactics of attacking equals. What he was concerned with was not equality of force, but equality of technology and intelligence; not equality of desire or fear, nor even the sameness of creativity, but equality of the raw materials of warfare, in terms of capabilities. Thus, a torpedo was smaller and perhaps less complex than the submarine it was designed to destroy, yet it was equal in *technological origins*.

A simple device could be made clever at the same level as a more complex, far more powerful or *forceful* device; it could be effective against the greater force, preventing its use or destroying it.

A superior adversary was best not confronted directly, or at all (though that was not a choice here; they must bat against such a force like a moth against a glass window, if necessary, dedicated but all-uncomprehending). But the superior adversary was likely also best at concealment, deception, and diversion. A far superior adversary might not be an adversary at all, as much as a supernatural force, a Godlike potentiality that could brush aside the most careful planning and the most concerted assault like the whims of a child.

Still, the moms insisted—and Theodore agreed—confronting a technologically superior adversary was not necessarily folly. Killing Captain Cook.

The tactics of dealing with superiority were largely those of silence and attrition, like an infected flea creeping into a human's clothes to spread plague. The makers and the doers could act as bacilli.

But repeatedly, Martin was reminded by Theodore's writings that any comparisons they made—even the comparison to killing Cook—were faulty.

It was possible the superior adversary could nullify or escape any of their weapons.

Martin closed his eyes and tried to subdue his frustration, his conflict. There would never be enough information. And he—Martin—would never be sufficiently prepared . . .

The *Dawn Treader* used every method at its disposal to slow over the long days of space, and to conserve its fuel, girding for battle.

Martin led the children outside the ship again, and this time he felt they were prepared. He had set up a particularly nasty adversary—one suggested by Theodore years before.

Martin stayed within the ship, directing the efforts of this adversary with two others—Harpal Timechaser and Stephanie Wing Feather.

Outside, forty of the children flew their craft around the *Dawn Treader*, preparing for entry into a simulated system configured very much like Wormwood.

The five unknown masses around the yellow star were hidden defense stations, in Martin's plan; and Theodore's adversaries, pure machine intelligences that had long since replaced their biological creators, were in command.

Martin watched the scenario play itself out.

Planets met their end in compressed time, surfaces molten slag, and most of the children survived. *Hare*, portrayed by the still-intact *Dawn Treader*, came through with minimal damage.

The farthest-scattered craft came in fifteen minutes after the simulation's end.

Stephanie licked her index finger, stuck it up to an imaginary breeze, swayed her arm toward Martin, and smiled. Confidence was returning.

The children gathered in the first homeball's cafeteria and analyzed their performances, Martin and Hans overseeing. The self-criticism flowed steadily, without hurt feelings, and Martin felt a knitting of the teams that had gone out on drill.

Afterward, they ate dinner, then listened to music performed by Joe Flatworm and Kees North Sea: raucous, lively folk music from the Ukraine and Tennessee, barely slowed by the extra weight.

Their bodies had grown stronger, stockier. No need to ask if the moms were responsible.

The performance lasted less than half an hour; they rested after, Martin in Theresa's quarters, in the heavy darkness, watching the ceiling, mind passing over the day's events.

He slept peacefully, without dreams.

Two days until coasting resumed; five days from passage through the pre-birth material.

Martin exercised in the second neck, climbing along the ladder fields instead of letting them haul him up or down. He had climbed almost the entire distance from the second homeball to the third, enjoying the exertion, almost used to the heaviness, when he heard the screaming, thin and far away, sliced into ghastly echoes by the shapes in the wormspace.

Theresa was in the third homeball, above him, doing private practice in a bombship. She quickly descended on a field, pausing beside him where he hung, and listened, frowning. "Did you hear that?" she asked.

He nodded, hoping it was nothing. It did not sound like *nothing*. It sounded horrible, even more horrible when distorted, and they were used to the distortions of voices in the necks.

Nothing for seconds. Then, a barely audible keening, voices of concern, two or three people trying to comfort.

They descended quickly, ladders dropping them to the second homeball.

In the main corridor, they found Rosa Sequoia weeping, surrounded by five others, two Wendys and three Lost Boys. Her broad, strong face wet with tears, Rosa could not catch her breath, and she could not speak beyond a few gasped words.

"We didn't see anything," Min Giao Monsoon said, patting her on the shoulder. "There is nothing in the halls!"

"What's wrong?" Martin asked.

"Rosa saw something," Kees North Sea said, narrow face nervous, eyes shifting. "She's scared out of her wits."

"What did you see?" Theresa asked, moving in closer to Rosa. Rosa kneeled in a tighter crouch, large frame forming a round obstruction in the corridor.

"Rosa, stop it," Martin said, an edge in his voice. "Please get yourself together." She had piloted a ship outside and performed well in exercises; he had thought she was coming around. Now he was irritated, and then ashamed of his irritation. *Doesn't she know she makes this more difficult for us?*

But that was truly beside the point, and he buried his resentment at her weakness. He knelt beside her, touching her wet cheek.

"No!" she shouted, starting up, falling back painfully on one arm. She looked so clumsy, so pitiably overwrought, that Martin's anger surged almost too quickly to be hidden. "You didn't see anything," she said. "You won't believe me . . . But I saw!"

"*What* did you see?" Martin asked, teeth tight together.

Resonant, almost silky, Rosa's voice carried down the hall to other children gathering, ten, then twenty, coming from both directions. "Something large and dark. It wasn't a mom."

Martin looked up, shoulders and neck tensing, less at Rosa's proclamation than at an intuition something was going to go very wrong, and he could not stop it.

"I've never seen anything like it," she said.

"Did it do anything?" Theresa asked. Martin winced inwardly at her implicit affirmation that there had been something.

"It stared at me . . . I think. I couldn't see any eyes. It left marks."

"Where?"

Rosa got to her feet, wiped her eyes with the palms of her hands, swung her shoulders back and stood tall. She apologized in a barely audible voice. "I was in the C wing, coming down for my team exercise . . . The lights were down. I don't know why."

"Lights are always down in C wing," Martin said. "Nobody has quarters there."

"That's the way I come here," Rosa said, glancing at him resentfully. *She avoids the place where she saw Theresa and me making love.* "It was in the dark, just . . . being there, sitting or standing, I don't know. I've never seen anything like it."

"Show us," Martin said. He turned to the children gathered on both sides and said, "I'll handle this."

"We'd like to help," Anna Gray Wolf said, face eager— something different attracting her, attracting all of them. She stared owlishly at Rosa.

"It's okay," Martin said. "Theresa and I will take care of it." *In case they doubt the masculine touch is sufficient.*

The children dispersed, and Martin took Rosa's elbow.

"You don't think I saw it?" Rosa asked as she led them along the hall to the empty C wing.

"I don't know what you saw," Martin said. Then, trying for a joke, "Maybe you saw a mom without makeup."

Rosa looked at him resentfully, sadly, then straightened and pointed to the area of the hall where she had seen the shape. Martin ordered the hall to brighten—wondering why Rosa had not already done the same.

He examined the walls. Never dirty, never dusty, the surfaces within the Ship of the Law cleaned themselves; it was taken for granted by the children. The walls showed no marks.

"I saw scuffs when I came through here," Rosa said.

"It was dark," Martin said.

Quietly, desperately, Rosa began to weep again.

"You could have turned the lights on and seen whatever it was," he said.

"We don't disbelieve you," Theresa said, holding Rosa's shoulder firmly, massaging it with her fingers. "But why didn't you turn the lights on?"

"I was afraid! I didn't want to see it, whatever it was . . . I didn't want it to see me."

"How big was it?" Martin asked. *Dangerous, dangerous.*

"It filled this part of the hall," Rosa said, stretching her arms to the ceiling. The hall was two meters wide, marked with blue circles where quarters might be chosen and doors made by the ship on request.

The entire ship had completely adapted itself to deceleration. The circles that had once marked doors in the ceiling and floor had been absorbed by the ship; only circles on the walls remained. Perhaps Rosa had misinterpreted some function of the ship, or seen something nobody else had witnessed.

He tried to express that diplomatically. "The ship usually cleans up or changes when we're not watching; maybe it accidentally allowed you to see something."

"It wasn't part of the ship . . . I don't think it was," Rosa said. She had lost her tone of hysteria. Her face appeared calmer now, puzzled, and she seemed willing to cooperate, to help them solve the mystery.

"Was it metal, or something else?" Theresa asked.

"It was like a shadow. I didn't see any details. I don't know what it could have been. It seemed alive to me." Rosa folded her arms. Martin saw her as she had been when the journey started, five years before, sixteen and not fully grown, slenderer, with a rugged attractiveness, now become a vulnerable burliness. He wondered again why the moms had chosen her. They had rejected so many others, many Martin had thought were good choices. She swallowed hard, looked, with her large black eyes, more and more lost. "Maybe it wasn't part of the ship. Maybe it doesn't belong here."

"Hold on," Theresa said sternly. Martin was grateful to her for taking a critical tone he dared not use. "We shouldn't jump to any conclusions."

"I saw it," Rosa said, stubbornly defensive.

"We're not questioning that," Theresa said, though Martin certainly thought they should, and she had. "We've all been under a strain lately, and . . ."

Rosa was turning inward again.

"I saw it. I think it might be important," she said.

"All right," Martin said. "But for now, until we know more, or somebody else sees it, I'd like to keep this quiet."

"Why?" Rosa asked, eyes narrowing. Martin saw more clearly the depth of her problem. She was not going to react well to his next request, but he saw no way around it.

"Please don't talk about it," he said.

Rosa tightened her lips, jaws clenched, eyes reduced to slits, face radiating defiance, but she did not say anything more. "Can I go?" she asked, as if she were a little girl requesting dismissal from class.

"You can go," Martin said. Rosa walked on long, strong legs down the hall toward the central corridor, not looking back. Martin inhaled deeply, held it, watching her like a target, then exhaled when she was too far away to hear.

"Jesus."

"No, I don't think so," Theresa said. She grinned. Martin felt the walls again, as if there might be some mark remaining, some trace of Rosa's shadow.

"I don't think there actually was anything," he said, trying to be extra reasonable, extra careful, even with Theresa.

"Of course not," Theresa said.

"But we shouldn't be *too* certain," he said without conviction.

"You think she's . . . let's not use the word hysterical," Theresa said. "That has the wrong sexual connotations. Let's say stressed out. She's been working up to something. That's what you think? Don't be a hypocrite, Martin. Not with me."

Martin grimaced. "If I tell it like I think it is, we might both reach the wrong conclusions. If I say Rosa is losing it, well . . . there's evidence, but it's not a sure thing. Maybe she saw a trick of the light. Something we don't know about.''

"Ask the War Mother," Theresa suggested.

That was an obvious first step. "Rosa should ask," he said. "It's her sighting. Let's make her responsible for it.''

Theresa touched index finger on one hand to little finger on the other, bent it back until it was perpendicular to the joint, a gesture she sometimes made that fascinated Martin. "Good idea. Do you think she'll keep quiet?''

"She doesn't have many good friends.''

"Poor Martin. On your watch, too.''

"Maybe it's just a temporary aberration, and she'll pull out of it. Just to be safe—''

Theresa caught his meaning before he expressed it. "I'll have some Wendys keep watch on her.''

Martin lowered his hands from the unmarked walls. "Right," he said.

"Maybe Ariel . . .'' Theresa said. "She seems to be the only friend Rosa has.''

"We're all friends," Martin said.

"You know what I mean. Don't be obtuse.''

Theresa, as their time together lengthened, was becoming more and more critical, more and more judgmental, but in a gentle way, and Martin found that he liked it. He needed another voice now.

There were things he could not directly express, even to Theresa: a growing fear. *Rosa expresses it her way. I almost wish I could be so direct.*

In the central glow of the schoolroom, the War Mother contemplated Martin's report. They were alone in the large chamber, Martin standing and the War Mother floating, both in a spot of bright light. The doors had closed. Nobody else could hear them. Rosa had refused to go to the War Mother, had seemed insulted they would ask her to. And inevitably, word about her experience had spread.

"No such phenomenon has been noticed within the ship," the War Mother said.

"Rosa didn't see anything?"

"What she saw is not apparent to our sense," the War Mother said.

"Is it possible that we could see something aboard the ship, something with an objective reality, that you would not?"

"The possibility is remote."

"Then it's a psychological problem . . ." Martin said. *And you won't or can't do anything about it.*

"That is for you to decide."

Martin nodded, less agitated by such an attitude than he might have been a few tendays before. Other than providing an interface with the ship, the moms did little now. He could issue direct instructions, request direct answers, but critical judgments from their former teachers were not forthcoming. This was independence and responsibility with a vengeance, and he had to complain, however weakly and uselessly.

"The strain is intense. We're drilling day in, day out. The drills are going well, and everybody's doing their job—no more absentees, not even Rosa. But I don't like the way the children reacted to Rosa's . . . sighting. Vision. They were fascinated by it."

The War Mother said nothing.

"There hasn't been much talk since, but it worries me."

The War Mother said nothing more. He looked at the black and white paint on its facelessness. He wanted to reach out, just once, and strike it, but he did not.

The tenth drill on ship division went as smoothly as the first. In the nose, Martin projected the schematic of the *Dawn Treader*'s practice preparations. Paola and Hans and Joe crowded closer to see from his wand, somehow more special than viewing the same through their own.

The picture of the changing *Dawn Treader* loomed large in the corridor, a vivid ghost in three dimensions. The ship had contracted, necks reduced in length, tail and nose become blunt nubbins, grooves indenting the circumference of the second homeball like the cell divisions of a blastula. The third homeball also revealed grooves, an inscribed portion of the second neck connected to an orange-slice of the second homeball.

The drives would break down into two units, of sizes proportional to *Tortoise* and *Hare*, *Hare* being approximately twice the size of *Tortoise*. *Tortoise* claimed most of the second homeball and the shortened neck between.

Within the image, new bulkheads glowed red against the general green, spreading like wax in hot water over designated spaces, until the units were completely marked out, ready for separation.

"Show me status," Martin said. Partitions melted away, necks lengthened, homeballs became ungrooved and round. Whiskers of magnetic field vanes streamed out from the third homeball; inner traces of the scoop field glowed red around the nose.

"Looks good," Hans said. "When do you want to do final strategy?"

"The search team has more to show us. We'll listen to them, then you and I and the ex-Pans will pow-wow."

"Palaver," Paola said, smiling.

"Jaw. Chew the fat," Hans added, also smiling.

Martin was pleased that some excitement had returned.

Rosa Sequoia had performed her latest duties flawlessly, and there was little more talk about what she had seen. The incident seemed to have become an embarrassment to her, and she did not respond to inquiries from the children.

Hakim Hadj's face was less beatifically calm, his manner less polite, though hardly abrupt. He looked tired. He seemed at most mildly irritated, perhaps by a tiny itch he could not get at. The transparent nose of the *Dawn Treader* showed stars now instead of abyssal darkness; the chamber was crowded with projection piled upon simulation upon chart and those piled upon neon finger-scribbles hanging wherever space allowed. Hakim and two assistants, Min Giao and Thorkild Lax, seemed to know their way through the confusion. Martin stood back and let Hakim approach him.

"We are close to knowing enough for a judgment," Hakim said, black eyes rolling. "We shall have to withdraw our remotes soon, before we enter the cloud, but I think we will have enough evidence by then. Our information about the system is immense,

Martin. I have abstracted important details for you. You can look
at the orbital structures between planets two and three. They are
very interesting, but do not seem active—not inhabited, perhaps.
We still have no clue what the five inner masses are.''

"Close-in power stations?" Martin suggested.

Hakim smiled politely. "They may be reserves of converted
anti em, but if so, they are very heavily shielded. They are
practically invisible, much less reflective than fine carbon dust
and non-radiating, and that makes little sense if they are stores
of anything."

"What's your best theory?" Martin asked.

"I posit nothing," Hakim said quietly. "The unknown troubles me, especially something so prominent."

"Agreed."

Hakim continued, moving simulations of the inner planetary
surfaces closer to Martin, out of the stacks of projections. He
mildly chided Thorkild and Min Giao for their contributions to
the clutter. They seemed to ignore him and went about their
work, adding even more projections, lists, charts, simulations;
blinking, flashing, moving, blessedly silent displays.

"These worlds are not very active, even for a quiet and advanced civilization. Seismic or other noise through the crust is
minimal. The planet seems old. No large-scale activities below
ground, natural or unnatural. Such movement would produce
vibrations from crustal settling. There is no planet-altering work
being done, Martin; perhaps they finished all that thousands of
years ago."

"Go on," Martin said.

"Radiation flux from the planets does not exceed expected
natural levels. Both rocky inner worlds are either dead, or quies-
cent, pointing perhaps to a solid-state civilization, that is, all
activity confined to information transfer through quiet links, or
using noach, as we do."

"No physical bodies? Nothing organic?" Martin asked.

"None visible. If there are organics below the surface, they
produce no traces on the surface itself, and that is odd. At this
distance we might miss extremely light organic activity, but
judging from the telescope images . . . Here." He pulled up a
projection. Smiled at Martin as the image wavered. "My wand

works overtime. Thorkild, clear some capacity, please, or shunt it to the moms' systems!''

Thorkild looked up, lost in momerath and graphics. A few of the stacks dimmed or winked out.

The second planet rotated once every three hundred and two hours, surface temperature of one hundred and seventy degrees Celsius, albedo of point seven, light gray and tan, no oceans of course, thin atmosphere mostly carbon dioxide and nitrogen, no oxygen, no geological activity, mountain chains old and worn with no young replacements, no visible structures over a hundred meters in size. Or no structures with a height of more than ten meters . . .

"All right," Martin said, deliberately quelling his enthusiasm. "Both inner planets are quiet."

"In keeping with the biblical turn of phrase," Hakim said, "I suggest we call the inner planet Nebuchadnezzar, the second Ramses, and the third, Herod."

Martin made a face. "Might be a bit prejudicial, don't you think?"

"Mere suggestion," Hakim said. His face brightened. "Ah, yes, I see what you are getting at. Herod destroying the first born . . . Ramses overseeing the captivity of the Jews. Nebuchadnezzar having destroyed the first temple in Jerusalem . . . I see."

"The names are fine," Martin said.

"Good." Hakim seemed pleased. "Ramses . . . the next rocky planet, second planet out, is like this . . ." He drew forth another chart, put it through its paces. "Similar to the first, but cooler—minus four degrees Celsius average temperature, albedo of point seven, atmosphere again contains no oxygen or water vapor. No seismic activity, old mountains—old worlds."

"They might be deserted."

"We do not think so. The strongest evidence of continuing artifice lies in their temperatures versus their distances from Wormwood, and their atmospheric compositions. They are actively controlled environments, but for what sort of organisms or mechanisms—if any—I cannot say."

"Very small machines," Martin mused.

Hakim nodded. "That is difficult to confirm, of course. If they exist, their work is isolated from the surface."

"But the worlds *are* active."

"Active, yes, but they do not have large numbers of physical inhabitants—living creatures. The moms teach us that many civilizations reduce their presence to information matrices, abandoning their physical forms, and living as pure mentality."

"About half of all advanced civilizations . . ." Martin remembered, stroking his cheek with one hand.

"Yes. That could be the case here."

Maybe they've become ghosts. Martin shuddered at the thought of abandoning physical form; like spending forever in neural simulation. What would they gain? A low profile, a kind of immortality—but no need to physically colonize the systems they "sterilized" for future use. "You said we could almost make a judgment."

Hakim's face brightened. "I have been teasing, Martin. Withholding the best until last. This is very good. But you judge."

He ordered a series of charts on debris scattered throughout the ecliptic between fifty million kilometers and seven hundred million kilometers from Wormwood. "Dust and larger particles heated by the star, chemical reactions excited by the little stellar wind that does get through . . . Very interesting."

The dust and debris pointed to intense spaceborne industrial activity in the system's past. Much of the debris consisted of simple waste—rocky materials, lacking all metals and volatiles, heavy on silicates.

Manufacturing dust from shaping and processing: trace elements inevitably mixed into the dust, reflecting even more precisely than in the spectrum of Wormwood itself the proportions of trace elements in the killer machines.

"It's more than a close match," Martin said.

Hakim revealed his excitement in a mild lift of eyebrow.

"It's exact," Martin said.

"Very nearly," Hakim said.

"They made the killer machines around Wormwood."

"Perhaps around Leviathan, as well. We are not close enough to judge."

"But certainly here."

"The evidence is compelling."

Martin's skin warmed and his eyes grew moist, a response he

had seldom felt before, and could not ascribe to any particular emotion. Perhaps it came from a complex of emotions so deeply buried he did not experience them consciously.

"No defenses?"

"None," Hakim said. "No evidence of defenses on the surface of the inner worlds. The depleted gas giant shows even less activity, a large lump of cold wastes and rocky debris, with a thin atmosphere of helium, carbon dioxide solids, bromine, and sparse hydrocarbons. Here is a list."

"Where did the volatiles go?" Martin asked. The list was devoid of hydrogen, methane, and ammonia. The thin haze of helium was so diffuse as to be useless. *No swooping down to scoop up fuel, like Robin Hood swinging out of a tree to snatch a purse.*

"Good question, but I can only guess, the same as you. The star is well over six billion years old. The volatiles could have been lost during birth, with the cold outer worlds getting correspondingly thinner envelopes of atmosphere. But this would be unusual for a yellow dwarf in this neighborhood."

"Even in a multiple group?"

Hakim nodded. "Even so. The volatiles might have fueled early interstellar travel within the group. The pre-birth cloud is also very low on volatiles, remember. Or . . ."

Martin looked up.

"Most of it could have been converted to anti em for making killer probes."

"That's a lot of probes," Martin said.

Hakim agreed. "Billions, fueled and sent out across the stellar neighborhood. Depleting the outer cloud, the comets, the ice moons, the gas giant, everything . . . If I may say so, a massive and vicious campaign with great risks, at great expense. To be followed logically by a wave of stellar exploration and colonization."

"But we don't see any settled systems beyond the group . . . It wouldn't make sense to launch such a campaign, and not follow through."

"Ah." Hakim raised his finger. "Centuries must pass while they wait for the probes to do their work. What if the civilization changes in that time?"

"Seems certain they'd change some," Martin agreed.

"A change of heart, perhaps, or sudden fear of the wrath of other civilizations. Cowardice. Many possibilities."

"What percentage of converted volatiles could be stored in the five masses?"

"A minuscule amount of the total estimated gases lost from the system," Hakim said. "We're not yet certain of the size, but each of the masses appears to be several thousand kilometers in diameter, which would rule out neutronium, if their densities were uniform."

Thorkild Lax said, "I'm finishing work on the outer cloud, and Min Giao is redoing our work on the inner dust and debris."

"Dust and debris . . . how long would it take to push most of it away from the system?"

"Wouldn't happen," Thorkild said. "Most of the dust grains and larger rubble are too big to be cleaned out by radiation. Remember, the stellar wind has been channeled up and out through the poles."

"A good point," Hakim said.

"How much more time do you need?"

"A day?" Hakim asked his colleagues.

"I'll need a break," Min Giao said. "My momerath is fading now."

"A day and a half," Hakim said.

"Fine," Martin said.

They would enter the outer pre-birth material in three days. They would make their decision. Martin had no doubt how the children would decide. The *Dawn Treader* would split just beyond the diffuse inner boundaries of the cloud. *Tortoise* would begin super deceleration immediately after splitting.

They could disperse their weapons, carry out the Law, and at the very least, *Hare* would be outside the system before any defense could touch it.

The second stage of deceleration ended. Martin felt his stronger body jump free, like a highly charged battery. Some of the children felt mildly ill for a few hours, but the illness passed.

Jennifer Hyacinth was a slim, chatty, energetic woman who had not impressed Martin upon their first meeting; triangular of face, neither pretty nor unpleasant to look at, with narrow eyes and a habit of wincing when spoken to, as if she were being insulted; thin of arm and large-chested, breasts sitting on her ribcage as if an afterthought. Jennifer had gradually acquired Martin's respect by the wry and sharp observations she made about life on ship, by her willingness to volunteer for jobs others found unpleasant, and most of all, by her extraordinary command of momerath.

Like Ariel, Jennifer Hyacinth did not trust the moms any more than she had to by working with them or living in an environment made by them. But she had concentrated this distrust into a kind of mental guerrilla action, using her head to gain insight into those things the moms did not tell the children.

Martin put her request to see him into a short queue of appointments for the first half of the next day, and met with her in his early morning, while Theresa organized torus transfer drills for the bombship pilots.

Jennifer laddered into his quarters in the first homeball, face taut, clearly uncomfortable.

"What's up?" Martin asked casually, hoping to relax her. She widened her eyes, shrugged, narrowed them again, as if she really had nothing to say, and was embarrassed by having called the meeting in the first place.

"Jennifer—" he said, exasperated.

"I've been thinking," she blurted defensively, as if he were to blame for her discomfiture. "Doing momerath and just thinking. I've reached some conclusions—not really conclusions, actually, but they're interesting, and I thought you'd like to hear them . . . I hoped you would."

"I'd like to," Martin said.

"They're not final but they're pretty compelling. I think you can follow most of it . . ."

"I'll try."

"The moms aren't telling us everything."

"That seems to be the popular wisdom," Martin said.

She blinked. "It's true. They haven't told us how they do certain things—convert matter to anti em, for example. Or how they compress ordinary matter into neutronium. Or how they transmit on the noach without possibility of interception."

"They don't seem to think we need to know."

"Well, curiosity is reason enough."

"Right," Martin said.

"I think I know how they do some things. Not how they actually *do* it, but the theory behind it." Her eyes widened, defying him to think her efforts were trivial. "It's good momerath. It's self-consistent, I mean. I've even translated some of it into formal maths."

"I'm listening," Martin said.

Martin knew his momerath ability was dwarfed by Jennifer's. She was probably the fastest and most innovative mathematician on the ship, followed only by Giacomo Sicilia.

"I've been putting some things together by looking at the moms'—I mean, the Benefactors' technologies. What they did on Earth and on the Ark. On Mars. They have ways of altering matter on a fundamental level—that's obvious, of course, since they can make matter into anti em. I *don't* think they have spacewarps or can rotate mass points through higher dimensions—that would imply faster-than-light travel, which they don't *seem* to have."

"Okay," Martin said.

"The way momerath is constructed—the formal side I mean, not the psychological—there are branches of the discipline that suggest human information theory. There's an argument that physics can be reduced to the laws governing transfer of information; but I haven't been working on that.

"What I *have* been doing is looking at how the moms treat basic physics in their drill instructions. We have to know *certain* things, such as repair of maker delivery systems using remotes, in case they're severely damaged in a fight. It's funny, but the *Dawn Treader* can repair itself, and the bombships can't . . . not without remotes, at any rate. I guess they don't want bombships going off on their own, mutating—"

"Yes," Martin said, in a tone that urged her to come back to the main subject.

"About the anti em conversion process. I think they've worked out ways to access a particle's bit structure, its self-information. To do that, they'd have to tamper with the so-called privileged channels. *Channels* isn't the right word, of course. I'd call them bands—but—''

Martin looked at her blankly.

"Some more radical theorists on Earth thought spacetime might be a giant computational matrix, with information transferred along privileged bands or channels instantaneously, and bosons—photons, and so on—conveying other types of information at no more than the speed of light. Baryons don't expand when the universe expands. They're loosely tied to spacetime. But bosons—photons, and so on—are in some respects strongly tied to spacetime. Their wavelengths expand as the universe expands. The privileged bands are not tied to spacetime at all, and they convey certain kinds of special information between particles. Kind of cosmic bookkeeping. The Benefactors seem to know how to access these bands, and to control the information they carry.''

"I'm still not following you.''

Jennifer sighed, squatted in the air beside Martin, and lifted her hands to add gestures to her explanation. "Particles need to *know* certain things, if I can use that word in its most basic sense. They need to know what they are—charge, mass, spin, strangeness, and so on—and *where* they are. They have to react to information conveyed by other particles, information about their own character and position. Particles are the most basic processors of information. Bosons and the privileged bands are the fundamental carriers of information.''

"All right,'' Martin said, although the full implications of this were far from clear, and he was far from agreeing with the theory.

"I think the Benefactors—and probably the planet killers— have found ways to control the privileged bands. Now that's remarkable by itself, because privileged bands aren't supposed to be accessed by *anything* but the particles and bosons they work for. They might as well be called *forbidden* bands. They carry information about a particle's state that helps keep things running on a quantum level—bookkeeping and housecleaning, so to speak. They have to carry information instantly because . . . well, in some experiments, that kind of bookkeeping seems to happen instantly, across great distances. Most information can't travel faster than light. Well, that sort can, but it's very special, the exception to the rule.

"Bosons travel at the speed of light. They carry information about changes in position, mass, and so on, like I said. If you can change their states and information content, you can make them *lie*. If you control all the information carried by bosons and along the privileged bands, you can *lie* to other particles. If you tinker with a particle's internal information, you can *change* that particle. I think that's what they do to make anti em.''

"They just tell an atom it's anti em?"

Jennifer smiled brightly. "Nothing so simple, but that's the gist, I think. They mess with privileged bands, they tinker with the memory stores of huge numbers of particles within atoms, all at once, and they create anti em. I've got the momerath . . .''

"How long would it take me to absorb it?"

She pursed her lips. "You, maybe three tendays.''

"I don't have time, Jennifer. But I'd like to have the record anyway . . .'' Her theory seemed less than important to him now. "Sounds impossible, though.''

Jennifer grinned. "It does, doesn't it? That's what's so neat. Given certain assumptions, and running them through the momerath, the impossibilities *go away*. It becomes a coherent system, and it has huge implications, most of which I haven't worked out. Like, what sort of coordinate system would a particle use? Relative, absolute? Cartesian? How many axes? I'm not really serious about it being Cartesian—it couldn't be—and remember, the coordinates or whatever you want to call them have to be *self-sensing*. The particle has to be what it knows it is, and to be *where* it knows it is. Unless we start calling in observer-induced phenomena, which I do in my momerath . . . though that isn't finished, yet.''

"How much information does a particle have to carry?'' Martin asked.

"To differentiate itself from every other particle—a unique particle signature—and to know its state, its position, its motion, and so on . . . about two hundred bits.''

Martin looked to one side for a moment, frowning, getting

interested despite his weariness. "If the universe is a computer, what's the hardware like?"

"The momerath explicitly forbids positing a matrix for this system. *None can be described*. Only the rules exist, and the interactions."

"There's no programmer?"

"The momerath says nothing about that. Just, no hardware, no explicitly real matrix. The matrix is, but is not separate from what takes place. You *are* interested, aren't you?"

He was, but there seemed so little time to think even the thoughts he needed to think, and make the necessary plans. "I'll look the work over when I can. You know I'm bogged."

"Yes, but this could be important. If we see something that fits, something around Wormwood maybe, something high tech that doesn't make sense unless I'm right, then we can apply whole new ideas."

"Obviously," Martin said. "Thanks."

Jennifer smiled brightly, then leaned over and kissed him on the cheek. "You're sweet, but I thought you'd ask about something . . ."

"What?"

"About the noach—how we communicate with nearby craft and the remotes."

"Along the privileged bands?"

She shook her head. "Not exactly. There wouldn't be any distance limitations if the moms used the privileged bands to chat. Remember, we can't chat beyond ten billion kilometers."

"All right, how, then?"

"By setting up a resonance. You could change the bit or bits that distinguish one particle from another. The particles seem to resonate, to be somewhere else for a very short time. Signals could be sent that way. But there's a limit how far. I don't know why, yet, but I'm working on it."

"Let me know what you come up with," Martin said.

"Can I talk about it with the others? Get others to work on it?"

"If they have time," Martin said.

She smiled again, bowed ceremonially in mid-air like a diver, and laddered through the door.

* * *

There was little time for anything but work, drill, sleep. Theresa slept with him, but they were too tired to make love more than once before sleep, down from their coasting average of two or three times per day.

Martin curled up against her in the warm darkness of his quarters, in the net. His limp penis nested between her thighs, just below her buttocks, slight stickiness adhering his prepuce to her skin. His hand on her hip, finger caressing lightly; she was already asleep, breathing shallow and even. Her hair in disarray tickled his nose. He moved his head back a few centimeters, opened his eyes, saw a dim memory of the momerath that had absorbed him in most of his time outside drilling and attending to the active teams. The personal momerath; what all the children were doing now, trying to think their way through to an individual judgment, to the most important decision of their lives.

There was much more than just analyzing the data Hakim provided. There was the intuition beyond rational thought; the unknown process of personal conviction, of human faculties at work, that made their judgments different from what the moms might have decided by themselves.

They probably had the power to destroy whatever life existed around Wormwood. The system did not look strongly defended; and in strategy, appearances could count for everything. An appearance of strength could be important . . . To appear weaker than one actually was could *invite* assault, never useful.

Going over it again and again. Gradually sleep came.

The universe is made of plateaus and valleys, stars nestled in valleys, the long spaces between the stars creating broad, almost flat plateaus along which orbital courses approach but never reach straightness. Martin floated in the nose of the *Dawn Treader*, the sleeping search team scattered in nets and in bags behind him. Through the transparent nose, peering into the valley around Wormwood, Martin contemplated their target, now the brightest star in their field of view.

Within twenty hours, they would begin separation into *Tortoise* and *Hare*. Martin would be in charge of *Tortoise*, Hans in command of *Hare*. Thirty-five children would accompany Martin, including Theresa and William and Ariel; Hakim and the search team would go with Hans. *Hare* would plunge through Wormwood's system ahead of them, collecting information to be relayed back to *Tortoise*.

Martin felt someone behind him and turned to see Ariel. She looked angry or frightened, he could not tell which, and she was out of breath.

"What's wrong?" he asked.

"Rosa's seen the dark shape again. In the second homeball. Alexis Baikal saw it before she did, in the third homeball, close to the neck and the stores."

"Shit," Martin said.

"Both think it's real. They're talking to others . . . I was the first to get here."

"Why in Christ's name now?"

"Maybe it is real," Ariel said. "Maybe it knows when to disrupt us."

"Where are they? Did they see it do anything or go anywhere?"

"I don't know. I came up here as fast as I could."

"Why not use the wand?"

"The moms . . ." She seemed slightly abashed, but still defiant. "Nobody wants them to know."

"Why in hell not?" Martin said.

She shook her head briskly. "I'll take you to where they are. They think maybe the moms have been . . . taken over. That we're being forced to suicide."

Martin took his wand and called for Hans and the five ex-Pans. "That's so slicking *stupid*," he said under his breath, following Ariel down the long nose to the central corridor passing through the first homeball. He noted the fissures already formed, stretching in thin grooves along the walls of the necks and around key pipes and protrusions, as the ship carved itself ahead of time for the likely partition. "If people are going to be this paranoid, they should at least use their heads . . ."

"I know," Ariel said, echoing ahead, then using ladder fields to propel herself quickly up the long corridor. "Most of what they're saying doesn't make sense. Martin, I don't agree with much of it. But some . . . it's frightening. They saw *something*."

Martin laddered grimly behind her.

She preceded him to the corridor leading to Rosa's quarters on the outer perimeter of the second homeball. Hans joined them, glancing at Martin inquisitively. Martin shrugged and said, "Shadows again." Hans pulled a disgusted face.

Stephanie Wing Feather and Harpal Timechaser waited outside the closed door to Rosa's quarters. Martin took up his wand and tried to communicate with Rosa.

"She won't be listening," Ariel said. "They're very frightened."

"They can't cut themselves off." Martin and Hans banged on the door, creating a dull, hollow boom. He did not know whether those inside would hear.

The door opened silently and Rosa stood before them, her face radiant with some new-found assurance, tall and stately, red hair tied back, dressed in an opaque gray gown that made her appear massive, formidable.

"What in the hell—" Martin began, his anger getting the best of him.

"You shut up," Rosa said, her deep voice cracking with emotion like a boy's. "You made me feel like a fool, and now somebody else has seen it. What can you say to that? It's *real*."

Martin tried to push past her, but she blocked his entrance with an arm. "Who told you to come in?" she said. "Who do you think you are?"

He suddenly realized the extent of the problem and backed away, throttling his anger. "If you saw something, I need to know what it is."

"Martin is Pan, Rosa, and he hasn't done anything to you at all," Stephanie said. "Don't be an ass. Let us in."

"Let them in," Alexis called behind Rosa. Rosa reluctantly moved aside, glaring at them as they entered her quarters. Martin had never seen the inside of Rosa's quarters before; few had. What he saw now startled him.

The cabin was filled with flowers, profusions of pots and bouquets, real flowers and synthetic, made of cloth or paper on wire stems. The air was warm and moist. Sunbright lamps glowed from the center to the periphery, where the flowers surrounded the walls in tiers.

Ten Wendys and two Lost Boys waited in the quarters with Rosa and Alexis. Two budgerigars played at hide and seek among the potted flowers.

Martin realized the disparity in sexes and his concern grew almost to befuddlement. "Alexis, what did you see?"

Alexis Baikal, swarthy and sandy haired, of middle height, with powerful legs and large hands, hung cross-legged from a net near the floor, despondent. "A big dark shape in the main corridor, heading toward the stores."

"What did it look like?"

Rosa advanced on him threateningly, for no apparent reason, and Martin lifted his arm. Her smile spread immediate and triumphant. "He doesn't believe any of us!" she called out, voice like a horn.

"Stop it, Rosa," Ariel said quietly. "He's trying to listen."

"It was bigger than four or five people," Alexis said, "but it didn't have any real shape."

"Did you ask the moms?" Hans asked. Rosa glared but did not move; Ariel's hand rested on her elbow. Martin wondered about this; Ariel should have relished a chance to discomfit him, to discredit the moms, but instead, she was acting on the side of reason—at least as he perceived it. More befuddlement, shifting of mental gears.

"No," Alexis said. "*We saw something.* We didn't make it up!"

Alexis had been talking with Rosa for some time, Martin surmised; had come to Rosa first with her report, before going to any of the other children. No wonder Rosa was defensive; Alexis' sighting was confirmation, vindication.

"Was it something alive?" Hans asked, stooping to be more on a level with Alexis.

"It was alive. It flowed like a liquid."

"Did it have any features—face, arms, legs, whatever?" Stephanie asked. They were trying to distance Martin from the confrontation that had broken out, and Martin approved—for the time being. Best to listen impartially until the few available facts were sorted out.

Rosa looked at them, worried, but kept quiet.

"It was black," Alexis said with an effort. "Big. Alive. It

didn't make any sound." *She knows it isn't credible, what she saw.*

"That's all you saw?"

Alexis Baikal fixed on Stephanie's eyes and nodded. "That's all I saw."

Hans stood and stretched his arms, flexing his shoulders as if they had cramped. "Where did it go?"

"I don't know," Alexis said. "I turned to run, and it was gone."

The door opened and three Wendys came in, Nancy Flying Crow, Jeanette Snap Dragon, and leading them, Kirsten Two Bites. Kirsten said, "These two have something to report."

"We are *not* cowards," Nancy Flying Crow said.

"You should have told us," Kirsten Two Bites chided. "Martin, they've seen things, too."

"We didn't see anything we could identify," Nancy said.

"Did you see anything while you were together?" Stephanie asked.

"No," Jeanette said.

"Ask them what they saw," Rosa interjected.

Martin pointed to Nancy. "You first."

"It was a man," Nancy said. "Not one of us. Not one of the children, I mean. He was dark, wearing dark clothes."

"Where did you see him?" Martin asked.

"In the second homeball. In the hall outside my quarters."

"And you?" Martin asked Jeanette.

Jeanette Snap Dragon shook her head. "I'd rather not say, Martin."

"It's pretty important," Martin said gently.

"It doesn't make any sense. I can't fit it into anything," Jeanette said, face wrinkling in anguish. "Please. Rosa started this . . . I didn't see what Rosa saw."

"What do you mean, Rosa started this?" Hans asked.

"Don't gang up on me!" Jeanette wailed. "I didn't want to see it, and I don't even know if I *did* see it."

"I didn't start anything, sister," Rosa said in a hissing whisper, shaking her head. "Don't blame me."

"I saw my mother," Jeanette said, looking down. "She's

dead, Martin. She died when I was five. I saw her dressed in black, carrying a suitcase or something like a suitcase.''

"That's bolsh," Rosa said.

"Be quiet," Stephanie said.

"Rosa, please," Ariel pleaded.

"This is all crap! She couldn't have seen that," Rosa said.

"Why the hell not?" Ariel said, face red. "Does everybody have to see what you saw?"

"They just want to be in on it. They're making it up. What Alexis and I saw—"

"That's enough," Martin said, raising his hand.

"We saw something!" Alexis cried out. "This is all crazy!" Hans muttered, "Righto."

Martin raised his hand higher, nodding his head forward, lips tight. "Quiet, *everybody*," he said. "Rosa, nobody's accusing anybody of anything, and this is not a competition for weirdness. Understand?''

"You don't control me," Rosa said. "You—"

"Smother it, Rosa," Ariel said. She looked sharply at Martin—*Don't take this cooperation for granted.*

"Why is everybody down on me?" Rosa screamed, tears flying. "Everybody get out of here and leave us . . . leave Alexis and me alone.''

"No thanks," Alexis said. "I don't know what I saw, or what it means. I just reported it."

Martin smelled the sweetness of flowers from Rosa's garden, tried to think of some way to conclude this meeting without damaging delicate egos.

"Nobody knows what anybody saw," he said. "Nobody blames anybody for seeing anything. Rosa, you reported what you saw, and that's according to the rules. Whatever anybody sees, they come to me and tell me right away, understand? No embarrassment, no hiding, no shame. I want to know.''

Stephanie nodded approval. Hans seemed less than convinced.

"Have there been other sightings?" Martin asked. "This is not snitching. Have there?"

Nobody answered.

"I'm going to talk to each of you individually for the next

hour, in my quarters," Martin said. "There's no time to waste
now. We have to be disciplined, and we have to think of the
Job. Got that?"

Heads nodding around the room, all but Ariel's and Rosa's.

"We have to make a judgment—if we're going to make one
before partition—by tomorrow morning. This is a very serious
time, this is why we came here. Not to worry about our sanity
and our egos. Think of Earth."

One by one they came to his quarters. Martin recorded their
words in his wand. Alexis Baikal came first, full of doubts,
tearful in her apologies for having seen *anything*. Martin tried
again to convince her there had been no crime, but his efforts
seemed less than successful.

Ariel was cool, as if regretting her tacit support of Martin in
Rosa's quarters. "I think the moms are doing something," she
said, folding and unfolding her hands. "I think they're experi-
menting with us, like when they made us screw up the first
external drill."

"You'll never trust them, will you?" Martin asked.

Ariel shook her head. "We're trapped. That's what Rosa
thinks, too, but she hasn't said it directly. She's desperate."

"You think she's seeing things, making them up?"

Reluctantly, Ariel nodded.

"That doesn't make sense. You think the moms are fooling
with us, but you think *Rosa*'s making up things, too?"

"I think they're weeding out the weak ones," Ariel said.
"They might jeopardize our doing the Job. I don't say I know
what's happening. You just wanted our ideas."

"Rosa's weak?"

"I don't want to get her into trouble."

"Ariel, she's having real problems."

"I know that."

"Can she do her work?"

"She's been doing pretty well, hasn't she?"

"Will she keep it up?" Martin asked.

"I think she will. But the children need to accept her."

"I get the impression she isn't accepting the children."

"Whatever," Ariel said.

"You're her friend. Can you bring her in?"

"We talk. She doesn't tell me everything. I don't think she's anybody's friend. I just make it a point to talk to her. You don't. Nobody else does."

Martin could not deny that. "I'm talking to her next."

Ariel lifted her chin back. "Are you going to be her friend?" *You are a bloody-minded bitch.* "I'll try," he said.

Ariel left. Rosa Sequoia came into his quarters a few minutes later, face set like stone, eyes wide with fear and that ever-present defiance, an expression that made Martin want to kick her.

"Tell me what you think you saw. Just me," Martin said.

She shook her head. "You don't believe any of us."

"I'm listening."

"The others . . . they saw something different. Why should you believe any of us?"

Martin lifted his hand and crooked his finger encouragingly: Come on.

"You think I started it," Rosa said.

"I don't think that. Do you think you started it?"

"I saw it first." Under her breath. "It's mine."

"If it belongs to you, can you control it?" The conversation was getting looser and loonier. How far would he go to bring her in? Rosa was too sharp to be deceived. "Do you claim it?"

"I don't have it. I don't have anything." She hung her head. "I don't know what I've been doing."

This reversal caught him by surprise. He opened and closed his mouth, then folded his legs beneath him. "Jesus, Rosa."

"I'm not saying I . . . I'm not saying that we haven't seen anything."

"No . . . Sit. Please. Just talk."

Rosa looked to one side and shook her head. "I don't want to go against the Job. I'm afraid this might hurt us. Hurt the Job."

"What is it? Do you know?"

She sobbed and held her head back to keep the tears in her eyes from spilling. "I didn't make it up. I swear to Earth, Martin. I wouldn't do that. I don't know about the others."

"Is it real?"

"It is, to me. I've only seen it once, though. It was more real than I am. It was more real than the Job. It scared me, but it was beautiful. Should I be ashamed of that?"

"I don't know. Talk."

"I do my work," Rosa said, "I try to be competent, but I don't belong here any more than I belonged on the Ark. Or on the Earth. You don't think much of me because I'm causing trouble . . . But nobody thought *anything* of me when I was nothing at all."

"You can't own a . . . Whatever it is. It can't be yours alone."

"If it was important, it would make me useful. People wouldn't look through me."

Martin asked her to relax and again she refused. "I want to go back. I want this forgotten."

"What about Alexis? What she saw?"

"I don't know what she saw. It sounds like what I saw, but it may not be."

"You didn't make this up, I know that. But is it real?"

Rosa shook her head. "Alexis thinks it is."

"Then maybe it is," Martin said. "I'm not going to doubt what my fellows see. You and Alexis. You'll continue to do your duties and attend all the drills. When you're off-duty, you can keep a look out. Look through the ship. Until partition. If it doesn't show up any more after that, we forget it. All right?"

"Jeanette and Nancy?"

"Jeanette saw her mother," Martin said. "Nancy saw . . . a man. They didn't see what you saw."

"Maybe it can take different shapes . . . read our minds."

Martin controlled his shudder. This was a real risk. Lancing the boil—acknowledging its existence—might do more than just drain the infection; it might spread it.

"You're a part of us, and whatever happens to you is important."

"I'm a large . . . thing," Rosa said, holding out her arms, fingers clutched into fists. "I was large when I was a child. Everybody stared at me and avoided me. I thought by coming here, doing the Job, I could be important to the girls and boys who ignored me and who died on Earth."

Martin took one of her fists and tried to massage it into openness. She stared at his hands, her fist, as if they were disembodied. Her voice rose.

"I wanted to be important to them. When I got on the *Dawn Treader*, nothing much changed. I knew there wasn't anything I could do to make anybody think I was important."

"You're part of us," Martin said. He reached out and brought her to him, wrapped his arms around her, felt her hard, thick—fleshed shoulders, broad ribcage, small breasts against his chest, the strength and tension and the damp warm skin of her neck. He hugged her, chin on her shoulder, smelling her, sharp like a large, frightened animal. "We don't want to lose you, or anybody. Do what I ask, and we'll see if it comes to anything."

She pushed him back with strong, large hands and blinked at him. "I will," she said. She smiled like a little girl. Possibly no one had hugged her in years. How could all the children have so ignored one of their own? Seeing the pain and hope in her eyes—a forlorn, lost hope—Martin wondered if he had done the right thing, used the right kind of influence.

So little time.

Rosa left, subdued to her old quietness, and Alexis Baikal came in, and then Jeanette and Nancy. They did not say much, and he did not push the issue. Somehow he felt he had broken the chain of events, that everything would go more smoothly now; but had he sacrificed the last of Rosa?

Only hours. Time flying by more swiftly, more in tune with the outside universe. Another partition drill; equally successful. One last brief external drill, also successful. The children seemed as prepared as they would ever be.

Hour by hour, Hakim's search team produced more and more information.

The time of judgment had arrived.

In the schoolroom, in the presence of the War Mother, Martin set up the rules for the judgment. In the first year, Stephanie Wing Feather and Harpal Timechaser had prepared the rules, trying to catch the resonances of the justice systems established on the Ark, based on human laws back to the tablets of Hammurabi . . .

A jury of twelve children was chosen by lots. Each child could refuse the assignment; none did. With more qualms than satisfaction, Martin saw Rosa inducted as a juror, taking the oath Stephanie herself had written:

I will truly judge based on the evidence, and what I will judge is whether the evidence is sufficient, and whether it proves guilt beyond a reasonable doubt. I will not allow prejudice or hate or fear to cloud my judgment, nor will I be swayed by any emotion or rhetoric from my fellows, so help me, in the name of truth, God, the memory of Earth, my family, and whatever I hold most dear, against the eternal guilt of my soul should I err . . .

The choosing and swearing-in lasted a precious hour. A defense advocate was appointed by Martin; to Hakim's dismay, Martin chose him. "No one knows the weakness of your evidence more than you do," Martin said. He was acutely aware of the roughness and arbitrariness of this system they had chosen; they could do no better.

As prosecutor he appointed Luis Estevez Saguaro, Hakim's second on the search team. Martin himself presided as judge.

The War Mother listened to the trial silently, its painted black and white designs prominent in the brightly illuminated schoolroom. All eighty-two children sat in quiet attendance as Martin went over the rules.

Luis presented the older evidence, and then outlined the new. Their data on the debris fields had increased enormously. The assay matches seemed indisputable.

Hakim questioned the conclusiveness of the data at this distance. Luis Estevez called on Li Mountain to explain again the functioning of the *Dawn Treader*'s remotes and sensors, the accuracy of observations, the science behind the different methods. The children had heard much of it before. They were reminded nevertheless.

Luis Estevez withheld his trump card until the final phase of the six-hour trial. Hakim fought vigorously to discredit this last bit of evidence, explaining the statistics of error on such observations at this distance, but the news made the children gasp nonetheless, more in horror than surprise.

Less than two hours away, at their present speed of three

quarters c, the cloud of pre-birth material surrounding Wormwood offered one more startling confirmation.

The residue of Wormwood's birth, a roughly shaped ring around the system, with patches and extrusions streaming billions of kilometers above the ecliptic, had been extensively mined, as suspected, and few volatiles remained. No cometary chunks were left to fall slowly around Wormwood; the civilization had many thousands of years before depleted these resources as part of a program of interstellar exploration.

Some leftovers from that program still floated amid the scoured dust of the irregular ring, spread here and there across the billions of kilometers like sand in an ocean tide.

The search team, probing the nearest extent of the ring, had found artificial needle-shaped bodies, the largest no more than a hundred meters long; inert now, perhaps experimental models, perhaps ships that had malfunctioned and been abandoned after being stripped of fuel and internal workings.

Luis projected for the jury, and all the children, graphics of what these needle ships looked like in their cold dusty junkyards. He then produced pictures they were all familiar with: the shapes of the killer machines when they entered Earth's solar system, when they burrowed into the asteroids between Mars and Jupiter, and into the Earth itself:

Long needles. Identical in shape and size.

Hakim valiantly argued that these shapes were purely utilitarian, that any number of civilizations might produce vessels such as these, designed to fly between the stars. But the shapes of Ships of the Law, including *Dawn Treader*, countered that argument. Space allowed many designs for interstellar craft.

The conclusion seemed inevitable: dead killer machines orbited the extreme perimeter of the Wormwood system.

Hakim's next suggestion was that this system had itself been entered by Killers, that the inhabitants had been wiped from their worlds, and that the worlds were not perpetrators, but victims. Luis countered that in such a case, it was their duty to expunge the final traces of the Killers from the victim's corpse.

And if there were survivors?

That did not seem likely, judging from Earth's experience.

But the Earth, Hakim argued, had been an extreme case; the Killers had been faced with strong, eventually fatal opposition. Perhaps they would behave differently with more time to perform their tasks. Perhaps there were survivors.

Luis pointed to the natural composition of Wormwood and its planets, the apparent origin of the machines themselves.

And if the machines had merely been manufactured here?

The debate went around and around, but these arguments were not convincing, however Hakim worked to make them so.

"If Wormwood is indeed the origin of the killer machines, why leave these wrecks out here for evidence?" Hakim asked, making his final attempt at a sound defense. "Why not sweep the cloud clean, and prepare for the vengeance of those you have failed to murder? Could there not be some other explanation for this evidence, allowing a reasonable doubt?"

No one could answer. No one doubted the evidence, however.

The jury was sequestered in unused quarters near the schoolroom.

The verdict was two hours in coming.

It was unanimous.

Wormwood must be cleared of all traces of Killers and their makers. Even if they had become ghosts, lost in their machines . . .

Hakim seemed perversely despondent that he had not presented his case more strongly. He moved to the rear of the room and curled behind the children, eyes wide and solemn.

Martin stood before the children, the weight of the judgment on his shoulders now. The hush in the schoolroom was almost deathly: no coughing, hardly a sound of breathing. The children did not move, waiting for him to issue the orders.

"We start dispersal as soon as we split," he said. "Shipboard weapons team will launch makers into the Wormwood system. There are no visible defenses, but we'll be cautious anyway. Instead of trying for three or four large-mass gravity-fuse bombs, we'll let the makers create a few thousand smaller ones out of the rocks and debris. If we fail, makers in the outer cloud will assemble their weapons and send them in later."

"That'll cost much more fuel," Hans said.

Stephanie and Harpal nodded.

"There aren't enough volatiles to make enough bombs and escape quickly. We should act as soon as possible. We'll destroy the rocky worlds first, then concentrate on the bald gas giants . . ."

"Destroy them, too?" Ariel asked from the rear.

"If we have enough weapons," Martin said. "We can gather the remaining volatiles for fuel from the debris clouds afterward."

"All of them?" William asked.

"Every world," Martin said.

The children thought this over somberly. They would reenact the battle fought around the Sun, centuries past. This time, they would be the murderers.

"It's not murder," Martin said, anticipating their thoughts. "It's execution. It's the Law."

That didn't make the reality any less disturbing.

"You didn't need to put me in your crew," Theresa said as they ate together in her quarters. This was the last time they would have together, alone, until the Job had been completed. These were the last four hours of the *Dawn Treader* as a single ship, as they had always known her. If they survived, they might reconstruct the ship again, but chances were, they would have to make her much smaller, perhaps a tenth of her present size, and live in comparatively crowded conditions . . .

"I had no reason *not* to have you with me," Martin said.

Theresa watched him, eyes bright.

"The Pan needs to think of himself now and then," Martin said softly. "I'll work better, knowing you're with me."

"When we finish the Job, where will we go?" she asked, finishing her pie. The ship was an excellent provider; this meal, however, tasted particularly fine. There would be little time to eat after partition, and the meals would be fast and small.

"I don't know," Martin said. "They've never told us where they'll send us."

"Where would you *like* to go?"

Martin chewed his last bite thoughtfully, swallowed, looked down at the empty plate. He smiled, thumped his knuckles on the small table, said, "I'd like to travel very far away. Just be free and see what there is out here. We could travel for thousands, millions of years . . . Away from everything.''

"That would be lovely," she said, but she didn't sound convinced.

"And you?" Martin asked.

"A new Earth," she said. "I know that's foolish. All the Earth-like worlds are probably taken, but perhaps the moms could send us to a place where nobody has been, find a planet where we could be alone. Where we could make a new Earth."

"And have children," he said. "Where the moms could let us have children."

"No moms," Theresa said. "Just ourselves."

Martin considered this, saw nations arising, people disagreeing, history raising its ugly head, the inevitable round of Eden's end and reality's beginning. But he did not tell Theresa what she already knew. Fantasies were almost as important as fuel at this point.

"Do you think they'll know when they die?" Theresa asked. Martin understood whom she meant. *Down at the bottom of the gravity well, on the planets. The Killers.*

"If they're still alive . . ." Martin said, raising his eyebrows. "If there's anybody still there, still conscious . . . not a machine."

"Do you think they can be conscious if they've become machines?"

"The moms don't tell us about such things," Martin said.

"Can they be guilty if they're just machines now?"

"I don't know," Martin said. "They can be dangerous."

"If there are a few still in bodies, still *living* as we do, do you think they are . . . leaders, prophets . . . or just slaves?"

"Machines don't need slaves," Martin said, grinning.

Theresa shook her head. "That's not what I mean. I mean slaves to their own bodies. The others might be so much more free, immortal, able to think and do whatever they please. Haven't you ever felt as if you were a slave to your body?"

Martin shook his head. "I don't think so."

"Having to urinate every few hours, shit every day or two or three . . . Eat."

"Make love," Martin said.

"Have periods," Theresa said.

Martin touched her arm.

"I've never had a period," she said. "I've grown up, but they've taken that away from me."

"The Wendys don't seem to miss them," Martin said.

"How would we know?"

"My mother didn't miss them on the Ark," he said. "She told me she was glad." *Has she had any children since we left . . . on Mars?* He had never thought of having brothers or sisters he would never know.

"What if they were thinking very deeply, solving very large problems, just working all the time, without worrying about bodies?"

"No passions, no sorrows," Martin said, trying to stay in tune with her musing.

"Maybe they feel very large passions, larger than we can know. Passions without physical boundaries. Curiosity. Maybe they've come to actually *love* the universe, Martin."

"We don't know anything about them, except that they're quiet," Martin said.

"Are they frightened?" she asked. "Hoping not to be noticed?"

Martin shrugged. "It's not worth thinking about," he said.

"But all the strategists say we should know our enemies, be prepared for anything they might do by knowing what they must do, what they *need* to do."

"I hope they die before they even know we're here," Martin said.

"Do you think that's possible?"

He paused, shook his head, no.

"Do you think they already know?"

Shook his head again, acutely uncomfortable.

"We have an hour before you go back," Theresa said. "Pan must take his scheduled free time, too. To be healthy."

"I wouldn't deny myself that. Or you," Martin said.

"Let's love," Theresa said. "As if we were free, and our own people."

And they tried. It worked, partly. At the very least it was intense, even more intense than in their first few days together.

"When I'm free," Martin said, as they floated beside each other in the darkness, "I will choose you."

"I *am* free," Theresa said. "For this minute, I'm free as I'll ever be. And I choose you."

One hour before partition, Rosa stood in the schoolroom, next to the star sphere, less than twelve meters from the silent War Mother. Her eyes were heavy lidded, head bowed. Her hands shook slowly like leaves in a small breeze. She was naked but for a scarf tied around her neck. Dull light from the star sphere limned her pale skin.

Liam Oryx came into the schoolroom looking for Hakim, saw her, and immediately called Martin on his wand. He also called Ariel.

Martin arrived with Theresa, but William had gotten there first. William approached Rosa slowly, saying nothing.

"I don't need you," Rosa told him.

"Something wrong?" Ariel called from behind William. "Rosa?"

"I've seen it again," Rosa said. "There's something in the ship with us. It spoke to me. I can't stop seeing things that are real."

William stopped three meters from where she stood, beside the War Mother, which did not speak or move. "What did it say?" he asked.

Martin bit his lip, watching, his stomach sinking. *So little time. Every child precious.*

Theresa climbed around the schoolroom, hovered beside Ariel. Other children arrived until finally fifteen occupied the chamber, all Rosa's Tree family and five others besides.

"What did it say?" William repeated.

"It's alive," Rosa said. "It lives out here, and it sees and hears things we can't. It's very large. I think it might be a god. Sometimes it hates us, sometimes it loves us."

Martin closed his eyes, knowing now—in his flesh and bones—what he had only known intellectually. *She saw herself inside. She saw nothing real to us.*

"It said Martin is a bad leader." She raised her head. "He

doesn't know what he's doing. He's going to lead us to our death. He doesn't understand."

"How could anybody else know how good Martin is?" William asked.

"Stop it, Rosa," Ariel said.

"It isn't true," said Alexis Baikal. "That isn't what I saw."

"Quiet," William said, gaze fixed on Rosa. "Rosa, everybody saw something different. That means they saw what they wanted to see."

Rosa shook her head stubbornly.

"I think we are having a bit of panic," William said. "Only to be expected. We're young, and this is all very strange and difficult."

"Be quiet," Rosa said, tilting her head back, a large, naked Valkyrie in an opera. She appeared so vulnerable, and yet Martin could feel her threat to the Job as palpably as if she were a wasp stinging his flesh. *No time to waste.*

He said nothing, watching William.

William nodded to Ariel. "She's your friend, Ariel," he said. "She needs your help."

"She's a victim," Ariel said.

"Stop it," Rosa said.

"It's panic," William pursued. "You're feeling our panic, our anxiety. You're very perceptive. You see what we feel, Rosa."

"Come with me, Rosa," Ariel said.

"I will not fight," Rosa said. "None of you should fight. The Pan is wrong. He's—"

"Enough, please," Ariel said, voice thick with emotion.

Martin saw Theresa crying, and Alexis Baikal; but only when William turned back to look at him, and Martin saw his face was damp, did his chest hitch and his own eyes fill. He stepped forward.

"You don't have to fight, Rosa," he said.

Rosa Sequoia looked at the fifteen companions around her, clasped her trembling hands together, said, "But I've trained. I deserve it as much as any of you. Pan can't take my duty from me."

Pan/panic. The words danced. *If she goes on it will spread and we'll all go mad. We're that close.*

"I hate you," Rosa told Martin, eyes slitted, lip curling. "I hate everything you stand for."

Ariel took her by the arm. William took her other arm. Together, they led her away.

Theresa stood by his side as Rosa left the room. "Who'll take her tasks?" she asked him.

"Ariel can do them," he said, looking at the empty space where Rosa had stood. "Rosa will be confined to quarters."

"And when we split?"

"She stays on the *Hare*. *Tortoise* can't afford her."

"You'd better talk with Hans, then," Theresa said.

"Why does she hate *me*?" Martin asked.

"That's silly," Theresa said, taking his hand. "You can't take what she says personally . . ."

"William was right," he said. "I don't want anybody to hate me. I want everybody to love me . . . Hell of a thing for a Pan. Hans wouldn't have this problem."

Theresa tugged on his arm, pulling him toward the door. "Forty-five minutes," she reminded him. Martin stared at the War Mother before yielding to her pressure. During this entire episode, the War Mother had done nothing. *So little time.*

The War Mother preceded Martin and Hans down the second neck as they made final inspections of the points where the *Dawn Treader* would split. The War Mother would go with *Tortoise*.

Hans and Martin shook hands, clasped each other. "Do it, brother," Hans said. "We'll come back for the mopping up. I envy you, Martin."

"I don't envy myself," Martin said, then blushed. "I wish they'd chosen you Pan."

"I voted for you," Hans said, smiling, not very sincere. "I'm just a born slacker. You'll get the Job done."

William waited behind Martin. The children mingled to say their farewells, hugging, kissing, patting shoulders, even singing one round of the wordless hum.

Rosa was not present.

In a few minutes, in the narrow space around the weapons

store, all the children divided, *Hare* team to the right behind
Hans, *Tortoise* team to the left behind Martin. William and
Theresa hung beside each other as the teams parted again. Martin
felt a sudden misgiving, taking both of them with him. This time
brought nothing but qualms.

The teams backed farther away, around the curve of the weapons store. Already the children in the rear of each group could
not see each other.

They parted.

Throughout its length, the Ship of the Law made a sound like a
sigh, as if it laid down some tremendous burden, only to take up
another. The children of the *Tortoise* crew surrounded Martin in
a newly made space beside the weapons store. They waited
apprehensively, listening to the ship's noises, some holding on
to each other. Despite the drills, they were afraid, and Martin
was certainly not least afraid among them. He remembered Theodore's words: "*No machine works perfectly. Every machine can
fail. Every day we are in danger.*" But Theodore had added,
"*No planet lives forever. Every day on Earth, our lives were in
danger . . .*"

No safety anywhere. And the Ship of the Law had never failed
them before . . .

Nor had it broken in two before.

Martin sat above a low couch in the center of the room. All
around him, the children floated, squatted, stretched out, looking
at each other or at nothing, trying to sleep, playing games with
their wand projections, waiting, waiting.

The sigh turned into a strong wind moaning through the halls
outside their chamber. Air pressure was being distributed before
the walls closed.

Theresa came close to Martin. He held her in front of all,
acknowledging this bond. No one seemed to mind; few seemed
to notice, not even William, who played a game of matching
colors with Andrew Jaguar.

"How are you doing?" he asked Theresa. She shook her head
briskly as if shivering away the question.

"Waiting," she said. "You?"

The floor beneath them vibrated. Their cabin rotated as the

orientation of this part of the dividing *Dawn Treader* changed.
Again the wind outside the walls, roaring like a storm; this
was their only safe place, their calm cell within the turbulent
body.

"What will it feel like, the super deceleration?" Patrick
Angelfish asked, standing beside Martin.

"Like what we feel in the craft, I suppose," Martin said.
"Only more. Longer."

"I don't like the way that feels," Patrick said.

Martin looked at him with mock-sternness. Patrick smiled
back.

"I know," he said. "I'm a wimp."

"Let's hope you're a strong-stomached wimp," Martin said,
examining and reexamining his tone to see if it was right, if it
was not too sarcastic where he did not mean it to be, if he was
hiding from his words the complex of worries and fears he
himself felt; if he was adopting the proper tone of command
mixed with reassurance and comradely banter. *I am not a
natural leader. A natural leader would not even worry about
such things . . .*

The children drew closer as the vibrations continued, the
sounds of the new ships being made: belling and scraping, humming and faint rasping, heat in the cabin increasing for a few
minutes, then cool returning. The air smelled different. Martin
sniffed but did not mention it; Ariel came forward, frowning,
and said, "Smells funny."

Paola Birdsong and Stephanie Wing Feather agreed.

"Smells like rain," Theresa said.

" 'Tut tut, it looks like *rain*,' " Theresa quoted.

"We need a Pooh," Andrew Jaguar said. "Who should be
the ship's Pooh?"

"Who's most popular?" Martin asked, glancing around.
"Not me," he said.

Mei-Li groaned. "Pans are never Poohs," she said.

"How about Ariel?" William suggested.

"Bolsh," Ariel said quickly.

"She's very cuddly," Mei-Li agreed.

Ariel looked around the circle, unsure whether to be angry or
to shrug this off.

"We think it's a fine idea. You have to be Pooh," Hakim said, smiling serenely.

Ariel made a sound of disgust. "Cut the crap."

"We mean it," Mei-Li said with uncharacteristic force, and Andrew Jaguar added with a tone of implied threat, "You're chosen."

Martin did not know whether to interfere or let the game continue. He did not know if Ariel understood that the teasing was a display of affection. *Leveling the road; no bumps.*

"All right." Ariel swept her arms out, stalking the children in the circle, starting with Mei-Li, who giggled and backed away. "Come to *momma*. Come hug the Pooh." She mugged, menaced and threatened with a grim smile. No one offered themselves to her arms until she came to William, who sighed, cast his eyes to the ceiling, and said, "Take me, I'm yours."

"Oh, oh, *Christopher Robin!*" the children cried out.

Ariel embraced William, and expertly, they waltzed and flew around the cabin, swinging through the children as if they had rehearsed for months. A marvel; Martin had not known William could dance, much less Ariel. In truth, he saw they surprised themselves.

"May I butt in?" Mei-Li asked, tapping Ariel on the shoulder.

"Buzz off," she said with a haughty shudder. "I'm Pooh."

"Buzz off! You can *fly*," Andrew Jaguar sang. "You can fly, you can fly, you can fly!"

William took Ariel around the waist and swung her legs up over the heads of several squatting children, who ducked and laughed.

"Bravo!" Theresa cried.

Martin clapped his hands in time to the loops of the dance, and the children joined in, making music, humming a waltz. Ariel assumed a pose of dignified involvement in her art, chin lifted, nose out-thrust, eyes half-closed, fingers tipping along William's fingers, swirling, swirling.

Martin noticed the War Mother had entered the room. The dance continued until William said, "Oh Lord, enough, I'm worn out." Ariel let him go and he echoed off the wall, grabbing a ladder field, laughing and waving one hand in time with the hummed waltz.

"Who's next?" she called, swinging closer to the center. Her face glowed with exertion, eyes on fire, and she focused suddenly, unexpectedly, on Martin, hooded her eyes seductively, leaned back in an abbreviated S with fingers extended. "You, Pan? Dance with Pooh?"

Martin blushed, laughed, and extended his hand. Ariel touched it with an expression of anything but addle-headed Pooh-bear affection, and was about to swing him off when the cabin lurched violently. The children instinctively dropped to the floor, fingers clutching uselessly. Martin felt their weight increase: a tenth of a g, half, three quarters . . . He glanced at Ariel, sprawled across from him, eyes wide, scared, then rolled over to find Theresa on his other side; the couches had collapsed into the floor, leaving an unobstructed, cushioned environment.

The War Mother grounded against the floor, fastening itself. Ladder fields sprang up and the air vibrated with milky rainbow colors.

Martin tuned his wand to show *Tortoise*'s exterior. Like a wooden stake shivered by the tap of an axe, the *Dawn Treader* had split from the third homeball forward. The last tissue of connection—Martin noticed the flexibility of that connection, so unlike metal—parted, and *Hare* leaped with new freedom.

"Separation?" Theresa asked, though the answer was obvious. Belief did not necessarily follow seeing.

"The Ship of the Law is now two ships," the War Mother said. They had already moved a dozen kilometers from *Hare*, and the distance quickly increased.

"We made it," Martin said.

"Shit," said Ariel, crossing her legs on the soft floor.

The children squatted and clasped their hands in front of them like so many Buddhas. Martin reached for Theresa's hand, gripped it tightly. She smiled at him.

All so very brave. No choice.

"Let's do it," Martin said.

"Super deceleration will begin in one minute," the War Mother said.

"Count!" Andrew Jaguar shouted, and they counted as the numbers from Martin's wand gleamed in the air above them.

Five, four, three, two

Martin took a deep breath and closed his eyes. Like a soft electric hand probing his body, the volumetric fields diffused through him. He heard a tiny distant whining noise in his ears, felt the blood stop in his veins, all the protoplasm in his cells pause, then the blood start again, pause, start: the vibrating jerkiness of fields controlling the path of each molecule, adjusting to allow normal vectors, to cancel the effects of the deceleration, temporarily paused thought, jammed his mind with half-aware impulses, threw him into blankness.

He could not see. His eyes hurt but he could not be fully aware of the pain. They would be in this state for days, but fortunately, the fields would soon give them a semblance of normality. They could see, move, talk, eat, however slowly and carefully.

If all goes well. No machine works perfectly. Every machine can fail.

The wands would not work under super deceleration. The War Mother would be inactive. They would have only themselves, in this small space, for days as they dropped from the top of the universe to the bottom, as they drained their momentum into massive sumps . . . as they let themselves be guided like pigeons in the head of a bomb, pigeons ready to peck their final destination, coo their final judgments, hoping to put out the eyes of those who had eaten their eggs, their young, their very coop.

Theodore came into the room where Martin sat alone with just the drip of thoughts to occupy him.

"Is it sadness then that makes you think of our enemy so?"

"Ah, Christ, Theodore. I miss you. Why did you kill yourself?"

"Because we're just pigeons, that's all."

"You never said so."

"I was never omniscient, Martin. You have original thoughts, you know, some better than mine ever were. Death just makes me larger, and that's silly. I'm actually very small now, being dead; a dust mote in your mind."

"I'd like to have you back in more than just dreams . . ."

"Hardly a dream. You're awake."

Martin sighed, shook his head. "I think we've gone through the worst part, and this is me, sleeping and dreaming, waiting for the whole thing to end. Boredom can do this to us. I think we're all sleeping now, tired of each other, bored with being in a tiny room.''

"You've been thinking of Ariel, haven't you?"

"I suppose . . . What can you tell me about her?"

"Nothing you don't already know. The disadvantage of being dead. I can only be the image of your thoughts.''

"So what do I know about her that I can't recognize?"

"She's tough, she keeps her mind about her, she believes in very little, and she has a capacity for great"

love

Theresa lay next to him, snoring lightly. Martin stroked her hip, feeling the tingle of field adjustment in his hands, the constant bind of constraints as the fields decided (if such was the right word) what motion was permitted, and what might be the beginning of a disastrous tumble into one-thousand-g deceleration.

love

for individual, for family, for group, for companions, for ship, for world, for Earth.

How does one come to love a world? Born into it, suffused with it, the world is part of everything and not differentiable. The *Dawn Treader* was a world, as large in its way as any human lifetime; plenty of places to live, plenty of dreams to dream, even allowing them fragments of Earth. Scientific, curious Theodore Dawn, always observing, making notes, bent over his lenses and clear tanks of pond water in the quarters he shared with Martin, his personal equivalent of the cats and parrots other children kept as mutual pets and mascots. The lenses—the moms' equivalent of microscopes—hovering in the air before Theodore's face like tiny white jewels, light-refracting fields of optical strength and clarity far better than fluorite. Caught in a small spherical field that allowed in oxygen, but kept water from escaping, several *chaoborus* specimens, the larvae of phantom midges that Theodore favored so highly. The specimens were kept from escaping by gentle fields . . . fields within fields, allowing Theodore access to these living creatures that would have been impossible on old Earth.

"Quite lovely," Theodore said. "And even better—harmless. Aren't you glad I'm not raising mosquitoes? You'd sneak in at night and destroy my tanks.''

''We'd put up with it,'' Martin said.

''No you wouldn't,'' Theodore said. ''You're much too judgmental . . .'' *Chaoborus*, zooplankters, phytoplankters, varieties of beautiful algae, and above the pond, flying about the room, adult phantom midges buzzing, almost invisible, preening themselves on the walls; ignorant that they were no longer on Earth.

''Do you think we understand where we are?'' Martin asked.

''You think we don't and can't, not where it counts. Not in our guts and cells. We always carry Earth with us. When a parent dies, the genes remain, and the memories, which are only lesser and weaker threads.''

''My parents are alive, probably, but I can't feel *them*.''

''We're on opposite sides of a gulf of physics difficult for us midges to understand, in our guts,'' Theodore said. Musing over his spherical field-bound pond, stirring it with a glass rod, watching the algae twine on the rod, making history among the micro-organisms, the paramecia and rotifers, the euglenoids and diatoms, the desmids, amphipods, ostracods, wreaking havoc among the daphnia.

The comparatively large *chaoborus* larvae thin as ghosts with vicious curved beaks and black-eyed heads, pairs of beautifully patterned buoyancy organs fore and aft, whisking themselves away with a wriggle to avoid the currents.

Martin rolled over and opened his eyes and felt the tingle in his lids. Sometimes he made moves that were resisted: sudden moves, alarming the fields perhaps, though dropping his substance only a few ten thousandths into the forbidden chasm of one thousand g's.

It was best not to move at all, and so most of the children did not.

Theresa and Ariel sat talking quietly about Hans the Eternal and others; as they talked, Martin saw Hans and Theodore together, though they had not been close friends, had rarely spoken to each other. Hans asked Theodore what he thought of Martin, whether Martin had what it took to be Pan.

''He doesn't think so,'' Theodore said, winking over his shoulder at Martin. ''He thinks he cares too much.''

"Do you think I have what it takes?"

"Nobody who wants to be Pan should be," Theodore said.

"I don't *want* to be . . ." But there was something like hope on Hans' face.

Theresa and Ariel discussed the gowns the Wendys would wear when all was done, and they married another world.

Theresa wore this gown as she marched down a vast cathedral aisle. The gown draped white, like a weave of quartz crystals and diamonds, supernaturally supple and beautiful, and in her hair threaded rubies, emeralds, opals, beryls, flowers of sulfur, selenite, celestite, amethyst, garnets, agates, sapphires, and on her hands she wore constellations of Iceland spar, white aragonite, green azurite, blue lapis, representing the dowry of her Mother, and Theodore gave her away, dressed in a suit woven entirely of shimmering midges and butterflies and moths, and Martin waited at the altar. Behind him opened the arms of another world, even more beautiful than Earth, and that meant a guilt of unfaithfulness.

Now the women were talking about having children someday, and Ariel shaking her head stubbornly, saying she would not be a good mother, she was too tough on others, no sympathy, but Theresa said instincts will kick in and they will be tender.

Three days, top to bottom, in this small room, sleeping and talking, eating only a few times, for food did not digest well under the tyranny of volumetric fields grumpy about adding new molecules to the body's equation.

The bottom of the universe, perversely, was bright, and the top was dark. The *Dawn Treader* had fallen out of the darkness, away from the muddy twisted ring of stars, but there was still this vast cliff to descend, from three quarters of the speed of light to less than one hundredth of one percent c, a profligate excretion of momentum that must later be regained from fuel in the very system they would try to kill.

They tumbled toward the central furnace, their almost straight-line course gradually curving like an expertly drawn wire. They slowed to one half c, one quarter, one tenth, one hundredth, and now, one thousandth, one ten thousandth.

Breaking and entering. Intent to murder.

The enormous burden of momentum passed away, and the

children were no longer fast gods, but pigeons in the head of a very quiet, dark bomb, stealing through the house, the solar system of Wormwood.

Martin opened his eyes and spread his arms, his fingers, savoring the freedom of no tingle, no tyranny.

Theresa leaned over him, already awake. "It's over," she said. "We're here."

In the first few hours of freedom from the cramped super deceleration space, the children reacquainted themselves with the ship. Martin led them stem to stern, following the map projected by his wand.

Tortoise had taken the shape of a squat dumbbell, the third homeball having split into two hemispheres, absorbing and redistributing the second neck to become a connecting bar between them. The nose was a mere blister on the blunt face of the fore hemisphere, and there was no tail.

Hakim set up the search shop in the nose of *Tortoise* to see what there was to see. The new star sphere quickly filled with information, and Hakim immediately reexamined their target worlds one by one as Martin observed: rocky Nebuchadnezzar, innermost, Ramses next, and far beyond, on the opposite side of Wormwood, Herod, the massive depleted gas giant. There were still no major surprises at this distance, half a billion kilometers from Nebuchadnezzar, but the images in the star sphere were gratifyingly crisp and clean.

"It's very good," Hakim told Martin. "What would we like to know?"

"The makers in the outer cloud should be ready in a few tendays," Martin said. "We need to confirm our first target, or inform the makers by tight-beam whether we've chosen another." The makers were beyond noach range; a tight-beam message would take days to reach them. "We need to know which is the most active world, and whether there are any defenses."

Tortoise was one sixth the size of *Dawn Treader*, but still large enough for the children to rattle around in. The unfamiliar corridors smelled new, like fresh clothes made by the moms. Martin took in as much of the new design as he could, judging its suitability for their needs, finding it adequate, but with an intense, childish kind of disappointment, missing the huge spaces of the *Dawn Treader*. He put that disappointment aside.

Martin leading, the thirty-five children in the *Tortoise* crew echoed and laddered down a smaller, shorter neck to the redesigned, rearranged weapons store, where the pods containing the makers and doers that would infiltrate the inner rocky worlds of Wormwood had been moved to prominent position.

Paola Birdsong and Stephanie Wing Feather moved the first pod groupings into six bombships, part of the ritual demanded by the moms—that as much as possible, the children should take responsibility for their weapons, for their assigned tasks, to complete the Job. Martin confirmed the loading, and the War Mother inspected the results. Training was paying off; the work had been done perfectly.

With the first part of the Job done, Martin gave them permission to establish new quarters and manufacture those things they needed. No personal goods or pets had been transferred to *Tortoise*.

The first group meal would begin in an hour.

Within three days, as *Tortoise* slid farther down the well of Wormwood's gravitation, all their familiarization, establishment of quarters, manufacturing of goods, might go for nothing; the ship might have to change again, to deal quickly with whatever defenses the planet killers could muster . . .

But until that time, Martin wanted to establish a sense of normality, to keep his children as stable and contented as he could.

Still, they all knew that their home had fled. The chances of *Dawn Treader* being reassembled as it had been were nil. The chances of all of them surviving . . . of Wormwood having no defenses, no sensors able to detect their presence . . . were also nil.

Hakim came to Martin in the weapons stores as he finished his inspection, waited patiently, approached the Pan with face alight with enthusiasm. "There's news," he said. "More information, and very interesting, too."

Martin looked at the arrays of craft in the stores, at the bombships on their pylons and the pods of doers attached to toruses. Stephanie Wing Feather and Paola Birdsong floated between the ships like birds between two gray footballs, listening. All the children in the stores listened.

"We should all hear the news together," Martin decided. "We'll update at mess."

Hakim projected his information after their hasty meal. He showed them Nebuchadnezzar first, as seen from *Hare* as it streaked through the system: a tan world with spots of reddish-brown and thin ribbons of green.

"As we observed from farther out, this is the more active of the two planets, judging from its crustal vibrations," Hakim said. "Nebuchadnezzar is very quiet, but it is definitely inhabited—if only by machines. *Hare*'s sensors tell us, on its pass through, that there are very likely some sorts of machines within the planet. We think the machines occupy the upper crust, nothing below, and they are very efficient. They use fields to transfer substances—possibly gases, water and other cool liquids, molten rock, molten metals, solids, slurries. We cannot judge how many individual biological creatures might be served by these machines, but there are none apparent on the surface. The surface is deceptively calm. Too quiet, as a soldier or cowboy hero might have observed. Perhaps they feel a need to hide . . ."

Martin shook his head. "They're not very good at hiding. If we can detect something, others can, as well."

Hakim acknowledged that, and continued. "The planet, as we noticed earlier, lacks obvious weather patterns. Its air currents are fixed and stable, a highly unnatural situation. What were once ocean basins have been empty for thousands of years, and there are no reservoirs. For the most part, except for some ancient construction activity, the entire surface seems to be abandoned desert. We conclude that the water in the old oceans was either lost through abrupt weather changes—unlikely—or sacrificed to provide volatiles across thousands of years."

"For conversion to anti em?" Martin asked.

"Perhaps," Hakim conceded. "Here is our surprise for the day. Ships much too small to have been noticed before, much too few to really be called commerce—perhaps ten ships traveling in low-energy orbits between Nebuchadnezzar and Ramses, and only one traveling outward to Herod. They all appear to be trailing radioactive particles, indicating primitive anti em drives or perhaps fusion. The ships may be trivial, toys, like . . ."

"Yachts in a bathtub," Stephanie Wing Feather suggested.

"Yes. If they are mere toys, then there is no longer spacefaring commerce in the Wormwood system . . . none that we can detect."

"If there are any inhabitants, are they physical?" Martin asked.

"My guess is they are not. Not in discrete biological bodies, at any rate. All the moms' profiles of other worlds and their development characteristics tell us that Nebuchadnezzar and Ramses are old, perhaps a billion years older than Earth, and that their civilizations, if any remain—if there are any intelligences in control of the planetary activity—have transferred to a non-biological matrix."

"Perhaps they've fled Wormwood entirely," Paola Birdsong suggested.

"Something's going on down there," Hakim said, the merest frown crossing his brow. "If the primary civilization has abandoned Nebuchadnezzar and Ramses, they've left machines to perform some task or other."

"It doesn't make sense. If nobody's here, and if we destroy these worlds, what do we accomplish?" Ariel asked.

"I believe there are intelligences here," Hakim said. "There is activity—it is just very low-key. Perhaps they have been hiding for a long time, and they are simply growing lax . . ."

Martin pondered this for a few seconds. "We go ahead," he said. "We drop the planetary makers and doers, and if possible, we reconnoiter. Still no evidence of defenses?"

"None," Hakim said.

"And the five masses inward from Nebuchadnezzar?"

"Still unknown," Hakim said. "I'm giving them full priority now."

The system of planets around Wormwood spanned fifteen billion kilometers, the major axis of the outermost planet's orbit. The *Tortoise* would not resort to extreme acceleration except in an emergency, and that made the system as vast, with regard to their present flow of time, as the spaces between the stars. It could take them years to explore, reconnoiter . . . Or they could do their Job and get out as best they could, to rendezvous with *Hare*, and perhaps begin the new life.

Martin made his quarters small and spare, just large enough to suit two comfortably. He did not request many goods, hoping to set an example for the others.

There were still tough choices to be made, but they would not be made by vote of the children. The decisions were his alone now. The judgment had been passed; the system was condemned. But how much could they contribute to the total effort against the planet killers? How much could they learn here about the development and growth of such civilizations, about intelligences so inclined to destroy and murder?

If Wormwood contained clues to the morphology of such civilizations, Martin argued with himself that they had a duty to learn as much as they could, to help the Benefactors. That meant time, and study—and greatly increased danger.

"I'd like to speak with the War Mother," he said to his wand. A few minutes later, the War Mother appeared at the hatch to his quarters, and he asked it to enter. The black and white paint on its surface had started to flake. They might have to renew it soon.

He expressed his thoughts about exploring in a few brief sentences, and asked for advice.

"Any knowledge gathered could be most useful," the War Mother said. "Should we ever be in a situation to pass on what we learn to another Ship of the Law."

"Would it be *crucial*?" Martin asked.

"That is impossible to judge until the knowledge is gathered."

Martin smiled wryly, wondering why he engaged in such conversations at all. As Pan, it was all up to him—to his instincts, which Martin did not trust.

He bit his lip reflectively, sucking in a lungful of cool air. If things went bad on Mars and Venus, if the solar system was (or *had been*) attacked again and the Benefactors had lost, then the children and records of Earth contained within the Ships of the Law would be all that remained . . .

Far more than just their individual selves could be at stake. He wondered if, at some crucial moment, all Earth might scream through him, the world in his genes reaching up to his mind, the spirit of terrestrial creation demanding survival at any cost.

Martin sleeved sweat from his forehead.

I fear the ghost of Earth.

"Then we concentrate on doing the Job," he said, "and we learn what we can."

For once, he was grateful for the War Mother's silence.

The *Tortoise* coasted more quietly than any stone. Within, the children prepared, watched, listened to the natural whickerings of Nebuchadnezzar and Ramses and Herod and the high buzz and squeal of Wormwood, tracked the slow courses of the tiny points of light that were ships.

Drifting, drifting, around the shallow well of Wormwood, across its vast gently curved prairie of gravitation.

The children became quieter, more somber.

Theresa and Martin still found occasion to make love, but the love was peremptory, more necessity than enthusiasm. Ramses, slightly larger than Nebuchadnezzar, had once been covered with thick volcanic haze, high in sulfuric acid, still evident in traces in its soil. Some internal anomaly—a huge undigested lump of uranium, perhaps—had kept it hot and heavy with volcanism even into its late old age. It had been tamed only by the action of civilization, perhaps from Nebuchadnezzar if that was where life had first formed around Wormwood—perhaps from Leviathan, the closest star system, or even Behemoth before it became a red giant.

Martin studied the search team's reports on Nebuchadnezzar hour by hour. Hakim did not sleep; Martin ordered him to rest finally when he found Hakim slumped on a ladder field, hardly able to move.

Down, down . . .

Time passed quickly enough, too quickly for Martin; there was no time to think the thoughts he needed to think, to reach the conclusions that had to be reached.

The purpose of their journey, perhaps the main purpose of their existence, approached all too rapidly.

The makers deposited in the pre-birth material around Wormwood converted rocky rubble into neutronium bombs sufficient to melt a single planet's surface.

After reporting their status to *Tortoise* along channels mimicking the cosmic babble of distant stars, in low-information drones lasting hours, the makers became silent. Not even *Tortoise* could detect them, or learn where they were; the time for giving them alternate instructions had passed.

Whether *Tortoise* succeeded or not, the makers would stealthily drop their weapons into the system. The weapons' journeys would take years . . .

Martin floated in a net beside Theresa. Both lay awake. For a long time—fifteen, twenty minutes—neither spoke, content, if that was the word, to merely stretch out next to each other, flesh warm against flesh, listening to their breath flow in and out.

"We're doing it," Martin said finally.

"You mean, it's almost done," Theresa said.

"Yes. The moms have trained us well."

"To destroy."

Martin snorted. "Destroy what? The Killers burned themselves out. Or they've left. How many thousands of years more advanced were they?" He snorted again, and stroked her arm. "Why did they kill Earth, when they still had their home worlds, and they couldn't even fill *them*? Was it just greed?"

"Maybe it was fear," Theresa said. "They were afraid we would send machines to kill *them*."

"Everybody's afraid in the forest," Martin agreed. "Kill or be killed."

"Kill and be killed," Theresa said.

"I don't like what I've become," Martin said after a pause. "What I'm doing."

"Do you like *me*?"

"Of course I do."

"I'm doing the same thing."

He shrugged, unable to explain the contradiction.

"Do you feel guilty?" Theresa asked.

"No," Martin said. "I want to turn their worlds into slag."

"All right," Theresa said.

"Do you?"

"Feel guilty?"

"No. Want to watch."

She didn't answer for some time, her breath regular, as if asleep. "No," she said. "But I will. For those who can't."

* * *

Falling, falling. Into the bright basement of Wormwood, around
the furnace, a hundred million kilometers from Nebuchadnezzar,
silent as a ghost, smaller than a midge, with snail-like slowness,
observing, Hakim and his team concentrating on the five inner
dark masses, Martin concentrating on the discipline, on the Job,
keeping their minds tightly wrapped around this one thought.

Going from child to child, Wendy to Lost Boy, talking, encouraging, until his throat was hoarse and his eyes bleary; talking
across the days to all at one time or another, maintaining the
contact, as his father would have done, across that unreachable
spatial and temporal gulf, where simultaneity had no meaning
but in the deceived, dreaming mind.

All like a dream, eerily unreal; the new spaces of *Tortoise*
working against their sense of having belonged, triply removed
from the realities their bodies had come to understand: Earth,
Ark, *Dawn Treader*. They belonged nowhere but in their work.

Theodore Dawn would have hated this, Martin thought. He
would have chafed at the single-minded life-in-illusion; he would
have demanded some bridging truth, some connectedness of
purpose between what they had once been, on the Ark, and were
now, purpose and connection gone missing.

He would have done poorly, or he would have changed as
they all had changed, as Ariel had changed, subduing her obvious
doubts, hardly ever complaining, drifting with the rest of them
on the descending sweep of Tortoise's orbit.

But later Martin thought, *Theodore would have done well;
better than I have done, he would have been chosen Pan, he
would have this responsibility; he would miss his ponds and*
chaoborus, *wonderfully glassy ugly denizens of Earth, but he
would bear down and focus his energies. The children would
respect him and he would not expect them all to like him.*

The Earth did not speak for revenge. It spoke for survival.

Down, down.

Martin went from child to child through the *Tortoise*, the
image of his father and mother leading, trying to be to the
children what the moms could not.

Strangely, Martin found old experiences opening to him as he
spoke to his shipmates, flowers of memory suddenly revived:

sucking on his mother's breast, the warm rich smell of her like roses in a gymnasium, the smile on her face as she looked on him, cradled in her arms, an all-approving smile the moms could not produce, all-forgiving, all-loving, the soft ecstasy of her milk letting down.

He remembered the discipline and love of his father, less gentle then his mother; the guilt of his father when he punished Martin, especially when Martin provoked a spanking; his father's solemn depression for hours after, locking himself away from wife and son while his mother sat quietly with Martin. The later years, spankings much less frequent—none after he was six— and the days of togetherness in the summers before Earth's death, after his father's return from Washington, D.C., investigating the river in a raft, exploring the forest around the house, talking, his father taciturn and solemn at times, at other times ebullient and even silly.

Arthur's love for Francine, filling Martin's childhood as a constant like sunlight. Martin did not forget the arguments, the family disputes, but they were as much a part of the picture as wrinkles in skin or mountains on the Earth's surface or waves on the sea . . . ups and downs of emotional terrain.

The memories helped Martin keep that sense of purpose they had had when they left the Ark and climbed out of the sun's basement, up into the long darkness.

"We still haven't found anything that is obviously a defense," Hakim pronounced on the eighteenth day. The children of *Tortoise* floated around him in the cafeteria, listening to the latest search team report. "Planetary activity hasn't increased or decreased. We haven't been swept by electromagnetic radiation of any artificial variety we can detect. We seem to be catching them by surprise."

Martin hung with legs crossed at the rear of the group, Theresa beside him. He laddered to the center of the cafeteria when Hakim had finished.

"We have some choices," Martin said. "We can drop makers and doers into Nebuchadnezzar first, then the same to Ramses, and hope they find enough raw material to do the Job. Or we can convert all of our fuel and most of the ship into bombs and

concentrate on skinning one planet. Because of the lack of volatiles, we probably can't do much damage to more than one, not
right away. Just to skin one planet will probably take most of
our fuel and large chunks of *Tortoise* itself. Or we can sleep and
wait for the makers and doers in the pre-birth cloud to send their
weapons down.''

"Let's vote," Ariel said when he paused.

"No." He shook his head patiently. "This isn't a matter for
voting."

"Why not?" Ariel asked, her expression languid, without
passion. *We all wear killing faces. Faces showing nobody home,
nobody responsible.*

"Because the Pan makes all decisions now," Stephanie Wing
Feather reminded her.

Martin half-expected Ariel to leave the cafeteria in anger, but
she did not. She relaxed her arms, closed her eyes, sighed, then
opened them again and watched his face intently.

"This is a tough one," Martin said. "If we wait long enough,
we might learn whether we should hit Herod, or even focus on
it. If there are no defenses, if the risk is low, we can suck out
all of Nebuchadnezzar's atmospheric volatiles *before* the planet is
destroyed—much easier and faster than after blowing it up . . .''

"Strip the atmosphere . . .'' Andrew Jaguar said, shuddering.
"Like vampires.''

"We're going to blow it to dust anyway," Mei-li reminded
him, small voice like a bird's chirrup.

"Hakim, how close do we need to be to investigate?"

"I don't think there's any real gain from being closer than a
few thousand kilometers. If need be, we can send out remotes
at this distance and create a bigger baseline, gather as much
information as we would if we flew right down to the surface
. . . But obviously, we could make a bigger blip in whatever
sensors they have.''

"What kind of baseline?" Martin asked.

Hakim conferred with his team for a few seconds. "We think
at this distance, about ten kilometers. We could resolve down to
bugs in the air, if there are any.''

"The makers and doers have to be delivered from a distance

of no more than one hundred kilometers,'' Stephanie said. ''The bombships, fully fueled, have a range of forty g hours, and that can translate into however many kilometers of orbit we wish, if we're patient . . . We know that none of us can live in a bombship for more than about four tendays without going crazy. We could induce sleep, but that wouldn't be optimum.''

The parameters were now clear to all the children. Each advantage had to be weighed against risk; Martin had worked through the momerath days before, and found several courses equally matched for danger and benefit. Theresa had checked his calculations, as had Stephanie Wing Feather and, he presumed, Hakim Hadj.

''We send out remotes and expand our baseline,'' he said. ''That seems to involve the lowest risk. We can gather all the information we need in a few days. We pull in the remotes, coast in quietly, release the bombships, pick them up again after they've injected the weapons into Nebuchadnezzar, drop our doers to gather volatiles in the ruins, accelerate outward to Ramses as fast as possible, and execute again. If we haven't found any further signs of activity on Herod, we rendezvous with the robots after a fast orbit around Wormwood. Then we measure our resources, report to Hare, drop doers to mine what few resources there are on Herod, and boost out. The best estimate for a rendezvous with Hare is two years. Another year to swing back to Wormwood to gather up the robots and their gleanings.''

The children groaned. They had done much of the momerath themselves, but hearing it from Martin—losing all hope of fast action and sacrifice of fuel to boost up and out, knowing what they had already suspected, that he would choose the most conservative and practical course, however time-consuming— brought the truth home hard.

Over three years. Awake and vigilant. And then, unlikely to have enough fuel to accelerate to near-c, perhaps centuries to move on to Leviathan . . .

At the very least, under those circumstances, they would have to sleep. There were dangers in such a long sleep; even a Ship of the Law could grow old.

Saying the plan aloud, when he had hardly thought it through

clearly himself, made it seem both more real and strangely beyond real. Young human beings saying such words, planning
such things.

As if to highlight the absurdity, Mei-li giggled. Her giggle
died quickly and was not picked up around the room.

"We will be in position to release the bombships in six days,"
Hakim said.

Nebuchadnezzar was easily visible to the naked eye, a bright
diamond among the lesser points of stars. Day by day, it became
even brighter, and Martin ordered a star sphere expanded in the
cafeteria. As they ate their meals, or gathered in quiet social
groupings, they watched their target grow.

The remotes spread their photon-intercepting fields like webs
and gathered in clear images of the brown world, as if opening
an eye ten kilometers wide.

There were no bugs in the atmosphere—no life crawling on
the surface, no organic chemical activity within the upper layers
of soil.

Nebuchadnezzar's subtle motions resembled a feeble, irregular heartbeat, but the profiles of the internal vibrations did not
match tectonics. Unlike Ramses', Nebuchadnezzar's heart was
cool; any internal heat had fled long before.

Martin finished examining Hakim's figures while the other
children slept, two days from H-hour.

The five inner masses remained enigmatic. From this angle to
the ecliptic, they could not measure the objects in transit across
Wormwood, but a chance star occultation allowed Hakim to
confirm that one of the dark objects was three thousand kilometers in diameter, with a mass of approximately fourteen billion
trillion kilograms, and only as dense as water. The dark objects
might be clusters of neutronium with large spaces between, surrounded by a shell . . . or they might be balloons filled with
water, a tantalizing idea, but unlikely.

"I have no idea what they are," Hakim said, shaking his head,
expression grim and exhausted. "They worry me greatly, Martin."

Martin replayed the inner mass star occultation and associated
graphics and measurement reports, trying to glean with supernat-

ural intuition what could not be seen. "The War Mother has no suggestions?"

"The objects are outside the moms' experience, I think," Hakim said. He looked as if he were thinking, but would not say, *Or they will not tell us.*

But that would be absurd.

"We should pull in the remotes now," Martin said, shivering slightly.

"Still no signs of defense, no awareness of our presence— no preparation to fight," Hakim said.

"Nothing we can detect," Martin added.

"I would appreciate more time with the remotes—more time to find something . . ."

Martin thought that over for a few seconds, then nodded. "Another twelve hours. But let somebody else keep watch. You sleep."

"No," Hakim said. "This is my only duty. I watch, I calculate, I keep you informed . . . For now, I do not need to sleep." His eyes stared up at Martin out of sunken orbits. His hair tufted on his scalp, his face gleamed with oil, he smelled faintly sour.

"Sleep for five hours, and get cleaned up," Martin said, touching his cheek with one hand. "You'll make mistakes if you push yourself too much. We don't need mistakes."

"I will get along with two hours of sleep," Hakim said. Then, smiling his angelic smile, "And I will take a shower, not to offend."

"All right. Put Jennifer in charge. She'll keep an eye out."

"It is because I am so worried," Hakim said. "What we do not know . . ."

When the remotes had been withdrawn, Martin conferred with Stephanie Wing Feather and Harpal Timechaser. Theresa and Jorge Rabbit hovered on the periphery in the otherwise empty quarters, representing the children aboard *Tortoise* in this final meeting of Pan and *Tortoise*'s share of ex-Pans.

"Stephanie . . ." Martin said. "Your thoughts. Twelve hours and we release the bombships. What have I neglected to do?"

"Nothing," Stephanie said.

"Harpal?"

"Nothing. We've done everything we've been taught to do, everything we know how to do . . . But . . ."

"It's too good," Stephanie said. "No defenses, no reaction, quiet and almost dead. Nothing like what we've been led to expect, what we've trained to fight. And . . ."

"No volatiles," Harpal said. "It's going to be damned difficult to refuel."

"Right. If there's anything here at all, it's a tired old civilization dreaming in its own high-tech grave," Stephanie said. "Not much satisfaction killing an old codger who doesn't care."

"Wormwood doesn't fit any profiles, does it?"

"It doesn't," Martin said. "The War Mother has nothing to suggest, except that this could be—"

"A sham," Stephanie said. "Something to draw us into a dead system we can't pull out of, something to waste our energy and time. Flypaper, baited with nasty evidence of past sins."

Martin touched finger to nose, shrugged. "The War Mother thinks the evidence is pretty conclusive." He glanced toward Theresa. She seemed to be daydreaming, staring at the wall beyond him.

"What if it is a trap, and we are wasted completely for nothing?" Jorge Rabbit said. Martin didn't answer.

"We've made our decision," Stephanie said quietly. "We have no proof it's a trap. We just don't know everything for sure."

"The five masses," Jorge said.

"Nothing's ever for sure," Harpal said.

Martin covered the unmagnified image of Nebuchadnezzar with his hand, edge of palm to edge of palm sufficing; or fist. Soft brown world like a dirty rubber ball. The search team conferred among themselves in the cafeteria, leaving the nose temporarily empty, and Martin had chosen this opportunity to see their target alone, photons reflected directly to his eyes.

We can kill you, whatever you are or were. Why don't you react? Why so silent?

"I don't think it's a sham," William said. "I think they've left Wormwood as a kind of sacrifice." He had entered the nose behind Martin without his noticing. "I think this was their home world, but it's old now, and they're old. Maybe they've left behind the responsible types, the builders and planners, to wait for execution.''

Martin frowned over his shoulder at William.

William smiled a fey smile in reply to the frown, lifted a hand as they floated beside each other, looking through the transparent nose. "If we were to land and explore their . . . caverns, tunnels, whatever they have, we'd find the guilty ones waiting for us, ready for justice.''

"Jesus, William,'' Martin said, turning away.

"It's a freaky thought, isn't it?''

"You said it.''

"The planners would give themselves to us, and the entire world . . . And it wouldn't be enough. We want *all of them* to die, don't we? Just getting the planners, the leaders, wouldn't be enough.''

Martin said nothing, growing angry. This kind of fantasizing was more than useless; it was counter-productive, perhaps even bad for their morale.

"I hope you haven't told anybody about this.''

"I keep my stupid ideas to myself . . . except for you.''

"Good,'' Martin said, perhaps more firmly than necessary.

"Don't be too hard,'' William said. "Can you imagine the kind of guilt the Killers feel, if they feel guilt at all? Maybe they grew up after launching their machines, when it was too late. Or perhaps one tyrannical, fanatic government built and launched the machines, and then fell out of power, and others came in, and they decided the best thing would be to leave all this here for us, to let us destroy their home world, maybe the leaders . . . That would be nice, wouldn't it?''

"Nice isn't the word,'' Martin said, his anger subsiding. William was always willing to play this peculiar game, somewhere between Devil's advocate and unbridled imp.

"I'm not really kidding, Martin,'' William said. "I think that's what it must be. If this is a trap, we're in too close already . . . What sort of trap works only once, when there might be dozens, even hundreds of Ships of the Law closing in? We've come too far for this to be a trap. We've got them.''

Martin gave the merest nod.

"You must be feeling very strange now," William said softly, cocking his head to one side. "It's so close."

"We're here. It's what we've waited and trained for."

"We never trained for something this easy," William said. "If they're sitting ducks, if they just bare their breasts or whatever and shout *mea culpa* . . . What will that do to us? Like getting ready to jump over a high wall and finding it's just a curb. Then waiting years in space, thinking about it. We might go mad. I might go mad."

"We'll make it," Martin said. "How do *you* feel?"

"Numb," William said. "I'll be on a bombship with Fred Falcon. We'll actually drop the makers and doers. We'll be out there."

"I wish I could be with you," Martin said.

William nodded. "I suppose we're privileged. Pulling the triggers to avenge the Earth."

They said nothing for a time, the conversation having swung through so many curves, and no central issue apparent.

"I'm doing fine, William," Martin said to an unspoken question. "It's not much fun, but life isn't supposed to be fun now. Is that what you're getting at?"

William caressed the back of Martin's neck. "It shouldn't be like this. There should be noise, action, danger, excitement."

"You're lonely, aren't you?"

William closed his eyes. "I feel like Rosa Sequoia," he said. "I wonder how they're getting along on *Hare*. They have even less to do than we. Second-line troops."

"Are you lonely?"

"No, Martin, actually, I'm not very lonely. I've kind of given up on the old slicking. It seems so trivial. I think I'll just shut down the libido and absorb these ambiguities. Not that there aren't possibilities for exercising the old libido. Very thoughtfully you included a couple of compatriots on this side of the split. They're less inhibited than I seem to be. There have been offers."

"But no love," Martin said.

William closed his eyes again, nodded. "There's not much love among any of us now. How about you and Theresa?"

"Still love," Martin said, watching his friend's face closely.

"Must be a comfort."

"I never stopped loving you, William."

"I still don't need comfort slicks," William said testily.

"That's not what I mean. You're part of me."

"Not an exclusive part," William said, looking at Martin from the corner of his eyes, self-deprecatory smile flickering on his lips.

"Pretty exclusive," Martin said. "Making love to you is like having a wonderful . . . *was* like having a wonderful kind of brother, a double, not dangerous, just accepting."

"Like jerking off by remote," William suggested. Martin knew that tone; sharp but not mean.

"Not at all."

"Men know men. Women know women. The great justification of homosexual slicking."

"William, stop it."

"All right," William said, subdued again.

"When I think about things, you're in my head, and I try to think about what you'd say or do in a given situation. I talk to you in my head, and I talk to Theresa. Brother and sister, and more than that." He was not actually lying, but this was not strictly true; he had given little thought to William, but did not want William to know that, or to acknowledge it to himself; that he could have passed over William with so little trauma, and yet still regard him with immense affection. What sort of love was that?

"You say you think about me, but you live with Theresa."

Both stared at Nebuchadnezzar, the planet whose real name they did not know, if it had a name at all.

"Did they ever love?" William asked.

"I don't give a damn," Martin said. *My friends and my home. They killed the fish in the seas and the birds in the air. They took away our childhood. They killed my dog.* "It's time to get this behind us and start living our own lives. We'll become shadows if we do this forever."

"Amen," William said. "You want Theresa to wear that gown, on another world, our world?"

"I do," Martin said.

"I'd like to see that. I want to wear something special, too."

"We all will, I think," Martin said.

"But first . . ."

Martin noticed William's lips working, as if in silent prayer. *For safe passage, or forgiveness?*

Will safe passage be a sign of forgiveness?

No signs, no consolation, no forgiveness; no blame. The forest was full of wolves.

No God of kindness and justice could allow such a thing. Nature could, but nature kept a balance.

The forest was also full of hunters.

The bombship pilots gathered in the weapons stores, Martin and the War Mother presiding. Between them hung a projected image of Nebuchadnezzar, its aspect changing as it slowly rotated night into day, the crescent orb visibly growing: two hours until release.

Theresa and William floated beside their craft, faces blank. Fred Falcon joined William. Stephanie, alone beside her ship, and Yueh Yellow River beside his. Theresa would fly a bombship alone. Nguyen Mountain Lily and Ginny Chocolate together; Michael Vineyard and Hu East Wind; Leo Parsifal and Nancy Flying Crow. Seven ships for this sortie.

Martin kept his face blank, hiding the gut-knot within, that nausea of excitement and naked fear, that urge to tremble and run and beg forgiveness of whatever nasty supernatural being controlled things. In his sporadic journal, Martin had written:

We have hugged and made love this morning, eaten breakfast together. I have seen her wrapped in the final gown, and we have sworn that we are married, that we are bound. "We will make children," she said, and I agreed; when we are out from under the moms, there will be fertility and we will make children, and we will love and live and argue and feel despair and feel brightness, but nothing like this will come to us again; we will have done our Job, and nothing more like this will be asked of us again, please God, we do not understand the Why . . .

The children gathered in the reduced space of the weapons store, fields dimmed almost to invisibility so as not to obscure the ranked Wendys and Lost Boys. It came time for Martin to speak; awkward, expected pep talk before the cosmically deadly game.

His throat seized and for a moment he could say nothing, just stare at his people with throat and jaw working. *Do it.* He cleared his throat painfully, swallowed, and said, voice cracking, "You are the finest people I've ever known. You are all volunteers, and my friends. We've been friends and lovers for over five years now, and we've always known that what we are about to do—that's the reason why . . . we're here. We are the best there is, and the moms know that."

He turned to the War Mother. There had been no rehearsal, no previous discussion between them of what this ceremony should be like, and Martin thought, *Damn you to hell if you don't commit yourself now and say something.*

The War Mother did not fail him. "You are indeed the best," it said. "You have been trained and given tremendous responsibilities, and you have done exceptionally well. There is not a race of beings among all those who made and enact the Law who would not have their sympathies with you now."

They have sympathies? They feel as we do?

"The Ship of the Law is pleased to be associated with you, to work with you," the War Mother said. "You are no longer children. Today you are partners in the Law."

"Good," Ariel said.

"We've voted and judged and now we must act," Martin said. He raised his fist, acutely conscious of the symbolic nature of this act, and its disturbing connotations, and most of him filled with passion and energy as the fist rose higher, until his arm pointed straight above his head. "For Earth," he said. "And for us, and all our memories, and our future lives."

His eyes were moist, warm. Theresa did not weep; William did, and through the crowd of children, others as well, including Ariel, whose eyes met Martin's briefly. She wiped her tears with her sleeve, stiff gesture and anguished face seeming to say: *God damn it, I'm human, too, you bastard.*

The children not assigned to weapons backed out of the chamber. Martin was the last to go, after the War Mother, and his eyes lingered on Theresa's for three long seconds, as if they could live their lives in that moment. They looked away from each other simultaneously. The hatch closed. In the projections of their wands, they saw the pilots enter the bombships.

They saw the ship's outer hatches open. Glowing fields pushed the bombships outside *Tortoise*.

The children quickly climbed to the first hemisphere and the cafeteria. Martin, for once unable emotionally to fulfill his duty, left them in the cafeteria and went to the nose. Hakim was there, and Jennifer, but none of the rest of the search team; they were all congregated in the cafeteria, watching the craft outside *Tortoise*.

Hakim smiled weakly at Martin. Jennifer floated curled behind the star sphere, now showing the bombships trailing *Tortoise* by a few hundred meters.

"They are all gathered in the cafeteria?" Hakim asked, perhaps more pointedly than he had intended.

Martin nodded. "I can't be there," he said softly. "I feel like shit right now. I can't be in a crowd."

Hakim put his hand on Martin's shoulder. Jennifer uncurled and recurled near the transparent nose. The nose was turned away from Nebuchadnezzar.

"Are they going to make it?" Martin asked.

Jennifer shrugged. "I'm not psychic."

"They will make it," Hakim said with calm confidence.

"Are *you* psychic?" Jennifer asked with a kind of innocence, as if he very well might be.

"No," Hakim said.

Jennifer frowned and concentrated on the star sphere. "Maybe Rosa would know," she said.

Martin made himself as comfortable as possible in the nose, unfolding a net and hooking it to the wall, then wrapping himself in the net. Andrew Jaguar poked his head through the hatchway, saw Martin, and said, "We're waiting."

"I'll stay here," Martin said.

"I mean, we're waiting for orders."

"There aren't any for the next hour," Martin said. "We drift in close, the *Tortoise* is on automatic. The bombships do their job and we gather them and we retreat and watch. You know that."

"We know that," Andrew said, "but we're still waiting. We need everybody together, Martin. Everybody."

Jennifer sniffed. Martin closed his eyes and with a tremendous effort, wanting nothing more than solitude or at most the company of a select few, released himself from the net.

Nothing was appropriate or inappropriate; nothing was condemned. In the cafeteria, four couples made love with theatrical noisiness. Martin skirted them and drifted toward the place the crew of Tortoise had made for him near the cafeteria star sphere. Most eyes were on him, and his weariness and frustration gave way to the numbness of a lamb under the knife. Sacrificing the needs of the self to the needs of the group down to even the smallest impulse to privacy.

The Why. This is the Why.

Hakim and Jennifer followed. Harpal Timechaser sat next to him by the sphere, the only other ex-Pan aboard *Tortoise* now that Stephanie led the bombships.

Tortoise sharpened all its passive sensors. The star sphere divided to show the bombships, the planetary surface, the heavens beyond, then concentrated on the bombships.

"Still no defenses," Hakim marveled, head shaking.

"Maybe they're cowards," Jennifer said.

Martin looked around the room, suddenly disliking his companions intensely. He shuddered the feeling away and settled into a restless neutrality of emotions, waiting.

The War Mother floated near a wall, still as a monument. *After all this is over, can we take a mom with us and set it up in the middle of our town, on the new world, on a pedestal?*

The view changed. They saw the bombships up close, all six of them, one by one. Martin recognized Theresa's ship. He fought to keep the neutrality, but his chest seemed stuffed with straw and his palms were damp. *No defenses.*

"This is *cruel*," said Andrew Jaguar. "We have to *do* something!"

Martin said nothing. There was nothing for them to do; best to keep them all in one place, all vigilant, all aware of what was happening.

The bombships had descended to within four thousand kilometers of Nebuchadnezzar's surface. Still, the planet had not changed its aspect; dusty brown with gray patches and green mineral stripes and black spots of reservoirs. Atmosphere clear and calm.

"Hakim," Martin said softly, "report on seismic disturbances."

"Nothing new. Same low-level rhythms," Hakim said.

"Project it for us."

The traces of crustal and mantle activity moved in graphic display beside the star sphere.

"Can you turn it into sound for us?" Martin asked.

"I will have to increase its frequency, repeat it like an echo."

"Fine," Martin said.

So treated, the deep susurration of Nebuchadnezzar became very like a heartbeat, booming and ticking, the repetition false but still informative, ears providing a more natural interpretation of this information than eyes. Martin quickly picked up the actual rhythms of sound as the series of beats rose at once to a higher frequency, dropped back, rose, dropped.

"Small ship between Nebuchadnezzar and Ramses is firing thrusters," Jennifer reported. With a scowl of concern, Hakim projected the picture, checked the images and interpretation, nodded, glanced at Martin, eyebrow raised.

A very small reaction.

"Pod release in ten minutes," Harpal said, stating what they all knew, tracking the numbers on their wands.

The room fell quiet. Three of the four couples stopped making love. The fourth became subdued, though still active.

Martin felt sick.

Nebuchadnezzar's heartbeat changed. Hakim cycled the signal through several enhancements and interpretations, meaning little to most of the crew, and said, "Subsurface activity seems to have decreased."

"Decreased?" Martin asked.

Seen in the star sphere, Nebuchadnezzar's atmosphere shimmered. Something sang through the *Tortoise*'s hull, between a bell tone and the screech of a fingernail on slate.

Martin's entire body tensed and he rubbed his eyes with one hand. Nobody moved. The War Mother did not move. Seconds passed.

"Jesus Christ," Harpal Timechaser murmured.

"Quiet," Martin said.

The fourth couple had separated and put on overalls. It would not be decorous to die naked and in the clinch.

Long minutes passed. Two minutes to releasing the pods and scattering the mines.

The atmosphere rippled again. The simulated beat changed abruptly to a chirp-thud and another bell-screech hurt their ears.

"The planet's crust has risen and fallen a few centimeters," Hakim reported.

"The entire crust?" Andrew Jaguar asked, incredulous.

"All that we can see," Hakim said. "I presume the entire—"

The surface of the planet seemed to shatter, hot white lines racing from the poles to meet at the equator, marking off jagged polygons, then dying into racing small reddish lines, fading again to normal brown.

Hakim's face blanched. "I don't know what that was . . . The mines are released."

"All eleven of the ships in the outer solar system have turned on thrusters," Jennifer said.

Martin surveyed the room, working to steady his breathing. "Something's up," he said.

The star sphere followed the progress of a pod of mines from a bombship. The pod dropped, exploded in a puff, and thousands of mines spread out in a shimmer, disappearing rapidly. Thirty seconds later, massive blossoms of light spread across the atmosphere. Spinning fireballs cascaded like fireworks, dazzling the eye, too many to count.

That was not supposed to happen.

Some of the bombships seemed to ignite with burning halos.

"Strong traces of anti em reactions," Hakim said. "Extreme gamma ray production, split nuclei forming alpha particles and larger ions. Cherenkov in the atmosphere . . . I think perhaps the entire planet is made of anti em . . ."

"No," said the War Mother. All faces turned to the painted robot. "The sensors do not support this interpretation."

"Still, there are anti em reactions," Hakim said, voice trembling. "The mines have detonated prematurely . . ."

"Have any mines reached the surface?"

"None," Hakim said.

"Are the bombships pulling away?"

The star sphere showed that the ships were indeed pulling away, four of them surrounded by glowing halos. The halos faded as they gained altitude.

"Four of our craft show strong anti em traces," Hakim said.

"That doesn't make sense," Martin said. "Is there a layer of anti em in the atmosphere . . . ?"

"Not possible," Hakim said, looking to the War Mother for support. The War Mother agreed.

Tortoise had passed beyond Nebuchadnezzar and was now dipping below the ecliptic. The bombships, one by one, had dropped their loads. Three of the ships, upon spreading their mines filled with makers and doers, had produced merely the flowering of immense atmospheric explosions across thousands of kilometers, leaving turbulent scars on the planet's surface.

The fresh scars made very little difference.

The planet looks like one huge scar, smoothed over by time.

"It's been attacked before, hasn't it?" Harpal Timechaser asked.

Martin shook his head. "I don't know."

"That's it. We drilled on that. Nebuchadnezzar has been attacked before. It's always survived."

But three of the ships' weapons had found their marks and dropped to the surface, leaving no flowers of radiation behind; falling and entering, unseen from this distance but tracked by the bombships responsible. These ships rose from their close approach, clearly visible to anyone watching on the planet, to *Tortoise*, but minus halos of light.

The bombships began their acceleration to be picked up by *Tortoise*. Nothing followed them; nothing attacked. The defense craft around *Tortoise* stayed in formation, unchallenged.

"How long until we pick up the bombships?" Martin asked.

"Twenty minutes," Hakim said. "They have to accelerate and decelerate on combat schedule—they will be almost out of fuel. We could be more leisurely about it, perhaps." But he didn't sound convinced. Unexplained things had happened; not all the mines had made it to Nebuchadnezzar's surface.

Martin bit his fingernail.

"We've gotten ourselves into something," he said softly.

"What?" Hakim asked.

They waited, the crew in the cafeteria silent, or whispering softly. Harpal approached the star sphere, examining the planet closely. "We've failed, haven't we? The seeds from the outer cloud will have to do the Job now."

"That will take years," Martin said. He turned to the War Mother. "We can't get volatiles from Nebuchadnezzar. We'll have to move on to Ramses and try again. Do you know what happened?"

"There is deception here," the War Mother said.

"No shit," Harpal said.

"Bombships are returning. Something's wrong," Hakim said.

In the sphere, Martin could see them outlined by tiny sparkles of white light.

"What's the discharge?" Martin asked the War Mother.

"Not known," the War Mother said. "The effect produces intense gamma rays, much like anti-matter reactions."

"Do we keep the bombships out?" Hakim asked.

Martin masked his face with intense concentration, eyebrows knit, lips tightened and pushed out, breath harsh in his nostrils. "That doesn't make sense," he said.

The six bombships drew closer to *Tortoise*, came into position for pickup, signaling their status on noach. All were intact, all weapons dispersed. The first ship in line-up for retrieval was William and Fred Falcon's.

William's voice came over the noach. "Mines discharged. I've got sparkles all around me. I think I picked something up in the upper atmosphere. Why would my mines discharge? *Tortoise*?"

Martin asked, "Is it possible the mines were defective?"

Hakim shook his head. "I think not."

"We've never been in combat. Could something on the planet deactivate the mines?" He turned to the War Mother.

"No conclusions are possible. Deactivation of the mines is not inconceivable, but simple deactivation would not cause an explosion. The atmosphere may contain seeker and doer systems designed to attack incoming weapons, but we have detected nothing of that nature. Shielded anti-matter dust does not seem a likely possibility."

"The weapons could be disguised, or hidden, like our own ships," Hakim suggested.

"That is possible," the War Mother said.

"Then they *do* have defenses," Harpal said. "Maybe the defenses are trying to break through to the bombships—maybe they're carrying some back with them."

"Are they carrying anything?" Martin asked.

Hakim examined the bombships again. "There is no atmospheric residue around them. We are trailing a residue ourselves—a very faint cloud of discharged ions and molecules . . . That is all I detect. I do not know what the sparkles are. The craft look clean otherwise."

Martin gritted his teeth, relaxed his face, opened and closed his eyes slowly, found his chest bound with tense muscle, relaxed the muscle and exhaled.

"Bring them in, one at a time," he said. "Fred and William first. Keep them isolated in a one way field—nothing gets out."

"Martin, I don't feel very good," Fred said over the noach. "My skin's changing color, or my vision is going bad. William's sick, too."

Something was very wrong. *Don't let them in.*

Hakim and Jennifer floated nearby. "Bring Fred and William in," he instructed the War Mother. "Isolated, like I said."

The bombships took formation behind the *Tortoise*'s aft homeball, awaiting instructions. Fred and William's craft was first in line.

Hakim inquired on the other bombships: "Theresa, Stephanie, any reactions? Problems?"

Their ships also sparkled as if surrounded by fireworks. The other four did not sparkle. Martin thought: *The mines from these ships did not explode in the atmosphere.*

Stephanie Wing Feather responded: "I feel a little ill. We might have been swept by radiation. The fields should have kept it out, but there was such a burst from our mines . . ."

"Theresa?"

"I'm okay. I'm a little dizzy but I'm not sick."

The first bombship entered the hatch. The arresting boom, glowing with a bubble isolation field, reached out to attach to the craft.

Hakim switched the star sphere to a view of the weapons store. Martin's eyes narrowed.

The War Mother said: "There is danger of—"

Time ran out.

The arresting boom touched William's bombship. The star sphere filled with light and winked out, leaving dark dazzles swimming in their eyes. Hakim cursed loudly in Arabic.

A violent shudder slammed the crew against the walls. Fields rose instantly between them, suspending them from further harm, but already there were screams of pain and smears of blood.

Anti em, Martin's inner voice said, too late. *The bombships and mines were changed into anti-matter.*

The star sphere flickered back for a fraction of a second, showing a lump of twisted, torch-bright wreckage careening through the weapons store, setting off violent blasts and shrapnel wherever it touched. The bombship disintegrated into hissing, sizzling shards; ambiplasma filled the weapons store, and again the sphere disappeared.

Martin's wand sang with warnings and messages, too many to be projected at once. *The ship will do something without consulting us.*

"Weapons store and the whole hemisphere is going," Theresa said from outside. "What happened?"

The other bombships contributed to the chatter.

Stephanie Wing Feather was the last to be heard: "*Tortoise*, the aft hemisphere is cracking—"

Tortoise spun violently like a whirled dumb-bell, accelerating out of control. Messages from the bombships ceased.

The noise that sang through *Tortoise* now was more than he could bear. Screaming, Martin shut his eyes and waited for death.

The protective fields around them abruptly vanished and they were shoved into an agonized mass in one corner of the cafeteria, arms and knees and heads and torsos interlocking with the force as if manipulated by a giant puzzlemaker. Bones cracked and blood misted.

The fields came on again, but jammed the crew against one another, unable to pick them apart and suspend them separately. All was failing; control was gone, they could see nothing and feel nothing but their crush and pain.

The ship twisted like a snake. Martin opened his eyes and tried to move but could not. He lay meshed with Andrew Jaguar, Hakim pressed behind him. Martin's face threw globules of blood against a bulkhead in the flashing twilight. Barely three or four seconds had passed; he still clutched his wand, and Hakim's fist and wand ground into his calf. He could not move or think.

All had returned to the animal, to protoplasm.

Fear and the smell of blood and pressure like an enormous hand grinding them into the cafeteria wall

I'm sorry
Theresa
William
Relief. Blessed nothing.

I suppose it picked us apart and put us here, was his first thought on awakening and finding himself surrounded by a green net and a gently throbbing field. Suspended in the field, all his body a huge bruise, medical doers like tiny golden worms criss-crossing, touching his bruised flesh, nothing touching him but the golden worms, mouth dry but not parched, top of head burning.

They all hung in darkness. A cool breeze pricked the hairs on his head and chest. For a moment Martin thought of being dead, corpses laid out for ejection into space. But all the green fields pulsed gently and doers wove around them all. He could not see to identify the faces and he could not count all the bodies so suspended.

William is dead. And Fred Falcon.

There were others awake now, making sounds not like moans, more like sighs and whimpers. All too weak to talk.

A mom floated beside Martin. He did not know whether it actually appeared out of nothing, or whether his attention had flagged; consciousness was a sometime thing under the ministration of the golden worms.

"How long since we were hurt?" he asked.

"Two tendays," the mom said. He noticed a remnant of black and white paint on the front; this was still the War Mother.

"Where are we?"

"We have moved to a wide orbit around Nebuchadnezzar. There has been no further attempt to damage the ship."

"Why not? They could kill us."

"I do not know," the War Mother answered.

"How many of us died?"

"No one who remained aboard *Tortoise* has died, but all are injured. Half of *Tortoise* was destroyed. William Arrow Feather and Fred Falcon died first. Yueh Yellow River's craft disintegrated."

"They were turned into anti em, weren't they?"

"Yes."

"Anti-matter doesn't behave exactly like matter . . . Their chemistry was going wrong, wasn't it? I should have known that. I should have seen the clues, the sparkles . . . Our outgassing and fuel remnants reacting with the bombship. I should have *seen* it."

"I also did not draw the right conclusions until it was too late. You are not to blame," the War Mother said.

"There were four. The other two . . . What happened to Stephanie and Theresa? Can you convert them back to matter?"

"We cannot," the War Mother said. "*Tortoise* collided with one of the unconverted craft during the explosion. Nguyen Mountain Lily and Ginny Chocolate died. Stephanie and Theresa survived. Hu East Wind, Michael Vineyard, Leo Parsifal, and Nancy Flying Crow are back aboard and safe.

"Stephanie was killed later by my unsuccessful attempt to convert her craft back to matter. We do not have the technique or the understanding of how the conversion was accomplished—"

Martin turned his head away from the War Mother, knowing now that Theresa was dead, too.

"Stephanie Wing Feather's craft was only partially converted, or converted unevenly. It exploded, causing yet more damage to *Tortoise*."

"Then you tried again with Theresa."

"No. Theresa is still in her craft."

Martin jerked his head around. "She's alive?"

"She is still alive."

Martin's weak grip on consciousness wavered and the War Mother seemed to shimmer before him. He pushed the dark pressures away and said, "Let me speak to her."

The War Mother raised his wand to his hand with a slender

green ladder field. The wand projected an image of Theresa's bombship into his eyes. The skin of her bombship still sparkled, but sharp pulses of light occurred much less often. The craft drifted a hundred kilometers from *Tortoise*.

Martin saw Theresa's face, wrapped in the folds of her couch, ladder fields glowing fitfully around her.

Martin spoke her name. She fumbled to complete the noach connection.

"You're awake," she said listlessly. Her face had yellowed, her hands ulcerated; her anti-matter chemistry, tuned to a slightly different physics, did not match her biological makeup. She was very ill. "I can't see you too well," Theresa said. "Were you badly hurt?"

"I think I'm healing. So are the others." His voice wobbled with emotion and he swallowed to control it. "I screwed up, Theresa."

"You couldn't have known."

"The ship's badly hurt, I think."

"The War Mother tells me about half of it is left," Theresa said. A picture of *Tortoise* from her perspective grew above Theresa's image; one hemisphere, a blunt-ended, debris-scarred pylon, drives gone. "Some amazing things," Theresa said. "The moms actually used the explosion—William and Fred— to propel the ship away from Nebuchadnezzar. The ship turned into it, used it. I followed . . . we all followed."

"How . . . How are you feeling?" Martin asked.

"I've been in this can for two tendays. It wouldn't be so bad, but I can't eat. I'm pretty weak. I've been waiting—"

"I'll ask the War Mother. We'll try everything."

Theresa shook her head. "They got us good. They know things the Benefactors don't."

Or aren't willing to teach us, Martin thought, but that didn't make sense; the War Mother could have converted the craft while the injured crew slept and nobody would have been much the wiser. Theresa was right. *We've been aced.*

Martin looked at the War Mother. "You tried, and it didn't work?"

"Stephanie Wing Feather agreed to an experiment. She is dead. We cannot turn anti-matter into matter."

"You're supposed to understand," Martin said. "How can you be ignorant about this?"

"The techniques are unknown to us."

"Jesus, I'm not asking for so much, just *learn how to do it!* She's dying!"

The War Mother said nothing. Martin wrapped his face in his hands.

"I've been waiting for you to wake up," Theresa said. "I'm glad you did before . . . I have a plan, and it's not much, but it's something. I've asked the War Mother to make a strong field and put pellets of matter into it, with me. I'm behind the field. You're protected. The explosion could be even more powerful than Stephanie's. That's what Stephanie asked for. If the experiment didn't work. It didn't. She helped push you—"

"No!" Martin shouted.

Theresa closed her eyes as if to sleep. "I've stayed this long to talk to you. Maybe it would have been easier to just do it while you were asleep. The War Mother says it would be useful."

"We'll take you with us, carry you in a field," Martin said. "We'll work on some way to convert you. Jennifer can think of something if the War Mother can't."

"I was being selfish," Theresa continued, as if she hadn't heard him. "I wanted to say some things to you, make sure you were all right. I wanted to see you again and talk with you."

"Please," Martin wailed, suddenly back in the crowded chamber aboard the Ark, watching the Earth die, and knowing even as a young boy what he was losing. He struggled but all he could do was twist in the field.

"Right now I'm good for nothing and I hurt. I thought about going back to Nebuchadnezzar, looking for a target, but the War Mother and I agreed, I'd just fizzle out and give the planet another useless scar."

"God damn it!" Martin screamed.

"Please," Theresa said, laying her head against the neck rest. "Let's just talk while there's time."

Martin felt immediate shame and sobered. "I love you," he said hoarsely. "I don't want you to go away."

"I can't come back to you, Martin, and that means I'm dead already."

He struggled against the fields again but kept his face under control. "We need to think." He stared at the War Mother, face wreathed with a child's bitter disappointment. "Nothing?"

"She is suffering and will not survive much longer," the War Mother said.

"I was selfish," Theresa said. "I'm hurting you more than if I just—"

"No, no. I'm glad you stayed." He pushed to be closer to her image. "I'm . . . I'll tell you something. I'm going to tell you about the new home." He made a supreme effort to put on a face of expectancy and joy. "It's going to be far away from here and so beautiful, Theresa. We'll make it. We're going to do the Job, and we'll go there, and I swear it will be beautiful.

"I'll wear my suit. All the Lost Boys will wear their suits. All the Wendys will wear gowns. We'll step out on the planet, and we'll marry the new home. We'll remember everybody, and they'll be with us, and we'll grow food, and make wine, and babies, and we'll . . . Oh, Jesus, it will be such a party, Theresa."

Her face relaxed. "I can see it," she said.

"You'll be there with me, honey."

"I think I will."

"We'll do it," he said. He had run out of words.

"Martin, *Tortoise* tells me it's ready. I'd like to go now. I want to help you get to the new home. Can I do it now, my love?"

Martin could not speak. He could hardly see. He pushed against the field like a fly in a web. The healing doers hummed.

"Goodbye." Theresa blew him a kiss.

Her image was replaced by a view from the rear of Tortoise. Theresa moved her bombship into position.

Martin shook his head, disbelieving.

He wanted to keep her alive as long as possible, to make up for the awkwardness and inadequacy of his last words to her. He wanted to scream but did not.

Martin closed his eyes and turned away, but he could not keep them shut; he wanted to see, to feel and *appreciate* the push, to realize for her sake as the first step into grief that Theresa was becoming something so absurd and simple as acceleration.

He whispered her name. She might have heard.

Theresa's bombship hung steady as pellets of mass approached. The stars moved behind her, peaceful and constant; Wormwood's corona flared in silence beyond a shadowed, ripped edge of *Tortoise*'s tail.

The pellets closed.

Ambiplasma bloomed brighter than Wormwood. Theresa's bombship wasped within the fields, frenzied by inequalities of blast. Light ate her. She was eaten by light clean and uncompromising, the opposite of space, of night and ending, all light, all colors.

The hull sang high and sweet like the tremolo of a flute.

Martin's scream came and he choked on it, struggling against the mercy of the healing doers.

Tortoise moved slowly between the worlds, her children ignored by Nebuchadnezzar, by Ramses, by Herod. The silence of these grim barren worlds proclaimed defeat.

Within, as the ship repaired itself, as the Wendys and Lost Boys healed, Martin thought about the Killers, the tricksters, impersonal, unseen.

As on Earth, so it was with the traps of Wormwood. Luring, testing, destroying.

He slept to the humming of the golden doers, finishing their work.

Came William this time. "You're dreaming of me, aren't you?"

"I guess so."

"I'm glad, Martin. I was pretty sure you wouldn't forget."

But he could not dream of Theresa.

Until now, Martin had wanted revenge, but he had not felt the extraordinary burn of *hatred*.

These monsters had cost him too many worlds, too many loves.

The children had been brushed away with a casual swat, crippled by an enemy who knew more tricks than their Benefactors. The survivors had been left to starve in a depleted void.

Tens of billions of kilometers away, *Hare* fell downward to the brightness.

Martin came out of his healing field to arrange things, to talk on the noach with Hans, who suppressed emotion in his voice, as Martin expressed no emotion in his. And then he led the children into a long sleep. No dreams, just coldness.

Tortoise rose from the pit of Wormwood to meet her sister. There would be no defeat, no giving up.

And no peace.

PART
TWO

TEN YEARS IN COLD, TRACKING EACH OTHER ON THE RIM OF A shallow well: *Tortoise* and *Hare*. In defeat, caution, conserving resources. Ten years would not matter in this war of centuries.

While the crew slept, the ships came together again and made a new *Dawn Treader*, half its previous length, only two home-balls connected by a short neck. Some old spaces came back, though empty of pets and personal effects.

The schoolroom and cafeteria remained. No damage showed, but the fuel reserves wrapped around the neck were much reduced.

Martin awoke a month after the rejoining, to consult with the moms. Field-wrapped in a cushion of warm air, he laddered through the cold, evacuated chambers of the Ship of the Law, approving or suggesting changes. He was not sure why he had been awakened; perhaps the moms were interested in the changed psychology of a crew facing defeat and death, and sought to study one individual's response. If so, they found Martin taciturn.

He had suffered no ill effects from the long cold sleep. He thought he much preferred sleep to years between the stars, these brief silent deaths between bright lives.

But there was a handicap to cold sleep. They would all awake with disaster fresh in their minds, their emotions raw, and immediately have to go to work. Martin was angry and frightened and twisted to such an extent he wondered if he was ill. How much psychological damage had he sustained? He could not know; there was no time for grieving and readjustment.

None of the moms carried a mark of paint. Either the marks had flaked away completely during the ten years, or the War Mother had returned to the bulk of the ship, emerging with Martin from a different kind of sleep.

Martin completed his inspection in five hours. A mom accompanied him to the chamber where the crew slept. "It is time to awaken everyone," it said. "Final deceleration will begin before they are revived. We will approach the inner worlds within two tendays."

"Good," Martin said. "Let's go."

He listened to the winds blowing through the ship as atmosphere and warmth returned. Isolated in a small room next to the sleep chamber, he felt weight return, and stood on his feet for the first time in ten years.

The others came awake in groups of five, were tested by the moms for any health problems, cleared, and gathered slowly, quietly, in the schoolroom.

The ship's floor felt cool to their bare feet.

Martin stayed away from the crew until they gathered in the schoolroom. His mind wandered; he thought of the children's pets, which would not return; *Dawn Treader* did not have reserves to spare. Martin did not know how this would affect morale; he thought they had other and larger griefs to deal with first.

He could hardly bring himself to face the crew and tell what had happened; he did not want to feel their grief as well as his own.

But duty at least remained, if no direction or feeling, and he spoke to them, to start and to finish, to do what he knew must be done.

"We're no longer children," Martin told them. The schoolroom at least had changed little, with a star sphere at the center, filled with thirty-eight men and thirty-seven women. "We've fought and lost. We may not be mature, or very smart, but we're no longer children."

The crew listened in silence.

"*I've* fought and lost," Martin said. "I missed what should have been obvious."

"The moms missed it, too," Hakim said, but Martin shook his head.

"A decade has passed. My term as Pan has long since expired. It's time to choose a new Pan. We should do that now."

Ariel sat looking at her folded hands.

"I nominate Hans," Martin said. "Hans is my choice for Pan."

Hans stood in a group of *Hare*'s crew, big arms folded, lips tightening slightly, pale skin reddening. "We usually measure time by how long we're awake," he said. "By that measure, you still have some months left."

"Hans did a fine job commanding *Hare*," Martin said, ignoring the comment. "His instincts are better than mine." He looked briefly at Hans: *Do not make me say it more clearly*. Hans looked up at the ceiling.

Alexis Baikal seconded the nomination.

"We'll take any other nominations," Martin continued.

The crew looked among each other, then Kimberly Quartz said, "I nominate Rosa Sequoia."

Rosa's broad face flushed but she said nothing. *Decline*, Martin silently suggested, swallowing back an even deeper sense of dread. *No sane person would nominate Rosa.*

"I second the nomination," Jeanette Snap Dragon said.

Martin surveyed the crew.

"I nominate Hakim Hadj," Paola Birdsong said.

That was a pretty good choice, Martin thought. Hakim looked up in surprise and said, "I decline. I have my place, and it is not as Pan."

"I renominate Martin son of Arthur Gordon," Joe Flatworm said.

"Decline," Martin said.

There were no further nominations.

"Vote through wands," Martin said. The voting was quick: sixty-seven for Hans, eight for Rosa. Martin projected the results, then laddered forward to offer his hand to Hans. Hans shook it lightly and broke the grip quickly.

"Hans is the new Pan," Martin said.

"I don't want any ceremony," Hans said. "There's work to do. I appoint Harpal Timechaser as Christopher Robin."

"Decline," Harpal said.

"The hell you will," Hans said. "We've had about enough emotional shit. Take the job or we're all damned."

Harpal gaped. Without waiting for his answer, Hans pushed through the crew to the edge of the schoolroom and the door, twisted around with feline grace, and said, "Martin's right. We're not children. We're scum. We've failed and we've lost friends. I condemn us all to hell until we kill these goddamned worlds, all of them. We're already dead; there isn't enough fuel to get out of here and go any place decent. Let's take these sons of bitches with us."

The crew began to look at each other now, shyly at first, then with a few reckless grins.

"God damn it," Paola Birdsong said, as if trying out the word for size. It was much too big a word for her, but the solemnity passed from her face, replaced by a grim, lively determination.

Rosa Sequoia floated as still as a statue, face as impenetrable as a mom's.

"Let's go see what's up," Hans said.

Hakim approached Martin as the crew echoed and laddered out of the schoolroom. "There have been changes," he said conspiratorially. "I would like you to be on the search team."

"Hans should—"

"Hans has no say, unless he wishes to disband the search team and start over. I do not think he will ask for that, Martin. I would enjoy working with you."

"Thank you," Martin said. "I accept."

Hakim smiled. "My friend," he said, touching Martin's shoulder.

There had indeed been changes. "I do not think we wasted our time," Hakim said as Hans, Harpal, and the search team gathered in the nose before the star sphere.

Nebuchadnezzar was no longer a brown world. Marked by streaks of bright red running longitudinally from pole to pole, dark lines like cracks covered the surface.

"It looks sick," Thomas Orchard said.

"It *is* sick," Martin said in wonder. "Some of our makers and doers got through."

Hans regarded the star sphere image with chin in hand, frowning. "I thought everything we sent down turned to anti em and blew up."

"Three pods got through," Martin said. "We assumed they were destroyed some other way, but apparently they weren't."

Hans said nothing for a few seconds.

Hakim glanced at Martin almost shyly, as if preferring still to think of him as Pan. "Perhaps not all is lost," Hakim said.

"Bullshit. We're dead," Hans said. "But we may not die in vain."

"Perhaps that is what I mean," Hakim said.

"All right," Hans said. "How long would it take for seeds to come down from the outer haloes?"

"Nine or ten years," Martin said. Harpal concurred.

"The planet's still there. Either they haven't come in yet, or they were deactivated. Can we signal them?"

"They should pick up the noach," Harpal said. "If they haven't been destroyed."

"Let's do it," Hans said. Hakim made the arrangements on his wand. The results were almost instantaneous; a signal sent out, a signal returned from a seed carrier to the ship's noach receivers. The carrier reported that eleven seeds had been delivered to Nebuchadnezzar's interior, sufficient to cook the planet's entire surface to a depth of fifty kilometers. Detonation of the seeds was imminent. Seeds would be delivered to Ramses within two tendays.

"I'll be damned," Hans said. "We've come to just in time for a *show*."

The search team and Martin moved closer to the star sphere.

"Let's send out remotes and take a closer look," Hans said. "We're how far?"

"Four hundred million kilometers from Ramses. Two hundred and fifty million from Nebuchadnezzar. Nebuchadnezzar must be a very sick planet," Hakim said. "We were more successful than we ever hoped."

"I trust in nothing," Hans said. "Martin didn't make any obvious big mistakes, and we still got whipped badly. I have to be that much better." He smiled almost shyly at Martin, suggesting that they might share some secret joke, and his smile actually took a weight from Martin's shoulders; he was not anathema, at least not to Hans. "If the planet's sick, and if our doers have jammed its defenses, we don't have to worry—but we haven't dropped doers on Ramses, and anything could happen there when the seeds arrive to be inserted. Am I right?"

Harpal and Martin nodded. Hakim was busy releasing remotes to increase their baseline. "What about those orbiting dark masses?"

"They have not changed," Hakim said, interrupting himself. "The same orbits, the same masses, the same sizes, judging by occultations."

"And the small craft?"

"We are actually not far from one such," Hakim said. "They are still in orbit. They have returned to status quo."

"I'd like to see the close one," Hans said.

"I have records from the past few tendays, recorded by the ship," Hakim said. "I will play them back." The star sphere sectioned and they watched a small bright point grow in size in compressed time to a long, blunt cylinder, gray in color, featureless, barely ten meters long. "It is coasting," Hakim said. "Quiet, no drives."

"Can we take it out?" Hans asked.

Hakim looked to Harpal and Martin.

"I suppose," Harpal said dubiously. "Why waste the effort?"

"I want to try," Hans said dryly. "I guess I give the order, am I right?" He lifted his wand. "We're how close to this little slicker?"

"Two million kilometers."

"I want two rifles to waste a little fuel, see if we can destroy it. That'll wake the sons of bitches up if they're still sleeping, or if they're just logy from dealing with our doers. If they don't react, we know something . . ."

"What?" Martin asked.

"That these orbiting ships aren't important, or . . ." Hans shrugged. "That the planets are sitting ducks."

"Or something else," Harpal said.

"Keep it up," Hans said, not unkindly. "Keep badgering me. What else?"

He's getting into this much more quickly than I did. Good, Martin thought.

"Or they've got another trap set."

"That's what I think. But . . . I'm about to make the same mistake Martin did. I'm going to spring their trap and see what they can do to us. We survived the first one. Maybe we can survive the second. And if not, well . . ." He rubbed his palms together, as if scrubbing away dirt. "Our grief is shorter, hm?"

Martin shivered. Here was something he had never felt as Pan: fatalism. Hakim sensed it too, and looked away, swallowing. It was a reaction the others might embrace; a Wagnerian dedication to duty, a mighty blow against the enemy, valiant but useless, ending in death.

"Too strong, huh?" Hans asked, as if Martin had said something. "All right. I'll tone it down, but I still want two rifles out there. Kill it." He looked to Harpal. "Go to it, CR."

Harpal left the nose. Hans concentrated on the cylinder for a moment, frowning. "I can't imagine what purpose they serve, except . . . Hakim, could they work as mass detectors? Very sensitive to orbital changes caused by anything large entering the system?"

Hakim considered this. "I cannot say for sure, but I think there would be better ways to do that . . ."

"You could ask Jennifer," Martin suggested.

"She gives me the shivers," Hans said briskly. "But you're right. What other purpose? They accelerated hours before our assault . . . Psychological weapons. I can't buy that. These things don't give a damn about our psychology. They just want us dead."

"I have an idea," Thomas Orchard said. The other members of the search team had been keeping a low profile, taking Hans' measure now that he was Pan.

"Give it to me," Hans said.

"I think they're remote signaling stations. Something goes wrong in the trap, they survive a little while longer . . . They don't attract much attention because they are small, because they seem to have primitive drives."

"And . . ." Hans said, tapping his little finger again, "they accelerate just before an attack to be ready to zip out of here, if everything goes to hell . . ." He smiled and ran his hand through his stiff blond hair. "God damn. I like that. It makes sense."

"But we can't be sure," Thomas said, proud to have Hans' approval.

Born leader, Martin thought with a twinge.

"We can be sure of nothing in this miserable place," Hans said. "I say we try to take one out, and if they're vulnerable, we'll take them all out. Meanwhile, one planet down . . . maybe. I'll be interested to see how Ramses responds." He lifted his fist and grimaced. "Slick 'em all!"

Away from the nose, going with Harpal to choose two rifle pilots for the job, Martin broke into a sweat. He lingered a few meters behind Harpal and wiped his face on his sleeve.

Ten years. Theresa and William had been dead ten years—and the others. Yet he had seen Theresa just a few days ago. She was fresh in his mind, her words were fresh.

A private and selfish bitterness came over him. He stood on the edge of a mental gulf filled with emptiness. He closed his eyes and actually saw this gulf, melodramatic imagery nonetheless real and painful. Guilt at this private bitterness could not drive it away. Others grieved; why should his grief be any the worse?

Martin told himself to catch up with Harpal, now almost one third of the neck ahead. His body refused to move.

"What are you doing?"

He turned and saw Ariel. The despair on his face must have been obvious. She backed away as if he were contagious. "What's wrong?"

Martin shook his head.

"Tired?" she asked tentatively.

"I don't know. Bleak."

"Be glad you're not Pan," she said, not forgiving but not accusing.

"Hans will do a good job," Martin said automatically.

"Something's wrong," Ariel pursued. "What is it?"

"Nothing for you to worry about."

"You're having a reaction, aren't you?" she said. "You were strong and stalwart, and now you're paying for it."

He grimaced. "You were always so full of bullshit," he said before he could think to keep quiet.

"That's me, bullshit babe," Ariel said softly. "At least I don't get trussed up like a lamb for my own slaughter."

"I'm okay," he said.

"Where are you going?"

"With Harpal. To pick rifle pilots."

"Then let's go," Ariel said. "We have to keep moving."

She treated his pain as something trivial. His hatred for her burned like fire. But he followed her along the neck to the aft homeball, still bleak, but at least moving, doing.

Paola Birdsong and Liam Oryx volunteered to take the rifles out. Their journey would last a day, as planned by Hans and Harpal.

Hans and Ariel accompanied the chosen pilots to the new weapons store. There were only thirty craft in the smaller space, all newly made after the destruction of William's bombship. The designs were familiar, however. Martin and Ariel watched the two volunteers enter the slender craft, checked out their systems through the wands, stood behind ladder fields as the ships pushed through the hatch on pylons.

The rifles began their journey of hundreds of thousands of kilometers.

"I feel guilty about keeping my room temperature above freezing now," Ariel said. "We have so little fuel. I hope this is really worthwhile."

Martin shrugged and left the weapons store for the school-room.

"Where are you going?" Ariel asked. He told her. "Can I come with you?"

Martin was surprised into a long, even a rude, silence. "You can go wherever you want," he said. "We're gathering to see if anything happens to Nebuchadnezzar."

"You need company. I don't want to see you bleak again."

He closed one eye, squinted at her, and again, without thinking, said what was on his mind: "I can't figure you. You were such a bitch when I was Pan. Now it's sweetness and light. Are you crazier than I am?"

She backed away, stung, then said, "Probably. What's it matter now?"

To that, he had no answer.

The crew gathered around the star sphere in the schoolroom, all but Hakim and Luis Estevez Saguaro, who stayed in the nose to keep working. "What we learned in training makes us think this planet's really sick with our doers," Thomas Orchard explained, pointing out large brown and red patches on Nebuchadnezzar. "Whatever turned our people into anti em may have been failing to start with—it didn't stop some pods from dropping doers. And it didn't convert all our ships. Now we think the machinery, the defenses, are completely gone."

"How long until it blows up?" David Aurora asked.

"It won't blow up," Harpal said. "It's just set to cook."

"That's what I mean," David said, smirking. Martin watched the crew closely, uneasy, still bleak despite Ariel's company.

"Any minute now," Thomas said.

"Then we got a win," David continued, raising his fist in a victory salute.

"Fat lot of good it does us," Ariel said. "Two more planets to go, and so little fuel we can't escape."

"It's something," Harpal said.

"I don't think it's much," Erin Eire said at the rear. Martin had not even seen her since the awakening, not closely enough to pull her apart from the crowd. "I think we all know this place isn't the real target."

"What makes you think that?" Thomas asked.

A mom entered the schoolroom. The crew fell silent as it floated to the center, but when it said and did nothing more, they resumed.

"Wormwood's a tar baby," Erin said. "We got stuck. We might blow off the tar baby's arm or leg. But it will still be sticky enough to get those who come after."

"A seed carrier signals by noach that demolition is beginning," the mom announced. The crew cheered, but not as lustily as they might have. "We will see the results visually within ten minutes."

Thomas shifted from the planet view and caught the rifles on their way to the nearest orbiting cylinder. His wand sang and a message appeared for his eyes only. "That's Hakim," he said. "Things are happening again . . ."

Martin followed Thomas to the nose. Hans floated with arms wrapped around legs, watching the search team put together their information.

Hakim played the wands and the data banks like musical instruments.

"Get Jennifer Hyacinth up here," Hans said. Thomas called Jennifer to the nose.

Martin quickly read the information projected by Hakim's wand. The five inner orbiting masses had diffused into elongated clouds.

Harpal had closed his eyes. The air smelled of tension. Hans seemed a still point in the swirl of motion around the star sphere. He faced the projected information with unmoving eyes, not really seeing it. Martin knew what Hans was up to: he was trying to put together a clear picture through the clutter and uncertainty.

Jennifer Hyacinth arrived in the nose a few minutes later. She squeezed in beside Hans to be in the best position to see the information.

"The masses are the next part of the trap," she said, frowning.

"Good girl," Hans said. "We're in close, the planet is going, so we're obviously dangerous and they don't want us to escape. They don't know how much fuel we have left, or what we're capable of . . ."

"We've done better than previous contenders," Martin said.

"Maybe," Hans said. "Harpal, what—"

"The dark masses could be loose-packed neutronium bombs," Jennifer said. "The measurements are about right."

"Good Christ," Harpal said. "That many bombs could wipe out every planet in the system five, ten times over. If we could gather them—"

"They're falling into Wormwood," Hakim said.

Fresh diagrams floating in the air showed the rearrangements of the inner masses, their drift toward the star, estimates of time of entry into the heliosphere. "They're being pushed in," Jennifer said. "I think—"

"Wormwood's going to go," Hans said. "Jennifer, work up

some momerath on what that will mean for us. Martin, coordinate with the moms. Tell the rifles to come back in, fast."

"Wormwood's particle wind is partially channeled to the poles," Jennifer said. "There must be powerful fields controlling its interior. When it blows, if those fields are still in place—and I don't think they could just be switched off—it won't expand as a sphere . . ."

Martin pulled back and spoke through his wand to the moms.

Hakim pulled up a picture of Nebuchadnezzar's surface glowing from the internal plasma of their seeds, but that seemed inconsequential now; the second part of the trap was indeed about to close.

The *Dawn Treader* orbited less than two hundred million kilometers from Wormwood. If the star went supernova, a tremendous burst of neutrinos would blow away the star's outer layers.

Neutrinos in normal quantities were less substantial than any ghost, capable of traveling through light year thicknesses of lead unimpeded. But if they were present in such huge numbers, their interactions with matter—with the *Dawn Treader* and everything else in Wormwood's vicinity—would become deadly.

Martin had no idea what so many neutrinos would do to their chemistry, but the sheer force of the neutrino blast could tear them to pieces.

Jennifer seemed lost in an ecstasy of calculation.

A mom appeared in the nose. "If this information is correct," it said, "there is both danger, and extraordinary opportunity."

Jennifer's face lit up. "There could be channeling of the blast in different areas," she said. "Neutrinos will pour out in all directions, but most of the star's mass may push through the poles, making two jets, like a quasar." She linked her hands and used two thumbs up and down to show the flow.

"I concur," the mom said.

Hans looked between Jennifer and the mom, biting his lower lip, and slowly uncurled, stretching his arms. "What do we do?"

"We use all available fuel for rapid acceleration into a new orbit to pass over the star's south pole," the mom said.

Jennifer laughed as if this were the funniest thing in the world. Tears came to her eyes. "Right, right!" she said.

"We can protect the ship's contents against most of the effects of a neutrino storm," the mom continued. "We will use neutrino pressure to propel us out of this system."

"We'll be like a seed in the wind," Jennifer said. "If we hold together, we'll be blown out into deep space."

"The post-explosion environment will be rich with volatiles from Wormwood," the mom continued. "We will gather volatiles even as we are propelled outward."

"They want to destroy us, but they may save us!" Jennifer said.

"Then why are they doing this?" Harpal asked. "Why give us this gift?"

"Very likely, they *will* destroy us," the mom said. "But the opportunity exists, if we are skillful, and very quick. Alert the crew to field confinement and super acceleration. We will begin in a few minutes."

Martin watched the star sphere. Haze covered Nebuchadnezzar's surface now, shot through with flashes of intense white light. The neutronium and anti-neutronium seeds deep within heated the body's surface to plasma; there would not be sufficient energy released to place any of the planet's material in orbit about itself, as had happened with Earth; indeed, Nebuchadnezzar would keep its spherical shape. But for the next few million years, the planet's surface would consist of cooling magma.

Martin could not exult at this small victory. Assistance in a suicide was no triumph; self-immolation designed to trap arsonists was comically absurd. But to have the fire offer them a chance at life, a chance to move on and finish the Job . . .

He began to laugh. Jennifer joined him. Harpal grimaced and left the nose to coordinate the crew. Hans stared at them as if they were crazy, then shook his head vigorously, and whooped.

Theresa would have appreciated this, Martin thought. *William would have simply loved it*.

They recovered their craft and prepared for the storm.

Wormwood's death-throes took seven hours. The star's magnetic field—restructured to push the solar wind up through the poles—whipped about like hair blown in the wind, clearly visible as the surface layers boiled and churned and cast up dancing streamers. The star began to resemble a fiery turnip with leafy top and frantic roots.

Within, billions of neutronium weapons ate through the star's dense inner layers and ended their unseen, unknown orbits, mated positive to negative, anti em to matter. The ambiplasma generated by these deadly copulations marched steadily outward.

The moms timed everything.

Hans ordered the crew into the schoolroom and fell silent, sitting beside the star sphere, watching with half-lidded eyes as things beyond his command and control—beyond his comprehension—began to happen.

Martin sat nearby, his body frightened but his mind too lost in sorrow to care what would happen next. He watched Rosa Sequoia, who squatted in an awkward lotus in one corner, rocking gently, eyes closed. He envied her personal treasure of spiritual solace, her ability to be lost in an inner reality that did not match the external. What had she found, that Martin would never find?

The images in the star sphere conveyed only an abstract meaning. What were the energies of a dying star if not incomprehensible? A human life—all their lives—could be snuffed with a paltry fraction of the energy about to be released.

They had climbed to the top of an enormous wave, years before, and now the wave crashed down, and any slight bubble in that foaming maelstrom would be sufficient to snuff their candles utterly and completely, forever darkness, no amens.

The peculiarity of Martin's state of mind was that he did not so much think these things as *feel* them, joined to his body's fear like an anatomical footnote.

Fear made its own opiate. Emotions cannot ride forever at high intensity; within an hour, terror declined to numbness, with clear and selfless perception. Certainty of death was replaced by light curiosity, an intensity of unattached thought impossible only a few minutes before.

Scattered parts of his overwhelmed self made ironic commentary: *This is the dark night of the soul Not hardly, this is just panic carried to its extreme Look at them they do not experience this the way you do They must They must*

Visceral moans filled the schoolroom as they felt the fields lock down. Martin's body tingled and all internal motions slowed.

Waves of darkness passed as the fields subdued their eyes, all their physical senses.

Yet something remained. What could possibly be left to him? Undefined memory, perhaps an illusion; who could say where that memory began? During their sequestering, or after, as a balancing of his brain's chemical bookkeeping . . .

What he later remembered was a fairy tale thread of personal continuity, all thought reduced to parable, and an extraphysical awareness of the star in its last stages. That such memory and perception were not possible did not make it less compelling.

Wormwood

blossomed like a daffodil

with twin streamers of intense blond hair

and a sigh of neutrinos, phantom particles now in such numbers they blew millions of times stronger than hurricane winds

above the tingling in his body, the battle of the neutrinos to change his chemistry, pushing denser than matter through the ship; a subtle whisper of persuasion, like a crowd of autistic children never heard, never seen, suddenly screaming in his ear at once, the silent ones of space and time gaining a voice in their liberation, that voice changing from a whisper to a propulsive scream

the remade *Dawn Treader* having reached a point above the southern pole of the star allowed itself to be pushed, very slowly at first, its own fuel depleted, on the rush of neutrinos, its crew held in place against the persuasion of those winds, against the subnuclear argument for deadly change, accepting only the force and not the persuasion

The fox speaks with the hurricane and says, "I need to travel far and fast. Can you take me?" The hurricane regards the puny fox with its huge, calm eye and asks, "What can you do for me?" "Why, I will let you whisper your dreams to me." "But I must kill whatever I carry. You are a living thing and do not wish to die." "If you do not kill me, I will listen to your inmost self, and tell all the animals, that they may feel sympathy for you." "What do I care for sympathy? I am all-powerful." "Yes, but someday, your winds will die, and my kits will tell this tale even when you are gone, of the time Great-great-great-grandfather Fox was carried by the winds and lived and learned their secrets." "But then they will not be afraid of me, and what good am I if I do not inspire fear?" "Oh, no living thing could ever be so strong they would not fear you. I give you something more. I give you a voice throughout time that is more than a wordless bellow of rage."

Dawn Treader spiraled through the plumes of gases rising south from Wormwood's pyre, and gathered fuel. It scooped hundreds of thousands of tons of hydrogen and helium and lithium, compressing them, storing them in envelopes around its waist as a bee stores pollen.

There was a kind of joy in its flight away from the dying system; it had subverted the last-ditch attempt by the Killers. The Killers' trap became a cornucopia.

The crew spent a silent, still year in the schoolroom, another chunk of time reassigned.

Behind them, receding into a reddened hole, Wormwood's nebula engulfed the system's farthest reaches. All traces of ancient crimes were obliterated; planets, orbital warning systems, clouds of depleted pre-birth material, needle ships.

The tar baby burned to cosmic ash. That alone was worth their deaths, but they did not die.

The ash of gases flowed around and ahead of them and they breathed their fill, as a drowning man draws long, grateful breaths of air.

Martin accepted a glass of water from Hakim.

Ten bodies lay in parallel around the outer perimeter of the schoolroom. Hans stood over them, chin in hand, silent, as he had stood for the last half hour. Every few minutes he would shake his head and grunt, as if in renewed astonishment. The new dead, Jorge Rabbit, David Sasquatch, Min Giao Monsoon, Thomas Orchard, Kees North Sea, Sig Butterfly, Liam Oryx, Giorgio Livorno, Rajiv Ganges, Ivan Hellas. The bodies bore no marks of violence but for faint purple blotches visible on the face and hands; they lay with eyes closed.

They had died in confinement.

Twenty-three of the survivors kneeled by the bodies, still dazed.

With a start, Martin realized they were standing in full gravity. The *Dawn Treader* accelerated again.

"How did this happen?" he asked, throat still dry and sore.

Hakim drank deep from his bulb of water. "Their volumetric fields must have weakened . . . Neutrino flux may have transmuted some of their elements. They were poisoned, or perhaps just . . ." He swallowed. "Burned. I have only looked at them briefly. There are no moms to talk with."

"The moms couldn't keep them alive?"

Hakim shook his head.

Rosa Sequoia walked among the crew, making weird and meaningless hand-gestures that most of the others ignored. Jeanette Snap Dragon and Kimberly Quartz followed her, heads bowed.

Cham approached Martin and pointed to Sig Butterfly's body, still and gray in the lineup. "One of our own," he said.

"They're all our own," Martin said.

"That's not what I mean." Cham screwed up his face. "We're losing the experience of our own leaders. We should arrange a full inquiry. We need to know what happened. Why the moms failed us again."

"I don't think they failed us," Martin said. "We're here. Most of us are alive."

"We need to know the facts," Cham said, getting more irritated.

"I agree," Martin said. "But Hans is Pan, and he calls the shots now."

"Not if he's too stunned to move," Cham said. "Where's Harpal?"

They looked for the Christopher Robin, but he was not in the schoolroom. Most of the surviving crew had gone elsewhere, perhaps to recover in privacy. Martin itched to get things moving, but he resisted. "I'll find Harpal," he said. "Hakim, tell Hans we need to inspect the nose and the star sphere." He pointed with his chin. "Let's give him something concrete to think about."

"Then I will gather the search team," Hakim said.

* * *

The ship's corridors smelled cooked, as if a fire had swept through the *Dawn Treader* while they were in confinement. The neutrino storm of dying Wormwood had done them more damage than Martin had first guessed; and that meant their escape had been something new for the moms, something experimental.

They could have lost many more.

I should be arranging for the burial of the bodies, Martin thought. The moms had always disposed of bodies before; why were they left out in the open now?

He stopped in a corridor and referred to his wand. Where were the moms? He called for one. None appeared. The wand itself acted fitfully, its projections weak and flickering.

He waited several minutes, beginning to shiver with a new fear: that the ship itself had suffered substantial damage, that its resources were diminished, that they might all die in a vessel without a ship's mind or the moms.

He was about to continue toward Harpal's chambers when a mom floated into view several meters ahead of him. "Thank God," Martin said. He embraced the robot gently, as if it might shatter. The mom did not react to his relief.

"I'm looking for Harpal," Martin said. "We have a lot of organizing to do, a lot of . . . psychological work."

"A description of damage is necessary," the mom said. "We will present an assessment before the entire crew."

"The bodies . . ."

"We cannot recycle for the time being. Repair work is under way now. Some of our facilities are limited or inoperative until the work is done. The dead will be kept in fields—"

Martin shook his head and held up his hand, not wanting to hear the minute details. "We just need reassurance," he said. "There could be a bad reaction if we don't have a meeting soon."

"Understood," the mom said.

"Where is Harpal?"

"He is in the tail," the mom said.

"I'll go get him."

Ariel came up behind them, sidled around the mom as if it

were a wall, looked directly at Martin. "Hans is fuguing out," she said. "He's scaring the crew. Let's find Harpal, and fast."

They walked aft, not speaking until they were in the spaces of the second homeball. Here, the peculiar singed odor was even stronger.

Ariel wrinkled her nose. "Are we as bad off as it smells?" she asked.

"You heard what the mom said."

"You know how I feel about the moms," Ariel said.

Martin shrugged. "They saved us."

"They put us down there in the first place. How grateful should I be that they got us out?"

"We chose—"

"Let's not argue," Ariel said. "Not while Hans is sucking his thumb and Rosa is back there acting like a priestess. We have to move, or we're going to be in more trouble than we ever imagined—our own kind of trouble. The moms aren't going to pull us out of a fugue. They don't know how."

"Hans isn't sucking his thumb," Martin said. "He's . . . putting it all together."

"You sympathize with everyone and everything, don't you?" Ariel said. She smiled as if in admiration, and then the smile took on a tinge of pity.

Harpal Timechaser looked at them with a frightening blankness as they approached. He had hidden in a dense tangle of pipes.

Martin's temper had worn thin; now he was angry at Harpal, angry at everybody, not least angry at this woman who mocked him at every step and followed him for reasons he couldn't understand.

"What is it?" Harpal asked too loudly, as if using the question as a wall or a defense.

"We have to get the crew together," Ariel said before Martin could speak.

"Slick it," Harpal said. "We could have died. We could have bought it while stuck in those goddamned fields."

"Most of us survived," Martin said.

"Jesus, I was right next to Sig," Harpal said. "It's never

been that close for me. Whatever cooked him could have cooked me.''

"I was next to Giorgio Livorno,'' Ariel said. "The moms have some explaining to do.''

"The ship is damaged,'' Martin said.

"Tell them to *fucking get it over with*!" Harpal screamed, tears streaking his cheeks. "Nobody should have died, or we all should have died!''

Martin and Ariel stood among the thick twisted pipes, the silence interrupted only by Harpal's faint, constrained, helpless weeping. Ariel glanced at Martin, put on a resigned look, and went to Harpal. She wrapped him in her arms and rocked him gently, eyebrows arched, lips puckered as if to croon a reassuring song to a child, and she meant it.

Martin was impressed. He could not have predicted this nurturing side of Ariel.

His wand chimed. The communications at least worked now. He answered and heard Cham.

"We've got problems,'' Cham said. Noise in the background; Hans shouting, weeping. "Hans is freaking.''

Harpal wiped his face and pulled from Ariel's embrace. "Shit,'' he said. "Time to zip it.'' He crawled out of the curl of pipe. They laddered forward.

When they got to the schoolroom, Hans had left for his quarters. The ten bodies had been rearranged haphazardly on the floor, as if kicked. Five of the crew, including Jeanette Snap Dragon and Erin Eire, wore bruised faces. Half the crew had left. Martin felt sick foreboding; this was the beginning of something Theodore had talked about long ago, something Martin had refused to consider possible: the breaking strain.

Rosa Sequoia had stayed. Hans had not touched her. Now that Harpal, Hans, and Ariel had reappeared, she carefully rearranged the bodies, positioning their arms and legs, closing eyes that had opened, straightening the overalls.

Watching her pushed Martin very close to the edge, and he pulled himself back with considerable effort, swallowing, pinching his outer thigh until he bruised.

"What happened?'' Harpal asked.

Cham nursed a cut cheek. "Wendys started mourning. Rosa led them. Hans told them to stop. They kept on, and a few Lost Boys joined in, started weeping, carrying on, and Hans . . . kicked them. David Aurora fought back and Hans really laid into him. David—"

"Where is he?" Ariel asked.

"He's fine. Cut, bruised, but as I was saying, he got some good licks in. Hans pulled out."

"Where is Aurora?" she asked again.

"In his quarters, I assume."

Martin could hardly bring himself to move. He shivered suddenly, casting away the paralysis of fugue, and said to Ariel, "Get water and make some bandages and help Rosa nurse the crew. Keep her away from the bodies."

"Right," Ariel agreed.

"I'm not Pan," Martin said, as if to make that clear; the crew in the schoolroom had focused on him with expectation when he spoke. "Harpal, find Hans and let's get all the past Pans together. I want a mom there."

"Who's ordering what?" Harpal asked, neither grim nor accusing.

"Sorry."

"Understood," Harpal said. "Let's go."

Ariel gently coaxed Rosa away, speaking to her softly; was she trying to impress him? He could not deal with that now. He allowed himself a few seconds of closed eyes, trying to push Theresa's remembered features into a complete portrait. The pieces would not combine.

He followed Harpal.

Hans had not locked his door. They entered his quarters, prepared for anything but what they found. He sat in the middle on a raised section of floor, sipping from a bulb of water, and greeted them with a weak smile.

"I've really slicked it," he said, almost cheerfully.

"That you have," Harpal agreed.

"Are you going to vote me out?" Hans asked.

"Why did you do it?" Martin asked.

Hans looked away. "They started keening. Women and men. I couldn't believe it, coming out and finding bodies. It was more than I could take. I'm sorry."

"Say it to them," Martin said.

"I'm saying it to you."

Cham and Joe Flatworm entered. "You bastard," Joe said. "You slicking bastard. We should kick you out now. Give it back to Martin and stick you away like a rat."

Hans' face flushed and his jaw muscles tightened but he did not say anything, or move from his seat.

"We've all gone through hell," Martin said, feeling how pitifully reduced the *Dawn Treader*'s group of leaders had become, and so quickly. "Hans agrees to apologize."

"Apologize hell. He should resign. Martin, you take the title again."

"No," Martin said. "Hans, convince us. *Now.*"

"I don't know if I want this mess on my head," he said lightly, standing and stretching his arms. "I'm giving serious thought to the old Big Exit. Cut my wrists and be done with it." He glanced at Martin. "The moms don't seem to give a slick what we do. We're just tools."

"I'm not satisfied," Joe said. He seemed on the verge of punching Hans; his arms crooked, fists clenched, chin thrust out.

"All right," Harpal said. "Stop this shit now and talk straight. Hans, tell us what you're going to do. And don't flex your ego."

Hans shrank a bit at Harpal's tone and unyielding choice of words. "I'll pick it up again," he said. "I know we're in trouble if we let it slide now. Bigger responsibilities."

"Good for a start," Harpal said. "What else?"

"I'll do penance," Hans said. "I'll put myself in solitude for a week after we get back on our feet. I'll tell the children—"

"Crew," Martin said.

"I'll tell the crew. If . . ."

"If what?" Joe shot back.

"I want the mourners to spend time in solitude, as well. A day. The ones who set me off."

"That's crap," Joe said.

"That's how they coped," Harpal said.

"I have a different way of coping . . ." Hans began, but let it go with a shrug. "All right. Just myself. In solitude for a week. I'm still Pan, I still give the orders. I agree to that, too. Harpal, can I lean on you for help—lean hard?"

"I'll do whatever I can," Harpal said.

"That's all I ask," Hans said.

We start fresh now, Martin thought, and with that thought came a kind of relief. They had cut cleanly from the disastrous past. In a way, Hans had taken the perfect course, allowing a clean break, expiation by the leader, a new game starting from this point.

If Hans had known this from the beginning, from the time he had come out of confinement—if Hans had planned this—then he was far more canny than anybody had given him credit for.

Martin shivered. He hoped it wasn't so.

The single mom—all the ship could produce now—told the crew what had happened to them and to the ship. They had survived the explosion of Wormwood with major damage—up to half the ship's capabilities reduced by failure of confinement fields under extreme neutrino bombardment; ten of the crew had died, and only now were their bodies being recycled. They had sufficient fuel to move on to Leviathan—if they voted to do so. The journey would take a minimum of one year, ship's time.

"Because of damage, you will not be able to face the antici-pated defenses alone," the mom explained. "For that reason, we suggest a combining of resources."

Martin raised his eyes. This was the first he had heard of such a thing.

"There is another Ship of the Law about two light years distant. We can match course with this vessel and join forces. This ship has suffered damage as well, and will benefit from joining forces."

"How do you know all this?" Hans asked. "You couldn't have heard about it on the noach."

"We detected the results of their skirmish, and correlated their probable path of escape. When remotes extended this ship's sensing abilities, we used them to confirm the ship's path."

"Without telling us," Hans said.

"It was not important at the time."

Hans shrugged, looked down at the deck. "If we know, then the Killers know as well," he said.

"The Killers do not know that we have escaped, though they may know of the survival of this second vessel. They do not know its present position, however. With both ships combined, we will have the capabilities of a fully equipped Ship of the Law."

"On the other ship . . . are they human?" Erin Eire asked.

"They are not human," the mom said.

"Do they need the same things we need?" Paola Birdsong asked. "I mean, do they breathe oxygen, and so on?"

"With slight adjustments, environments can be joined," the mom replied.

"What do they look like?" David Aurora asked.

"More information about this ship and its inhabitants will be available before we join forces."

"Do we take a vote?" Ariel asked.

"A vote is not forbidden. But you must understand that we cannot fulfill our mission in our present condition."

"No shit," someone said in the back, out of Martin's sight; it sounded like Rex Live Oak.

"Do we really need to vote?" Hans said. "I'm still ready to fight. If this is our only chance, we should take it."

"Vote," Ariel insisted, and Rosa Sequoia, in a calm, deep voice, as if speaking from a cave, agreed.

"All right," Hans said. "Martin, Harpal, take the count."

The crew voted quickly, without energy. Of the sixty-five remaining, thirty voted no; thirty-five voted yes. Ariel voted to go; Rosa Sequoia voted against further action.

"That's close," Hans said, standing before them. "Now I'm here to take my licks. I screwed up today. I really fouled the nest. I apologize. I'll go into solitary for a week. I appoint Harpal as Pan in the interim. He'll work with Martin. I suggest we all take a rest. Let the mom finish its work. We say our farewells to everybody we lost around Wormwood, and we think things through."

He nodded to the closest members of the crew as he passed them, heading toward the door. Harpal looked at Martin; this was hardly what they had hoped for. Martin felt sick inside; sick with his unresolved pain, and sick at the dissolution that seemed to be upon them.

"We need to talk this out," Harpal told Martin.

Martin declined. "Rest," he said. "We've been through too much, and I can't talk sensibly now. Aliens!" He trembled suddenly, whether with excitement or exhaustion, he could not say. Harpal's shoulders slumped and his chin dropped.

"We'll all rest," Martin said, touching his arm delicately. "And mourn."

Martin's quarters were bare and cold. Still the smell of burning lingered; the odor of neutrino-singed matter. He entered and the door slid shut behind him and for this moment at least, ignoring the smell, he might have been at the beginning of his journey, when first the *Dawn Treader* had been presented to the children, and they had made their new homes here.

With some relief and some sorrow, he knew that these were not the same quarters in which he and Theresa had made love. The ship had rearranged and repaired itself too extensively; the deck on which their bed had rested might now be shifted meters away, or recycled completely. What connection did he have to the past?

None.

Martin closed his eyes and curled up on the floor, laid his cheek against the smooth cool surface, flexed his fingertips against it, and waited for sleep.

He thought on the edge of that desired sleep of Jorge Rabbit's bruised body, and what it had once held: language and laughter and sharp reliability, a favorite of the children. The crew.

Jorge Rabbit and the others might soon be in the air they breathed, the food and water they took in. But not William or Theresa.

Martin reached out for Theresa's hand. He could almost feel it, his fingers brushing the air where it would be, faintest rasp of sensation. Then, deliberately, he withdrew his hand and folded it under his chest. "Goodbye," he whispered, and slept.

Behind the *Dawn Treader*, the corpse of Wormwood expanded as a many-colored vapor, like milk swirling in water and illuminated by many lights.

Hakim watched the stellar corpse with cold curiosity, arms folded. Beside the image in the star sphere scrolled and flashed figures, charts, condensed images, conveying the qualities of the corpse in an interstellar autopsy of incredible depth and complexity.

"If I were back on Earth now," he told Martin, "I would be an astronomer, but never in my life would I see something like this. Where would I rather be, do you think? Here, now, seeing this, or . . . ?"

"You'd rather be on Earth," Martin said. They were alone in the nose; the rest of the crew awaited the end of Hans' self-imposed week of isolation, going through their own isolations, their own regroupings, reassessments.

Hakim agreed. His face had changed since the Skirmish, as Erin Eire called their costly victory. His expression had hardened, eyes shining brighter, perpetual smile tighter, lines more deeply grooved around his lips and eyes.

"It was a fair exchange, perhaps," Hakim said. "How many Ships of the Law were trapped by Wormwood and destroyed?"

"We were lucky," Martin said. "The trap was getting rusty."

"You know as well as I, war is a matter of luck as much as strategy. We should not deny ourselves satisfaction because we came upon a weakened enemy."

"We don't know the *enemy* is weak," Martin said. "They might still be strong."

"Then why do they hide behind traps?"

"To avoid trouble. Maybe this was no more significant to them than the loss of a bug zapper in a front yard."

Hakim's smile curled wickedly. "I like this metaphor," he said. "We are mosquitoes, but we bring yellow fever . . . And now the bug zapper is down, we fly freely toward the house . . ."

"About to join with a group of moths," Martin suggested.

"I would prefer wasps." Hakim chuckled, and then suddenly his voice caught and he turned away. "Excuse me," he said, clearing his throat.

"Someone you loved," Martin said after a moment. He had never followed Hakim's romantic affairs, partly out of respect, partly because Hakim and his partners had always been extremely circumspect.

"It was hard for me to call it love," Hakim said. "Min Giao Monsoon. She was my equal, and I couldn't . . . I didn't know how to digest that. But she was very important to me. We were not very open." For an instant, Hakim showed simple and enormous pain.

Martin watched the beautiful display, greens and reds dominating, cinders of planets visible only in the graphs and enhancements at this distance. Spirals of plasma from the poles had quickly spread and whipped in arcs to encompass a vast sphere; the artificial fields that controlled Wormwood giving way and rearranging in the violence. Wormwood's corpse had finally assumed an aspect of natural star death. Perhaps that had been planned by the Killers, as well . . .

No need to light any brighter a beacon in the forest than absolutely necessary.

"However you loved, you loved," Martin said.

Hakim agreed to that with a measured nod. "I have high hopes that our new Pan will grow into his position." He spoke quietly, as if Hans might be listening.

"It's not easy."

"There are many challenges even before we get to our destination. I wonder how I will react to new and inhuman colleagues . . . perhaps better to say nonhuman."

"The ship and the mom don't know an awful lot about them," Martin said. "Otherwise they'd tell us more."

"I agree," Hakim said. "I have never believed the moms hold things back from us."

"Oh . . ." Martin said, "I wouldn't go that far. They always tell us what we need to know, but . . ."

"Pardon my saying so, but you sound like Ariel."

Martin scowled. "Please," he said.

"Not to offend," Hakim added with a touch of his old impishness.

Rosa Sequoia sat in the cafeteria among a group of twenty-two of the crew, conducting a ceremony for the dead, following—

as far as Martin could tell—her own rules and her own rituals.
He could not object; ritual was healthy at this point.

She had made up hymns or borrowed from old songs and
projected lyrics for the crew to sing. Martin watched from the
outside, near the door, and did not sing, but felt his heart tug at
the swell of voices.

Rosa looked up, and her eyes met his, and she smiled—
broadly, without resentment; beautifully.

In our grief and pain, she finds herself, he thought. But
perhaps that was too unkind.

Hans came out of his isolation after six days, somber and un-
shaven, blond beard bristling and face wreathed in a dreary scowl
that gave nobody confidence, least of all Martin. He asked for a
private session with Hakim and the remains of the search team.
After, he emerged from the nose to brush past Martin and Erin
Eire in the corridor, saying nothing.

"He hasn't taken a lover since he became Pan," Erin said.

Martin looked at her. "So?"

Erin blinked. "So it's unusual. He's not exactly been chaste,
Martin. A lot of Wendys go for bulk over brains."

"He's not stupid," Martin said.

"He's still acting like a jerk," Erin said.

"Maybe he's waiting for the right girl to come along," Martin
said, aware how silly that sounded.

Erin hooted. "Oh, sure. Somebody he's never met before."

"We'll have visitors soon," Martin said, face straight.

"Spare me," Erin said, grimacing over her shoulder as she
departed.

Ariel laid her meal tray on the table across from Martin in the
cafeteria. New watch schedules posted by Hans had placed her
in an opposite sleep cycle; he was having dinner, she breakfast,
but the food appeared much the same.

The ship was not yet up to the broad variety of meals it had
once offered; what they were served now was bland but filling,
a brownish bread-like pudding varied occasionally by soups.

They exchanged minimal greetings. Ariel made him uncomfortable by focusing on him when he wasn't looking.

"What do you think of Hans now?" she asked when their eyes met.

"He's doing fine," Martin said.

"Better than you?" she asked.

"In some ways," Martin said.

"How? I'm curious. I don't mean to embarrass you."

"I'm not embarrassed. He's probably more canny than I am, more sensitive to the crew's swings of mood."

She tipped her head in a way that implied neither agreement nor disagreement.

"And you?" he asked.

"Reserving judgment. He is more canny than some Pans we've had. Rosa approves of him. She talks about the duty to our leader in her sermons."

"Sermons?"

"I haven't been to one, but I hear about them."

"She's preaching?"

"Not yet," Ariel said, "but close. She's counseling. Helping some of the crew face up to the Skirmish and what it means."

"Blaming the moms?"

"Not implicitly."

"Blaming them at all?"

"She doesn't even mention them, from what I've been told. She talks about responsibility and free will and our place in the broad scheme. Maybe we should go and listen."

"Maybe I will," Martin said.

"Maybe Hans should go, too."

"Do you want me to spy on her for Hans?"

Ariel shook her head. "I just think it's significant, what's happening."

"It's inevitable, maybe," Martin said under his breath, and got up to go to his quarters.

Theodore Dawn visited his dreams, and was full of talk, some of which Martin remembered on waking.

They sat in a garden, under an arbor in full flower, Theodore in a short white tunic, his legs tanned from long exposure to the summer sun now at zenith over their heads. They were eating

grapes; they might have been Romans. Theodore had been fond
of reading about Romans.

"Something terrible is about to happen to Rosa," Theodore
said. "You know what it is?"

"I think so," Martin answered, letting a grape leaf fall to the
pebble gravel at their feet.

"The worst thing that can happen to a prophet is not to be
ignored and forgotten; it's to have her cause taken up and chewed
by the masses. Whatever she says, if it doesn't fit, will be chewed
some more; some opportunist will come along and forge a contradiction, polish a rough edge of meaning, and then it will fit.
People believe in everything but the original words."

"Rosa isn't a prophet."

"You said you knew what's happening."

"She isn't a prophet. Just look at her."

"She's had the vision. This is a special time for you."

"Nonsense!" Martin said, angry now. He got up from the
marble bench and adjusted his robe clumsily, not used to its
folds. "By the way, is Theresa here with you?"

Theodore shook his head sadly. "She's dead. You have to be
alive to die."

Paola Birdsong and Martin found themselves alone in the tail of
the ship, having completed a wand transmission test for the mom,
and with no further instructions, they sat and talked, glad to be
away from the glum business of the crew.

Their talk trailed off. She looked away, olive skin darkening,
lips pressed together. Martin reached out to stroke her cheek,
make her relax, and she leaned into the stroke, and then tears
came to her face. "I don't know what to do or how to feel," she
said.

She had been loosely bonded with Sig Butterfly. Martin did
not want to inquire for fear of opening wounds, so he kept silent
and let her talk.

"We weren't deep with each other," she said. "I've never
really been deep with any lover. But he was a friend and he
listened to me."

Martin nodded.

"Would he want me to feel badly for him?" she asked.

Martin was about to shake his head, but then smiled and said, "A little, maybe."

"I'll remember him." She shuddered at the word "remember," as if it were a realization or betrayal or both, remembrance being so different from seeing directly, remembrance being an acknowledgment of death.

It was natural for him to fold her in his arms. He had never been strongly attracted to Paola Birdsong, and perhaps that was why holding her seemed less a violation to his memory of Theresa. Paola must have felt the same about Martin. The embrace became more awkwardly direct, and they lay side by side in the curls of pipes, the burned smell almost too faint to notice now.

Where they lay was dry and quiet and isolated. Martin felt a little like a mouse in a giant house, having found a place away from so many cats; and Paola was herself small, mouselike, undemanding, touching him in a way that did not discourage, did not invite. The momentum of the situation was carried by instinct. He did not undress her completely, nor himself, but rolled over on top of her, and with a direct motion they joined, and she closed her eyes.

Neither of them cried.

Martin made love to her slowly, without urgency. She had no orgasm to match his, which was surprisingly powerful, and he did not press her for one; it seemed this was what she wished, only a little betrayal of memory at a time, a little return to whole life. After, with no word of what they had just done, they rearranged their overalls.

"What have your dreams been like lately?" he asked.

"Nothing unusual," she said, drawing her knees up in her arms and resting her chin on them.

"I've been having pretty vivid dreams. For a long time now. Pretty specific dreams, almost instructive."

"Like what?"

Martin found himself much more reluctant to describe the dreams than to characterize them. "Memories with real people in them. People from the ship, I mean, saying things to me. Giving advice as if they were alive."

Paola bumped her chin on her knees as she nodded. "I've had dreams like that," she said. "I think it means we're in a special time."

Martin jerked at that phrase.

"What do you mean?" he asked.

"It just seems right. We're so far away from our people. We're losing more and more connections. Something's bound to change."

"What will change?" Martin asked.

She uncurled, pulled up a bare foot to inspect a toenail. "Our psychologies," she said. "I don't know. I'm just talking. A special time is when we learn who we are all over again."

"Shrugging off the past," Martin suggested.

"Maybe. Or seeing it differently."

"Does Sig come to you in your dreams?" he asked.

"No," she said, dark eyes watching him.

He thought it unlikely they would make love again.

After, in his quarters to prepare for a watch in the nose, he felt melancholy, but that was an improvement. It had been only weeks in his personal, conscious time, but the clouds thinned, and he could think clearly for moments at a stretch without the shadow of Theresa or William.

In the nose, Hakim slept while Li Mountain and Giacomo Sicilia tracked the corpse of Wormwood. In a few months, they would see the shroud of gas as no more than a blotch in the receding blackness.

"Any sign of a neutron star?" Martin asked Li Mountain.

"None," she said. "Jennifer doesn't think one will form. She thinks the star's interior was deeply disturbed, that everything was flung out."

"It must have been quite a blast," Giacomo Sicilia said. Almost as adept as Jennifer at momerath, he had replaced Thomas Orchard on the search team.

There was little else for them to do but science, which Hakim enjoyed, but Martin found vaguely dissatisfying. Knowledge for the sake of knowledge was not their Job. But Hakim insisted that studying the corpse of Wormwood could teach them about Killer technology.

They would be many months traveling to meet with the second ship; training was not an option in their present situation. Healing and reknitting the crew would be their major occupations.

Martin recorded the figures with Giacomo, and stared back into the past, at the beautiful tendrils and shells of gas and dust.

No sign of Killer activity around Wormwood.

The tar baby was truly dead.

The following months passed slow and hard in their dullness. The state of comparative luxury they had known before the Skirmish and the neutrino storm did not return; the solitary mom merely told them that the ship was damaged in ways not quickly mended. Food was nourishing but bland; access to the libraries was limited to text materials, and wand graphics were severely curtailed.

Martin suspected the Ship of the Law had lost portions of its crucial memory, and was merely a shadow of its former self. The mom would not elaborate; it, too, seemed lost in a kind of dullness, and dullness was the order of things. In a way, Martin did not mind this difficulty; it gave them all plenty of time for thought, and he used that time.

Hans was clearly made uneasy by it.

The ex-Pans held colloquium every five days in his quarters.

"I'd hate to be known as the exercise Pan," Hans said. "We have three more months until we rendezvous with our new partners. We've done about all the science there is to do with Wormwood—at least, everybody has but Jennifer and Giacomo . . . We're bored, there's still only one mom, and that worries me. Am I right?"

Hans had been asking that more and more lately: a slightly nasal "Am I right?" with one eyebrow lifted and a perfectly receptive expression. "We need some mental action, too. The ship isn't going to be much help." He looked to Cham, but Cham shrugged.

"Martin?" Harpal asked.

Martin made a wry face. "Without the remotes, we can't learn much more about Leviathan."

"The food is dull," Harpal offered. "Maybe we can cook it ourselves."

Joe Flatworm snorted. "The mom won't let us near raw materials."

"Any suggestions, Joe?" Hans asked.

"We're stuck in a long dull rut," Joe said softly. "We should be asleep."

"I'm sure if that were an option—" Martin began.

"Yeah. The mom is concerned." That was another phrase Hans used often now, and others in the crew had picked it up. The proper form was: *stated problem or dissatisfaction*; reply, "Yeah, the mom is concerned."

"I think we should—" Martin began again.

"Slick worrying about the ship," Hans said.

"That wasn't what I was—"

"Fine," Hans interrupted.

"Goddammit, let me finish!" Martin shouted. Joe and Cham flinched, but Hans grinned, held up his hands, and shook his head.

"You have the floor," he said.

"We can't blame the ship for saving our lives," Martin said, expressing not a shred of what he had meant to say, and now realized was useless to say under the present circumstances.

"I don't think any of us Pans have actively enjoyed our rank," Hans said, drumming his fingers on the table between them. "Am I right? But I'm faced with problems none of you faced. Political problems. Psychological problems. We don't have any real work to do. We have plenty of time on our hands. The only thing I can think of to keep us occupied is sports. I don't like it, but there it is."

Cham raised one hand to shoulder level.

"Yes?"

"We should begin thinking about after," he said.

"After what?"

"After the Job is done. We should work on a constitution. Laws, and so on. Get ready for when we look for another world . . ."

Hans considered with a thoughtfulness that somehow did not convince Martin. "Right," he said. "Joe, get on it. Cham, for your sins, organize some games and competitions. Start with races from nose to tail, like we used to do. Think up rewards.

Shake them up, get their blood moving. Martin, perhaps you should work on intellectual games . . . More your speed, no? Get together with Hakim. Jennifer. Whoever. Competition. If we're cast on our own resources, we have to be resourceful."

Am I right? Martin predicted. Hans smiled and said nothing.

Rosa Sequoia sat comfortably in the middle of thirty-two of the crew—a broad selection, including Erin Eire and Paola Bird-song. Martin stood to one side of the schoolroom, listening, observing.

With all of her words, she made gentle, sweeping hand gestures, drawing in but not demanding or assertive. Her voice soothed, low and soft, yet authoritative. Something had come together for her, Martin saw; and her newfound grace and ease of expression worried him. A special time.

Hans entered behind him, leaned against the wall next to Martin, nodded in greeting, folded his arms, and listened.

". . . To have lost the home we all cherished, we all grew up with, is like the farmer who lost his farm, when the wind came and blew it away. One day he awoke and walked out his door to see barren dirt, the crops smashed flat, dead and brown, and he told himself, 'I have worked this land all my life, why didn't the wind take me as well? This farm is like an arm or a leg to me—why wasn't I snatched away with it?' "

Martin listened intently, waiting to see if Rosa's fairy tale or parable or whatever it was came close to those he had experienced in the volumetric fields.

Rosa looked down, lowered her arms as if resting. "The farmer became bitter. He thought he would fight the wind. He built walls against the wind, higher and higher, making them out of the dust and straw and the mud that ran in rivers across the dead fields. But the wind knocked the walls down, and still the farmer was alive. The wind took his family one by one, and still the farmer lived, and cursed the wind, and finally he began to curse the Maker of Winds—"

"He became a wind breaker!" Rex Live Oak called out.

Rosa smiled, unperturbed. "He tried magic when the walls wouldn't work. He chanted against the wind, and sang songs, and all the while, he grew to hate the land, the wind, the water.

He cursed them all and he became more and more bitter, until it seemed bad water ran in his veins, and his mind was poisoned with hate and fear and change. He no longer missed his family; he no longer missed the farm. It seemed nothing meant anything to him but revenge against the wind—''

"Sounds subversive to me," Hans whispered to Martin.

"And he grew thinner and thinner each day, more and more wrinkled, until he looked like a dead stalk of corn—''

"I don't remember what corn looked like, growing on a stalk," Bonita Imperial Valley said. "I grew up in a farm town, and I just *don't remember*."

"He couldn't remember, either," Rosa continued smoothly. "He couldn't remember what the crops looked like, or what had been important to him. He fought the wind with the only weapon he had left, useless empty words, and the wind howled and howled. Finally, the farmer became so bitter and dry and dead inside, the wind sucked him up through the air like a leaf. He lived inside the wind, empty as a husk, and the wind filled his dry lungs, and reached into his dry stomach, and then into his dry, rattling head.''

"So what's the point?" Jack Sand asked, looking around the assembled group with a puzzled expression.

"It's a story," Kimberly Quartz said. "Just listen."

"I don't listen to stories unless they have a point. It's a waste of time," Jack said. He got up and left, glancing at Hans and Martin and shaking his head.

"In the wind," Rosa continued, hardly missing a beat, "the farmer knew what he was up against, and that he had no power. He stopped cursing and he started listening. He stopped resisting—I mean, how can you resist something so powerful?—and he began to live in the wind, as part of the howl and the whirl and the swirling. He saw other people in the wind—''

Hans motioned for Martin to follow him outside. Martin walked through the door and they stayed in step down the corridor, past Jack Sand, past Andrew Jaguar and Kirsten Two Bites.

Out of the others' hearing, Hans said, "When I was a little kid, back on Earth, my folks took television and video games away from me for a week to punish me for something I did. I went nuts. I even started to read books. Well," he said, "our

TV's gone now. Rosa is better than nothing." He shook his head. "But not much."

"Did you slick Paola Birdsong?" Ariel asked. Martin picked up his tray of food and walked away from her, face pinking.

"Did you?" she asked innocently, following with her own tray.

He sat, got up when she sat next to him, moved to another table, started to get up again as she kept pace with him, and finally dropped the tray a few inches to the table, slapped the tabletop once with his fist, and said, "Who the hell cares?"

Martin ate and tried to ignore her.

"I'm not trying to be nosy," Ariel said. "I want to know what it means to be devoted to someone for a long time, even after they're dead."

Martin found the situation intensely uncomfortable. "I'd like to eat in peace," he said.

"I'm sorry. I'm bothering you. I apologize." She got up, carried her tray out of the cafeteria, and left him feeling guilty, mad, and confused.

That sleep, he cried again, thinking of Theresa, but he did not remember any dreams.

Two moms appeared in the schoolroom for the next crew tenday report. There had been no announcement, no fanfare, but the crew cheered, taking it as a sign that things were improving.

Hans announced the results of the previous day's nose-to-tail races.

Hakim had five minutes to squeeze in a report on science.

Jennifer Hyacinth came up to Martin after the meeting.

"Maybe you'd like to be in on what we're doing," she said. She sounded almost conspiratorial, but he could not imagine Jennifer involved in intrigue.

"About what?" he asked.

"The noach. We're having a little conference to share results."

"Oh." He had planned to attend the next trial for the main race, but that was certainly trivial enough to ignore.

"Sure," he said.

"In the nose in ten minutes. Hakim Hadj, Giacomo Sicilia and Thorkild Lax are coming."

"I'll be there," he said.

Hakim, Giacomo, Thorkild and Jennifer had formed a Noach Studies Society some tendays before. Martin had not attended the meetings—they were reportedly dry and mathematical, the chief excitement being momerath challenges.

The reports were wrong.

Jennifer, with Giacomo's help, had put together a comprehensive description of how the noach could work, how matter could change character under the influence of noach-transmitted information, and what that meant for the ultimate shape of Benefactor society as they imagined it.

Hakim spent a few minutes projecting graphics for Martin, filling him in on the key points.

Jennifer and Giacomo held hands and contemplated momerath until the meeting was convened by Thorkild.

"We've been trying to piece together an overview of Benefactor technology," Thorkild began. "Jennifer's done most of the tough work, laying a foundation for the rest of us. Giacomo has erected the frame on that foundation . . ."

Giacomo smiled.

"You might say they work together intimately," Thorkild added. Hakim clapped his hand on Giacomo's shoulder as if in congratulations. Jennifer's face remained set in solid neutrality, but her eyes flashed.

"Hakim has put on the siding and I've painted," Thorkild concluded. "Mind you, none of what we've come up with has much meaning for our mission. It's all theoretical—"

"I disagree," Jennifer said.

"Which I was about to add," Thorkild said.

"I think it could have a lot of meaning for the Job," Jennifer said. "We were caught by surprise when the Killers converted our craft to anti em. We assume the moms were caught by surprise. The more we can guess about the technology and theory behind our weapons, the more we can contribute to planning."

Martin rubbed his nose. "So what's the house look like?"

Hakim projected a list. "First, the noach—instantaneous communication at a distance. This is made possible by confusing two particles—in this case, atomic nuclei—into 'believing' that they are the same. Second, actually creating a particle at a distance—deluding the matrix into believing that a particle exists at a certain position, and has a certain history attached. This could be how fake matter is created—resistance to pressure, but no resistance to acceleration; extension, but no mass."

"Noach could be the key to all of this," Jennifer said. "To send a noach message, you have to confuse a particle's bit makeup, its self-contained information about character, position and quantum state."

"What do you mean by a particle 'believing' something?" Martin asked.

"The particle's bit makeup determines its behavior," Hakim said. " 'Behavior' is a bad word, like 'belief.' We do not think particles are alive or think. But they do exhibit simple behavior, of course—a nature or character, which is the same for all similar particles, and a history in spacetime."

"Given that," Martin said, "how do we get to the rest of the abilities in this list?"

"To create fake matter," Giacomo said, "basic elements in the matrix are convinced they have some of the properties of matter. To noach messages, you tamper with the privileged channels used by particles to convince one particle at some distance to believe it is the same as, or in resonance with, another particle under our local control.

"There could be several ways to convert a particle to an anti-particle. A boson, approaching a particle, carries information from its source, some of which has already been conveyed by information following so-called privileged bands. The boson also conveys energy, which acts on the particle's data, changing a particular bit sequence."

"Energy is information?" Martin asked.

"Energy is a catalyst for information change. It's information in only a limited sense. To convert a particle to an anti-particle, you can change its bit makeup either by perverting the privileged band information, say by sending it a boson tailored to react falsely, which might compel it to switch a series of bits to be consistent, or by creating a resonance with outside anti-particles.''

"Resonance . . . ?"

"Imposing the data of an anti-particle on a particle in another position by making them congruent, coextensive," Hakim said. "It is similar to how the noach works."

"We *think*," Jennifer cautioned.

Martin could not keep up with their projected momerath, or even all of their explanations. "I'll have to take some of this on faith," he said wearily.

"Oh, please no," Hakim said. "Work it out for yourself, in private. We may be wrong, and we need criticism."

"Not from me, I'm afraid."

"We are all out of our depth here, actually," Hakim said. "We must not accept this as anything more than playful theory."

Martin poked at a few expressions in the momerath that he could just begin to riddle. "Would they have to have a lot of anti em to convert something else to anti em—match a mass particle for particle?"

"We do not think so," Hakim said. "In Jennifer's momerath, a single particle could be used as template to confuse and convert many other particles. Possibly, simply knowing the structure of a particle would be enough."

"Even at a distance," Thorkild said.

"But just how it's done, we haven't a clue," Jennifer said. "The difference between theory and application."

"Oh," Martin said.

"Neat, huh?" Thorkild asked.

Martin closed his eyes and shook his head.

After, Martin sat alone in an empty quarters space, dabbling with the momerath but not able to concentrate on it, thinking instead about how much the crew had changed in just a few months. They acted like passengers enduring hard times on a down-on-its-luck cruise ship, or like students in a particularly lax high school with a principal too hip for their own good.

He longed for time to speed up, for the rendezvous to occur, for *anything* to happen that was significant and not theoretical.

* * *

Rosa's storytelling improved.

The races were concluded, with Hans pitting himself against the fastest of ten trials, Rex Live Oak, and winning by two seconds, the races being run nose to tail within the ship. Hans was inordinately proud of the victory, and took two Wendys to his quarters after for a private free-for-all, the first partners he had taken since becoming Pan.

Martin did not notice who the Wendys were; he had tired of the growing reliance on gossip for excitement. He did not care who Hans was slicking, or whether Hans had stolen Harpal's love interest, or who was going to attempt Rosa soon.

Rosa, thinner by five kilos, face austere and happy at once, was becoming, for Martin, the most interesting and at the same time the most disturbing person aboard *Dawn Treader*.

Martin came to the nose when it was empty and collapsed the star sphere to see the outside universe without interpretation. The stars ahead had not yet changed noticeably; bright, frozen forever against measureless black.

Jennifer's theories had upset him on some deep level. He had dreamed about enemies they could not see, malevolent beings confusing and perverting them from a distance like puppetmasters.

"What the hell are we doing here?" he asked. He had come to the nose to pray, but he could not conceive of anything or anyone to pray to. Nothing touched him; nothing felt for him, or knew that he was in the nose, that he was alone. Nothing knew that he was confused and needed help, that Martin son of Arthur Gordon had lost whatever path he had ever known, and that merely doing the Job seemed a highly inadequate reason for living.

His father might have thought this view of deep space the most spectacular and beautiful thing one could wish for; Martin could not see it as anything but scattered light impinging on exhausted eyes.

He had fought the end of his pain for many tendays now, but his grief followed its natural course like a healing wound. Finally even the itch would be gone and Theresa would truly be dead— and William—

He groaned softly, for he owed William so much more than he could give emotionally, now or ever.

With his grief knitting its torn edges, there would be nothing left to define him but the dreary nothingness at his core, more blank than any black between stars, a comfortable emptiness to fall into, a gentle negation and dissolution.

He thought he would gladly die if death were an end in itself and not something more.

What he would pray to, then, was a weak candle of hope: that in these horrible spans of contesting civilizations, there was something, somewhere, that oversaw and judged and sympathized; that was wise in a way they could not conceive of; that might, given a chance, intervene, however mysteriously.

Something that cradled and nurtured his dead loves in its bosom; but something that would also acknowledge his unworthiness and allow him a finality, an end.

He thought of the powerful orgasm with Paola, stronger by many degrees than he remembered experiencing with Theresa.

Confusion and stars. What a combination, he thought.

He encouraged the pain to return and let depression settle over him, until his heart seemed to slow, his eyelids drooped, and he was surrounded by a comfortable blanket of despair, so much more palpable than memory or responsibility or the day-to-day dreariness of shipboard life.

Nothing intervened.

Nothing cared.

In a way, that was reassuring. There could be an end to the universe's complexity, an end to the strife and confusion of intelligence.

In the middle of the sports and competitions, in the middle of Martin's despair, Rosa Sequoia disappeared.

Kimberly Quartz and Jeanette Snap Dragon found her naked and half-dead from thirst five days later. They brought her to the schoolroom. Ariel kneeled on the floor and gripped her hair, pulling her head back and forcing her to drink water. Her eyes wandered to fix on points between the people in the room. "What the hell are you doing?" Ariel asked.

Rosa smiled up at her, water leaking from her mouth, cracked lips bleeding sluggish drops. Her face was smeared with dried blood. She had bitten her lower lip. "It came again and touched me," she said. "I was dangerous. I might have hurt somebody."

Hans entered the schoolroom already in a rage and brushed Ariel aside. "Get up, damn you," he said. Rosa stood unsteadily, smelling sour, drips of dried blood on her breasts.

"Are you nuts?" Hans asked.

She shook her head, her shy smile opening the bites. They bled more freely.

Hans grabbed Rosa's arm, looked around the room for someone to come forward of the ten crew that had gathered. Ariel stepped up again, and Hans transferred the unresisting arm to her hands, as if passing a dog's leash. "Feed her and clean her up. She's confined to quarters. Jeanette, guard her door and make sure she doesn't come out."

"I should be telling stories later today," Rosa said meekly. "That's why I came back."

"You won't talk to anybody," Hans said. He brushed past them all, ridding himself of the mess with a backward wave of his hands.

Martin followed him from the schoolroom, anger piercing his gloom. "She's sick," he told Hans. "She's not responsible."

"I'm sick, too," Hans said. "We're all sick. But she's slicking *crazy*. What about you?" He whirled on Martin. "Christ, you mope like a goddamned snail. Harpal's no better. What in hell is going on?"

Martin said, "We've fallen into a hole."

"Then let's climb out of it, by God!"

"There is no god. I hope. No one listening to us."

Hans gave him a withering, pitying glare. "Rosa would disagree," he said sharply. "I'll bet she has God's business card in her overalls right now. Wherever her overalls are." Hans shook his head vigorously. "Of all the women on this ship, *she* has to shed her clothes when she feels a fit coming on." He stopped a few meters down the corridor, shoulders hunched as if Martin were about to throw something at him.

Martin had not moved, wrapped in a wonderfully thick and protective melancholy, feeling very little beyond the fixed anger at Hans.

Hans turned, frowning. "You say we're in a hole. We're losing it, aren't we?" he asked. "By *damn*, I will not let us lose it." He tipped an almost jaunty wave to Martin, and skipped up the corridor, whistling tunelessly.

Martin shivered as if with cold. He returned to the schoolroom. Rosa talked freely with the five who remained. Ariel had brought her a pair of overalls that did not fit. She looked ridiculous but she did not care.

"I'm sorry," she said. "I apologize for my condition. I couldn't even think. I was wired to a big generator. I wasn't human. My body didn't matter." She faced Martin, large powerful arms held out as if she might try to fly. "I felt so ugly before this. Now it just isn't important." The light went suddenly from her eyes and she seemed to collapse a couple of inches. "I'm really tired," she whispered, chin dropping to her chest. "Jeanette, please take me to my room. Hans is right. Don't let me out for a while, and don't let anybody but you—or Ariel—in to see me." She raised a hand and pointed at the three, including Martin. "You are my friends," she said.

"It's a very weak signal," Hakim said. He unveiled the analysis for Hans, Harpal, and Martin, all gathered in the *Dawn Treader*'s nose. "With our remotes out, we could have picked it up months ago . . . Maybe even when we were orbiting Wormwood. But we weren't focusing in this direction . . ."

"All right," Hans said impatiently. "It's a ship. It's close to us. How close?"

"Four hundred billion kilometers. If we do not alter course, we will pass within a hundred billion kilometers. It is following a course similar to our own, but traveling much more slowly. It is not accelerating."

Hans said. "It seems odd to find such a needle in the haystack. Why is it close to our course?"

Hakim ventured no guesses.

"Maybe it's a reasonable course between the two stars," Harpal suggested. "Give or take a few hundred billion kilometers . . ."

"Bolsh," Hans said. "They could have swung wide either way. We came up out of the poles . . . a reasonable course would have been to use least-energy vectors between the planes of the ecliptic. What's our relative velocity?''

Hakim highlighted the figure on the chart: the difference in their velocities amounted to one quarter c, about seventy-five thousand kilometers per second.

''Even if we could change course, we wouldn't want to shed that much speed to rendezvous . . . We'll just have to pass in the night. You're sure it's a ship?''

''The dimensions are appropriate. It is less than a kilometer long. We were fortunate enough to get a star occultation.''

Hans hummed faintly and rubbed his cheeks with his palms. ''Why send out a signal? Why not just hide and get your work done? Whatever the work is . . .''

Nobody had an answer.

''Can we interpret the signal?''

''It is not language of a spoken variety. That much we know. It may be a series of numbers, perhaps coordinates.''

''You mean, telling rescuers where it is?''

''I think not. If these pulses are numbers, they are repetitive . . . There are about a hundred such groups of numbers, assuming that a long pause—a few microseconds—means a new group. Giacomo and Jennifer are working on the possibilities now.''

''What kind of coordinates?'' Hans asked.

''Jennifer thinks they may describe a two-dimensional image.''

''You mean, television?''

''Digital, not analog—not modulated.''

''A crude picture,'' Martin suggested.

''Perhaps only a few dozen pictures in sequence,'' Hakim said. ''We just can't be sure yet.''

''Call me when you are,'' Hans said.

Jennifer entered the nose and stood for a moment, blinking at them, grinning with canines prominent: Jennifer's wolfish expression of intellect triumphant. Giacomo came in behind her. She lifted her wand and said, ''We've got it. Too simple to see, actually. Polar coordinates, not rectangular, spiral within a circle, a sweep point, angle theta, radius measured from the center, groups of numbers in sequence: theta, radius, gray-scale value. Theta changes every one hundred and twenty numbers. The gray-scale value gives about thirty shades. The signals translate to about a hundred graphic images before it starts to repeat. It's clumsy but simple enough for almost anyone to decode.''

"Want to see?" Giacomo said.

Hans patted his arm with strained gentleness, impatient. "Show us."

Jennifer lifted her wand.

The first picture was difficult to make out, a series of blurs and blocks of shadow. Harpal pointed to a mottled oval white blur and said, "That's a face, I think. It's very low resolution, isn't it?"

"We can interpolate, do some so-called Laplace enhancements," Giacomo said. "But I thought we should see the original images first."

"Enhance. We'll worry about distortions later," Martin suggested.

Giacomo picked out simple enhancements, stabbing with his finger expertly at a menu of selections only he could see. The picture became at once more contrasting and easier to perceive, but reduced to blacks and whites with few shades of gray. "Five faces, I think," Harpal said, pointing them out slowly. Martin nodded; Hans simply looked with hands folded, frowning.

"They're not human, but they're bilaterally symmetric," Harpal said.

"I think there are more faces, but they're too blurred to make out," Giacomo said.

"Eyes," Jennifer said. "A mouth perhaps."

"I don't give a slick what they look like," Hans said, scowl deepening. "What do they *mean*?"

"Maybe these are the crew of the . . ." Jennifer said, and stopped.

"The crew of the other Ship of the Law. Our future comrades," Martin finished for her.

"If they are, they're awfully stupid, radiating a signal like this for anybody to pick up."

"This could be more of a last testament," Hakim said. "A dying ship, channeling power to send out a weak but detectable signal . . . Someone who no longer cares about being found."

"The moms would tell us at least that much—whether they're still dead, or alive. Wouldn't they?" Harpal asked.

"These aren't our partners," Hans said. "They're just some other poor sons of bitches lost out here."

More faces. Dark interiors with brightly lighted figures. They began to see the overall shape of the beings: round bodies with four thick stubby legs, elongated horse-like heads on long necks, a pair of slender limbs rising from the "shoulders" and tipped with four-fingered hands. They wore harness-like outfits more useful for carrying things than as concealment.

"Centaurs," Jennifer said.

"They look more like dinosaurs to me," Giacomo said. "Sauropods."

"Tweak it again," Hans ordered.

Giacomo and Jennifer worked together to interpolate more detail. For a moment, the picture fuzzed into grayness, and then it stood out in artificial clarity, all shapes reduced to plastic simplifications. "I'll enhance shadows, since the light source seems to be from this angle," Giacomo said, pointing his finger in toward the picture experimentally.

Hans' scowl did not change. *Something new and he doesn't like it*, Martin thought.

Giacomo poked the unseen menu and keyboard and spoke short verbal commands, all interpreted by his wand.

The image's contrast became more dramatic, shadows more pronounced, and the scene suddenly took on depth. Five of the sauropod beings floated in an ill-defined interior, joined in a five-pointed star, heads toward the middle, linked by hand-like appendages.

"Group portrait," Martin said.

"Next picture, and tweak it the same," Hans said.

More figures appeared, arrayed with machines as difficult to riddle as the interiors of the *Dawn Treader* might have been to fresh Earthbound eyes. The tenth image was a diagram: stars and larger balls against mottled dark sky. Arrays of dots and slashes that might have been labels for the image seemed to be compromised by the enhancements, but when Giacomo removed the enhancements, the symbols made no more sense than before.

Hakim leaned closer to the picture and said, "I can make out a familiar constellation. Familiar to the search team, at least . . . We have called it the Orchid. It has been with us for a year now. It looks a little different, however . . . The brightest star, there . . ." He gestured to Giacomo, who surrendered control of the image to him. Hakim brought up a crystalline starfield, live, and rotated it until he found the constellation he wanted. Then he flash-compared the blurred chart with the fresh image, adjusted for scale, and the corresponding stars jumped in and out, the brightest jumping the farthest.

"Time has passed," Hakim said, "but these are the same stars. Notice that stars in the distant background do not jump."

"I noticed," Hans said. "How long has it been?"

Hakim worked his momerath quickly. "If estimates of proper motion are correct, this image would have to be one, perhaps two thousand years old."

"They've been out here two thousand years?" Harpal asked, whistling.

The next few images showed the spacecraft itself from several angles: three spheres linked by necks.

"It's like our ship," Jennifer said.

Harpal whistled again. "It's a Ship of the Law, all right."

More pictures: cabin interiors, what might have been a social or even a mating ritual, sauropods holding up pale ovoids for examination, breaking the ovoids and appearing to consume the contents, beings in repose or dead, twenty blocks of what was probably text, then a series of ten individual portraits.

The next ten images were simple charts of a stellar system. Hakim compared these charts with the charts they had made of Leviathan. The numbers and orbits of the planets were very similar, though not exact. "Puzzling," Hakim said. "There is strong similarity, but . . ."

"Maybe the system has changed," Martin suggested.

"Not natural changes. Twelve planets are shown in these charts, but we have detected only ten. The largest planet is not shown in the earlier charts. Where could it have come from?"

"You're saying they didn't visit Leviathan? This is another system?" Hans asked.

Hakim frowned. "I do not know what to say. The resemblance

is too close to be coincidence . . . these six similar planets, congruent masses, orbits, diameters . . .''

"Forget it for now," Hans said.

The next forty images showed planets and planetary surfaces, details too muddied to be very useful. Hints of mountains or large structures with regular, smooth surfaces; a lake or body of water; dramatic cloud formations over a flat-topped mesa, sauropods in suits exploring a broad field.

The last image was startling in its directness.

Three sauropods in suits on a planetary surface confronted a being of another kind entirely; three times more massive than they, barrel-bodied, standing on two massive legs like an elephant's, with a long, flat head topped by a row of what might have been eyes, nine of them.

They were exchanging ovoids. One sauropod appeared to be kneeling before the larger being; offering up an ovoid.

"What in the hell happened?" Hans asked, frowning, fixed on the final image. "They've picked a mighty poor choice of pictures to tell a story."

"Perhaps the sequence is incomplete," Hakim said. "What could be left after such a time?"

"Are we going to change course and find out?" Giacomo asked.

"Hell, no," Hans said immediately. "They're dead. This isn't a distress call, that's clear; they must have known they were dying."

Silence settled. Then, very distinctly, the ship's voice spoke—the first time they had heard it since a year before the Skirmish, before Martin served as Pan.

"There will be an expedition to examine this ship," it said in a rich contralto. "It would be best if members of the crew accompany the expedition."

Hans' face reddened as much with surprise as anger. "We don't have the fuel to waste!"

"There is sufficient fuel," the ship's voice said. "A vessel will be manufactured. It can carry three people, or none, depending on your decision."

"You can make another ship now?" Hakim asked in a small voice.

"Why do it at all?" Hans said. "The ship is dead—it must be! Two thousand years!"

"It is a Ship of the Law," the ship's voice answered. "The transmitted information is likely to be much less than what is stored aboard the ship itself. It is required for all Ships of the Law to rendezvous and exchange information, if such a rendezvous is possible."

Hans lifted his eyes, then his hands, giving up. "Who wants to go?" he asked.

"We can draw lots," Hakim said.

"No—we won't draw lots," Hans said. "Martin, I assume you'd like to go?"

"I don't know," Martin said.

"I'd like you to go. Take Hakim and Giacomo with you." Jennifer's breath hitched.

"How long a voyage?" Giacomo asked.

"Your time, one month," the ship's voice said. "Time for this ship, four months. There will be super acceleration and deceleration."

"A lot of fuel," Hans said under his breath.

Giacomo touched Jennifer's hand. "Nothing like a side trip," she said. "Makes the heart grow fonder."

Giacomo did not look at all convinced.

"If people go, it will use more fuel," Martin said. He wondered if Hans wanted him out of the way.

"That is correct," the ship's voice said. "But it is not a major consideration. You will learn much that cannot be learned by sending an uncrewed vessel. Your observations will be valuable."

"There it is," Hans said. He wrapped his arm around Martin. "It'll cheer you up," he said.

"How?" Martin asked. "Visiting a derelict . . ."

"Get your goddamned glum face off this barge," Hans said.

"Doesn't sound like I'm being given a choice."

"I could send Rosa," Hans said.

Martin stared him down. "All right," Martin said. Hakim tried to break the tension.

"It will be a very unusual journey. While we are gone, the crew will have something to do. They'll study these pictures and—"

"Bolsh," Hans said. "We don't show them to anybody now.

We can't avoid letting them know there's a ship, but everything else . . . zipped lips."

"Why?" Jennifer asked, astonished.

"Our morale is so low the pictures might kill us," Hans said. "Martin, Giacomo, you study them with Hakim and Jennifer. Nobody else sees them for now. I don't even want to look at them. Report only to me."

"Hans, that's deception," Jennifer said, still astonished.

"It's an order, if that means anything now. Are we agreed?"

Jennifer started to talk again, but Hans interrupted.

"Slick it. If everybody wants to choose another Pan now, let's go to it. I'll be glad to go back to a relatively normal life, taking orders instead of giving them," he said evenly. "Am I right?"

Nobody was willing to push the issue. They agreed reluctantly. Jennifer transferred the images to their private wands.

For the first time in their journey, one group would withhold information from another.

Numb, his gloom deeper and more perversely comforting than ever, Martin returned to his quarters and looked through the images again, trying to fathom the seriousness of what had just happened, and whether he had gone along with Hans too quickly.

He did not look forward to the journey. The pictures were devastating. The Benefactors apparently could not save this Ship of the Law; the sauropod beings were almost certainly thousands of years dead.

The Benefactors could have known about Wormwood and Leviathan for millennia.

They had sent others here before. They had surmised that much around Wormwood; now it was confirmed.

The *Dawn Treader* was just another in a series.

No ship had succeeded; none had even gone so far as to burn the tar baby, until now.

But what awaited them around Leviathan might be even more deceptive, even more complex, playing for much higher stakes . . .

The craft created within the second homeball was slightly bigger than a bombship—ten meters long, with a bulbous compartment four meters in diameter, within which Martin, Giacomo, and Hakim would spend one month—much of that time asleep or wrapped in volumetric fields.

They said their farewells. The crew still knew next to nothing—only that there was another Ship of the Law, probably a death ship, and that the three of them would investigate.

Hans withdrew from the interior of the new craft, looked at Martin with narrow eyes, and said, "You can back out if you want. This is no picnic."

Martin shook his head. He felt foolish, being manipulated so blatantly—challenged to back away, refusing to be so weak in front of Hans. Hans cocked his head to one side. "Giacomo, keep your brain running. Maybe we can learn something they don't want us to know."

"Why would they have invited us to come if they wanted to keep secrets?" Hakim asked.

"I don't know," Hans said. "Maybe we're being paranoid."

"Maybe," Martin said.

"But I doubt it."

He shook hands with each of them. Giacomo and Jennifer had said their farewells privately.

"We're ready," Martin said. *A journey of a trillion kilometers begins with a single step.* He pulled himself into the craft, kicking free of the ladder field, into the spherical interior. Giacomo followed, then Hakim.

As they settled, Hakim said, "The *Dawn Treader* is giving us one quarter of its fuel."

Martin nodded. Such profligacy seemed beside the point now.

"We will be like a fish carrying a yolk sac," Hakim continued. "Very ungainly. And this craft is sixty percent fake matter . . ."

"Please," Giacomo said. "I'm queasy enough."

"Big adventure," Hakim concluded with a sigh. His skin was pale and he shivered a little.

The hatch smoothed shut.

They eased out of the weapons store. *Dawn Treader* receded to no more than a pinpoint against the stars.

A mom's voice spoke. "We begin super acceleration in three minutes."

The ship was little more than an enlarged mom, Martin thought, given seven-league boots.

"You might want to see this," Hans' voice came over the noach.

They witnessed their departure from *Dawn Treader*'s point of view, a tiny dart with bulbous middle surrounded by pale green fuel tanks.

Volumetric fields wrapped the three passengers in smothering safety. Martin's eyesight suffered, as usual, but he still watched the noach transmission. A sump swallowed their flare. Little more than a rim of intense white showed, and quickly faded.

"Bon voyage," Hans said.

Martin passed the acceleration in a slice of nothingness in which only a few incoherent dreams surfaced—meeting girls at dances on the Central Ark, Mother and Father, basement sweepings from his brain, exhausting in their banality. When they had reached near-c, they coasted, their fields folded, and they faced each other balefully, cramped shipmates. Outside, space twisted and stars huddled into a blurred torque. The ship restored the star fields to a normal appearance for their benefit.

"How long until we arrive?" Giacomo asked, clearly not comfortable in the close quarters.

"A tenday," Hakim said.

"You may sleep for the first six days if you wish," the mom's voice told them.

"Earth's astronauts did this for months at a time," Hakim said.

"Yeah, but we're spoiled," Giacomo said.

"Let's sleep," Martin said.

Sleep came and went, another longer slice of oblivion. Martin awoke disoriented, drank a cup of sweetened fluid, exercised in the weightlessness, observed his companions surface from their slumbers.

He had expected the journey to add even more weight to his burden of gloom. Instead, he experienced exhilaration and freedom he had never known before.

Hakim behaved as if the burden had shifted from Martin to him. He worked quietly but without enthusiasm. Giacomo spent much of his time contemplating the small star sphere.

"We're further away from our fellows than anybody's ever been before," he said at the end of their second day awake. The derelict was now two days away.

"Farther," Hakim said softly.

"Whatever," Giacomo said. "I don't feel isolated. Do you?"

"The *Dawn Treader* is pretty isolated," Martin observed.

"Yes, but they have each other . . . too many to keep track of. We have just three."

In natural sleep, Martin saw Rosa's dark shadow entity walk through an impossibly green field, wind knocking pieces of it away like fluff from a black dandelion. It towered over trees and hills, yet it was fragile and somehow vulnerable . . .

Awake, he helped Hakim prepare for their investigation. The craft mom briefed them on designs of Ships of the Law launched over the past few thousand years, though without any indication of their origins or destinations. Martin thought this was make-work; indeed, he was coming to believe their presence on this journey had more to do with ship-crew relations than practical function.

But the crew was the entire reason for the *Dawn Treader*'s existence. Perhaps the ship's mind recognized the impact of crew fears and suspicions, and was working to reduce them.

"Let's try something," Hakim said when boredom had set in at the end of the second day of coasting. "Let's float by ourselves in the middle of nothing, and see what we think about."

Giacomo gave Hakim a pained look. "You want us to go nuts?"

"It will be amusing," he said. Hakim's gloom had lifted, but his sense of humor had taken on a strange tinge, part fatalism, part puckishness; his face stayed calm, eyes large and inoffensive, but his words sometimes aimed at targets neither of his companions could see.

"I'm not so sure," Giacomo said.

"You're big and strong, a strapping theoretical fellow," Hakim said with a smile. "Catholic cannot take a dare from a Muslim?"

Giacomo squinted. "Bolsh," he said. "My parents didn't even go to church."

"Nobody mentions my religion," Martin said. The conversation was becoming too ragged for his taste, but he could not just stay out of it.

"We don't know what you are," Hakim said.

Martin thought for a moment. "I don't know myself," he said. "My grandparents were Unitarians, I think."

"I challenge us all to sit in the middle of a projection of the exterior, unaltered, and speak of what we experience," Hakim said.

Giacomo and Martin glanced at each other. "Okay," Martin said.

The craft mom obliged. Within a few minutes the exterior enveloped them: intense speckled darkness ahead, twisted torque of blurred stars, muddy warmth behind.

Martin experienced immediate vertigo. The weightlessness had never bothered him until now, and he clutched the arms of his seat and felt sweat break out. They did not look at each other for several minutes, afraid of showing their discomfort.

Strangely, it was Hakim's voice that dispelled Martin's sense of endless falling. "It is worse than I thought," Hakim said. "Is everybody all right?"

"Fine," Giacomo said tersely. "Who's going to clean up if I vomit?"

"Hakim dared us," Martin said.

"Hand me the mop," Hakim said. Nervous giggles almost got the better of them.

"It's pretty strange," Giacomo said. "I look to my left, and . . . Jesus! That's weird beyond belief. Everything twists and spins like a carousel."

Martin tried looking to his right. The torque shivered, an infinity of stars cowed into being social, like little knots tied in strings of dissolving paint. It all seemed oceanic, the glow of an underwater volcano behind and the queer glimmer of deep water fish ahead. Galactic fish, X-ray fish in the depth of beginning time.

"What are you thinking?" Hakim asked after a few minutes of silence.

"I think I want to go inside," Martin said.

But they remained "outside," minutes following one on the other, and their hands crept out and grasped, their breathing came in synchrony. "Wow," Giacomo said. "I'm not asleep, am I?"

"No," Martin said.

"I keep seeing things out of the corner of my eye, where the star necklace tries to be. Things reaching out to touch me. Pretty spooky."

"I hear the muezzins calling the faithful to prayer," Hakim said. "It's very beautiful. I wish you could hear it."

"Are you still a Muslim, Hakim?" Martin asked.

"We are all of us Muslims," Hakim said. "It is our natural state. We must give ourselves to Allah at some point, become obedient. Allah is looking out for us, that I feel . . . And Muhammad is his prophet. But what shape Allah is, who can say? And it is no use bowing to Mecca."

"I think that means you're a Muslim," Martin said.

"The Pope died with Earth," Giacomo said. "Isn't that something? The moms didn't save the Pope. I wonder why."

Martin saw grass growing on the rim of a tunnel, the greenness bright and welcoming, blending toward the center.

"Remember volunteering?" Giacomo said.

"A difficult time for me," Hakim said. "My mother did not want me to go. My father spoke to her sternly and she cried. I decided I had to go, and my mother . . . she ignored me from that day. Very sad."

"The tests?"

"I didn't take a lot of tests," Martin said.

"I remember a lot of tests," Giacomo said. "Physical—"

"Oh, those," Martin said. He remembered being wrapped in fields that tingled while the moms floated in attendance, never telling whether the results were good or poor.

Martin remembered his father's face, proud and sad, on the last day. The families in the Ark gathering at the berthing bay for the new Ship of the Law, stars visible beyond the curve of the third homeball. Some of the children barely into their teens getting caught up in the excitement. Martin remembered Rex Live Oak throwing up and a hastily spread field grabbing the expelled contents of his stomach and whisking them away. He smiled. The moms did not disqualify the children for nerves or fright.

Sleepless nights as the *Dawn Treader* rose into darkness, climbing for almost a year on a torch dipped into a sump. The classes, momerath refreshers, Martin's first tryst with Felicity Tigertail, awkward and delicious, a little scary to him, how much he fixed on her. With a little more innate physical wisdom, she did not fix on him, gently repulsed his further advances, introduced him without embarrassment to her other boyfriends . . .

Strange that he did not feel attracted to Theresa much sooner. Eighty-five young crew, given subtle guidance or no guidance by moms intent on letting their charges come to wisdom the human way, not the Benefactors' way, whatever that might be . . .

"Martin," Giacomo said. "Do you remember first meeting Jennifer?"

"Yes," Martin said.

"Was it on the Ark?"

"No," Martin said. "On the ship."

"What was she like then? I just don't remember much about her . . ."

They talked into the weirdness for hours, and gradually their talk fell silent, and they simply stared, or slept fitfully. The universe seemed to quiver with Martin's heart, flinching, star necklace alive, a thinly spread tissue of life. His own scale increased to match; Martin became galactic and with his new size came a nervous euphoria.

How long they sat, Martin couldn't tell at first. But Giacomo broke the vigil and said, "That's enough for me."

Hakim made a little grunt. "Why?" he said.

"Because I just had a wet dream, damn it," Giacomo said.

They agreed to stop, and the projection folded into a small star sphere, returning them to the narrow and much more comfortable confines of the craft.

* * *

Their deceleration was brief, merely two hours, to match course
and speed with the derelict. As volumetric fields faded, they
waited eagerly for a first glimpse of the ship from a few kilometers.

What first appeared was almost impossible to comprehend.
The ship resembled a twisted, crisped piece of paper in a fire,
covered with holes, the edges of the holes burning orange and
red; homeballs skeletal, debris drifting in a cloud.

"Dear God," Giacomo said.

"What happened?" Hakim asked.

The mom took them around the derelict in a slow loop. "This
ship is very old," it said. "Central control of its shape has failed.
Fake matter is decaying. Within a few hundred years, there will
be only the shells of real matter."

"There are no survivors?" Hakim asked.

"We guessed that much already," Martin said.

"Not with certainty," Hakim persisted.

"There are no survivors," the mom said. "The ship's mind
is inoperative. We will search for deep time memory stores."

A hole opened in the side of their craft. Martin pushed himself
through first, wrapped in a spherical field with a green balloon
of life support.

"It's like being in a soap bubble," he said. They had not
practised with these fields before. Martin pulled down an ephem-
eral control panel and touched arrows to indicate the direction
he wanted to move. The bubble thrust away from the craft with
a barely audible *tink* and a tiny flash of light—individually
matched atoms of anti em and matter, their explosions cupped
against a mirror-reflective field the size of his hand.

Giacomo emerged next, then Hakim. Except for their few
words and the sounds of breathing, again they were enveloped
by the universe, although in the form of an undistorted field of
stars. Martin saw the constellation of the Orchid. In that direction, visually aligned within a degree of the star known to humans
as Betelgeuse, lay the *Dawn Treader*, two hundred billion kilometers away.

He rotated his bubble toward the constellation Hakim had
named Philosopher. The derelict crossed the sweep of the Philosopher's hand.

"What was its name?" Giacomo asked.

The craft mom's voice answered, "I do not know."

They pushed slowly across the two kilometers. Martin trailed Giacomo's balloon, watching the staccato, firecracker punctuations of dying atoms.

"I feel like an angel. This is incredible," Hakim said, following Martin.

Martin's attention focused on the disintegrating hulk looming before them. He could make out the three homeballs, reduced to psychedelic leaf-skeletons, all edges glowing red and orange and white.

"I knew it took energy to maintain fake matter . . . I didn't know it would just fizzle out," Giacomo said. Martin spun around and urged his bubble toward the third homeball, leaving Giacomo and Hakim near the middle. He had spotted a hole big enough to squeeze his bubble through, and with the craft mom's approval, he was going to attempt entry.

Beside him followed a half-sized copper-bronze mom; he had not seen the craft produce the little robot, but no explanations were necessary. The diminutive mom advanced on its own firecracker bursts.

"What do I look for?" he asked the little mom.

"Ship's mind will have left a marker that will interact with close fields. The deep time memory store will probably reside within the third homeball, in the densest concentrations of real matter."

His bubble passed through what must have once been the hatch to the weapons store. "This ship wasn't attacked, was it?"

"No," the little mom said. "It ceased performing its mission."

"Why?"

"We have insufficient information to answer," the little mom said. Martin watched an extrusion of glowing scrap push against his bubble. He slowed and moved deeper, through layer after glimmering layer; walls, distorted cubicles, warped structural members. Sheets of disengaged matter—real matter, not subject to deterioration—hung undisturbed, brushed against his bubble, bounced aside silently, rippling like cloth. He could see now

how little real matter actually coated the fake matter within a
Ship of the Law; no thicker than paint.

"I'm inside the second homeball," Giacomo said.

"I'm entering the first neck," Hakim said. "It's really thin-
ning out here—not much holding it together. I'll go forward."

Within a dark cavity, wrapped by sheets of pitted matter,
Martin saw an intriguing shadow, something that did not appear
to be part of the ship. He extruded a green field to push aside
the sheets. A shriveled cold face stared at him, eyes sunk within
their orbits, long neck desiccated to knots of dried skin and
muscle around sharply defined bone.

"I've found one of the crew," he said.

"Freeze dried?" Giacomo asked.

"Not exactly. Looks like it died and mummified, then was
exposed to space, maybe centuries later."

"One of our sauropods?"

Martin transmitted an image to satisfy their curiosity. A flap-
ping sail of matter tapped the corpse and knocked lines of powder
free.

He maneuvered around the corpse and pushed deeper.

His bubble pulsed suddenly, glowed pale green, returned to
normal.

"That is the beacon," the little mom said. "We are near a
deep time memory store."

"I've found more bodies," Giacomo said. "Dozens of them.
They look like they fell asleep, or died quietly—like they're
lying down."

"The ship must have been accelerating when they died,"
Hakim said. "Unless we are seeing peculiar patterns of rigor."

Martin wiped his eyes with a sleeve. "Really awful," he
murmured.

"Do you think they just gave up, or did they run out of fuel?"
Giacomo asked. Nobody could answer. "What happened to
them?"

Martin's bubble advanced through curving pipes and conduits,
the ship's drive, real matter, not fake. He had come to the very
bowels of the ship.

The bubble pulsed again. The deep time memory store was a
white dodecahedron surrounded by an intact cage of real matter,

near the center of the third homeball. "Found what we're looking for," he said. "I think."

The half-sized robot pushed closer, used fields like hands and fingers to disengage the dodecahedron, pulled it from its cage. "I will store it in the craft. You may explore more if you wish."

Martin's horror and pity had diminished enough to bring curiosity to the fore. He moved forward through the neck to the second homeball, saw Giacomo prying his way into what must have once been a large room—a kind of schoolroom—to get at what lay within. More bodies, some hidden by membranes of surface matter, all shrunken, limbs curled in death's rigor, necks pulled back as if they were in despair or agony—rigor also, he hoped—arranged against what might have been a floor. The floor rippled under the impact of dislodged particles. The bodies drifted centimeters from their resting places, illuminated by the spooky fireside glow of fake matter coming apart.

Giacomo kept muttering under his breath.

"Speak up," Martin said, irritated.

"It's so much more . . . obvious, how they do it," Giacomo said.

"Who does what?"

"How the Benefactors make Ships of the Law. There must be a kind of noach transmitter, and it makes a shape . . . fools the privileged bands into informing other particles that matter is there, but doesn't finish the job. Leaves out mass. Something paints real matter over the fake, and voila! A big fake matter balloon. That's all *Dawn Treader* is. Our ship could look like this in a few thousand years."

"I think there must have been fifty or sixty crew members," Hakim said. "I count thirteen where I am, near the nose. They all seem to have slept before they died."

"They sure as hell didn't die in *combat*," Giacomo said.

"Our mission is accomplished," the little mom said. "It is time to return."

Back in the craft, they sampled portions of the deep time memory store, what little was comprehensible to them. Martin confirmed what he had already suspected; the Benefactors' representatives, the moms, even on this Ship of the Law, interfered very little with their charges, and did not keep day-to-day records of activities. But they did store records kept by the crew, and that was what occupied Martin, Giacomo and Hakim in their free moments on the return voyage.

They decelerated, saw the two homeballs of *Dawn Treader*, and were welcomed back to the ship by a crowd of fit-looking crew.

Martin did not look forward to briefing Hans. Hans immediately took them to his quarters, with no time to recover. Harpal and Jennifer came as well, but no others.

"The moms let you see what you recovered?" Hans asked.

"They did, as much as we could understand," Martin answered.

"Most of the memory is ship's mind data," Hakim said. "We do not know what that contained."

Martin produced his wand. "We've tried to translate and edit. You can look over the crew records in detail . . . For purposes of a briefing, I thought this might cover the important points."

They watched in silence as picture and sound unfolded. The unfamiliar visual language of the recordings made viewing difficult; different color values, different notions of perspective and "editing," attempts at three-dimensional images which did not match human eyes, all added to their problems.

But the salient points were clear.

They watched hour after hour of sauropod crew history, rituals, ceremonies; and as the other Ship of the Law moved farther and farther from Leviathan and their encounters with the civilization there, the sauropod social structure became less and less firm.

Martin pointed out what must have been acts of murder. The sauropods needed a kind of reproductive analog without full reproduction; non-fertile eggs provided essential nutrients, apparently. But egg production dropped off, and the egg-producing sex—not precisely females, as three sexes were involved—underwent chastisement, isolation, and then death for their failures.

All of this was recorded with a solemn and unwinking attention to detail, a little slice of hell from human perspective, but day-to-day existence for the sauropods.

"Don't they see what they're doing?" Jennifer asked, aghast;

they saw the ritualized execution of the last egg-producer, multiple hammer-blows by a group of dominants, all of one sex.

Hans grunted, turned away from the flickering images.

"It'll take us a long time to riddle some of this," Giacomo said, clutching Jennifer's hand.

"Seems pretty clear to me," Hans said. "They went to Leviathan, they were given the runaround, they gave up and left. Play back the meetings."

In much clearer detail, they saw selected images and motion sequences of Leviathan's worlds, conferences with multiple-eyed, bipedal creatures that seemed to represent the civilization; these segments were particularly muddy, almost useless in terms of linear history.

A mom entered Hans' cabin. "The ship has translated all Benefactor and ship language records," the mom said. "We may call these beings Red Tree Runners."

"Why would we want to?" Hans asked.

"That is a close translation of their name for themselves. Their home system was invaded four thousand three hundred and fifty years ago, *Dawn Treader* frame of reference. They had already established a pact with representatives of the Benefactors. The killer probes were defeated and their worlds were not substantially damaged. Perhaps half of their original population survived, and they were able to rebuild. They were outfitted with ships and weapons suitable to seek out the Killers. They became part of the Benefactor alliance."

"But they weren't Benefactors themselves?" Hakim asked.

"No. You might call them junior partners."

Hans chuckled. "Higher rank than us."

"A different arrangement, under different circumstances. The Red Tree Runners traveled over one hundred light years, a journey lasting thirty Earth years by their reference frame."

"And?" Hans said.

"They arrived at Leviathan nineteen hundred years ago. Leviathan has changed considerably since then."

"We noticed," Giacomo said.

"Reasons for the changes are not clear. But they were convinced Leviathan was not their target, obtained fuel from the inhabitants of one of the worlds, and departed."

Martin shook his head. "That's all?"

"The memory store has undergone considerable decay. The Red Tree Runners may have discovered how to deactivate the ship's mind, or interfere with its operations. Over ninety percent of the records are too deteriorated for retrieval. One third of the shipboard recordings have survived, but all biological, historical, and library records of their civilization have decayed."

"Of course," Hans said dryly.

"They fell apart," Jennifer said. "They lost it and they killed themselves. Or decided to die."

Martin recalled the mummified corpses, the last of the crew, saw them lying down to accept the end.

"By God, that won't happen to us," Hans said.

"Will this information be made available to all crew members?" the mom asked.

Hans seemed startled by the question. He mused for a moment, squinted one eye, looked at Martin as if about to dress him down for some unspecified offense. "Yeah," he said. "Open to everybody. Why not. Warning to us all."

"It'll be our albatross," Harpal said. "I don't know what the others are going to think . . ."

"It's a goddamned bloody sign from heaven," Hans said. "Rosa's going to have a ball."

Wild Night was not, as the awkward name suggested, a free-for-all; boredom with lust had settled in. The occasion was treated as both a welcome home for the three travelers and a chance for the crew to let off steam after absorbing news of the death ship; to get back at authority—at the moms, and more implicitly, at Hans, with his planning and approval.

In the cafeteria, the crew enjoyed the first dinner they had had since the Skirmish that tasted like anything.

Martin had not participated in the Wild Night planning, and so was as surprised as anybody by the depth of vituperation Hans endured. Rex Live Oak cut his hair to resemble Hans', and performed a skit with three Wendys about Hans' sexual escapades. The jokes were explicit and not very funny, but brought hoots and cackles from the crew. Hans smiled grimly and tilted his head back in mock chagrin.

Martin wanted to leave before the third skit, but saw clearly that that would not have been appreciated. Group action was the call of the night, cooperation and coordination: laugh together, poke fun together, rise from the pit together. The entire atmosphere only deepened Martin's gloom; on Earth, he had never seen a social gathering turn sour, but this must have been what it was like: forced hilarity, insults and insincerity passing for humor, bitterness and sadness masking as camaraderie. Hans presided over it all with dogged equanimity, sitting slightly apart from the others at a table.

The unexpected came, of course, from Rosa Sequoia. She had been quiet for the months when Martin, Giacomo, and Hakim had been away, "Biding her time," as Hans said. Now, as the skit's players took a break, she climbed on top of the center table and began to speak.

The show's presenters could not intervene without breaking the fragile, false mood of all for one and one for all; they had started something, and Rosa took advantage of it.

"You know me," she said. "I'm the crazy one. I see things and tell stories. You think *Hans* is funny. You think you are funny. What about me?"

Nobody said a word. Uncomfortable shufflings.

"What about *us*?" Rosa's loose robe did not hide the fact that her bulk had turned to muscle, that while neither thin nor graceful, she had grown much stronger in the past four months, much more self-assured.

Her face radiated simple pleasure at being in front of them; of all the people in the crew, now only Rosa could manage a genuinely pleasant smile.

"We're flesh and blood, but we allow ourselves to be dragged across hundreds of trillions of kilometers, to fight with ghosts . . . to take revenge on people who aren't there. That's funny."

Hans' expression solidified, dangerous, head drawn back as if he might snap at a passing bug with his teeth.

But there was something about Rosa's tone that kept them in their seats. She was not going to harangue them for being foolish; nor play the doom-saying prophet, holding up the example of the corpse of a Ship of the Law to chasten them; she was up to something else.

"How many of you have had strange dreams?" she asked. That hit the mark; nobody answered or raised their hands, but a stiffening of bodies, a turning away of eyes, showed that most had. Martin looked over his crewmates, neckhair rising.

"You've been dreaming about people who died, haven't you?" Rosa continued, still smiling, still disarming.

"What about you?" Rex barked.

"Oh, yes, I've been dreaming; if you could call it dreaming, the crazy things that happen to me. I've got it bad. I don't just talk to dead people; I talk to dead ideas. I visit places none of us have thought about since we were little children. Now *that's* crazy!"

"Sit down, Rosa," Hans said.

Rosa did not flinch, did not shift her smile or narrow her eyes; she was oblivious to him.

"I've been dreaming about people who died on Earth," Jeanette said. "They tell me things."

"What do they tell you?" Rosa asked. Target acquired, audience responding, some at least warming to this change, welcoming relief from the previous cruel absurdity.

Kai Khosrau jumped in before Jeanette could answer. "My parents," he said.

"What do your parents tell you?"

"My friends when I was a little girl," Kirsten Two Bites called out. "They must be dead; they weren't on the Ark."

"What do they tell you, Kirsten?"

"My brother on the Ark," Patrick Angelfish said.

"What does he tell you, Patrick?" Rosa's face reddened with enthusiasm.

Martin's skin prickled. *Theodore.*

"They all tell us we're in a maze and we've forgotten what's important," Rosa answered herself, triumphant. "We're in a maze of pain and we can't find a way out. We don't know what we're doing or why we're here any more. We used to know. Who knows why we're here?"

"We all know," Hans said, eyes squinted, looking from face to face around him, shrewd, assessing. "We're doing the Job. We've already done more than all the others before us—"

He cut himself short, glanced at Martin, grimaced.

"We know up here," Rosa said, tapping her head. She placed her hand over her breast. "We do not know here."

"Oh, Jesus," Hans groaned. No one else said a word.

"We play and we try to laugh. We laugh at Hans, but he doesn't deserve our laughter. He's Pan. His job is tough. We should be laughing at ourselves. At our sadness."

Paola Birdsong cried out, "You're sick, Rosa. Some of us are still grieving. We don't know what to think . . . Stop this crap now!"

"We're all grieving. All our lives is grief," Rosa said. "Grief and vengeance. Hate and death. No birth, no redemption. We are like mindless knives and guns, bombs, pigeons in rockets."

"Make your point and get off," Hans said, sensing that taking her off by force would meet with strong disapproval.

"Something else speaks to me," Rosa said, chin dipping, shoulders rising.

"Monsters in the halls?" Rex Live Oak called out.

"Let her talk," Jeanette Snap Dragon demanded, angry.

Hans started to rise.

Rosa lifted her arms. "The things we fight against, we might have called gods once, but we would have been wrong. They are not gods. They aren't even close. I saw something last tenday that nearly burned me alive."

"The God of our mothers and fathers!" Jeanette sobbed.

Martin slipped from his chair and started to leave. He did not want to be here, did not want to face this.

"No!" Rosa cried. "It has a voice like chimes, like flutes, like birds, but it crosses this span of stars like a whale in the sea."

Martin froze, eyes welling up. Yes. So huge and yet it cares.

"It touches everything, and around it swirls parts of itself like bees around a flower. It . . ." She nodded self-affirmation and wiped her eyes.

"Stop this now!" Hans ordered. "Enough!"

"*It loves me!*" Rosa cried, hands held out, fingers clutching. "It loves me, and I *do not deserve its love!*"

A few of the men walked out past Martin, shaking their heads and muttering. None of the women left, though Ariel looked as if she might spit fire. Her body shook with anger, but she said nothing.

"It spoke to me. Its words ripped my head apart. Even when it was gentle, it overloaded me."

"Pray for us!" Kimberly Quartz shouted. Others yelled, "Back to the show! Get off!" Voices strained, bleating, angry.

"Then it showed itself to me," Rosa said in a stage whisper.

"What did it look like?" Kirsten Two Bites asked.

"It didn't come as a shadow. That was my preparation, my illness. I had to become sick to see, to want to see; sick and desperate and completely lost. It came to me when I was most ready, weakest and least myself. It was not a shadow, not a presence, but a folding-around. I cannot fold myself around this; it must wrap me. I saw it was not just a whale among the stars; it covered everything known. The parts of it that I saw buzzing like bees were bigger than galaxies, dancing so slowly in endless night, trying to return to the center . . ."

"They can't! We can't!" Kirsten Two Bites said.

Hans got up, caught Martin's eye, gestured for him to follow.

Martin followed him outside the schoolroom. "What the hell am I going to do?" Hans asked, shaking his head. "Some of them are into it. I should have kept the death ship secret."

"How?" Martin asked.

Hans shook his head. "If I ordered everybody out now, what would happen?"

"It would get worse," Martin said. He could still feel the tingle, the gooseflesh. He was confused; he feared Rosa, but part of him needed to hear what she had to say. He realized her message was crude, that she was undoubtedly crazy, but she had a message, and no one else did.

"If we don't do something, what'll happen to us?" Hans asked. "We might end up like those poor bastards, drifting for thousands of years!"

Martin lowered his head. He did not want to acknowledge what such an awkward, unattractive person had made him feel: the depth of their lostness.

Hans stared at him and whistled. "You too, huh?"

"No," Martin said, shaking his head. "We should break it up now."

"Just you and me?"

"I'll get Ariel and the past Pans. You stay outside. We'll meet here and go back in, announce . . ."

"Training," Hans said. "If we can get back to some kind of training . . ."

"All right," Martin said, unable to think of anything better.

Martin entered the cafeteria, Rosa started to step down, and collapsed into the arms of Jeanette Snap Dragon and Kirsten Two Bites.

The meeting broke up with a scatter of hard, fragile laughter. Jeanette and Kirsten supported Rosa out the opposite door, away from the crowd. Martin subdued an urge to follow them, to question Rosa; instead, he collected Cham and Harpal and Ariel, and told them they were meeting with Hans. Ariel was puzzled.

"Why does Hans want to see me?" she asked.

"Maybe he doesn't know yet," Martin said. "But I do."

"We're two months away from rendezvous." Hans folded his hands behind his head, leaning back on a chair that rose from the floor. Six gathered in his quarters; the past Pans, Ariel, at Martin's insistence, and Rex Live Oak, whom Hans had invited. "We're losing our edge. Martin sees this, and I'm sure the rest of you do, too. This is a shitty way to fight. Rosa isn't too far wrong; we fight ghosts, we lose our friends and gain nothing really deeply satisfying—just another step in the Job. And now we have nothing to do for months.

"We find a ship full of corpses, and the moms force us to go take a close look, stick our noses into the stink of failure. Meanwhile, we're waiting to receive strangers—new crewmates, not even human beings. Any wonder we start listening to Rosa?"

The six said nothing, waiting for a point to be made. Hans drew his lips together, said, "Am I right?"

"Right," Rex said.

Hans raised his hand over his head, spread the fingers, contemplated them.

Very melodramatic, Martin thought. *Child-like.*

Hans' mood was unreadable. Nobody else dared to speak. Martin felt some dreadful kind of grit being revealed in their Pan; tough, determined and perhaps a little perverse, even uncaring.

"The moms say we won't practise in simulations for a tenday, perhaps two," Hans said. "The hell with waiting. We forget games and free-for-alls. I don't want anybody slicking with anybody until this ship is fully prepared. I want some real tensions and angers, not these fake, shitty boredoms we have now. I'm going to have to slap this crew, hit them with work, busy work if necessary. Martin, can you figure the moms?"

Martin showed his surprise. "Beg pardon?"

"Any more insights into what they're up to?"

He fumbled for a second, shrugging, finally said, "They're making repairs still. I don't know what you—"

"Repairs hell. They made your goddamned racing boat to visit the death ship. They gave up a quarter of the fuel we gathered around Wormwood—at the cost of how many lives? Are they keeping anything else important from us?"

"I don't think so," Martin said. Ariel did not react. She seemed frozen, listening, waiting.

"We train ourselves, without simulations. We drill for discipline and to keep our blood flowing. We fight each other in physical combat. All of you will be drill instructors. Martin, Rex, and I will work up a schedule of physical endurance and combat. Hand to hand. Winners get to slick. Nobody else. We'll ask for volunteers to be rewards."

Only Rex returned his smile. The rest were astonished into blank expressions and silence. Ariel closed her eyes, swallowed.

Before now, except for his outburst following the neutrino storm, Hans' leadership instincts had always seemed acute. But Martin's gut reaction to this pronouncement was abhorrence. To go up against crewmates in zero-sum games, physical exercises, competing for the physical affection of a few—he could think of no other words for them—*prostitutes*, *whores*, seemed as far wrong as they could go.

But nobody objected, not Martin, not even Ariel. That horrified Martin more than anything else.

"Then let the games begin," Hans said.

Martin faced Jimmy Satsuma. They bowed to each other, circled warily, clinched.

In the schoolroom, fifteen other opponents faced off, circled, clinched. The room filled with grunts and shufflings, outrushes of air as bodies hit the resilient floor, slaps of flesh on flesh. Wendys wrestled Wendys, Lost Boys faced off against each other.

The family groups, already reduced and weakened by the deaths, became even weaker as Cats opposed each other, Trees and Places wrestled together, Fish and Flowers grappled with Fish and Flowers.

The ship was finding a new social order. Victors emerged; Martin came in sixth out of the top fifteen Lost Boys.

Hans picked out the top fifteen as instructors, and the next round began with additional competitions: running, variations on football, soccer, handball.

There was some satisfaction to Martin in seeing that most of the victors eschewed Hans' rewards, walking from the matches with wary, embarrassed glances. Rex Live Oak eschewed nothing, taking Donna Emerald Sea to his quarters.

Exhausted, bruised and sore, Martin spent half an hour in his quarters before sleep exploring the libraries of *Dawn Treader*. The libraries had re-opened in the past few days. There were gaps, but not large ones; about ninety-five percent had been saved or reconstructed from damaged domains. The libraries now integrated the remnants of the derelict's deep time memory store.

With the libraries restored, he felt some of the pressure of turning inward pass away. He could venture outward again, through the ship's information universe.

The zero-sum competition was not nearly as divisive as Martin had feared. There were casualties; there were abstainers. Rosa Sequoia and a few of her followers did not compete, and Hans did not compel them to. Some refused after a few attempts, and Hans did not subject them to ridicule.

Days passed.

Nobody talked much about the upcoming rendezvous. It would be like inviting strangers to join a family already having enough troubles; the thought frightened Martin, and he realized with some elation that at least now he could genuinely feel uneasy, that the journey and Hans' outrages had pulled him out of the gloom that had returned since the voyage to the death

ship, lifted that gloom sufficiently to have emotions other than
blanketing, all-too-comfortable despair.

Perhaps Hans had been right again.

Sixty-four of the crew listened to Rosa's storytelling. Hans was
not there; Ariel and Martin, at his request, attended.

Ariel had accepted Hans and Martin's attempt to bring her
into the fold of authority with surprising composure. Martin
thought of two explanations for her placidity: proximity to the
center of things gave access to crucial information, and Ariel
was no fool; and she would be closer to Martin.

Ariel sat beside Martin in the cafeteria. Martin was reasonably
sure she had been making her moves on him, in her peculiar
way, since the Skirmish.

He had been celibate since Paola Birdsong. The lure of the
flesh was nothing compared to the other conflicts he had to
resolve.

The crew came to the cafeteria singly and in triples; few
entered in pairs. The dyad structure had broken down in Hans'
exercises and rewards; those who had lost partners in the Skirmish had not yet made new matches, and only one or two new
dyads were apparent.

Rosa began her session with a parable.

"Once, back when Earth was young, three children came
upon a sick wolf in the woods. The first child was a girl, and
her name was Penelope, and she was sweet and younger than
the others, and spoke with a lisp. The second was Kim, her
brother, who did not know where to go in life, and who always
worried about fighting and winning. The third was Jacob, a
cousin, the oldest, frightened of his shadow.

"They circled the wolf and Penelope asked the wolf what was
wrong with it.

" 'I am in a trap,' the wolf said, and Penelope saw that this
was so; the wolf's paw was caught in a steel jaw chained to the
ground. 'Please release me.'

" 'Wait a minute,' Kim said. 'What if the trapper sees us?
We'll get in trouble . . .

" 'The trapper only comes once a week,' the wolf said.

" 'If you know that, then you must know where the trapper

sets his traps. How did you fall into a trap if you knew where they were?' Kim asked.

" 'You are a very smart boy, so I will tell you something,' the wolf said. 'Something very important. But first you must release me.'

" 'Are you a magic wolf?' Penelope asked. She had heard of such things.

" 'I am a sorcerer, pretending to be a wolf. I can change my shape at will, unless I am caught by iron—and this is iron.'

" 'I think we should release him,' Jacob said. 'I don't like to see live things in pain.'

" 'Wait,' Kim said. 'Maybe this is the wolf that's been killing our sheep. Maybe the trapper is doing us a favor.'

" 'That was the cougar, not me,' the wolf said. 'Have you no trust?'

" 'I trust nothing, and care for nothing, because I have been hurt when I trusted before,' Kim said.

" 'I trust you,' Penelope said.

" 'I don't know whether to trust him or not, but he's in pain,' Jacob said.

" 'What will you give us if we set you free?' Kim asked.

" 'I can grant no wish while I am trapped by iron,' the wolf answered.

" 'So you can't prove you're a sorcerer. I say let's leave him here for the trapper,' Kim said.

"But Penelope reached down to open the trap anyway. Kim saw her and tried to stop her, but Jacob fought with him, and she opened the trap, and the wolf crawled free, lay in the grass with its tongue out, and said, 'I am very ill. I will die now, because I have been in the trap so long, but I will come in your dreams and give you each what you have given to me.'

"And the wolf died. Penelope mourned, and buried its body in the woods where the trapper would not find it. Kim stalked away, angry at Jacob. And Jacob felt sad that they had not saved the wolf, and that he had lost Kim's friendship in the bargain.

"That night, the wolf came to Penelope in her dreams, but it was a slender old man wearing a wolf-fur robe, with sharp gray eyes and a wise smile. The old man said, 'To you I give long life and children, and in your old age, when your time comes to die, you will be content with the men you have loved, the children you have borne, the life you have lived . . . This I give to you.'

"To Jacob the sorcerer came as a wolf, and said, 'You will live a long life, and it will be rich and complex, with sadness and joy mixed so that often you cannot distinguish between them. Life will make you a wise soul, because it will be hard, and when you die, you will sit on God's favored side, to render advice on the affairs of men. All this you will have; but this you will lose. You will never know what is truth, and never know certainty. All things will be ambiguous, for this is the curse of wisdom.'

"To Kim, the wolf came as a wolf, and growled at him in his dreams, until the dreams became dark as nightmare. And the wolf told him, 'All your life the world will turn its hand against you. You will scheme and scheme, but gain no advantage, and learn nothing from your failures. You will not live to a ripe old age, but instead, you will die young, bitter and cheated, loved by no one. This I give to you.'

" 'And what do you give to yourself?' Kim cried out in his dream. 'You who have so much power, and can cause so much pain?'

" 'For my foolishness in being trapped, I can have nothing but oblivion. For to gain this power, long ago I sold my soul. I now have nothing. And when my ghost fades from your dream, I will be less than the echo of wind.' "

Rosa lowered her head. The crew seemed to appreciate the story, but did not applaud. They stood to leave, and Jeanette Snap Dragon said in a stage voice, "Rosa was visited again last night. Something came to her."

The crew stopped, stared at Rosa, who raised her head, eyes distant.

"We don't talk about it, but we think of the death ship a lot now," Rosa said. "We wonder why they all died, and there are no answers. I give no comfort this evening. Our greatest trial comes. Soon another kind of intelligence will join with us. We will be visited by innocents, and we will teach them pain."

Silent, without argument, the crew left the cafeteria.

Ariel followed Martin to Hans' quarters. "Well?" Rex Live Oak asked, beckoning them in as the door opened.

"She was . . . innocuous," Martin said.

"What kind of word is that?" Hans asked. "Nothing Rosa does can ever be innocuous. What did you think?" He stared at Ariel.

"She's getting better. Much stronger," Ariel said. "Jeanette and Kirsten are with her all the time now. She doesn't ask for me very often. She knows I talk to Martin and you. She's putting together disciples. I think she's building up to something."

Ariel gave Martin a fleeting smile, as if asking for approval but realizing he would not give it.

"Is that right?" Hans asked Martin.

"Whatever she's building up to, she isn't there yet," Martin said. "She spins a good story, but so far, it's just entertainment. Fairy tales."

Hans pondered for a moment. "She's not going to stick to telling stories. She's bound to have another revelation. I'm not sure we can afford to let her go off on her own. We're still close to the edge, and having visitors isn't going to make things any easier." He mused, squeezing his palms together, making small sucking sounds. "What Rosa needs is a good slicking. Any volunteers?"

The crudity stunned Martin and made Ariel's neck muscles stand out, but they did not answer.

"Not me," Rex Live Oak said casually.

"Just as I thought. I'll have to bell and feed the cat. Part of the old burden, am I right?"

"The libraries are open, the food's getting better, and the moms tell us we can use remotes to expand our baseline," Rex Live Oak said, looking around the cafeteria. "I think we're ready to meet our new comrades. Any comments, before I let the search team report?"

The crew moved restlessly for a few seconds, as if reluctant to push forward a questioner. Paola Birdsong raised her hand.

"The Pan is supposed to give us the report," she said. "Why isn't Hans here?"

"Hans is doing research now," Rex said.

"Then why not Harpal?" Erin Eire asked.

"I don't know," Rex answered flippantly. "Harpal?"

Harpal shrugged, refusing to be stung. "Rank hath its privileges. Hans can pick anybody he wants as a speaker."

"We don't need a speaker. We need the Pan himself," Erin persisted.

"I'll take your questions directly to Hans," Rex said.

Martin looked around the room. There were two conspicuous absences: Hans, of course, and Rosa Sequoia.

"Think he's giving Rosa her medicine?" Ariel whispered in Martin's ear. Martin didn't answer; if Hans was with Rosa, he must know their absence together would be noticed. If Rosa was giving in to Hans' "medicine," she was at risk of losing her unusual status, and perhaps that was Hans' intent.

Hakim cleared his throat and came forward as Rex cleared the way magnanimously with a sweep of his arm. "We are at least a half a trillion kilometers from the other ship," Hakim said. "We'll drop our camouflage in a few days. The moms think it's very doubtful anyone can detect us out here. We should be able to establish noach a few hours before rendezvous."

"Are we looking at the Cornflower?" Alexis Baikal asked.

Hakim affirmed that the Leviathan system was being studied.

"Anything new?" Bonita Imperial Valley asked.

"There are ten planets around Leviathan," Hakim said. "We have few details on the planets other than their mass and size: five rocky worlds less than twenty thousand kilometers in diameter. The sixth through the tenth planets are gas giants. They emit very little or nothing in radio frequencies. There has been no reaction to the destruction of Wormwood; no armoring, nothing. That is about all we can say for now."

"Are there other orbiting structures?" Erin Eire asked.

"Not that we can detect."

"Any explanation why they've changed since the death ship was there?" Rex asked.

Hakim shook his head. "Perhaps there has been massive engineering, as there was around Wormwood. That would be my guess. Two planets might have been broken down for raw materials."

"Are the planets inhabited?" Paola asked.

"No signs of habitation, but that is expected. We presume

they are," Hakim said, averting his eyes. "For now, there is not really much more to say."

"All right," Rex said, standing again, arms folded. "Comments? Anything for me to take to Hans?"

"We're tired of wrestling," Jack Sand said.

"I'll let him know," Rex said, smiling broadly.

Harpal came to Martin's quarters an hour after the meeting, Ariel following. "I'm going to resign as Christopher Robin," he said, stalking through the door, arms swinging loosely, fists clenched.

"I suppose I don't need to ask why," Martin said. Ariel sat with hands between her knees, lost in thought.

"I hope not. You're too smart," Harpal said. "He picks me, then he lights on Rex, and Rex does everything I should be doing . . . and I do nothing. Does that make sense?"

"He's feeling his way," Ariel said. Harpal turned on her.

"And where do you stand, Mademoiselle Critical?"

Ariel lifted her hands.

"Jesus," Harpal said. "When Martin was Pan, you were so full of bolsh we could grow mushrooms in your mouth!"

"Harpal," Martin said.

"I mean it! What's with the sudden quiet?"

"I trusted Martin," Ariel said. "He wouldn't hold things against me. Not enough to hurt me. I'm not an idiot."

This stopped Harpal cold. He simply stared at her, then at Martin, and threw his hands up in the air. "None of this makes sense."

Martin gestured with his fingers to her: *Come on, let it out.*

"Martin was sincere. He didn't calculate for effect."

"Thank you very much," Martin said with some bite.

"I mean it. You didn't measure everybody for his coffin. Hans hasn't changed . . . he's just grown into the job. Everything is weighed according to political advantage."

"Even when he blew up after the neutrino storm?" Harpal asked.

"That was genuine," she admitted, "but it put people in their place. Where he wanted them to be—a little afraid of him. He's big. He hits when he's angry. He's not exactly predictable. So people are more wary and they don't speak up. Big, smart bully. Or didn't you notice?'' She looked at Harpal accusingly.

"I don't see how he could plan such outbursts," Martin said.

"You can't tell me you haven't noticed his skills," she said, eyes glittering. Martin saw the former Ariel again, saw she was keeping her anger and dismay tightly wrapped, and felt a fresh surge of concern.

"He's a better Pan than I was."

"Maybe better at manipulating. He knows what he wants."

"He pulled us out of a pit," Martin said, realizing his Devil's advocacy. He wanted to see how much Ariel's views coincided with his—all unvoiced, even unconfirmed in his own mind.

"He put us there in the first place," she countered.

Harpal sat and crossed his legs. Martin and Ariel both looked to him for comment. "Good Pan, bad Pan," he said softly, in wonder.

"The crew puts a lot of faith in the Pan. Martin was good— if a little gullible—because everybody knew they could talk to him, and he wouldn't hurt them, wouldn't even think of it," Ariel said. "I spoke up because I thought I could argue him into seeing certain important things . . .''

"You went at it pretty forcefully," Martin said.

"I've never claimed to be subtle. When will you resign?"

Harpal squinted. "When the time's right," he said. "Can anybody tell me why he's courting Rosa?"

"He's doing more than courting her," Ariel said. "Rosa's still in his room. You know she hasn't had a real friend for years?"

Martin nodded. "He thinks she's on to something."

"What?" Harpal asked.

"Something we need," Martin said, and Ariel nodded.

"What?" Harpal asked again, genuinely puzzled.

"Faith," Martin said.

Harpal drew back as if bitten. "You're kidding."

"Not at all," Martin said. "She's getting closer and closer to the mark. I've felt it myself." He tapped his chest.

"I'm completely lost now," Harpal said. "I don't deserve to be second. I'm out of touch."

"Things are going to get a lot more complicated very soon," Martin said. "Let's see how he handles the situation."

Ariel surprised him by agreeing completely. "He's made mistakes . . . But he's still in charge, and we're still ready to do the Job."

Harpal stood in the door. "If he accepts my resignation, that's fine by me," he said. "But why did he pick Rex? Rex is not the smartest person on the ship. He knows nothing about leadership."

Martin held back the most obvious and the darkest answer he could think of: *Rex won't say no.*

Hans kept to the back of the cafeteria, smiling benignly. Rosa stood on a table; sixty-three of the crew listened intently.

"In two days," she said, "we'll meet our new colleagues . . . What will they be like? What will they think and believe? How can we accommodate them? Interact with them? What are *we,* to *them?*"

The crew did not answer. Martin sat a few meters from Hans, beside Harpal and Ariel. Hans winked at Martin.

Rosa looked radiant; the beauty of intense compassion, of selflessness. Awkward Rosa had melted finally, giving way to a new woman; had the defining moment occurred in Hans' arms? Hans revealed nothing.

"In the scale of things, we are the very smallest of intelligences, the very dimmest of lights. Yet like plankton in Earth's seas, we lay the foundations for all the complex glory above us. We are the food and eggs and seed of all intelligence, up to and including that radiant center beyond all understanding. A disturbance in the sea of little thinking creatures can move up the spiritual food column with disastrous consequences, though it may take an age; and so the highest regards the lowest with more than just disinterested love, for we are ultimately *them,* part of their flesh, if they have flesh, part of their histories, and their futures . . .

"The colleagues joining us have undoubtedly suffered as we have. They have lost their home world, have wandered for centuries in foreign shells, and have fought and lost loved ones, all to vanquish the poison, the death of the planet killers. We join with them now, and the little intelligences merge . . . And it is noticed by those high above us, those in attendance on the Most High, the galaxies of bright spirituality that rotate around the unimaginably vast center . . . And that notice is not just a kind of love, it *is* love, compared to which the love we feel for the parts of our own body, for our own flesh, is a cheap imitation.

"Our success or failure has a larger meaning. When we die, we are not just lost; I have felt the cradle of the Most High coming for our dead, to embrace their memories, their essence, and draw them to the center, where there is eternal motion and eternal rest, peace and the center of all action."

"She hasn't read her Aquinas," Ariel whispered to Martin.

But what Rosa said sounded good to him. Martin needed to know that Theresa and William were happy, that they had found rest; that sardonic and razor-sharp Theodore and all the others were appreciated somewhere, that perhaps they floated in a sea of painless interaction, showing their highest qualities to something that might finally appreciate them . . .

"When our ships join, we join purposes as well. All our goals must mesh. We are here not to satisfy the moms, but to clean the seas of a poison that could reach to the center itself. Call it evil, call it senseless greed, call it maladaptation . . . It is separate from the Most High, and the Most High does not cherish it.

"The cup-bearers of planetary death are not among the lights in attendance to the Most High; they are caught in a vicious cycle of pain and fear. We have felt their fear. It killed our home planet and it has killed our friends; the time has come for us to apply the burning iron to that fear, and to send the Killers back to where they can again become part of the column, rise in usefulness again to the Most High.

"But we will not receive divine aid. Though there are things repugnant to the highest intelligences, the greatest spirits, they do not give us their powers and insights when we fight the repugnant things. That would be a kind of interference even more evil than senseless murder; a confusion of scales, the Most High stifling the potential of the low, where all creativity, all creation begins. We are on our own, but our struggle is not senseless."

"What do the moms think of this?" Harpal asked Martin in a low voice.

Martin shook his head.

"The story I tell this evening is of war. Nothing gentle, nothing soothing, it reminds us of what we face still, and may face for centuries more, before we can lay down our weapons and take up the duties of living for ourselves."

"Why can't I feel the touch and see what you've seen?" Nguyen Mountain Lily asked.

Rosa looked puzzled for an instant, then smiled again and raised her hands, sweeping all around. "The Most High is never not touching us. But it does not tell us what to do, and it does not speak to us in words; its presence is the conviction we all feel, that there must be a loving observer to whom we are very important, and who loves us.

"The love the Most High feels is not the love of sexuality and reproduction—it is the love of one of us for our own bodies, our own cells, a constant love made of care and nourishment. But we do not interfere with our own cells."

Martin could poke holes in this like ripping a finger through rotten cloth, but he did not want to; he found himself explaining away the inconsistencies, the poor metaphors, as weaknesses in Rosa's perceptions, not in her message.

"I don't think anything watches me, or cares about me," Thorkild Lax said. "I watch out for myself and for my crewmates."

"I felt that way. I felt lost," Rosa said. "I thought no one cared—not my crewmates, certainly. I was slovenly, out of touch. I didn't really belong. No one was more lost than I was. But there was this final loving in me, this urge to reach out." She folded her hands in front of her, then swept them out and up like two parting doves, fingers spread. "I reached out in the middle of my pain—"

"Enough of this shit," a masculine voice called out. "Tell the story."

The crowd turned and Martin saw George Dempsey, blushing at the accumulated stares. He got up, started to leave, but Alexis Baikal reached up and held on to his hand, pulled him gently down, and he sat.

Martin felt a warmth, and then a tremor of unease. The group spirit, the bonding again—the wish for strong answers, for transcending love. *The special time.*

He thought of his father and mother, and the touch his father could give, and the warmth of his mother, large and all-encompassing, the way she wore full dresses to cover her ample figure, the sweetness of her round face wrapped in dark silken hair, the complex and giving love of both; and he thought of that love writ large, the beginning place for that sort of love.

"How do I reach up and out?" Terry Loblolly asked, voice small in the cafeteria.

"When you need to, you will do it as a hungry flower blooms beneath the sun," Rosa said. "If you do not need enough, you will not; your time is not yet."

"If we don't love, does the Most High blame us? Does he hate us?"

"The Most High is neither male nor female. It does not blame, it does not judge. It loves, and it gathers." She curled her arms as if to gather unseen children to her breast and hug them.

"I need that touch badly," Drusilla Norway said. "But I don't feel it. Is that my fault?"

"You have no faults except in your own eyes. All fault is human judgment."

"Then who will punish us for our sins?" Alexis Baikal asked, voice distorted with sorrow.

"Only ourselves. Punishment is our way of training ourselves for this level of life. The Most High does not acknowledge a court of law, a court of judgment. We are forgiven before we die, every moment of every day, whether we seek forgiveness or not."

Martin thought of Theresa waiting at the end of this long journey to explain these things to him, part of the all-enveloping warmth; he put Theresa's face over Rosa's, and wanted to sleep in the comfort of this thought, hoped it would not go away.

"Is Jesus Christ the son of the Most High?" Michael Vineyard asked.

"Yes," Rosa said, her smile broadening. "We are all its children. Christ must have felt the warmth like a fusion fire, even more strongly than I do. It glows from his words and deeds. The Buddha also felt the warmth, as did Muhammad . . ."

Hakim seemed displeased to hear the Prophet's name in Rosa's mouth.

". . . And the many prophets and sages of Earth. They were mirrors to the sun."

"All of them?" Michael persisted.

"All knew part of the truth."

"Do you know only part?" Michael asked.

"A small part. You must explain the rest to me," Rosa said. "Tell me what you find in yourselves."

In murmurs, in challenges and questions, in Rosa's parables and explanations, give and take, for the next two hours the crew spoke and confessed. A current went through the room as something palpable, as if she were a tree, and the wind of feeling passed around her, through her. When others in the crew cried, Martin found tears in his own eyes; when others laughed with a revelation of joy, he laughed also.

"I am not a prophet," Rosa said. "I am simply a voice, no better than yours."

"How can we hate our enemies, when they are just like us?" someone asked.

"We do not hate them; but they are not just like us, they are desperately *wrong* and we fight them with all our strength, for that is how we correct the imbalances. We must never be cruel, and we must never hate, for that damages us; but we must never forget our duties."

Martin felt the Job fall into place in his thoughts; nothing holy about death and destruction, but a necessary part of their existence, their duty. A natural act, action to reaction.

Nothing they did was sanctioned; nothing they did was judged except by themselves, and by the standards that flooded them from the light of the Most High. The passion of revenge had no place here; it was an abomination. But the duty of correcting the balance, that was as essential as the breath in his lungs and the blood in his veins.

Groups pushed in close around Rosa, hands linked. Together they sang hymns, the wordless Hum, Christmas carols, ballads, whatever they remembered, while others searched the libraries for more songs. All their musical instruments had been absorbed in the emergency, but their voices remained.

The singing lasted an hour. Some were hoarse and weary, and some fell asleep on the floor, but still Rosa ministered to them. Jeanette Snap Dragon brought her a chair and she sat in it atop the table, her red hair standing out in radiant frizz around her head. Jeanette and others sat around her, on the table, at her feet. Jeanette placed her head on Rosa's knees and seemed to sleep.

Others came, until almost all the crew filled the cafeteria. Some looked bewildered, feeling the current, but not letting it pass through them yet; hopeful but confused, resistant but needy.

The special time. Ariel came close to him and he hugged her as a sister. She looked up at him, head against his shoulder, and he smiled, loving all his fellows.

At Rosa's request, the floor softened. The crew lay together on the floor, around the table, as the other tables and chairs lowered and were absorbed. Jeanette's wand projected light behind Rosa and the room fell dark.

"Sleep," Rosa said, her hair an indistinct shadow in the rosy glow. "Soon we begin our duties again. Sleep in peace, for there is work to do. Sleep, and reach into your dreams to find the truth. When you sleep you are most open to the wishes of your friends, and to the love of the Most High. Sleep."

Martin closed his eyes.

Someone tapped his shoulder. Hans kneeled beside him. He shook Martin, whispered into his ear, "Cut it out. Come with me."

Martin rose, a shock like electricity tingling through him. He seemed stuck between two worlds, shame and exaltation. Hans' grim expression and tense marching posture seemed a reproof. Ariel followed, and at first it seemed Hans might send her back, but he said, "All right. Both of you."

Rex Live Oak stood in the corridor, smiling wolfishly.

"Fantastic," Hans said, shaking his head. "She's so good. She's got them all now."

Martin's head cleared as if with a dash of ice water.

"She just needed a little help and encouragement," Hans

said. Rex chuckled. "I damn near felt it myself. Didn't you? I think we have this situation under control now."

Ariel touched Martin's shoulder but he shrugged away the touch.

"All she needed was a little reason to live, something just for herself," Hans said.

"Don't slick her too much," Rex said. "Keep her lean and hungry."

Hans shook his head ruefully. "Got to ration my blessings," he said. "I only have so much to be generous with."

Rex and Hans walked along the corridor. Ariel watched Martin for a moment and saw the anger on his face. "You didn't know?" she asked, astonished. "He coached her, Martin. He's been whispering in her ear for days."

His eyes filled and he wiped them. He turned to stamp into another corridor, away from the cafeteria.

Ariel followed. "I'm sorry!" she said. "I assumed you knew! It was so obvious . . ."

"What was obvious?" Martin asked, still fleeing.

"He was turning Rosa, directing her to shore up the Job. Otherwise she could tear us apart. He thinks—"

"Thinks what?" Martin asked, stopping at the join to the neck. A ladder field appeared and he gripped it with his hand, preparing to descend.

Ariel caught up with him, still astonished by his naïveté. She dropped her voice, murmuring as if embarrassed. "Hans is very smart. He sees that this vision can help him control the crew. He told us so. Remember?"

"Yeah?" The word came out loud and harsh.

"She's warm and cozy in his arms. He says something, you know, about the Job, and our relation to God, something like that. She's happy, she's flattered. She's never been an ascetic by choice. She listens. She goes his way." Ariel spread her arms, eyes narrow, puzzled. "So for him, everything's great."

Martin felt like hitting out, and he went so far as to clench his fist. "Why are you following me?" he shouted. "Why don't you just stay the hell away from me?"

"Hans is dangerous," Ariel said in a conspiratorial, husky

voice. "He's hollow inside, and the more he settles in, the hollower he gets. He thinks the Wendys are cattle. He thinks we're *all* cattle."

"Crap," Martin said.

Ariel's face reddened and her eyes narrowed even more, to angry slits. She spat out, "What are you, *celibate*? Do you plan on being solitary for the rest of the journey? Is that why you hate me?"

Martin grimaced and laddered into the neck, leaving Ariel behind.

"God damn you!" she cried out after him.

Giacomo and Jennifer hung beside the star sphere in the schoolroom. The ship had stopped accelerating twelve hours before, and all drifted free now. Ladder fields crossed the periphery of the schoolroom and shimmered along what had once been floor and ceiling.

Hakim, Li Mountain and Luis Estevez Saguaro quietly arranged for echoes of the sphere to appear around the schoolroom.

Martin entered alone, stared at the central sphere, and took a deep breath.

They were nine billion kilometers from their future companions, about two days from a merger. The two ships had matched courses and now edged slowly closer.

Harpal came in behind Martin. "Why so many?" he asked, sweeping his arm at the five spheres.

"Hans aims for effect," Martin said.

Hakim climbed along a ladder field, hooked his foot, and hung beside them. He did not smile. "Races over?" he asked.

Hans was making sure the crew was exhausted before bringing them into the schoolroom.

"Almost," Martin said. "Ten, fifteen minutes."

"It seems silly to me, all this exercise," Hakim said. "We could be doing science, anything but rolling like squirrels in a cage."

"Hans has his plans," Harpal said.

"Who's winning?" Jennifer called from across the schoolroom.

"Rex," Martin said carelessly. He climbed in closer to the

main sphere. The image of the other Ship of the Law appeared distinct, about two hand-breadths wide, three eggs swallowed by a snake. "They don't look damaged," he said.

"The ship is smaller than *Dawn Treader* used to be," Giacomo said. "About half the size. It must have taken some pretty substantial hits. I wonder where they fought? What they did?"

"I don't see any fuel cells," Harpal said.

A mom entered the schoolroom. They had seen so little of the moms in recent tendays that Martin was startled by it. "Hans has not made a tenday report," it said to Martin and Harpal, matter-of-factly, no judgment implied. "Is there something wrong?"

Martin swallowed; for Hans to ignore the tenday was . . . What? What did they expect? Hans had restructured the society of the *Dawn Treader*, just as the ship itself had been rebuilt. Why should anything surprise Martin?

Hakim looked to Martin, no sign of natural cheer or even excitement; eyes wary. Betray nothing.

"I don't think so," Martin said. He no longer wanted to play the advocate for the office of Pan, to defend Hans, to judge the situation in the best light. He could not ignore the knot in his stomach whenever he saw Hans' confident, strong features, or Rosa's intoxicated beatitude.

"There is information to be presented to the crew," the mom said. "I am here to report. Is a meeting scheduled?"

"Yes," Martin said.

"Hans shouldn't shirk the reports," Harpal muttered.

"There are problems?" the mom asked. Martin's embarrassment turned to anger in a flash and he crossed his arms, shook his head.

"No problems," he said. *Nothing I can pin down in words. Hans does nothing overt; the worst he does is change things without consulting us . . . and why should he? The crew follows him almost without question. He doesn't act like a tyrant; he just glowers, and that's enough.*

We're back to being children again. Hans is Daddy; Rosa is Mommy. So what will we call the moms now? Auntie?

We're one big happy family.

"When will the crew convene?" the mom asked.

"In a few minutes," Hakim said.

"I will wait."

The Wendys and Lost Boys started filing in a half hour later, sweating and flushed. Hans had insisted on trying new sports in the weightless conditions. Three or four had arms in makeshift slings. They gathered in loose groups, no longer according to family or namesake; Hans had dissolved those connections.

Hans and Rex came in last.

All eyes turned to the spheres, weary, interested but shielding responses.

Hakim began his description: the second ship's length, mass, the approximate amount of fuel it carried. He glanced nervously at the mom, wondering if it would merely repeat what he was saying. He seemed to fear becoming redundant; Hans seldom conferred with the search team.

"I think the mom has something to tell us," Hans said when Hakim stammered into silence. Hakim nodded and backed away.

"We will now prepare you for the meeting with your new partners," the mom said. "Noach communications have been established with this Ship of the Law, which is called *Journey House* by its crew. We have many more details. May I take control of the displays?"

"Of course," Hans said.

The first image in the spheres puzzled the crew: a long black cable. Martin had to concentrate to understand what he was seeing. The first guess would have been a tentacle, or perhaps a snake, but close inspection showed that this was more than an individual being. The image moved, and the crew reacted with shock.

The cable disassembled into a squirming pile of serpents, and then quickly reassembled. Martin wondered whether this was a simulation or the image of a real creature.

"These are colonial intelligences," the mom said. "Such a configuration is not unusual. Many worlds support bionts that combine to form larger bionts, even in more advanced evolutionary phases. Your new partners are of this type. Between ten and twenty components come together to form an intelligent individual. The components"—A single blunt-ended tube with

grasping hooks at one end and millipede-like feet at the other—
"are seventy to eighty centimeters long, and are not in themselves intelligent, though they perform many social and practical roles. The components are responsible for gathering food, though not for agriculture or preparing food. They are responsible for reproduction and nurture their offspring. When the offspring are mature, they are instructed in the basics of forming combinations, and these combinations are then raised and educated by fully mature aggregates."

More images: aggregates ranging in size (a human silhouette for comparison) from two meters long, comprising ten intertwined components, to five meters, and fifty centimeters to a meter thick.

"They are oxygen breathers. An atmosphere conducive to both species, human and aggregates, will be maintained in all common areas of the ship, though separate quarters will also be available."

Martin glanced at Hans. Not a hint of shrewd speculation, not a trace of anything but shock. Here was strangeness that exceeded Hans' expectations.

"Their foodstuffs are not edible for humans, nor is your food sufficient for their needs. Contact is not dangerous, provided certain rules are followed. Components must not be molested or impeded in their duties; they can't respond socially beyond a limited—"

"Like my wanger," Rex Live Oak cracked. Some of the crew laughed nervously.

"A limited range of interactions with their kind, guided largely by instinct. Components can be dangerous if they are molested. They can inflict a painful bite. We do not yet know how toxins for this species might affect humans—"

"Christ, they're poisonous?" Rex asked, astonished.

"That is a possibility. But they will not attack unless severely molested. Aggregates are highly intelligent, capable of complex social interactions. We are confident they can mimic human speech better than humans can learn their methods of communication, which are chemical and auditory. To your senses, their variety of smells should be pleasant."

The promise of pleasant smell wasn't cutting much ice. The crew looked on the images with open mouthed amazement and half-controlled revulsion.

"What do we call them?" Ariel asked.

"Good question," Erin Eire commented. "I don't think calling them snakes is a good idea."

"Or worms," Jeanette Snap Dragon added.

"What in hell are they?" someone else asked.

"They are aggregate intelligences," the mom said, not making the mystery any shallower.

"But what the hell is that?" Rex asked. "How do they think? How do they fight?"

"The proper question," Hans said, "is how—and if—we're going to cooperate with them."

Martin stepped forward. "Of course we're going to cooperate," he said, as if challenging Hans directly. Hans took the challenge without hesitation.

"Martin's right. We're going to get along, whatever they're called. Which takes us back to an earlier question. What do we call them?"

"What will they call *us*?" Erin Eire interrupted.

Hans ignored her. "Suggestions? The moms seem to be leaving this up to us. I assume they don't use any name we could *smell*, much less pronounce . . ."

"Do they have sexes?" Rosa asked, voice sweet and clear over the murmuring.

"The components can be male or female or both, depending on environmental conditions. They give live birth to between one and four young every two years. Aggregates do not engage in any sexual activity; sex occurs only among separated components."

The crew mulled this over in silence; stranger and stranger, perhaps more and more alarming.

"We could call the components cords," Paola suggested. "The aggregates could be braids."

"Good," Hans said. "Anything better?"

"We'll call them Brothers," Rosa said, as if it were final. "A new part of our family."

Hans raised one eyebrow and said, "Sounds fine to me."

The names stuck. Cords, braids: Brothers. A new addition to the family of Wendys, Lost Boys, and moms.

Dawn Treader and *Journey House* would merge to make a single vessel nearly as large as *Dawn Treader* had originally been.

Communication between *Dawn Treader* and *Journey House* passed along the noach at a furious rate; hour by hour, the libraries expanded.

Martin, just before sleep, toured the libraries' new extensions and found himself in territories that had not existed before, filled with streaming bands of projected colors, tending to the reds and greens; sounds like aspirated music—haunting, sweet, and disturbing at once; and images of enormous complexity, swimming and flowing as if projected on dense fog. Some images were expressed in rotated and skewed multiples, as if they might be viewed by many eyes, each having a slightly different function.

He checked to see how many of the crew were exploring these fresh territories. The wand reported fifteen so engaged, including himself; the rest, it seemed, were waiting to be pushed.

The size of the libraries had trebled in just a day. If the libraries had been reduced by a tenth during the neutrino storm, then the Brothers' libraries had held just over twice as much information as theirs. Martin was eager to have that translated, if translation was possible; perhaps they would have to learn how to see and understand differently.

Before shutting off the wand, he requested a kind of judgment from the libraries: how the Brothers compared to other beings of whom the Benefactors were aware.

"In a range of deviance from your norm, the Brothers are perhaps halfway along an arbitrary scale of biological differences," the library voice responded.

Martin sensed something new in this answer; something fresh and perhaps useful. They might be dealing with the merged intelligences of both ships' minds; and he thought it more than a little possible that, for whatever reason, the new combination would be more informed, and more willing to inform the crews.

Before falling off into muddled dreams, Martin realized what this could mean, if true.

They're more confident. We're closing in; there aren't many surprises left.

Another voice—it might have been Theodore's—seemed to laugh ironically. *How wrong do you want to be? Keep working at it . . . You might break a record . . .*

Hans gathered the remaining ex-Pans—and Rex Live Oak. They met in the nose, with the search team absent, and looked across a few infinitesimal kilometers to *Journey House*.

"The ships join tomorrow at fifteen hundred. We'll all wait in the cafeteria," Hans said. His face looked drawn, older. Circles shadowed his eyes. "But we're going to meet a few of the Brothers first. They're coming over in one of their craft in two hours. Three of them, three of us. The moms say they can't predict how we'll interact. For once, I think they're being absolutely square with us. I'd like Martin and Cham to join me. We'll meet them together. Before then, the moms are going to give us background on the individuals." He looked around the group with one eyebrow raised, as if expecting a challenge. Quietly, he asked, "Any suggestions?"

Harpal said, "As Pan's second, I'd like to go."

"Cham is better suited to meeting live ropes," Hans said. It wasn't clear to the others whether that was a joke or not.

"Then I'd like to resign as Christopher Robin," Harpal said.

"Fine."

Harpal waited for someone to object, to rise to his defense. No one did. He nodded, jaw clenched, and backed away.

"Not that you haven't done a good job," Hans said. "I'm not appointing anyone in your place. Anything you'd like me to ask our new friends?" He made the inquiry with unctuous solicitation, rubbing the moment in.

"Ask them what they regard as a mortal insult," Harpal said. "I don't want to get on their bad side if they're poisonous."

"We'll get all this culture stuff straightened out. Right now—and I think that's a good question, Harpal, but it can wait—right now, I'd like to see just how much personality the braids actually have. How we connect, what sort of fellows they are."

"I think a woman should go with us," Martin said. "A different point of view."

Hans cocked his head to one side, considered for a moment, and replied, "Bad idea. I've watched the Wendys closely, and I think they're going to take longer to adjust than the Lost Boys. Maybe it's a snake or phallic thing. Just look at their faces when the Brothers move. Stephanie maybe, but she's not with us any more."

"They scare me, too," Rex said.

"Here's what I think we should do," Hans said, and he told them.

Martin, Hans, and Cham waited in the weapons store. The air in the hemisphere had cooled to just above freezing and smelled faintly of metals and salt. Hans straightened his overalls and cleared his throat. "We'll meet them casual," he said. "No hands out, nothing. Let them make the first gesture."

"What if we all just stand here?" Cham said.

"I'm patient," Hans said.

A mom entered the store and floated next to Hans. "The craft approaches now," it said.

"Christ, I'm nervous," Hans said.

A field glowed around the pylon, which pushed through a darkness in the bulkhead. Faint clunks and hums resonated throughout the chamber. The pylon returned, bringing at its tip like a fly on a frog's tongue a round craft about three meters wide with a conical protrusion, much like a squat pear. The pylon set the craft gently in a field, and the field wrapped it in purple, lowering it to the floor of the chamber.

"Our gravity will be slightly heavy for them," the mom said. "But they are very adaptable."

"Good," Hans said. His throat bobbed.

Maybe he's got a snake thing, too, Martin thought.

The pear-shaped craft opened a hatch. Within, like rope in a ship's locker, coiled three of the Brothers: red and black, cords gleaming like rich leather. They did not move at first. Then, with uncanny grace, a braid uncoiled from the mass and slid to the floor, the forward end rising and making a faint chirping noise, like summer crickets.

The second and third braids followed, and stood before the three humans separated by only a few meters of floor. Martin

smelled fruity sweetness, like cheap perfume. He did not feel
repugnance, or even fear; only child-like fascination, as if these
were wonderful new puzzles. *I like them.*

The central braid coiled its rear and lifted its front end two
meters above the floor. Then, in birdlike, chirping English, it
said, "We we are very pleased to be with you."

Hans swallowed again, eyes wide, and said, "Welcome to
the *Dawn Treader*. To our ship."

"Yes," said the central braid. "We we must all be curious
to know. I we do not see any of females. Odd must be very odd
to have two sexes when you together are thinking."

Cham grinned. Hans swallowed again. "Not so odd," he said.

"Let get closer, and touch," the Brother continued. "It is
perhaps best to know what we we are."

Cham and Martin stepped forward as the central braid swayed
and the other two lowered themselves to lie at full length on the
floor.

"You may touch any of we us," the Brother said. "I we am
speaking because this individual is most skilled this time at
your language. I we will pass this along to other individuals by
teaching and by giving parts of myself."

Martin bent down next to the leftmost braid and put out his
hand. The cords glistened, their smooth skins finely wrinkled.
Hans stood behind Martin, not stooping.

Cham touched the rightmost braid, stroked it with his palm.
"It's warm," he said. "Almost hot."

Martin could feel the heat even before contact was made, like
a dampered stove.

The braid shifted beneath his touch, and a cord slowly uncurled four legs, touching, scraping Martin's hand. Now he
shivered; the touch was like pointed fingernails.

The smell became tangy and sweet, like wine.

"You are not touching," the central Brother said to Hans.
"Touch."

Hans closed his eyes and gathered his courage. He reached
out, and in a move that surprised Martin completely, wrapped
his arms around the Brother and squeezed gently. The Brother
wriggled beneath the pressure.

The air smelled like fresh soil.

"How do we look to you?" Hans asked, glancing up at the front end. Cords made a kind of knot there, small black eyes—four per cord—rising as the knot undid itself and the cords splayed to inspect Hans' face.

"In your visible light, you are quite interesting," the Brother said. "Like nothing familiar to we us."

"We have creatures called snakes or worms," Hans said huskily. Sweat beaded his cheeks and forehead. "You remind us of them . . ."

"You do not like snakes or worms? They mean harm or negatives to you?"

"I'll get over it," Hans said, looking down at Martin. "Not too bad, huh?"

"You're doing fine," Martin said.

"Thanks," Hans said, stepping back. "You fellows would be great on a cold night."

"He means," Cham said, "that to us you feel quite warm, pleasant."

"You are pleasing cool," the Brother said. "Now companions will speak. Pardon language. Lacking tongues, we we make sounds with air expelled between parts of components, and with friction on legs interior we our fore part."

"Like horns and violins," Martin said.

"I'll be damned," Hans said.

"It is true that you always are," the rightmost braid said, the tone sharp and scraping, vowels mere lapses between tones.

Martin, Cham, and Hans looked at each other, puzzled. Martin pondered if the aggregate was echoing Hans' proclamation of damnation; Cham figured out that the statement was actually a question. "I think he's asking, are we always the same person. Do our arms and legs run away when we aren't looking."

Hans grimaced. "We're always the same," he said. The central braid issued a series of cricket chirps and the air smelled of something rich and perhaps not entirely fresh. "Our bodies stay together."

"We our guide tells us so," the middle aggregate said. "It is difficult for we us to think about."

"I understand," Hans said. "Your lifestyle . . . your life is difficult for us to imagine, too."

"But we we can friendly," the rightmost aggregate chirped and sang.

"Friendly we are," Hans said, smiling giddily at Martin and Cham.

"You do have no like we us?" the rightmost asked.

"Nothing like we us," the middle clarified.

"Where we . . . come, came from," Martin began, "colonial, aggregate creatures—beings . . ." He paused and took a deep breath. The three aggregates made a breathy noise as well. "Creatures made of parts existed only in simple animals and plants."

"Insects," Cham said.

"What?" Martin asked.

"Insects came together to make flowers," Cham said.

"Different," Martin said.

"Stuff it," Hans said under his breath.

"May we we see records of these colonials?" the middle asked.

"Certainly," Hans said.

"Do you regard them with disliking?" the middle asked.

"I've never met any of them, actually," Hans said. Martin admired the insouciance of the answer and hoped it wasn't lost on or misinterpreted by their new partners.

"Think in reality you are colonials, only individual is big social, society," the rightmost said.

"I think he means we're part of a social group, and that's the real individual," Cham said. "Interesting idea. Maybe we can discuss it when we know each other better."

"Do you fight each other?" the middle asked.

None of the humans answered for long seconds. Then Martin said, "Not usually, no. Do you?"

"Constituent parts may fight outside we our control," the middle aggregate said. "Do not interfere. It is normal."

Hans controlled a shiver. Martin said, "We play games, competition, to keep ourselves fit. They are a kind of fighting, but generally, nobody gets hurt."

"Components may be violent," the middle said. "No interference. It is normal. They have no minds alone."

"Make a note," Hans said to Martin facetiously. "Don't step on them."

"We we are interested how we our components react to you," the middle said.

"So are we," Hans said.

The rightmost braid touched "heads" with the middle braid and smoothly disassembled. The air smelled of vinegar and fruit. The components, fourteen of them, lay in an interwoven pile, like centipedes or snakes taught macramé. Slowly, the cords crawled apart, spreading out on the floor until they encountered the humans.

Hans' face dripped and he smelled rank. Martin felt no better.

"Shit shit shit," Cham said, but kept his place.

The cords gently nudged their feet and calves. Several cords used this opportunity to lock lengthwise and roll back and forth.

"Mating?" Hans asked.

"Dominance on their level," the middle braid responded. "It is not fighting to kill. You might call it rough play."

"Your English is wonderful," Martin said, trying to hide his fear.

"I have fine components, and am blessed with interior harmony," the middle replied.

"Congratulations," Hans said.

The two aggregates chirped and whistled to each other. The air smelled of baking bread and sulfur.

One component advanced up Cham's pantsleg, front feelers spread wide. Martin had noticed that the feelers fit into rear invaginations when the cords locked together.

Cham could barely control his trembling.

"Our companion is not comfortable," Martin said.

"I'm fine," Cham said.

"We we anticipate distress," the middle braid said. "Must you get accustomed."

"We must," Hans said, more to Cham than in answer.

"Right," Cham said. The cord crawled up his leg to his side.

"It is not behaving violently," the middle braid reassured.

"By the way," Cham said, his voice high-pitched and shaky.

"We use names to address each other." The cord advanced around his chest, slipped, grabbed hold of the overalls material.

"You may touch it," the middle braid said.

"How do we . . . what names can we use for you?"

"We we have discussed," the middle said. "As each of we our aggregates learn language, they will pick names. You may call I me mine Stonemaker. Disassembled braid, when together again may be Shipmaker. Other may be Eye on Sky."

"Enjoy stars," the leftmost braid said.

"Like Hakim," Martin said.

"Your names," the middle braid requested.

"Our names are sounds, sometimes without meaning," Martin said. "I am Martin. This is Hans. And this is Cham."

"Bread and jam food," the leftmost said.

"Cham, not jam," Cham corrected.

"Martin animal," Stonemaker observed. "From word lists."

"Hands for picking up with," said Eye on Sky.

Hans smiled stiffly.

"Do you like component, Jam?" the middle braid asked Cham.

"It hurts when it grabs," Cham said. "Can you speak to them?" The cord's feelers explored his face. Cham bent his neck back as far as he could.

"No," Stonemaker said. "But we we make them assemble. Looks it enjoys humans."

"Wonderful," Cham said.

"No biting," Stonemaker observed.

"Yes, we've had some concerns . . . about that," Hans said. "Can they hurt us?"

"That would be distressing," Stonemaker said.

"End of aggregate whose part did wrong," Eye on Sky added.

"Wouldn't want that, would we?" Cham said. He put his hands up to stroke the cord, which had crawled lower. It had wrapped around his chest, tail under right arm, head and feelers under left, and stopped moving.

"It likes the way you smell," Martin said to reassure his crewmate.

"Very true," Stonemaker said. "To me self my you smell friendly."

They don't know us very well. We stink of fear, Martin thought.

"Good," Hans said. "If Stonemaker agrees, we'll try a larger group next. Twenty of our crew, twenty of his individuals. Then we'll combine *Dawn Treader* and *Journey House* and carry on with the Job."

Stonemaker chirped and the room smelled of tea and lilac. The cord dropped abruptly from Cham's chest and landed on the floor with a hollow smack, then aligned with the other cords beside Stonemaker and reassembled. The braid reared and stretched until it touched the base of the pylon, twelve feet over their heads.

"We my components reproduced and made Shipmaker," Stonemaker said. "He is either brother or son, perhaps we we talk which sometime."

Twenty of the human crew and twenty Brothers gathered in the schoolroom. Martin could not tell the Brothers apart yet. Clicks and chirps and bowed violin speech; Rosa Sequoia, approaching and embracing a Brother; Paola Birdsong singing to another; there was a carnival atmosphere to the meeting that set Martin at ease. However strange the Brothers might seem, there was enough common ground and likable traits for both sides to demonstrate quick, almost easy friendship.

Ariel stayed close to Martin after the first ten minutes. "It's going well," she said.

"Seems to be."

"I thought it would take a while," she said.

"So did I. They haven't broken down into cords yet. Cords aren't quite as personable."

"So Cham told me. The difference between animals and people. Will that cause problems?"

Martin pushed his lips out, frowned. "Probably," he said. "I think we can adjust."

"We've been stuck with each other for so long," said Jennifer. "It's nice to have somebody new to talk to." She walked past Martin and Ariel, a Brother following closely, chattering in broken English about numbers. Martin smelled cabbage cooking and wrinkled his nose.

Giacomo played a finger-matching game with another braid. He lifted his closed hand, shook it twice, opened two fingers. The aggregate reared back, shivered with a sound like corn husks, weaved its head through a figure eight, said, "I we am wrong, wrong."

Rex Live Oak approached Martin. "Hans wants the past Pans to convene in a few minutes in his quarters."

Cham and Joe Flatworm accompanied Martin along the connecting hallways. Joe was ebullient. "Christ, they're snakes, but they're real charmers."

"Snakes charming us, is that it?" Cham asked.

"Ha ha. Much easier than I thought," Joe said. "We can work with them."

Hans seemed gloomy as they entered his quarters. They sat in a broken circle and Hans squatted to finish the loop. Rex Live Oak stood outside the circle, arms folded.

"Stonemaker and I talked a little," Hans said. "He still has the best English. I asked questions about their command structure. Here's what I've learned so far. Every few days—our days, not theirs—they create a command council by pooling cords, each braid donating two. The pooled cords make a big slicking braid called Maker of Agreement or something like that. This braid uses memories from all the cords and makes decisions. The cords take these decisions back to their braids. There's nothing like giving orders. That worries me."

"Why?" Joe asked.

"Because it implies no flexibility. What if we're in the middle of a crisis and we have to communicate with them? I think they'll stick with what Maker of Agreement told them, no matter how things have changed . . . Unless they can go through the whole process again, and we can talk to Maker of Agreement directly. I couldn't get a clear answer on that."

"You think they'd do that in battle?"

Hans shrugged. "It's too early to tell, but it's never too early to worry. That's all I'm saying."

"We should find out what their disaster was like," Cham said, looking down at his crossed knees. "Where they failed."

"I'm working on it," Hans said. "Martin, you don't seem to

have hit it off with any of them . . . Paola and a few others have made fast friends.''

"I haven't made friends, either," Joe said.

"The more we bond, the faster we can learn. Like marriage," Hans said.

"And we should help them improve their English," Joe said.

"They're quick, no doubt about it," Hans said. "They may be a lot quicker than we are. But there's still a hell of a lot to learn before we can mesh with them in battle. Am I right?"

"Absolutely," Rex said from the sidelines.

"I want to find out how our ship's mind and the moms are going to integrate with *Journey House*'s mind, whether there will still be moms, or some form acceptable to both groups . . ."

"The libraries have become huge," Martin said.

"Anything we can use?" Hans asked.

"Right now, it's just a big light show," Martin said. "I hope it can be translated."

Hans nodded. "I'm satisfied with our progress, for the time being. But I don't want the crew to be so ecstatic about our new friends that we lose sight of the problems."

Cham and Joe nodded. Martin fingered the cuff of his overalls leg.

"Something to add?" Hans asked, observing this fiddling.

"You're managing Rosa now," Martin said.

Hans hesitated, then nodded with a bitter expression. "I'm managing," he said. "It isn't easy, believe me."

Rex snorted. Hans looked at him with sharp disapproval, and Rex colored and backed away.

"How's Rosa going to integrate the Brothers into her world view, her . . . religion?" Martin asked.

"She'll find a way. She's good at that sort of thing."

"I know," Martin said. "But what you're doing is dangerous. It's a game that could backfire any day."

"Better than letting her run loose, am I right?" Hans asked.

None of the ex-Pans answered.

"Or getting rid of her," Hans said. "Of course, I'd hate to have to do that. But if worse comes to worse, there's always that possibility."

Martin's face paled. Nobody said anything for a long time, ten seconds—an impressive lull for such a conversation.

"Not very smart," Joe said finally. "Making a martyr."

"Well, shit, something will happen," Hans said. "We're facing a lot of problems more frightening than Rosa."

Hans invited Stonemaker to meet the full complement of *Dawn Treader*'s crew, to familiarize them with a Brother, and to explain, in person, the Brothers' history, in particular their experiences with the Killers.

Hans led Stonemaker into the schoolroom, laddering toward the central star sphere. The crew watched in polite, stiff silence as the Brother undulated through his own ladder field—a cylinder—into their midst.

Martin had learned to identify Stonemaker by the color patterns of two components in his "head"—bright yellow and black stripes on the anterior portion.

"Stonemaker is a friend," Hans said, arm around the braid's neck. Smell of burnt cabbage—a sign of affection, Martin had learned, and one he hoped he would find more pleasant as time passed.

Those of the human crew who had not yet met a Brother wrinkled their noses apprehensively. To hear tales was very different from direct experience.

"We we have similar lives, memories," Stonemaker said.

The repetition of pronouns was going to be unavoidable. By linguistic and cultural convention even deeper than religion, Brother language used two personal pronouns, the first referring to an individual braid or a group of braids, the second to the braid's or the group's component cords. *I we, we we*. Possessives became more confused: *we mine*, with cords first, individual's possessive second; *we our* or *we ours* for group possessives. Other complications—*this we, I we myself, we our ourselves*—crept in on an unpredictable basis.

Interestingly, references to humans always relied on single pronouns. Martin hoped this did not reveal prejudice on the part of the Brothers.

"I we myself will pass on to you some of we our lives," Stonemaker said. "When we we work together, to kill those who killed we our past—" smell of something like turpentine "—we will find common thought, strength.

"We we believe we our worlds were much like your Earth and Mars."

Inside the star sphere, images of two planets, the first a rich and almost uniform green, the second half as large and yellow ochre and brown in color. "We our kind grew young first on the world you can call Leafmaker. We our time past was long, hundreds of thousands of times year." Smell of dust and warm sunlight on soil. "Your time past shorter than we ours. But we we able to travel between worlds often, as you did not. We we made young on second other planet, Drysand I we will name it. Ten thousand times years we we lived there, not making weapons, having no enemies.

"Killers come to we us as friends, smelling we our innocent radiation. Killers come as long friends made of jointed parts."

Stonemaker projected an image of a collection of shining spheres beaded together, a giant chromium caterpillar. Martin was instantly reminded of the Australian robots, shmoos they had been named; these might have been variations on the same form. "Long friends like machines for you, but living, alive within. They tell of wide places beyond, full of interest, that we we are invited to join, to learn, and then we we smell we our world is sick with weapons, it is dying. We we make power-filled ships, leave our kind to die. We we can't travel between suns, but leave anyway, and watch we our worlds be eaten, made into millions of killer machines. Then come the ones you name Benefactors, and there is a war. We our worlds are gone, only a few alive, but we we are taken in by Benefactors, and removed from the war, to seek Killers. This is short version; long when library smells good to you.

"We our weakness comes when we find suns and worlds infested by Killers, too late to save, hundreds of times year past. We we are caught in this tide, *Journey House*, and many die, *Journey House* is damaged. Hundreds of times year past. We we flee." Smell of turpentine.

Martin saw tears on the cheeks of both Wendys and Lost Boys.

"We we hear there is another Lawship." Smell of lilac and

baking bread. "Hear we we will join and work with others not smelling of our own, singles not manyness. We we are fearful, for singleness is strange, manyness is accepted. I we am proud both can grow together, fight together. We we are all manyness, all aggregate, group brave, group strong."

Stonemaker, Martin thought, had the makings of a good politician.

"We our Lawship is watched over by machines. They are long and flexible like ourselves, but I we think they are the same as your machines. Ships' libraries will join and we will teach each other to smell, to read, to see.

"Our ships will be one ship, manyness made one, group strong, group brave." Smell of cooked cabbage, not burnt. "We all selves will wait in one space while ships aggregate," Stonemaker concluded.

The human crew rustled uneasily. Martin heard whispers of assurance from the familiarized, and saw nudges of encouragement. *Not so bad. Wait and see.*

Rosa stepped forward and raised her arms. Martin wanted to turn away, embarrassed for her, for all of them.

"They are truly our brothers," Rosa said. "Together, we'll be doubly strong."

Hans put his arm around Rosa, smiled, and said, "We're grouping here in the schoolroom. It's big enough to hold us all. The *Dawn Treader* can make food for the Brothers. We'll stay here, all of us, and all of the Brothers, until the ships have joined."

No grumbling from the crew. Martin sensed an electric anticipation that had only the slightest tinge of fear.

Joe stood by Martin as they awaited the arrival of the full complement of Brothers. "We keep using the masculine pronoun for them," he observed. "Is that justified?"

"No," Martin said. "But they are Brothers, aren't they?"

Joe gave him a quizzical look, one eye squeezed shut. "Martin, you're getting a bit . . ." He waggled his hand. "Cynical. Am I wrong?"

Martin zipped his lips with a finger.

"The comment Hans made about Rosa . . ."

Martin looked meaningfully at the crew a few paces away.

Though he had spoken in an undertone, Joe sighed and said no more.

Fifty Brothers, seventy-five Lost Boys and Wendys, for the time being separated, with a star sphere in the middle of the schoolroom, showing the ships already joined bow to stern, like mating insects:

The air smelling of cabbage and lilacs and all manner of unidentifiables:

The moms and the Brothers' robots, quickly called snake mothers, two of each in the schoolroom, the moms bulbous like copper kachina dolls, the others resembling flexible bronze serpents two meters long and half a meter thick in the middle, biding their time:

The schoolroom sealed off with an exterior sigh of equalizing pressure:

Martin: *We've been through this before. This is not new.*

Hakim saying to him: "I am learning to interpret their astronomy. Jennifer says they have marvelous mathematics. What a wealth, Martin!" Hakim is overjoyed:

Ariel not coming very close to him, keeping a fixed distance, watching him when he is not looking at her:

Have I truly gotten cynical, or am I just terrified? We are such a dry forest, any spark, any change—

Sounds throughout the ships, silence among the humans, and no smells now, the air swept clean of communications, the equivalent of Brotherly silence, and vibrations under their feet.

Rosa stood strong and quiet near the star sphere in a theatrical attitude of prayer.

One of the Brothers quietly broke down into cords. The cords seemed stunned and simply twitched, feelers extended, searching, claw-legs scratching the floor. Other braids quickly moved to gather the cords into small sacks carried in packs strapped around their upper halves.

Chirps and strings of comment; smells of turpentine and bananas. The cords struggled and clicked in the sacks.

"Fear?" Ariel asked Martin, moving closer.

"I've never seen the cliché brought to life before," Martin murmured.

She raised an eyebrow.

" 'Falling apart,' " he said.

She raised the other eyebrow, shook her head. Then she chuckled. Martin could not remember having heard her chuckle before; laughing, smiling, never anything between.

"Not a very good joke," he said.

"I didn't say it was," Ariel replied, still smiling. The smile flicked off when he didn't return it; she looked away, smoothing her overalls. "I'm not asking for anything, Martin," she said softly.

"Sorry," he said, suddenly guilty.

"I haven't changed," she continued, face red. "When you were Pan, I said what I thought you needed to hear."

"I understand," he said.

"The hell you do," Ariel concluded, pushing her way to the opposite side of the group of humans.

Another braid disintegrated. Hakim bent over a straying cord. A Brother clicked and swooped down to grab the cord, head splaying, extended clawed tail sections from two of its own cords closing on the stray. He paused with the limp cord hanging just under his head, then said, "Private."

"Don't mess with them," Hans warned Hakim. "We've got a lot more to learn about each other."

"Merging begins," a mom said, moving to the center, near the star sphere. Martin looked at the sphere intently, watching the two ships melt into each other, impressed despite himself by the Benefactors' capabilities.

The snake mothers chirped, sang, and released odors. Martin's head swam with the tension and the welter of scents; more bananas, resinous sweetness, faint odor of decay, cabbage again. Snake mother voices like a high-pitched miniature string orchestra, braids responding; stray cords mostly grabbed and bagged, the last few pulled from the air by Brothers coiling like millipedes in water.

So damned strange, Martin thought, feeling the hysteria of creeping exhaustion. *It's too much. I want it to be over*.

But he floated in place, one hand clinging to a personal ladder field, eyes blinking, head throbbing, saying nothing. Hakim also clung to a ladder, eyes closed, as if trying to sleep. Actually, that was sensible. Martin closed his eyes.

Giacomo patted his shoulder. Eyes flicking open, disoriented by actually having slept—for how long? seconds? minutes?—Martin turned to Giacomo and saw Jennifer behind him.

"Completion of merger in five minutes," the mom announced, its voice sounding far away.

"We can't wait to get into their math and physics," Giacomo said, round face moist with tired excitement. Humans were adding their own smells to the schoolroom, now seeming much too small with two populations. "Jennifer's spoken to their leader—if Stonemaker is their leader."

"Spokesnake," Jennifer said, giggling, punchy.

"Some fantastic things. Their math lacks integers!"

"As far as we can tell," Jennifer added.

"They don't use whole numbers at all. Only smears, they call them."

Martin's interest could hardly have been less now, but he listened, too tired to evade them.

"I think they regard integers, even rational fractions, as aberrations. They love irrationals, the perfect smears. I can't wait to see what that means for their math." Giacomo saw Martin's look of patent disinterest, and sobered. "Sorry," he said.

"I'm very tired," Martin said. "That's all. Aren't you tired?"

"Dead tired," Jennifer said, giggling again. "Smears! Jesus, that's incredible. I may never make sense out of it."

Martin smelled lilacs; dreamed of his grandmother's face powder, drifting through the air in her small bathroom like snow, spotting her throw rug beneath the sink. In the dream, he lay down on the rug, curled up, and closed his eyes.

When he awoke, the schoolroom was quiet but for a few whispered conversations. Hakim slept nearby; Giacomo and Jennifer lay curled together an arm's reach in front of Martin. Joe Flatworm slept in a lotus, anchored to a ladder field. The moms and snake mothers floated inactive.

The Brothers had all disintegrated. Cords hung from ladder fields like socks on a neon clothes net.

Cham was awake. Martin asked him, "Is that how they sleep?"

"Beats me," Cham said.

"Where's Hans?"

"Other side of the schoolroom," Cham said. "Asleep with Rosa holding his head."

Martin turned to the star sphere and saw for the first time their new ship, the merger largely completed. He judged it to be perhaps as big as the original *Dawn Treader*, with three home-balls again; but this time the aft homeball was larger than the others. There were no obvious tanks of reserve fuel; Martin assumed the fuel must now be stored in the aft homeball. That might reflect a design improvement; the more he saw, the more he was convinced that the Brothers' Ship of the Law was a later model, with major differences in equipment, tactics, perhaps even general strategy.

"I wonder if they dream?" Cham asked.

"They're *all* asleep?" Martin stretched out, peering between the fields and sleeping bodies. He could see no intact braids, only cords.

"Wonder if they ever get confused and end up with parts of each other? It's scary, how much we're going to have to learn."

Deceleration began. Up and down returned to the Ship of the Law; humans and Brothers explored the new order of things. The quarters were divided into human and Brother sectors in the first two homeballs. A buffer of empty quarters and shared hallways gave cords spaces in which to hide and conduct their private, instinctive affairs. Provisions were made for human capture of straying cords; boxes mounted in well-traveled halls were filled with specially scented bags (tea and cabbage odors) with which to sedate and carry any cords they might find in human quarters.

Some practise sessions were arranged; Martin learned where to pick up a cord, before and after it had been covered with a scented bag. The best place to hold a cord was along the smooth, leathery body forward of the claw legs and behind the feelers. The cord mouth parts opened ventrally just to the rear of the feelers. The only danger—as yet untested—was that a cord, away from its fellows, might defend itself if the pick-up and bagging ritual was not properly observed. It might then nip or chew on a human, and certain alkaloids in its saliva might cause a toxic reaction, perhaps no more severe than a rash, perhaps worse, so why take chances?

What the humans learned soon enough was that the Brothers' diet was simple. They ate a cultivated broth of small green and purple organisms, resembling aquatic worms, neither plants nor animals. These organisms—Stonemaker suggested they might be called noodles—grew under bright lights; they could move freely within their liquid-filled containers, but derived most of their nutrients from simple chemicals. At one stage in their growth, they ate each other, and the remains of their feasts contributed substantially to the broth.

Brothers always ate disassembled, the cords gathering around the vats like snakes around bowls of milk. While the cords dined, two or more braids watched over the diners.

The snake mothers had nothing to do with preparing the broth. Growing food was a particularly important ritual for the Brothers, and it was apparently an honor to be placed in charge of the broth vats.

This much the human crew was allowed to observe. Other aspects of Brotherly life were more circumspect. Because cords could die as individuals—it was normal, like shedding skin—reproduction continued after a fashion. Breeding cords were sequestered and their activities were hidden from the humans.

Three braids seemed to act as intellectual reserves for the entire group. These braids appeared slow, not particularly personable; they spoke no English, communicated not at all with humans, but occasionally disassembled, and some of their parts would be used for a time by other braids. Erin Eire called them Wisdom, Honor, and Charity; the names stuck, at least among the humans.

Stonemaker became familiar to all the humans; Shipmaker and Eye on Sky also mixed freely. Others came forward more gradually to interact with the humans. Within two days, twenty-three Brothers mingled regularly. Their English improved rapidly.

Within a tenday of the merger, rudimentary jokes could be exchanged. Brother humor was simple enough: sickly-sweet flower-smells marked a kind of laughter, brought on by simple stories whose punchline always involved involuntary disassembly. The Brothers particularly enjoyed stories or mimicry of humans passing gas or fainting.

With Hans' approval, Paola Birdsong appointed herself a special student of Brotherly language and behavior.

Giacomo and Jennifer volunteered to help coordinate human and Brother libraries, working with Eye on Sky and Shipmaker. Hans suggested they first translate and integrate what the libraries had to say about galactic history and battle strategy and tactics. Jennifer was disappointed by these practical priorities; she desperately wanted to explore Brother mathematics.

Martin observed, in his library visits, that the ship's mind was itself translating and correlating information.

Rosa Sequoia stayed in the background, watching everything intently, weighing and measuring the new situation.

The remnants of Martin's funk had passed like fog. For hours at a time he did not think of Theresa or William.

Hakim, Harpal, and Luis Estevez Saguaro joined forces with a Brother named Silken Parts, a large (five meters long) and dapper-looking braid whose cords were, indeed, somewhat silkier in texture than those of other Brothers. Together, they organized a combined search team in the nose.

Giacomo and Jennifer acted as search team advisors, but were now absorbed in their library work and theoretical activities.

Remotes were sent out and Leviathan came under close scrutiny.

After four days immersed in studying Leviathan, Hakim asked to speak with Martin, alone and in Martin's quarters.

They squatted beside each other and sipped strong sweet hot tea, Hakim's favorite.

Hakim was agitated. "I will speak of this with Hans soon," Hakim began, eyes downturned. "This is awkward, I know, but I do not know how he will react. I myself do not know how to react. I hope you can advise me."

"About what?" Martin asked.

"Silken Parts has gone to the Brothers now, and I understand they face similar difficulties. The information from the remotes is disturbing."

"How?" Martin asked.

"I am most embarrassed."

"Christ, Hakim—"

Hakim glanced at him sharply, disliking religious blasphemies of any sort.

"I'm sorry. Tell me."

"Our early information about Leviathan seems to have been completely in error. I don't know *how* it could have happened, but we have major discrepancies. Our new findings are different."

"How different?"

"Leviathan has fifteen planets, not ten, or even twelve."

"Fifteen?"

Hakim winced and shook his head. "The star itself has much the same characteristics—some not unexpected refinements in spectral measurements. Almost everything else seems to have changed."

"How wrong could we have been?"

"Not this wrong," Hakim said. "I am upset to think the ship's instruments could have misled us; even more upset to think we could have misinterpreted the facts so."

"Fifteen planets sounds awfully crowded."

"It is. I have referred the momerath to Jennifer and Giacomo. The orbital patterns as we see them are astonishing. We believe the system must be artificial, and artificially maintained—which would require great expenditures of energy."

"What else?"

"The system is rich with raw materials. Two of the planets, not four, are large gas giants, and they are not depleted. The fourth planet is a true enigma—about one hundred thousand kilometers in diameter, with a distinct and apparently solid surface, not a gas giant . . . but with a density comparable to the gas giants'."

"Hakim, I know you've checked this a dozen times—"

"We've made measurements more often than I can count, separately and together. The current information seems correct, Martin. I am mortified to possibly have been so in error before."

"The Red Tree Runners were inside the system. They saw ten planets. Their charts didn't match with our views from a distance . . . and they certainly don't conform now . . ."

"We could be in different universes, the differences are so great."

"Right . . ." Martin screwed up his face in thought. "Hakim—"

"We were not wrong!" Hakim shouted, pounding the mat. He glanced at Martin expectantly.

"I don't think you were, either. The Brothers took Leviathan's measure. Have you compared results?"

"They made measurements before our first efforts."

"And they saw . . . ?"

"From what Paola and Jennifer have translated, and what Stonemaker tells us—so difficult to interpret! They do not use numbers as we do—they saw a system of we think ten planets, with four gas giants."

"Then they got a picture similar to what the Red Tree Runners saw. The Brothers didn't pick up signs of civilization?"

Hakim shook his head. "Nor did they notice any reaction to Wormwood's destruction. From what we see even now, there is no sign of armoring, or any other preparation."

Martin felt at once a kind of dread and excitement, a chill of surprise and something he could hardly quantify. *This is no simple chase now, no sitting duck. We're close!*

"Leviathan is camouflaged," Martin said.

"I was hoping you would agree!" Hakim cried out, clapping Martin on the shoulder.

Martin could have laughed at Hakim's relief and joy, but he did not.

"We were not measuring improperly! The death ship saw what it saw! The Brothers did not measure improperly!"

"But how do you mask an entire star system?"

"Only planets," Hakim said.

"Are they ghost planets?"

"Perhaps," Hakim said, raising a finger. "One of these versions may be correct, but which?"

"The deception is not infinitely varied . . . and it changes across fairly short intervals, on the order of years."

"Yes!" Hakim said, face flushed with excitement. "The bastard Killers fool nobody!"

Martin touched finger to nose. "It's obvious some massive planetary engineering has been done . . . You'd think the closer an observer was, the more they'd want the system to look *empty*."

"With your support, I will take this to Hans," Hakim said, rising from the cushion. "He cannot become angry if you back us."

Martin stood. "Are you afraid of him?" he asked.

Hakim looked away, embarrassed. "I do not trust him as much as I trust you. Do you approve of him, Martin?"

"It isn't my job to criticize the Pan."

"I have felt badly about some of his actions, the way we have become. The games, with sexual partners as rewards. Martin, I have kept very quiet until now, but that was wrong."

"Well, it's stopped. We start training with the Brothers soon."

"You are not worried about what might happen?"

"Of course I'm worried."

"But not worried about Hans."

"Hakim, I know how difficult it is to be Pan. When I was Pan, people died. Hans was elected. That's that."

Hakim regarded him sadly, then arranged his overalls with smoothing gestures of palms down chest and legs. "I will go to Hans now. I hope he will be as understanding as you."

"He's no dummy," Martin said.

"He will not chastise us," Hakim said. "He will see, as well, that these are not our errors."

"I'm sure he will," Martin said. When Hakim had left, Martin rubbed his eyes vigorously with his knuckles, then looked up and around his quarters, as if seeing them for the first time; ribbons of light, bare brown and silver-gray surfaces, the single cushion large enough for two; why had he asked for it to be large enough for two?

He was not due anywhere for an hour. There would be a meeting of past Pans with Hans and Rex and two of Stonemaker's planners; they would begin to design drills, coordinate strategies.

Brothers and humans could and would work together.

Martin reached for his wand and idly tuned to the translated territories of the Brother libraries. Vast regions were still incomprehensible. The human wands did not supply scent; he could not interpret half of what might be stored. Even the best translations would never be ideal. As Hakim had discovered, even so simple a thing as numbers was subject to ambiguity. He wondered how the Brothers counted . . .

Perhaps counting was not important to them.

Perhaps they were better equipped to deal with Leviathan's changing nature than humans.

He searched for Theodore's texts in his wand, found them still intact after the disasters and merger. Randomly he leafed through the projected pages, hoping for some small insight or guidance.

Never underestimate the power of circumstance to grind your very bones, Theodore had written in the first three months of their journey. *Never underestimate the perverse power of everything to go wrong, to tend toward trouble. Always the problems seem to come from within; I judge myself to be at fault, for not anticipating the unforeseeable, not knowing the way a chaotic function will collapse.*

And elsewhere,

What I have lost does not make me greater, but it makes me deeper, like a hole. Take more away and I will come through to the other side, like a gaping wound. But then I will be the wound and the body will have sloughed away. Is it possible to lose more of what is not there?

Very adolescent, with the insight of resilient youth and none of the reserved silence of the experienced adult. If he had written these things, Martin might have felt a little embarrassed. But then he had always felt that way about Theodore's writings: strongly attracted to them, even admiring, but always discomfited by them. They explored territories, emotions, and ideas Martin was not comfortable with.

Theodore had been so *open*. It was what killed him.

He turned off the projected pages, lay back on the cushion and asked for the lights to dim. Soon there would be much less time for sleep.

* * *

"How in hell can anyone disguise an entire star system?" Hans asked. His hair stuck out in blond spikes; clearly, he had not slept much recently. Ex-Pans, Silken Parts, and Stonemaker's representatives, Eye on Sky and Shipmaker, gathered in the nose with the joint search team. The starfield expanded beyond, Leviathan bright and steady to one side, still too far away for planets to be visible to their naked eyes.

Silken Parts rustled; every few minutes, the braids would tremble, as if their cords needed to scratch some itch difficult to locate. Luis Estevez Saguaro had prepared a chart comparing the four views they had of the system—the view found in the records of the dead ship, the *Dawn Treader*'s view from just beyond Wormwood, the view obtained by the Brothers, and the present view. Hans regarded it dourly, chin in hand.

"How much energy would it take to broadcast such a disguise?" he asked.

Hakim calculated quietly. "Half the energy produced by the star itself, in one estimate," he said.

Silken Parts softly disagreed. With violin speech and a somewhat musty odor, he said, "We cannot assume the disguise is broadcast in all directions—"

"Wait," Hans interrupted, raising one hand. Silken Parts drew back, rustled again. Martin doubted that the Brother felt affronted, but he wished Hans could be less imperious. "You think something's being *broadcast*. What—an image of the system, altered somehow?"

Hakim cleared his throat. "Jennifer and Giacomo—"

"Spare me more goddamned momerath," Hans said. "I need something concrete."

"Please have patience," Hakim said, looking to one side, face darkening.

Hans lifted a hand, flicked a finger: go on.

"Jennifer and Giacomo have taken time from the work in the combined libraries. Jennifer believes that several regions of space may have had their ray tracing, their radiation-transit bit structures, interfered with. Photons could seem to appear out of nothing. These regions, each perhaps as wide as the star system itself, but having no depth—located perhaps at the periphery of the system—would act like giant projectors, revealing convincing full-spectrum images of . . . a nonexistent system.''

Hans poked his finger into a projected image of the fifteen-planet system. ''Like this one, but a lot bigger. You mean, if we were to enter, we'd pass through the deception, see what was really there?''

''Not at all,'' Hakim said. ''It would be possible to shift these ray-altered regions to continue to deceive. I admit, it would be a massive undertaking, but not nearly so great as wrapping the entire solar system in a sphere of deception.''

Silken Parts said, ''Our ideas cross difficult. Please project.''

Hakim quickly sketched in diagrams showing their positions, regions of ray-alteration shaped like shields, camouflaged or deceptive images perceived from great distances.

''Very powerful,'' Silken Parts said. ''Could change field of battle. Great blindness and confusion.'' He explained to Eye on Sky and Shipmaker.

''Scary stuff,'' Hans said. ''Any way we can penetrate it?''

''If it is constant, no,'' Hakim said. ''But if the images are maintained only at certain intervals, we may receive a correct image with constant vigilance.''

''But we wouldn't necessarily know which was correct.''

Hakim shook his head, eyes downcast.

''So what do we plan for?'' Hans asked.

''Stonemaker should be in on any planning,'' Harpal said. Martin agreed.

''Right. But what I'm asking is, how can we make plans, when we can't know what to expect, what is real and what is not?''

''Possibly nothing is there at all,'' Silken Parts said.

Hans' eyes seemed to glaze over. He put his hands behind his neck, shook his head slowly, said, ''I haven't the slickest notion what we can do, but we need a war conference.''

As they prepared to leave, Paola Birdsong arrived with a string of ten braids, all eager to see the unobscured stars. She smiled at Martin as they passed, happy with her new occupation. ''They feel better if they can see the stars once or twice a tenday,'' she said.

The braids rustled like leaves poured from a bag.

* * *

Martin learned from Silken Parts that Stonemaker would not be available for four days. Hearing the search team's latest information had caused quite a stir among the Brothers, and Makers of Agreement had been called for.

Donating two cords apiece, the Brothers had created three large new individuals, the Makers of Agreement. They served one function only: to look over the present situation and render fresh judgment, unclouded by whatever prejudices the former braids might have had.

Hans received this news from Martin and Eye on Sky with intense vexation. He conferred with Rex for a few moments in one corner of the schoolroom, then returned and said, "All right. We'll hold a conference with the Makers of Agreement. Is that okay with you?"

Eye on Sky smelled of cabbage and old tobacco smoke, showing intense cogitation, and replied, "It will be adequate."

"Maybe they'll give us a fresh perspective as well," Hans said. Martin watched from one side, arms folded behind his back.

The discussion took place in the Brothers' territory. It was dark in the corridors there; the air smelled moist and electric, like a storm. Sometimes Martin caught a tang of beach, salt and organic decay. Eye on Sky led Hans, Rex, Paola, Martin, Harpal, Cham, and Joe to a small, close chamber. Martin had requested that Paola join them, since she was most expert at Brother speech.

The walls were coated with dripping oil. On the floor of the chamber, three braids lay, undulating slowly to a steady wind of intensely organic, fishy smells and the sound of waves breaking on a shore.

The braids rose and coiled like cobras as the humans entered. Martin could not recognize any of them; all patterns had been rearranged. They did not even smell familiar. In the past few tendays, Martin had learned to pick up a few of the subtle odors of individual braids, even giving some of them code names: Teacake, Almond Breath, Kimchee, Vinegar.

Eye on Sky, the best of the Brothers at speaking English, would act as translator for the temporary braids. "Makers of

Agreement will seem disoriented for a time, but when the braids return cords to all, we they all will remember discussions."

"Not ideal," Hans commented dryly. "Still, we're coming into Leviathan in the next three months. We need to begin strategic planning. War councils. Understood?"

Eye on Sky translated, with Paola's help. While Paola could not make Brother sounds, she had modified her wand to provide a basic vocabulary.

Hans wrinkled his nose at the effusion of smells. "I've been studying your conflict. We all have, I assume."

"Conflict?" Eye on Sky asked.

"Your battle. When your ship was severely damaged."

"Yes," the braid said. "We might translate it more as the Sadness."

"You entered a stellar system ten light years from here, to take on what you assumed was a world colonized by Killers . . . And in fact, you were probably correct. You made an effort to be certain your judgment was correct. That took a year and a half, our time . . . An extraordinary effort. During that time, you were detected, but you maneuvered through the defenses, sterilized the surface of the planet, then encountered a squadron of killer probes fleeing from the destruction. You were subjected to a bombardment of neutronium weapons; you survived with high casualties and severe damage to your ship."

He paused. Eye on Sky added nothing to this summary.

"You accelerated out of the system, and with your available resources, looking back, you saw what might have been the surviving killer probes returning to the planet."

"Yesss . . ." said Eye on Sky, with the peculiar musical upturn in its voice. "Mostly correct."

"Anything incorrect?" Hans asked, eyebrow raised.

"Mostly correct."

"All right," Hans said, shoulders slumping, hunching his upper body over where he sat. He lifted his wand and projected some crude colored sketches of the Brothers' battle. "It seems obvious to me that you faced a decoy world, much as we did around Wormwood. It may have been a less sophisticated decoy—it was farther away from Leviathan—but that in itself could be important. We both got our asses wiped. Pardon me—"

"The analogy, for we us, is cords were skinned," Eye on Sky said. "I we understand." A steady progression of violin sounds, chirps, and smells wafted from Eye on Sky to the three temporary braids.

Hans smiled. "And after you were done, it seemed likely the killer probes would repair the decoy, start all over."

"Yes," Eye on Sky said.

"So in effect, your sacrifice was for nothing."

"Yes," Eye on Sky said.

"We're all pretty awful at anticipating what the Killers can do. But then, so are the moms—your snake mothers, too, I assume. The closer we get to Leviathan, the more sophisticated the traps, until Wormwood itself seemed to actually be the target. I think we can assume Leviathan is the real center of interest. And the deceptions and defenses are going to be extraordinary. Am I right?"

The three braids stirred as Eye on Sky conveyed this to them.

"There is general agreement we our survival not good chances," Eye on Sky said.

"But we have an advantage," Hans said.

"Combined resources and knowledge," Eye on Sky translated for the largest braid.

Martin added, "And the chance to compare notes and pool our minds. The Killers don't know that we intercepted the Red Tree Runners' ship. They don't know that we've combined forces with you."

"Right," Hans said. "Some of our best brains are working with some of yours, and we're getting along just fine. Now it's time to make serious plans."

The three braids moved closer together, heads almost touching. Smells of bananas and musty wine.

"I'd like our weapons crews to join with yours. I'd like the moms and snake mothers to make ships we can fly together."

Martin felt a sudden and unexpected renewal of respect for Hans.

"We're in this together," Hans said, rubbing his face with his palms and wiping them on his overalls as if they were greasy. He looked at Cham and Martin, smiled, turned back to the braids. "We're family. Am I right?"

"It is a good time for this," Eye on Sky translated.

"We're going to need a joint planning team," Hans said. "Myself, Rex, Harpal, Martin, will be on it from our side. As soon as possible, we'll need to know which braids will represent your side."

"Agreed," Eye on Sky said. "Makers of Agreement look sharply at we our crew, and choose, and then reassemble normal in two days your time. Stonemaker will announce to yours."

"Perfect," Hans said. He clasped his hands, bowed to Eye on Sky and the Makers, gathered up his party, and prepared to leave the Brothers' territory. The largest temporary braid suddenly screeched shrilly and all turned to look at him.

"I we sees water clear, air clear," he said, voice like a child's recorded on a bad tape machine.

Hans nodded, waiting for more.

"This is the one," the large temporary continued. "As you sound words, this is the one. Fine all if we we die for this."

"Right," Hans said.

"I we believes this one means—" Eye on Sky began.

"I understand him perfectly," Hans said, raising his thumb. "We are in accord. Am I right?"

The humans nodded. In the corridor, once in human territory and away from any Brothers, Hans murmured, "God damn, I love the way they talk. If we could only speak their lingo-smello half so well-o!"

Martin felt unexpected tears begin in his eyes. Hans was still capable, still a leader; his decisions and ideas were strong and forward.

The moms and snake mothers took the joint weapons team into the weapons store and showed them three modified craft. Each could carry a braid and a human in separated compartments; this, they explained, in case one was injured or suffered problems that might interfere with the other.

Meeting after meeting, planning session upon session, ruminations between Brothers and humans, preparations for joint drills, yet despite their best efforts, never a sense of resolution, of full understanding. If this was what the defenders of Leviathan had hoped for, they had achieved it in spades: a deep sense of unease, far worse than when *Dawn Treader* had descended toward Wormwood.

Leviathan hung three and a half light months distant, a steady image of fifteen worlds.

In the nearly empty schoolroom, Silken Parts coiled near the star sphere and spread three grasping cords from below the tip of its trunk, each grasping a human wand. The first three pairs of claws along each cord curled around the wands with impressive dexterity. Images flew through the air for the benefit of Stonemaker and Eye on Sky, faster than Martin could intercept; the Brothers had the advantage of multiple sensory systems, each capable of absorbing and holding for braid assimilation. The Brothers' briefing took less than a minute. Silken Parts than transferred all three wands to one cord and handed them to Hakim, Luis, and Jennifer.

"Thank you," Silken Parts said, leaning forward to the human observers: his comrades on the joint search team, and Hans, Harpal, Rex, Cham, and Martin.

Hakim sighed in admiration. "It is frustrating to be human," he said to Silken Parts and Stonemaker. Stonemaker made a sound like water over gravel and emitted a sickly-sweet flower scent, olfactory and auditory laughter, which Martin suspected was more politeness than true humor.

"I will present the results now for humans," Hakim said, lifting one wand. "Slower, but with no more joy. We have spread our remotes to their farthest position, as agreed to by Hans and Stonemaker, and we have seen the Leviathan system with much greater detail.

"Civilization is apparent. It is very, very busy. There is continuous commerce between the fifteen worlds, especially in the vicinity of the fourth planet. If this is a false projection or deception, it is a masterpiece.

"Every planet is occupied. The density of activity on each planet is marvelous, even from what we can see at this distance. Commerce between the worlds flows unceasingly, and it appears to be conducted by a variety of beings. At least, that is my intuition, and it is shared by Silken Parts." Hakim projected images of five of the planets, arrayed around his head like balls frozen in a juggling act.

"We are using numbers and Greek designators for each body," Hakim continued. "The first planet outward from Leviathan is a rocky world. Yet as you see, it is very fuzzy. We believe the fuzz is a heavy layer of tethered stations suspended in orbit. We are seeing this planet from an angle of sixty degrees, and the fuzziness increases on this, the southern, limb of the planet, which indicates to me much activity around the equatorial plane, perhaps out to synchronous orbit. The planet is heavily modified, but must at one time have been comparable to Venus in size and composition."

"I assume there will be more news on these tethers or whatever as our parallax changes," Hans said.

"Yes indeed. In fact, I will have a ninety-degree shifted view within a tenday, because of our speed, because of its precession—it has a natural polar angle of thirty degrees with relation to the ecliptic—and because of parallax change."

"Do you think they're defenses?"

"They do not appear to be defenses. If they are tethers, they may be extended surface habitats—hanging buildings. How such a network of tethered structures could be maintained in orbit presents an awesome challenge."

"Sounds like a bustling metropolis," Harpal commented. "Why do you think there's more than one intelligent species there?"

"Actually, we posit nothing of the sort—only that there are varieties of intelligent forms. For a civilization at this stage of development, the moms tell us speciation is not a useful concept. Biological forms, if any, may be entirely artificial and arbitrary."

Hakim sipped from a bulb of water and continued. "The second planet is very different from the first. It possesses no fuzziness and perhaps few if any tethered structures, yet has a dense atmosphere of carbon dioxide and nitrogen, high in water vapor, maintained at a steady planet-wide temperature of eighty-five degrees centigrade."

"Why?" Hans asked, frowning.

"To provide a different habitat, perhaps," Luis suggested.

"The planets are quite different, as if designed for some particular environment or function. To highlight the most interesting, the fourth is not a rocky world, nor a gas giant, but we do not know what it actually is. I once thought it might be a brown dwarf, but that makes no sense now. It has an enormous surface area covered by what appears to be a thin atmosphere of carbon dioxide and oxygen and argon, and an actual solid surface—a lithosphere, which would have to be artificially stabilized. The lithosphere may float on a fluid core, but the surface temperature is remarkably warm, twelve degrees centigrade, which would point to internal heating."

"All right," Hans said. "Why do they have lots of different environments?"

Silken Parts rustled his cords before speaking. "In we our records, we we see and smell of many species developing intelligence in a local area, and creating great communities. They are not common. They exist, but."

"It's all deception," Hans murmured. "Why worry about it?"

"If it is not deception . . ." Hakim said, lifting his hands.

Hans laughed. "We've faced nothing *but* deception from the Killers from the very beginning. This is perfect—something to make us hesitate, lose confidence. It's just goddamned perfect."

Stonemaker rustled now, then coiled and uncoiled. A single cord disengaged from his tail and crawled out the door. Eye on Sky retrieved and bagged it; it squeaked plaintively. "I we beg pardon," Stonemaker said. An odor of something akin to embarrassment—fresh salt air with seaweed. Minor spontaneous disengagement was not uncommon for the Brothers, but discomfiting if noticed.

"Think nothing of it," Hans said. "I detect a conspiracy here. Not just Hakim . . . does somebody else think this isn't a blind?"

Stonemaker rustled again. Clearly, something irritated the Brother. "The ship must be cautious, or I we is a Killer attitude."

Hans knit his brows.

"We must not rush into blind judgment," Hakim said.

Hans looked around the schoolroom, flabbergasted. "We're seriously thinking the Killers aren't here after all? This is what's

really here—a zoo of cultures, cooperating and prosperous, waiting for us to just drop in and visit?''

"The deception is incredibly dense," Hakim said.

"We know of no such deception succeeding over vast periods
of time," Silken Parts said.

Hans' face reddened. Rex started to say something, but Hans
cut him off with a raised hand. "So we should vote again . . .
pass judgment again."

"Yes," Stonemaker said. "All our crews."

"I'm for that," Hans said, stretching cat-like. "Anything to
build consensus. When?"

"After much more seeing," Silken Parts suggested. "Much
more research."

"We have time," Hans said. "Meanwhile, we should begin
drills and exercises. I'd like Martin, Paola Birdsong, Ariel, Giacomo, and . . . Martin, you choose three others. I'd like all of
you to go through the libraries and find whatever precedent there
is. Make a case. You'll be defense. Hakim, you take Jennifer,
Harpal, Cham, and three others, and prepare a case for prosecut-
ion. Stonemaker, I'm not yet familiar with the way your legal
system works, but I think something similar should be done by
the Brothers. Then we'll bring the entire crew together, humans
and Brothers, and judge."

Silken Parts gave off an odor of wet clay. Stonemaker said,
"We we will regroup, assemble Makers of Agreement, make a
decision."

"Grand," Hans said. He looked at Martin. "We need to
talk," he said. "Alone."

They went to Hans' quarters, passing four Brothers and five
humans as they exercised in a corridor. The humans tossed balls
to the Brothers, who passed them along their backs from cord to
cord and flipped them with their tails. The contest—a kind of
football—was desperately uneven; the Brothers were winning
handily, and the humans cheerfully shouted their complaints.

"Competitive, aren't they?" Hans said. He opened the hatch
to his quarters. Within, Martin saw a room as spare as his—
except for vases of flowers. *Rosa's touch*. Hans lay on a pad and
motioned for Martin to get comfortable.

"You've been quiet lately," Hans said. "I should be grateful . . ."

"Why grateful?" Martin asked.

"That you're not screaming your head off. The ex-Pans don't approve of my style, do they?"

Martin didn't answer.

"Ah," Hans said, nodding. "There it is."

"Not really," Martin said softly. "Every leader finds fault with the next in line. I argued with Stephanie."

"Never mind," Hans said, dismissing the subject with a wave. He stared up at the blank ceiling, as if talking to someone far away. "Harpal has resigned. I need a second—let's not use the name Christopher Robin any more, all right?"

"Fine," Martin said.

"Rex is loyal as hell, but I need somebody critical right now. A balance. Cham grates on me as much as Harpal. I keep coming back to you."

"Why?" Martin asked.

"Because when you keep quiet, I wish you'd talk. If you're my second, it'll be your duty to talk to me, and I won't wonder what you're thinking. Besides, Stonemaker already acts as if you're next in command. Might as well make it official."

Martin sat on the bare floor, crossing his legs. "That doesn't seem reason enough."

"I said it before, I'll say it now; you weren't responsible for the Skirmish going wrong. Nobody could have seen it coming. We got away. We did what we came to do. I think you got blamed for all the wrong reasons."

"I don't worry about it," Martin said.

"You lost someone you loved."

"More than one," Martin said.

"I think you were perhaps the best Pan we had, or at least a close match with Stephanie. She was hot, she had guts. You were quiet and deliberate. I'm flying on instinct through a thick fog. You know what my problems are."

Martin took a deep breath.

"We're friendly with the Brothers. That's a relief. They scared the hell out of me, just looking at them the first time. That

cord crawling on Cham . . ." Hans chuckled. "I would have
wet my pants. I think they're good for us. But they're different,
too. They screwed up royally in battle. They hesitated, they gave
the Killers every benefit of the doubt . . . And they're going to
do it again. I can just smell it coming from Silken Parts and
Stonemaker. They see this blind, this big cooperative solar system, all bustling and peaceful . . . And Christ, Martin, they
want to *hug* the slicker, not kill it."

"We can work around that," Martin said.

"Can we?" Hans turned to glare at him.

"I think so," Martin said.

"But you agree it's a blind."

"Hakim seems to have his doubts. Hakim's smart—"

"Hakim's too goddamned gentle," Hans said.

"He's not a coward," Martin said.

"I didn't mean that. He'll be turned by the Brothers. They'll
put all kinds of doubts into his reasonable head. I wish sometimes
they'd chosen a bunch of dumb-ass soldiers and not all these
mental high-performance types." Hans slapped the floor with
his palm. "I could lead a bunch of blockheads anywhere, do
anything, come out with most of us alive. But not thinkers and
doubters. And if I add Rosa . . ." He pointed to the flowers,
tossed his head back dramatically. "You noticed? God save me.
She's pretty good in bed, you know that?"

Martin shook his head.

"But I don't do it for my health," Hans said, tone softening.
"She scares me more than the Brothers. She's a cipher, Martin.
I think maybe she actually does talk to God. If so, God's on
their side, not ours. If I let her loose—and I can't control her
for long, Martin—I have no idea what will come out of her. A
whole new religion. Am I right?" He stood and stretched, restless as a caged leopard. "She almost sucked you in, didn't she?"

Martin's face reddened. "I was hurting," he said.

"Don't be ashamed. If I weren't so goddamned cynical, I'd
have got down on my knees, too."

"I don't want to be second in command. I served my time."

"You were cut short," Hans reminded him.

"It was fine by me," Martin said.

"Bolsh," Hans said. "You have as deep a sense of duty as

anyone here. You feel more deeply than anyone but maybe Ariel.'' Hans grinned. ''She's sweet on you, I think.''

Martin didn't respond.

''Well, I can choose my own second if the elected one doesn't work out. I've made my choice. It's you. You'll replace Harpal.''

''I don't—''

''Sorry, Martin,'' Hans said, putting his hands on Martin's shoulders. ''I need help. I need balance. I don't want to make mistakes now.''

The drills began first with physical exercise, humans and Brothers cooperating in gymnastics. The result was comic at first, and Martin worried the Brothers might be offended by the confusion, but they were not.

The entire crew involved in the exercises seemed to take it as a game, even while performing the drill to the best of their ability.

Cham served as drill leader. Eye on Sky translated for the Brothers.

''We're going to get used to each other, get formally introduced,'' Cham said. ''You can call me coach.''

The humans hooted and jumped around, pretending to shoot a few hoops or pass and intercept a clothes-wad football.

''First thing is, we have to know what we can do, and what we feel like, in terms of strength, resilience, where we're vulnerable, where we can be hurt, how we can help. Got that?''

Silence and attention indicated assent.

''We have no idea what we'll be getting into this time. Everything we've drilled for, all we've trained for, may have to be turned upside down soon. That's my feeling, anyway, and I think the bosses agree. Looks like Leviathan is going to be a corker. Target-rich, the old military folks on Earth used to call it. So we have to work together closely.''

Rich smells like a seashore filled the room. Martin noted a few who seemed to find the smells unpleasant: Rex Live Oak was among them, still made uneasy by the Brothers.

Harpal stood beside Martin. He had not said a word since resigning. At least he showed no resentment against Martin. Martin was grateful for that.

"First exercise," Cham said. "A carry. Two humans will take a single Brother across the schoolroom. The Brother will then carry the two humans back. I don't have any idea how you'll do these things; just do them, and learn."

Cham and Eye on Sky picked the teams. Each team had two Brothers and two humans; Martin and Ariel teamed with two braids, one a small individual called Twice Grown, the other a medium called Makes Clear. Neither of the braids had honed their human communication skills, and both often resorted to odors rather than human words, which added to the confusion and—Ariel seemed to think—to the fun. Martin had not seen her laugh so much before.

"We have a new second in command," Cham said gleefully. "The Brothers will pardon me if I push rank forward. Martin, your team goes first."

Makes Clear slithered forward. "Carry long ways," he suggested, then coiled like an upright spring. Martin and Ariel tried to find safe places to grab him, but the cords squirmed beneath their grasping hands.

"Be *still*," Ariel suggested.

"Not accustomed," Makes Clear sighed. The others watched with interest as Martin finally found the least ticklish section of a cord, about three quarters toward the rear, near the most firmly gripping claws. The skin of the cord changed texture beneath his hands, from hard slick leather to easy-to-grip rubber.

Makes Clear straightened and stiffened. Ariel fumbled, recovered her grip, and they hefted Makes Clear to hip level. "Let's go while we've still got him!" Martin shouted, and they started to run across the floor.

Makes Clear vented a particularly sharp turpentine smell that stung Martin's eyes. To let go and rub his eyes would be disastrous; but he was almost blind. Ariel was little better off. "Where are we?" Martin asked.

"You tell me!"

"I we tell! I we tell!" Makes Clear chirped. "Left, right, right."

"What?"

"Go to the left more," Ariel said. They narrowly missed a

line of Brothers, who arched like startled serpents, adding more turpentine scent.

Martin strained his head back, teeth bared, eyes almost shut, arm muscles corded with effort. The Brother weighed at least eighty kilos. Ariel was strong, but her grip was failing, and Makes Clear slipped lower on her side. Just as they finished the trip across the chamber, they all fell and slid into the wall.

Makes Clear rustled and rose upright, then swiftly bent down, unlimbering two pairs of cords along the sides of his upper body. The cords' claws grabbed Martin's and Ariel's arms and legs, and Makes Clear hoisted them from the ground with a loud buzz of effort, tossed them, and caught them around their mid-sections.

"Shit!" Ariel cried out. Makes Clear reversed course and undulated along the weaving track they had followed with comic exactness, again forcing his fellows to arch. Martin felt the claws pinching deep into skin and muscle and grimaced with pain.

The return trip was much faster. The traction of multiple cord claws along a Brother's underside was truly wonderful, like a living tank tread, or a supercharged caterpillar. Makes Clear lowered himself and they scrambled to their feet beside Twice Grown.

"They we did well?" Twice Grown asked, his head rearing to chest level on Martin, smelling like stale fruit.

"Well enough," Martin said, recovering his breath and feeling his ribs.

"Better next when," Twice Grown said, weaving toward Ariel and tapping her arm with an extended cord.

"That's affection," Martin said, looking to see her reaction.

"I know," Ariel said, glaring.

Cham announced the next team, and the exercise worked its way to a rather dull conclusion. By the end, they knew much more about each other, and even the most reluctant—Rex among them—had been forced to come in contact with, and to cooperate with, the Brothers.

Martin sat with his back against the wall. Ariel approached him, examining his face cautiously. "May I?" she asked.

He gestured for her to sit beside him.

"Hans didn't pick Rex," she said quietly.

In the middle of the schoolroom, several men and women showed the Brothers where they had been bruised, and suggested more gentle methods of handling. The Brothers, in broken English and with smells of onion and fresh bread, lodged more courteous, but no less pointed, complaints.

"My luck," Martin said. "Getting ready to jump all over me again?"

"You're a prick, a real prick," Ariel said. A child-like tone of pique took some of the sting out of her words. "You don't deserve my anger." She squatted, lay her back against the wall, straightened her legs one at a time, and slumped beside him.

Rosa had stayed apart from the exercises; Hans had privately instructed Cham not to include her. She seemed dreamy, unfocused; Martin saw her leave the room. "How's Rosa?" he asked.

"Like a volcano," Ariel answered. "Hans isn't helping her any. He may think he is, but she knows what he's doing."

"What do you think he's doing?"

"Typical masculine shit. 'What she needs is a good slicking.' "

"What do you suggest we should do?"

"About Rosa?" She lifted her shoulders, inhaled. "She has a mission. She doesn't pay attention to me now—I'm not in her circle, if you haven't noticed."

"I noticed."

"She doesn't pay attention to anybody, really, except Hans—she's like a tape-recorder with Hans."

"You said she knows what he's up to."

"She's using him as much as he's using her. He's given her official status, Martin. She's strengthening her position. If Hans thinks he's smarter than Rosa . . . But you're co-opted now, aren't you? You can't talk about Hans or what he's thinking."

"I didn't ask to be second."

"Right," Ariel said, nodding emphatically. "Do you disapprove of Hans?"

Martin didn't answer.

"Right," she said again, and stood. "Everything's working out with the Brothers. But there are some of us besides Rosa who are on the edge, and being with the Brothers isn't helping.

You know the ones I mean. They're traveling without any compass, Martin."

"Thank you for believing I have some intelligence."

"You're welcome." She rubbed her hands on her pants and looked at him with an expression between concern and irritation. "I know you won't swallow the bait," she said. "Spit it back. Rosa isn't the most dangerous person on this ship."

Martin pretended to ignore her.

Rex lost it first.

Martin was laddering between the first and second homeballs when he heard shouts echoing from below. He clambered down to the neck join and saw a radiance of cords streaming from a pile that had just seconds before been a braid.

Rex stood to one side with a metal baseball bat, face pale and moist. He stooped and swung the bat lightly from one hand. With the other hand he fanned a sharp odor of turpentine and burned sugar.

He turned and lifted his eyes to Martin's face. "Help me," he said, voice flat. "This slicker attacked me."

The braid had completely dissolved. The cords tried to climb the walls and fell back with sad thumps. Three cords lay writhing in the middle of the join, smearing brown fluid on the floor—the first time Martin had seen cords bleeding. "What the hell happened?" he asked.

"I just told you," Rex said, pointing the bat at Martin. "It grabbed me. I had to fight it off. "

"Who was it?" Joe Flatworm asked, dropping from a ladder field behind Martin. "Which Brother?"

"I don't know and I don't give a damn," Rex said, lowering the bat and standing straight. "It was a big one."

Two of the three injured cords had stopped moving. Two more Brothers wriggled through cylindrical fields from the level below. They immediately set about bagging the uninjured cords.

Ten more humans and three more Brothers gathered in the dome. Paola Birdsong stooped beside the still cords. Twice Grown slid forward and gently picked up one of the two, not bothering to bag it.

"Is it dead?" she asked.

"It is dead," Twice Grown said.

"Who did it belong to?"

"A cord of Sand Piler," Twice Grown said.

"What is this, a goddamned funeral?" Rex shouted.

Martin approached Rex carefully, holding out a hand and wriggling his fingers. "Give me that," he said.

Rex dropped the bat and stepped away. "Self-defense," he said. Martin picked up the bat and handed it to Joe.

"He was part of your training team," Martin said. "Are you sure he attacked you?"

"It put its claws on me and it pinched like it was going to break my arm," Rex said, backing away from Martin, who kept edging closer.

"Was he trying to do more exercises with you?" Martin asked, working to contain his anger.

"How the fuck should I know?" Rex said. "Stop pressing me, Martin, or I'll—"

"You going to knock his brains out, you slicking baboon?" Hans pushed through the humans and sidled around Martin, then grabbed Rex's sleeves and shook him once, twice. "You—are—a—piece—of—SHIT!" Hans shouted, then dropped Rex and turned back to the middle of the room. "Twice Grown, is Stonemaker coming here?"

Twice Grown consulted his wand. "I we have requested such," he said.

"I hope this one's not badly injured."

"Two cords still, one hurt," Twice Grown said. "Will not be complete Sand Piler."

"We're very sorry," Hans said. "Martin, Joe, take Rex to his quarters. Joe, watch and make sure he doesn't leave."

"What?" Rex cried indignantly. "I said it was self-defense, damn it!"

"Do it," Hans repeated coldly.

Rex did not fight them. Rosa watched, hanging from a field in the neck as they passed. "What happened?" she asked.

"Fuck you," Rex said.

Joe grabbed Rex's shoulder with his free hand. "You're swimming in sewage, buddy," he said firmly. "Don't stop paddling or you'll sink."

Rex wiped his eyes and forehead and shook Joe's hand off. He walked between them in silence.

The inquest was held a day later, Stonemaker, Eye on Sky, Hans, Cham, Joe, and Martin presiding. Rex stood between Cham and Joe, considerably subdued. Hans had interviewed him for an hour after the incident.

Stonemaker made the first remarks. "I we have asked the individual Sand Piler for a telling, but memory is degraded. Sand Piler does not see what happened. We we must rely on your individual for testimony."

Hans sat on a rise in the schoolroom floor and folded his arms. "Tell us, Rex."

Rex looked at the humans in the room, all but Hans. "It's a misunderstanding," he said.

"Tell us," Hans said, tone neutral, eyes downcast.

"We met in the neck join. I was going my way—"

"Carrying a bat?" Hans asked.

"The moms made it for our games. We were going to play baseball in the gym."

"We?" Hans asked.

"We were going to choose teams," Rex said.

"Who?"

"Four or five of us. We wanted to see how baseball was played. Do some normal, Earth-type games."

"You met Sand Piler in the join," Hans prompted.

"Yes. I didn't recognize it—"

" 'Him,' " Martin said softly. "That's the accepted pronoun. 'Him.' "

Rex swallowed hard but was not about to argue. Martin saw the apprehension in him, and something else—a blunt kind of defiance, no admission to himself that he had done anything wrong.

"I didn't recognize *him*," Rex said. "I didn't know who it . . . he was. He was big, though. We passed and he reached out to grab me. It hurt. He hurt me."

"Did he give you any warning?"

"He said something, but I couldn't understand. I can't understand any of them."

"Do you understand I we?" Stonemaker asked.

"Mostly, but you speak the best English," Rex said. "It was an accident. He frightened me."

"Did you figure out later what he might have been trying to say?" Martin asked.

"Gentlemen, we have procedures here," Hans interrupted with a heavy sigh. "I'll ask my questions, and Stonemaker will ask his questions."

Martin agreed to that.

"It's a good question, though," Hans said. "What was he trying to say?"

"I don't know," Rex said.

"Something about being on your team in the exercises, the grab races?"

"Maybe," Rex said. "I just didn't hear him clearly."

"Then what?"

"He got me with those claws . . . Grabbed me around the chest. It hurt like hell. I thought he was attacking me."

"And?" Hans pursued.

"I defended myself."

"Was there any reason he would want to attack you?"

"How should I know?" Rex said.

Here it is, Martin thought. *Plain as can be*.

"You mean, the Brothers are unpredictable," Hans said, face clouding.

"I don't know them," Rex said, smiling as if on firmer ground.

Hans turned to Stonemaker. "Rex Live Oak has been to Brother orientations. He participated in the grab races. He's carried Brothers, and been carried by them."

"It wasn't like that," Rex said. "It—he tried to crush me."

"You have bruises?"

Rex dropped his shoulder straps and showed livid bruises around his ribs and abdomen.

Stonemaker rustled, rearranged his coils. Hans put his chin in one hand and bent to examine the bruises. "Did you do anything to frighten him?"

"Nothing. I swear."

"No reason for him to attack you."

"Hey," Rex said, his smile broad now, shoulders lifted.

"Stop smiling, you asshole," Hans said. "Stonemaker, can you tell me how Rex might have frightened Sand Piler?"

"We we have not experienced aggression from our partners before," Stonemaker said. "We we do not understand capacity for being frightened, for giving fright."

"I don't think that's clear," Hans said.

"We we do not expect aggression from you," Eye on Sky said. "There is no reason for we us to be afraid, whatever you do, unless we we are injured. Then we we lose trust and may be afraid."

"Makes sense," Hans said. "It's a pity Sand Piler doesn't remember. I'm open to suggestions from our partners."

The Brothers said nothing, weaving and scenting the air with baking bread, new-mown grass.

"I don't have any guidelines myself," Hans said. "I'm very angry at Rex. Personally, I'd throw his ass outside, if the moms would let us. Would they, Martin?"

Martin shook his head.

"You don't know?" Hans pursued, as if shifting his anger to Martin now, Rex being such a pitiful target.

"I don't think they would let us," Martin clarified.

"Damned lucky for Rex. Stonemaker, I don't know how to make up for this breach, however it happened. I think we should be blunt and say that some of our people are still frightened by your people. Rex seems a simple-minded sort, and anything can happen with *idiots*." He fairly jammed the name down Rex's throat, standing with face pressed a few centimeters from Rex's nose. Surprise or emotion made Rex's eyes water and he stumbled back a step.

"It wasn't anything I planned," he said. "It just happened."

"Will Sand Piler recover?" Hans asked Stonemaker.

"Damage to Sand Piler will not mean breakdown and adoption by others. He will be an individual, and useful to his friends."

"That's . . . very good," Hans said, taking two sharp and broken breaths, as if he were about to hiccough. He seemed infinitely weary as he returned his attention to Rex. "We take care of our own. Brothers judge Brothers, and humans judge humans. You're banned from the Job. I suppose later you might try something really impressive and heroic, and get back your duty. But I wouldn't waste my time thinking about it.''

Rex closed his eyes. ''Hans—'' he said.

''Please go,'' Hans said.

''I was defending myself, for Christ's sake!''

''You're a liar,'' Hans said. ''I can't prove it, but you've lost my confidence, and while I'm Pan, you have no work to do. You're a free man, Rex. Leave before I decide to beat the shit out of you.''

Rex left the room, shaking his head, fists clenched. He slammed a wall just before stepping through the hatch.

Hans bowed very low to Stonemaker and Eye on Sky. ''I beg forgiveness for my people,'' he said. ''We must work together. We have no choice.''

''We we shall work together, and this shall be lost in we our minds,'' Stonemaker said.

''If we judge again, if we take a vote to enact the Law,'' Hans said, standing in the middle of a wealth of planetary images, ''the Brothers will probably vote to investigate. Am I right?''

Martin, Hakim, Joe, and Cham sat circled before Hans in the nose of the ship. Joe and Cham nodded. Hakim kept still and quiet.

''Martin? Will they vote to go in and learn more?''

Martin said he thought they would.

''Because the more we learn, the more ambiguous this all is,'' Hans said softly. ''I don't think it's going to get any better.''

''Terribly ambiguous,'' Cham said. He pulled down a more detailed image of Leviathan's third planet. Smooth, lovely green continents and blue oceans, no visible cloud cover, surface temperature about twenty Celsius, land masses checked with immense tan squares. Surrounding it like a fringe: huge puff-ball seeds, perhaps a thousand kilometers long, touching ocean and continent. The seeds did not limit themselves to the equator; a few even rose from the poles.

Fourth planet, huge and dark, surrounded by seas butting against dark continents spotted with glowing lava-filled rifts. The fifth planet: volatile-rich gas giant, surface temperature of eighty-five kelvins, two point two g's, hints of wide green patches and black ribbons, rotating storms. Again enormous structures studded the upper atmosphere, these shaped like giant nested funnels. The sixth: a smaller gas giant, about the size of Neptune, artificial constructs floating in orbit like braided hair, brilliantly reflective. Thick streamers of gas rose from the giant's surface along the equator, drawn up by the constructs.

"Looks like paradise for the fuel-hungry," Cham said.

"A very masterpiece of bullshit," Hans said. "Designed to do just what it's doing to us."

"Or—" Joe said.

Hans raised an eyebrow.

"I can think of two or three ways what we're seeing could actually be what's there."

"Camouflaged with real races and cultures," Hakim said, taking Joe's hint.

"Explain, please."

"Well, Hakim seems on my wavelength," Joe said.

"I think I see it, too," Cham said.

"Somebody should explain it to the poor old boss-man," Hans said.

"The Killers have given up sending out probes," Hakim said. "They have aligned with other cultures, made alliances, and now hide among them."

Hans cocked his head to one side, squinting one eye dubiously.

"Or they've died out," Joe said, "and other spacefaring races have taken over the system."

"If we don't accept that these planets are all projections or something as crazy as that," Hans said. He slumped his shoulders and closed his eyes. "Has anybody asked the moms what they think?"

"I've asked for a formal meeting with a mom and a snake mother," Martin said. "I've asked that Stonemaker and whoever he wants to bring should be there, too."

"Shouldn't I be there?" Hans asked, opening one eye.

"Of course," Martin said.

Hans pinned Martin with a fishy gaze, then smiled. "Good. We've been exercising for a tenday now. Everything's smooth."

"There are still problems with some of our crew," Martin said.

"But they're doing the work," Hans said.

Martin hesitated, then agreed.

"Let me deal with just a few hundred things at a time." Hans stood and stretched. He had put on weight around the stomach and his face seemed puffy. "Rex is staying out of sight. I hope his example keeps the others in check. I need a plan. What are we going to do if the decision is to investigate, get right in close before we drop weapons?"

"Split the ship," Joe said.

Cham agreed. "Maybe into two or three ships, dispersed to swing back at different times, from different angles. All black, all silent."

"My thoughts exactly," Hans said. "Martin?"

"The ship that goes in first . . . it's a fantasy to think it will stay hidden for long, if at all."

"So?"

"Maybe it should go in openly. Maybe it should be disguised. A Trojan horse."

Hans leaned his head back, looking at Martin over his short nose and open mouth. "Uh, Jesus is simple, Satan is complex. We come in openly, we're traveling merchants, we're not hunting killer probes. We've just come to show our wares—"

Cham cackled and slapped his legs. Hakim looked around, still bewildered. "Don't you see?" Cham asked him.

"I am not—"

"Slick them at their own game," Joe said. Hakim caught on but suddenly frowned.

"They know we were at Wormwood," he said. "They know—"

"They may not know anything," Martin said, energized by his own idea, and Hans' elaboration. "They could easily assume Wormwood killed us in the trap. They're more vulnerable, but for that reason, they can't afford to throw off their disguise—if it is a disguise—"

"Because traveling merchants might tattle on them, or be expected somewhere else, and missed if they don't show," Hans said. "And they have a reputation in the neighborhood to maintain. They let the Red Tree Runners go . . . Martin, my faith in you has paid off. Anything after this is bonus.''

"It is not a bad idea," Hakim agreed, smiling at Martin.

"But it needs development," Hans said. "I want a full proposal, with details, before we talk with the Brothers."

Giacomo and Jennifer picked up quickly around their compartment, embarrassed that Martin had come to visit unexpectedly. Clothing, scrap paper waiting to be run through the ship's recycling, sporting equipment for joint human-Brother games, were quickly stacked into piles and shoved aside. "This would be a real mess if we were coasting," Jennifer said.

"Don't worry about it," Martin said, waving his hand. "I'm just dropping by on my own initiative. Hans hasn't asked for a report on the translations, but I thought I'd inquire . . ."

"We're working with two of the Brothers now, Many Smells and Dry Skin," Jennifer said.

"Those are complimentary names," Giacomo said, smiling.

"Dry Skin has even chosen a human name. He wants to be called Norman. Sometimes Eye on Sky helps."

"So what do we have?" Martin asked. "Are their libraries better than ours?"

"They're certainly different," Giacomo said. "We've barely begun to translate the really technical stuff, but the snake mothers seem more open with their facts, more trusting. There's less fear of influencing the Brothers, I think—that is, taking away their freedom to choose by overawing them. The Brothers are pretty solid, psychologically."

"Can we learn anything more from their libraries?"

Jennifer looked at Giacomo. "Possibly, if they help us translate."

"Shouldn't you know one way or the other by now?"

"If their libraries stored key concepts in words, yes," Jennifer said. "I'm sure we'd know. But the reason we had to call on Many Smells and Dry Skin/Norman is because we were having such a tough time dealing with the synesthesia—with translating smells and music into human language. Their math is disintegrated, literally—no integers. They deal with everything in probabilistic terms. Numbers are smears of probability. They don't see things separated from each other, only in relations. No arithmetic, only algebras. How many planets around Leviathan? It's expressed in terms of Leviathan's history, the shape of its planet-forming cloud ages past . . . Only after a Brother understands everything there is to know, will he have an idea how many planets there are. Even their most simple calculations are mind-wrecking, to us—parallel processing of cords in each braid. It's math for much more powerful minds than ours."

"We talked about that already," Giacomo said. "But the definite article is also missing from their languages. They have three languages, auditory, olfactory, and written—but writing is supplementary to the rest. All we've gotten access to is the written, so far. Norman is trying to convert olfactory into written, but he says it's the most difficult thing he's ever done."

"What do the annotations tell us?" Martin asked.

"They're intriguing," Jennifer said, leaning forward, eyes narrowing with enthusiasm. "The snake mothers trust the Brothers—"

"Like we said," Giacomo interrupted.

"The snake mothers seem to think there's no chance the Brothers could ever turn into planet killers."

"But they're not so certain about us," Giacomo said.

"The Brothers were littoral, beach grazers—at least, in their earliest forms," Jennifer said. "Almost all their cities were located along coastlines. They made artificial beaches inland to feed the growing populations—that was the beginning of civilization for them. They seem embarrassed by their past, as if hunters and gatherers—us—might think beachcombers are inferior."

"I think their world had little or no axial tilt," Giacomo said. "No seasons, but with two moons—"

"We haven't heard any of this!" Martin said, astonished. "Why didn't you tell us about this sooner?"

"We were waiting to be absolutely sure," Jennifer said.

"Couldn't you just ask Norman or Many Smells?"

"Not nearly so simple," Jennifer said, looking away, fiddling with the overalls at her knees. "The snake mothers may have told them to be careful about telling us too much."

Martin let his breath out with a low moan. "Why?"

"Because while we've been exploring their libraries, they've been going through ours, and they're a lot better equipped to understand them."

"They're awed by our capacity for violence," Giacomo said ruefully. "They became *really* interested after Rex attacked Sand Piler."

"Our history is so different," Jennifer said. "Many Smells watched some of our movies. We tried to interpret for him."

"*The Longest Day*," Giacomo said. "*Ben-Hur. Patton*. He was particularly confused by *The Godfather* and *Star Wars*. Jennifer tried to explain *The Forever War*. He was pretty quiet afterward, and he didn't smell like much of anything."

Martin shook his head, puzzled.

"They don't release scents when they feel threatened and want to hide," Jennifer explained. "Sand Piler stunk things up because he was injured. That was his distress call."

Martin shook his head. "Why weren't you a little more . . . selective about what he watched?"

Jennifer blinked owlishly. "I don't see how we can expect them to be open with their libraries, if we aren't open with our own. We tried to find some movies we thought they might appreciate more," she added. "Domestic comedies. Family films. He watched *Arsenic and Old Lace*. We couldn't erase first impressions, and after Rex's attack, who would blame them?"

Martin let out his breath and closed his eyes. "All right."

"I think they're having a hard time accepting anything made-up," Giacomo said. "We had to explain the movies were not about real events. Except the history films—and even those were reenactments, fictionalized."

"What about literature?"

"They're just getting into some now. No reaction yet."

Martin felt a sudden rush of shame: collective, human shame. He rubbed his nose and shook his head. "We may be allies, but not trusted companions."

"Exactly," Giacomo said.

"We didn't want to tell Hans until we were sure. We thought he might take it badly."

"With him in charge, I don't wonder the Brothers are worried about us," Jennifer said.

"He's under a lot of pressure," Martin said.

"Hans has gotten us through some tough times," Giacomo said. "But he's fragile. Who knows what will happen when things get tough again?"

"Don't blinker yourself," Jennifer said.

Martin looked down at the floor, hands clasped. "Tell me more about the annotations, about whatever you think you've learned."

"Their information on other worlds is extensive. The snake mothers have told them more about types of civilizations, levels of technology, past encounters with different civilizations that went killer. We're still trying to work out the implications."

"Is it possible," Martin began, face brightening, "that the Benefactors simply built the snake mothers and the Brothers' ship after they built ours? Maybe things loosened up. Maybe the Benefactors became less concerned about the Killers getting strategic information."

Giacomo shrugged. "Possibly."

"Maybe we're being a little too self-critical," Martin suggested. "Letting our guilt complexes lead us by the nose."

"Let's not worry about it for now," Jennifer said. "What we need to worry about is how much in their libraries is new and useful to us. I think in a couple of tendays, we'll know enough to make a strong report to Hans."

"You should talk with the snake mothers," Giacomo suggested. "Not Hans. *You*."

"Bring Paola with you," Jennifer said. "They may think we're more stable in male-female pairs."

"Too bad Theresa couldn't be here," Giacomo said wistfully. "You and she, together, would have been just what they're looking for."

"They like working with dyads," Jennifer said. "They really like Giacomo and me."

"If we could all be in love and connected to each other—" Giacomo began.

"They'd feel more affinity for us," Jennifer concluded.

Martin grinned. "We'll try to make do."

PART
THREE

PART
THREE

MARTIN FOUND TWICE GROWN IN THE SCHOOLROOM, COILED IN deep discussion with Erin Eire and Carl Phoenix. Paola squatted on a cushion to one side and knitted a blanket, clarifying when necessary.

"But you don't have fiction in your literature," Carl was saying. "And you don't have poetry. You have these symphonies of odors . . . I suppose they'd be like music to us. But nothing comparable to literature."

"It has made things difficult for learning," Twice Grown said. "I we have adjusted to thoughts that things described in your literature, in fiction, did not actually happen. Even your recorded history is indefinite. Is it not better to know something is truth before communicating?"

"We like experiencing things that didn't happen," Erin Eire said. "There's a difference between writing fiction and lying."

"Though I'll be damned if I can pin it down," Carl said, smiling.

"Carl means," Paola said, lifting her chin but keeping her eyes on her knitting, "he can't easily describe what the difference is between writing stories and lying. But there is a difference."

Erin turned to Martin. "We're having difficulty explaining this to him," she said.

"We we do not create situations for our stories," Twice Grown said. "It seems possible to confuse, especially the young."

"I we—" Erin cleared her throat. "I think we know the difference. Fiction is relaxing, like dreaming. Lying, not telling the truth, is to gain social advantage."

"We we do not dream," Twice Grown said. "We our method of sleep is unlike yours. We we sleep rarely, and are not braided when sleeping, but we our cords are inactive for a time every few days."

"Do cords dream?" Paola asked, looking up from her knitting.

"Cords have mental activity not accessible to braided individuals," Twice Grown said. "They are not smart, but behave on programmed paths."

"Instinct," Carl Phoenix suggested.

"Does this make fiction a kind of waking dream, something two or more people do together?" Twice Grown asked, smelling of peppers and salt sea. He was intensely interested; but Martin also detected a whiff of turpentine, and that might have been nervousness.

"I suppose," Erin said. "One or more people make up a story—"

"But it is known to resemble the real?" Twice Grown interrupted, coils rustling.

"Fiction is based on real settings, sometimes," Carl said.

"We're getting into pretty abstract territory," Martin warned.

"Based on real behaviors, such that it is not unlikely for humans to behave in such a fashion?"

"Well . . ." Martin said.

"Characters in fiction sometimes do things real people would like to do, but don't dare," Erin said, pleased that she had scored a point of clarification.

Twice Grown did not understand. "I we have a question about this. I we have read short stories, and are now reading novels, which take long to eat."

"Finish," Paola suggested.

"To finish a novel. In some pages, I we see closeness with human behavior in a story, and in reality. But in other pages, other texts, behavior surpasses what I we have experienced. Are these behaviors not available to the humans we we know?"

"Which behaviors?" Erin asked.

Martin wished he could end the conversation now. The smell of turpentine had intensified. Twice Grown was either nervous, feeling threatened, or wanted to flee.

"Harming and other violences," Twice Grown replied. "The wishing to kill, to inactivate. I we have read *Beowulf*, and I we have read *Macbeth*. I we have also read *The Pit and the Pendulum*."

"Physical conflict is important in fiction," Martin said. "It plays a much smaller role in our everyday life."

Erin gave him a look that as much as said, *Always the politician.* "Some humans are capable of violence," she said. "Sometimes, when we're frightened . . ."

"This fear emotion, when you wish to flee or hide," Twice Grown interrupted, "it is different from we our fear. You not only wish to flee and hide, but to destroy the thing which causes fear."

"That makes sense, doesn't it?" Carl asked.

"But I we do not know this fear emotion. Is it akin to wishing to flee, or is it akin to a wish to do violence?"

"It's part of getting ready to run or fight back," Carl said. "An urge to protect oneself, or one's family and friends."

"But is it also awareness of the unknown? We we find the unknown powerful, like a stimulant. We we willingly sacrifice to the danger of unknown for experience in knowing, understanding. You do not?"

"We've had people willing to do that," Martin said.

"But they've been rare," Erin said. "Mostly, we try to conquer or protect ourselves against danger."

"That is difficult," Twice Grown said. "Are new friends not unknown? Do you wish to conquer new friends?"

"I think maybe we should put together a discussion group later," Martin said. "We need to think through our answers and not give wrong impressions."

"Need for more thinking, yes," Twice Grown said. "For looking at humans, there is a mystery not like looking at we ourselves; a wondering if perhaps there is death here, without cause, like a sharkness in the waves."

Erin's eyes widened. "Oh, no," she said. "Fiction is a way of letting off steam."

"What?" Twice Grown asked.

"She means, releasing personal and cultural tensions," Paola said. "I think Martin's right. We should think this over and let humans and Brothers debate and ask questions. We're just making things muddier."

Twice Grown grew still and tightened his coils. His odors had dissipated; Martin could smell nothing now. "I we would enjoy such a debate," he said. "To rid of the mud."

A snake mother and a mom awaited Martin, Paola, and Ariel, and two Brothers—Stonemaker and Eye on Sky—in empty quarters along the boundary between human and Brother territory.

Paola Birdsong seemed surprised that Martin had chosen her for this meeting, but Martin had grown more and more impressed with her skills in dealing with the Brothers.

Ariel was quiet, alert, and slightly nervous. Neither asked why they were chosen; he did not volunteer to tell them.

Martin had conferred with Hans about the meeting; he had been a little surprised when Hans had decided not to attend.

"I'm sure I'm a little tainted right now, having worked with Rex too closely," Hans had said. "You go. Ask some pointed questions." He had seemed subdued, even sad.

Martin put that from his mind as the snake mother and the mom settled themselves before them. Stonemaker and Eye on Sky sat in formal coils, rustling faintly. They emitted no scents Martin could detect.

"We may begin," the mom said.

"We have important decisions to make," Martin began. "But first we have to agree on overall strategies. And I think we have to . . . clear the air a little."

He hadn't meant to bring up the problem of trust; but now there was no way to avoid it.

Stonemaker said, "It is good we all we meet now. But for we us, clear air is ominous. Can you explain?"

"The more we learn about Leviathan, the more confused we become," Martin said. "It looks like a thriving stellar system."

"Like a shoreline marketplace," Paola said by way of enhancement for the Brothers.

"Yes," Eye on Sky said.

"We haven't seen visitors come from outside, so perhaps it's an isolated market," Martin continued. "But there's evidence many different races live there. If this isn't another illusion, or if we can't penetrate the illusion from this distance, what are we going to do next?"

"Do you ask us?" the mom inquired.

"Not really. I'm just throwing the question open."

"We we are opposed to passing judgment without conclusive evidence," Stonemaker said.

"So are we," Martin said. "But we're also fairly convinced this is another blind the Killers are hiding behind."

"We all we must be more than fairly certain to condemn these worlds," Eye on Sky said.

"I think we're in agreement," Martin said. *They still have no scent; what's going on?* "So we have to design the mission accordingly. How many ships can we make out of *Dawn Treader* and the *Journey House*?"

The mom said, "As many as are required. How many do you contemplate?"

"At least three. Humans have talked about entering the Leviathan system in disguise, as visitors. Could we create a different kind of ship, something that doesn't look at all like a Ship of the Law?"

"Yes," the mom said.

"Would it be within the Law for the ships' minds to help us create such a disguise?"

"An interesting question, I we agree," Stonemaker said.

"It would be no more inappropriate than providing you with the original Ships of the Law," the mom said.

"I think we should assume Leviathan is not what it seems," Martin said.

"A reasonable beginning," Stonemaker said.

"Just to be cautious," Martin added.

"Agreed."

"Acting under such an assumption, we also should assume that the beings behind the disguise are Killers . . ."

"Agreed," Stonemaker repeated.

"And the Killers probably have some knowledge, perhaps extensive knowledge, of the civilizations in this vicinity, and what they're capable of," Martin said.

"You wish to design a ship that might come from such a civilization," the mom said.

"Yes. A ship that couldn't be destroyed without interstellar repercussions," Martin said.

"You are assuming," Eye on Sky began, "that this disguise is meant for senses other than we all our own. That the Killers of worlds assume they are under scrutiny from others besides we all ourselves."

Martin nodded.

"He means yes," Paola said.

"It is remarkable insight," Stonemaker said. A faint smell of peppers and baking bread: interest, perhaps pleasure for one or more of the Brothers. "I we see this is related to your literature, as a fiction or strategic lie. Would all this joined Ship of the Law be part of play-act?"

"Hans and I believe the ship should divide into several parts," Martin said. "One part will enter the system, disguised but essentially unarmed, to investigate; the other two will orbit far outside. If a guilty verdict is reached, weapons can be released by the ships outside. We can try to finish the Job. If the Killers no longer live here—"

"Or if we can't hurt them without hurting innocents," Ariel said. Martin cringed inwardly. *Yes, but what if?*

"Or if we can't find them or recognize them," Martin amended, "then we'll rejoin and change our plans."

"That is feasible," the mom said. "Useful information will be made available. Do you wish to design the vessel that enters the Leviathan system, or do you wish us to design it for you?"

"We can do it, but I think we'll need assistance," Martin said. Ariel was about to add something, but he looked at her dourly and she clenched her jaw.

"Your designers should think about these things," the mom said. "The ship to enter Leviathan's system must not appear overtly threatening, nor should it appear to come from a weak civilization. It should not, however, appear to have technology equal to that possessed by the Ships of the Law, specifically, the ability to convert matter to anti-matter. Your crew must appear innocent of all knowledge of killer probes.''

Martin agreed.

"When will your groups make their decisions?" the mom asked.

"In a couple of days, maybe sooner," Martin said.

"Separation and super-deceleration will have to begin within a tenday," the mom said.

"Is there anything else we'd find useful?" Martin asked.

"There is no possibility that the Killers, if they still exist around Leviathan, have knowledge of humans," the mom continued. "No killer probes escaped Earth's system. There is a small possibility they have knowledge of the Brothers. Transmissions by the killer probes from the Brothers' system were monitored, information content unknown.''

"We we would like to be part of the crew of any entry vessel," Eye on Sky said. "This might be a difficulty?"

"It might," the mom concluded.

The snake mother arched and floated a few centimeters above the ground, a purple ladder field faintly visible beneath. In this, too, they differed from the moms; Martin had never seen a mom display its field. Its voice sounded like a low wind interpreted by the string section in an orchestra. "Brothers may play key roles in ships that stay outside the system," it said.

"Is that something they will vote on?" Paola asked, brow wrinkling.

"It is something to be decided by the Brothers in private," the snake mother said.

Eye on Sky and Stonemaker produced strong smells of salt sea air. "So is it," Stonemaker said. "There will be a Triple Merging for objectivity and decisions will be made before next day comes."

"I have one more question," Martin said, feeling his chest constrict. "It isn't an easy one, and I hope for a straightforward answer."

Silence from the robots. Eye on Sky and Stonemaker rustled faintly.

"Some of us have been given the impression—rather, we've observed—that the Brothers' libraries are much more extensive than our own. Why are they more extensive?"

The mom said, "Each race is given the information necessary to carry out its part of the Law."

"We feel the ships' minds may not think humans are as trustworthy as the Brothers," Martin continued.

"Every race differs in its needs and capacities," the mom said. "Information differs for that reason."

"Will we be denied any of the information contained in the Brothers' libraries?" Martin asked.

"You will be denied nothing you need, as a group, to complete your Job."

The snake mother said, "Your Ship of the Law is older than the Brothers' ship. There are design differences."

"I thought that might explain part of the . . ." Martin said, trailing off.

"Attitudes and designs change," the snake mother added.

"We have discussed this before," the mom said.

Martin nodded. "I'd like to have it made more clear. Do you trust humans as much as you trust the Brothers?"

"We are not designed to trust or distrust, or to make any such decisions regarding character," the mom replied.

"Please," Martin said through clenched teeth. Ariel reached out and touched his hand, and he gripped hers tightly, feeling her support, her strength. "We do not need evasive answers. The Benefactors could not have known our character before you sent your ships into the Earth's system . . . You must have made some judgment, reached some decision about our capacities."

The ship's voice spoke. Martin was startled. "The ships' minds can't make such decisions. If such a decision was made, we didn't make it."

He felt tears on his cheeks and gritted his teeth, ashamed at showing such emotion. "Are we inferior to the Brothers?"

Stonemaker became agitated. His rustling increased until his entire length vibrated. Eye on Sky coiled and uncoiled twice, weaving his head. "Offense is given here," Stonemaker said. "We we do not wish we our partners to feel offensed."

"Offended," Paola corrected automatically.

"We need to know whether we are trusted," Martin repeated, it seemed to him, for the hundredth time.

"Both libraries will be open to those who wish to conduct research," the ship's voice said. "What is shared and is not shared is up to humans and Brothers, not to the ships' minds."

"We came close to the edge," Paola said sadly as they walked toward Hans' quarters. "Maybe we don't want to know the whole truth."

"Maybe the Brothers are afraid of us," Ariel said. "Of what we might become."

"What do they think we'll do?" Paola asked.

Martin's voice shook with anger—and with more than a little guilt. "They might think we'll become planet killers," he said.

Ariel shivered to untense her muscles. "Rex certainly didn't convince them otherwise," she said. "What about the moms?"

"Maybe they think so, too," Martin said.

"Wouldn't they have dumped us or killed us or something?" Paola objected.

"Not if they're forced to enact the bloody Law," Ariel said. "We were victims. They rescued us. They need us to finish the Job."

"Why not push us aside, and let the Brothers do the Job?" Paola asked. "They only need one set of victims."

"So maybe we've scared the Brothers. What have we shown them to the contrary?" Martin asked.

Paola stared back at him, jaw quivering. "Me," she said, pointing to herself. "You. We're not all like Rex."

"How could they know?" Ariel asked. "Let's just ask ourselves that."

"By looking at me!" Paola said, crying openly now. "I'm not like that!"

"Do they expect to send pacifists out to kill worlds?" Martin asked, feeling his anger build, then deflate. He let his shoulders slump. "What are we? Allies, or just bad cargo?"

Hans examined the designs for the *Trojan Horse*, nodding and humming faintly. Martin, Hakim, Cham, Donna Emerald Sea, and Giacomo had spent the better part of two days working out the design and details with Dry Skin, Silken Parts, and Eye on Sky; even now, in the Brothers' quarters, Eye on Sky presented the design to Stonemaker for his approval.

"It certainly doesn't look like a Ship of the Law," Hans concluded. "It looks like a pleasure barge."

Eighty meters long, with a brilliant red surface, laser/solar sails folded and rolled along its length, two curving arms reaching from a spindle-shaped body, small, heavily shielded matter–anti-matter drives mounted fore and aft, the *Trojan Horse* would appear to be the product of a relatively youthful technology, star travel on the cheap.

Humans and Brothers had come up with something unarmed, innocuous—in so far as any starship could be innocuous, heralding the arrival of potential rivals or partners—and even jaunty.

"The moms say it can be built," Martin said. "They say it will fly, and it will be convincing."

"Do they say anything about our fitness to be allies?" Hans asked. The circles under his eyes had darkened. He spent much of his time alone in his quarters, as he sat now, in the center of the room, legs crossed.

A second cushion waited empty nearby; Rosa might still share his quarters occasionally. Yet the condition of a few vases of sickly flowers showed that she had probably not been here for several days.

"Are we fit for the Job?" Hans asked.

"I don't know what they think," Martin said. "Rex caused a lot of bad feeling. If the Brothers can experience something like bad feeling . . ."

"What would they have thought if I'd executed Rex right there, on the spot?" Hans said. "Would that have made them happy?"

"Would have made things much worse," Martin said.

"Well, if they don't like us now, they're going to really have it in for us in a couple of days," Hans said.

"Why?"

"Rosa's on her own," Hans said. "You should have been here, Martin. She refuses to slick. she looks me right in the eye, and she says," he began to do a fair imitation of Rosa's strong, musical voice, " 'I have been shown what you are. I have been shown that you are mocking me, and holding me back from my duty.' " Hans grinned. "At least it took her this long to catch on. Not bad for delaying action, right?"

Martin looked away.

Hans' grin vanished. "She's going to start up again, Martin, and this time she really has something good for us. She's damned near psychic, and she's tuning in to our inadequacy. 'We have sinned. We are not worthy of the Job.' Good stuff to toss out now, right?"

"Where is she?" Martin asked.

"I don't know."

"I'll ask Ariel to look out for her."

"Yes, but who will keep her under control? She should be the one banished and locked away. Before she's done, she'll have us all at each other's throats." Hans picked up the wand and projected the ship's design again. "Who's going to be on board?"

"The moms and snake mothers think there's a small chance the Killers might have information about the Brothers. The Brothers are willing to let the crew be human—"

Hans laughed with a bitter edge that set Martin's neck hair on end. "It's probably a suicide mission. How kind of them."

Martin's jaw worked. "Don't underestimate them, Hans. They want to go. They want to do the Job as much as we do."

"I'd rather survive to see it done."

"At any rate," Martin said, "I thought, subject to your approval, that it would be better psychologically and politically if we took the chance, and had Brothers on the crew."

Hans rotated the ship's image, poked his tongue into his cheek, rolled it over his teeth beneath closed lips. "How do we explain two species aboard, if we party with Leviathan's citizens?"

"Hakim and Giacomo are working up a whole fake history. Two intelligent species from one star system, cooperating after centuries of war. The alliance is still fragile, but the crew is disciplined—"

"We're better at making up stories than the Brothers, I hear," Hans said.

"After a fashion."

"Where's the origin?"

"Hakim has found a buttercup star about forty light years from Leviathan. For the *Trojan Horse*, that would mean a journey of about four hundred years. The crew will have just come out of deep freeze."

"They get this bucket up to, what, one fifth, one sixth c? What's the drive?"

"In theory, laser propulsion and solar sail to the outskirts of the home system, primitive matter–anti-matter beyond, no sumps, no conversion technology," Martin said.

"And the Killers won't know this is all crap? Can't they detect drive flares at forty light years? Didn't their probes hit on this star system?"

"For a ship this size, detection of drive flares at forty light years would be almost impossible. The moms say the chosen system shows no signs of being visited. They say the ruse probably will work."

Hans rolled his tongue across his teeth again, looked away. "If they say it, it must be so."

"Do you approve the design?"

Hans shrugged. "It looks fine to me. Who's going?"

"That's your decision, of course," Martin said.

"I'm glad you've left me something to do."

Martin did not rise to the gibe. "If you're having a problem with any of this, or with me, best to talk it out now."

Hans looked at Martin darkly. "I'm worried about crew morale. I'll be damned if I can find any easy solution, or any solution at all."

"Isolate Rosa," Martin said.

"There are about twenty Wendys and Lost Boys who would be very upset if we isolated Rosa. She's been quiet, but busy."

Martin raised his eyebrows, baffled.

"I'm working on it," Hans said with forced cheer. "You seem to be doing well with this stuff. Keep it up." He waved his hand as if shooing a fly and made a wry face. "Hell with it. Forget what I said. Brothers and humans. You choose the human crew. I'd like to be on the ship, but I don't think that will be possible. So pick yourself. You'll be number one again, at least aboard the *Trojan Horse*."

Martin stood beside Hans for a few more seconds, but Hans had nothing more to say, lost in his thoughts.

Two days before separation, humans and Brothers exhausted from endless drills and conferences, Leviathan a growing point of light and remotes spread to their farthest extent, Martin was overwhelmed by far more information than he could possibly absorb. In his rest periods—now reduced to one or two hours a day—he slept fitfully, images of Leviathan's bizarre coterie of fifteen worlds haunting his dreams.

Theodore Dawn sat in a wood-paneled library with him and pulled out book after book, opening them to pictures of ill-defined threats and dangers until, with a laugh, Theodore simply tossed the books into the air. "We always knew we'd die, didn't we, Marty?"

"You're already dead," Marty said.

"We're Brothers under the skin. But even if we die, *so will they*," Theodore said.

"Who?" Martin asked, wondering if he meant the Killers of Earth, or the Brothers.

He awoke with wand clutched in his hand, and no answer.

"Three ships, *Greyhound*, *Shrike*, and *Trojan Horse*," Hans said, projecting the designs of all three before the seven occupants of the schoolroom: Eye on Sky, Silken Parts, Stonemaker, Twice Grown, Paola, Ariel, and Martin.

Eye on Sky and Ariel would be going with the *Trojan Horse* and Martin. Stonemaker would be in charge of *Shrike*.

Hans said, "You've all worked out the *Trojan Horse*'s mission: envoy and explorer for a young, naïve two-species civilization, four hundred years in space. Enough clues to make the Killers think that in the four centuries since *Trojan Horse* left its system, the civilizations have probably become much, much stronger, and would not appreciate having their early explorers destroyed . . . Donna Emerald Sea and Silken Parts are designing costumes reflecting the cultures." He smiled. "Sounds like the Brothers are learning the art of fiction."

"But this is lying," Stonemaker said. "The difference was clear, we we thought."

"Strategically, no difference," Hans said. "*Greyhound* and *Shrike* have enough weapons and fuel to cook four of the fifteen planets, or enough to blow one planet completely apart, into orbit about itself if we aren't interfered with—no defenses—a big if . . . The human crews are ready."

"Brothers are ready," Stonemaker said, smelling of ripe fruit and cut grass.

"Then we bring the plan to both crews." Hans raised his hands and the Brothers lifted their splayed heads high. "Courage!" he said. "Does that translate well?"

"It is the smell of being born," Stonemaker said.

"Couldn't put it better myself," Hans said.

Martin came awake to a soft touch on his shoulder. He had fallen asleep in the schoolroom, leaning against a wall. He rubbed his eyes and saw Erin Eire kneeling beside him. "Too much drill?" she asked.

He stood and stretched. They had two days until the split; preparations had come flooding down on them, and he was embarrassed that his exhaustion had made him drop off in a public place. "Trying to sleep before super deceleration."

"Uh huh," she said, unconvinced. "Donna guided the Wendys and a few Lost Boys in costume manufacture. Moms provided the fabric and did some assembly. We thought you'd like to see them. I think they're pretty neat, myself."

"Sure," Martin said. Erin led him past groups of other humans, sleeping. Many Smells and Dry Skin conferred with Giacomo near the star sphere; everybody looked exhausted except Erin Eire, who as always was bright-eyed, calmly confident.

"Where's Hans?" Erin asked as she walked steadily ahead.

"Putting together battle plans with Stonemaker, last I heard," Martin said.

"*Trojan Horse*'s crew won't know the battle plans?" Erin asked. "In case they're captured?"

Martin shook his head. "No strategic weapons. What can we do?"

"Pray, I suppose," Erin said tersely. "We've been working in Kimberly Quartz's rooms, just up ahead . . ."

Rosa stepped from a side corridor, Jeanette Snap Dragon close behind. They blocked Erin and Martin's way. "We need to talk to Martin," Jeanette said.

Erin stepped aside. "Don't take too long. I'm going to show off the costumes."

"For a masquerade?" Rosa asked caustically. She looked if anything even more exhausted than Hans.

"You should leave," Jeanette said pointedly to Erin. Erin looked to Martin.

"If she wants, she can stay," Martin said.

"This is a private audience," Jeanette said.

"Who's giving the audience?" Martin asked.

"I thought you might have some promise," Rosa said. "Now I have my doubts. Let her stay, then. Word will get around faster." Rosa turned her full attention on Martin. "There's a separate crew forming. We're choosing a new Pan."

Martin folded his arms, too tired to express much surprise. "Oh?"

"I'm inviting you to join the crew. Some have said you'd be an asset."

"I said you would," Jeanette added, as if defying him to disappoint her.

"What good is a separate crew?"

"The ship is splitting," Rosa said. "Those who go with me have their freedom. Those who go with Hans . . . That's up to them. Will you join us?"

"We're dividing in three to perform a mission," Martin said. "There's no plan to let you or anybody take a ship."

"We've voted to split," Jeanette said, face flushed, left hand quivering. "You shouldn't stop us. Hans shouldn't. It would only prove how much freedom we've lost."

"I have concluded that Leviathan is innocent. We're in the wrong place," Rosa said.

"You've been *told*?" Martin asked without sarcasm.

"I've been told," Rosa said. Erin lifted her eyes and tilted her head to one side.

"Let's talk with Hans about it," Martin suggested.

"Hans is our enemy," Jeanette said. "He's—"

"Please," Rosa said, touching her arm. "Nobody's our enemy."

"How many agree with you?" Martin asked.

"Enough to make a difference," Rosa said.

"I'll meet with your people, then," Martin said.

"Without telling Hans?" Jeanette asked.

Rosa watched him closely, expression taut but not agitated.

"Without telling Hans. Erin, I'll see the costumes a little later."

Erin nodded and marched off.

"This is strictly between you and me," Martin called to her.

"Of course," Erin said. "Your secret."

"I'll call the people," Jeanette said.

"Do that," Rosa said. Jeanette ran down the corridor, vanished around a corner. "Hans taught me that extremes accomplish nothing. If I receive privileged information, I'm not about to give it to just anybody."

"Good," Martin said.

"You needed my words once, didn't you?" Rosa asked.

Martin saw no reason to lie. "They were attractive."

"But Hans' influence soured you. You thought I supported him and his plans, that he had co-opted me."

"It seemed that way."

"It wasn't that way. Hans took what he wanted from me, and I learned what I needed to learn. I must say, I miss the innocence of those first few weeks, when I could behave as the word took me."

"The word of God," Martin said.

Rosa shrugged. "Something speaks to me. Call it God if you need a name. For me, it's just a very powerful friend to all of us. We live in confusion . . . It clears away the confusion."

Jeanette returned. "We're meeting now," she said.

Rosa had made new quarters for herself on the perimeter of the ship's second homeball.

Fifteen Wendys and five Lost Boys had gathered among the flowers. Rex Live Oak squatted on the floor next to a potted rosebush, glancing at Martin, turning away after a brief staring contest. The air thickened with an unpleasant mix of flower scent and stress.

Rosa took the center of the room.

"I've brought Martin here to explain our position," she said. "We are not planning a mutiny. We are simply asking to be allowed to go our own way. We opt out of the Law."

How can they? Don't they feel it, the dying Earth, hear it in their blood and flesh?

"We'd hate to lose so many of you," Martin said. "I'm willing to listen, though."

"The aliens who have joined us are not acceptable," Rosa said. "They don't like us, and frankly, most of us don't feel comfortable with them."

"We're working with them," Martin said. "We're getting along pretty well, I think. Most of us." He looked at Rex, but Rex did not meet the challenge.

"I have been told their work does not fit with our own," Rosa said. "They have a different moral standard."

"If anything, their moral standard seems a little higher than our own, from what I've seen," Martin said.

"It is different, and that's sufficient. I have been told that it is not right to mix our destiny with the destinies of those not human."

So what is it, an abomination in the eyes of the Lord? That was Theodore Dawn talking in his head, tone bitter, voice nasal, a caricature of all that Theodore had hated.

"I don't see that at all," Martin said.

"I have been told, and for us, that's enough," Rosa said.

He conceded that for the moment. "We can't spare you. If you leave, we might not get the Job done."

"The Job is merely vengeance, and I have been told the races of Leviathan are innocent."

"I wish I had your sources," Martin said, trying to smile without showing his exasperation.

"You do," Rosa said, nodding. "I tell you."

"Does anybody else hear what Rosa hears?" Martin asked.

Five Wendys and two Lost Boys, Rex included, raised their hands. Jeanette said, "I don't hear the words myself, but I see the truth."

Others agreed with Jeanette.

"We won't punish the innocent," Rosa said. "Revenge is the straight road to spirit death. We cannot carry out the Law if the Law is cruel and wrong."

Martin could not think of a wise and circumspect method of dealing with Rosa now. "You've done this before," he began, conflicting impulses making the words thick in his mouth. He swallowed and held out his hands as if he might grab someone's neck. "Rosa, there's real danger here. You could tear this crew apart. You say you're talking to God—"

"I never said that," Rosa interrupted.

"You say you have direct access to the *truth*. That makes you . . . what, the fount of all knowledge, we have to come to *you* to be told what to do?"

"Better me than Hans," Rosa said.

"You want to take away everything we've worked for, everything we've devoted our lives to—"

"If it's wrong, it's wrong."

"But where's your evidence, Rosa? Divine authority?"

"That's enough for us," Jeanette said. "It makes more sense than you do."

"Are you all willing to throw in with . . . divine authority? Hand everything, your grief and your . . . will power, your self-respect, everything, to *Rosa*?"

Kai Khosrau said, "We're tired, Martin. Revenge is useless."

"Revenge against the innocent is evil," Jacob Dead Sea said. Attila Carpathia, Terry Loblolly, Alexis Baikal, and Drusilla Norway all nodded, looked to each other for support and confirmation, some with expressions of beatific obedience, human sheep having given up their higher selves.

Rosa had eaten them.

She had once come close to eating Martin. He shivered and wondered what would have happened had he tipped, had he undergone a conversion to Rosa's faith; would he be with them now, working to undermine the Job, to protest the enactment of the Law?

"It is not up to you alone to judge innocence or guilt," Martin said. "The crews make that judgment."

"We've judged already," Rosa said. "We will not abide by what others say."

"We can't afford to lose you," Martin said, realizing that he would lose this confrontation; that Rosa for the time being was stronger.

"You've lost us already," Kai Khosrau said. "What can you do about it—lock us up?"

"Lock us all up," Rex said. "At least you'll keep us away from the Brothers."

"None of us will have contact with the Brothers," Rosa said. "There will be—"

"What is this, a list of demands?" Martin asked.

"You listen to her," Rex said in his most threatening tone. Rosa lifted her hand.

"A list of facts," she said quietly, firmly. "We are autonomous now. We make our own rules. We will live apart, and have no contact with the Brothers. There are places in this ship where we can live apart, without hindering anybody."

"You won't prevent others from coming to us," Jeanette said.

"Anyone who needs to join us must be free to do so," Rosa said.

"No Brothers," Rex said. "We stick with each other." Kai Khosrau nodded.

"The family is dissolved," Rosa said. "Our new family is born."

Martin reported to Hans alone in his quarters. The vases and dead flowers had been removed, as well as the second pad. Hans lay in his net, arms behind his head, eyes closed tightly, wrinkles forming at their corners. "She's got me in check," he said gloomily. "I'm open to suggestions. Everything I've done this far has turned to shit. We don't have time to set up a tribunal. We split tomorrow—and who's going to take them? Kai had volunteered to go on the *Trojan Horse*."

"And Terry Loblolly," Martin added.

"We can get two to replace them, easily enough," Hans said.

"They won't work with the Brothers. They have to be isolated," Martin said.

Hans looked at Martin with an expression Martin might once have characterized as shrewd, but now realized was defensive. Hans could not look frightened; it was not in his repertoire, hadn't been since he was a child, since Earth's death perhaps. *What that took from all of us; bits of ourselves, our flexibility, our nature.*

"I could resign," Hans said. "I wish I could."

"Jeanette would suggest that Rosa take your place," Martin said.

"Then she could deal with herself. What would the moms do, I wonder? I mean, if we just stood down and refused to enact the Law. Would they drop us into space for being cowards?"

Martin didn't answer.

"Is this what happened to the death ship? They just ate themselves up, no fight left for the enemy? Jesus, I didn't expect this."

The narrowed eyes, the shrewd expression; not just defensiveness, Martin saw. Hans seemed expectant.

"Whatever happens, it will have to be fast," Hans said.

"You're Pan," Martin said.

Hans looked up at Martin and pulled himself from the net. "You're telling me Pans do what they must," he said. "I'm telling you, I'm open to suggestions."

Paralysis.

"If you give up, Rosa wins."

"Be a lot easier just to rush into her motherly arms, wouldn't it?" Hans said, crossing his legs and flopping back on the pad. "Let it all go. Slick the Job. Slick the Law. Just grab for whatever youth we have left. *Gott mit uns.*" Hans gave him a fey smile. "You think I'm pretty ignorant, don't you? Not nearly as well-read as you or Erin or Jennifer or Giacomo. But I've studied my share of history. Frankly, it's depressing as all hell, Martin. Just one long series of blunders and recoveries from blunders. Blindness and death. Now it's on a universal scale."

"You've done some startling things since you've been Pan," Martin said. "I know you're not stupid."

"That's some satisfaction. Truth is, I feel I march in your shadow. The crew judges me against your standard. That's why I asked you to be second when Rex wasn't making the grade. So it's good to know I can still surprise you."

Martin shook his head. "We're still not solving our problem," he said.

"Time wounds all heels," Hans said, his tone suddenly light. "One step at a time, am I right?"

"None of the planets around Leviathan seem affected by the explosion of Wormwood," Giacomo said, "but if *Trojan Horse* doesn't show some damage, I think they'll have reason to be suspicious. We'll come in broadcasting a distress signal."

"On radio?" Hans asked.

"Why not?" Giacomo said. "We're innocents, unseasoned voyagers, right?"

Hans grinned and acknowledged that much. "Will we use the noach to talk to each other?"

Giacomo looked to Jennifer, then to Martin. "I don't see why not. Secretly, of course."

"Noach can't be detected between transmitter and receiver. No channel, right?" Jennifer said.

"The ships should be close enough part of the time," Martin said.

Giacomo projected the orbits of the three vessels. "*Shrike* will be out of touch with *Trojan Horse*, beyond the ten-billion-kilometer range, for about four tendays, just when *Trojan Horse* goes into orbit around the green world. *Greyhound* and *Trojan Horse* will be out of touch for about a month, unless we arrange for a remote to act as relay."

"That can be arranged," Hakim said. "But it increases our chances of being detected."

"Otherwise, no transmissions of any kind. Complete silence."

Paola stepped forward at Martin's encouragement. She looked nervously between him and Hans. "Paola has the crew assignments," Martin said.

Paola projected the roster for each vehicle. "Twice Grown and I worked through our crew lists and picked out the best combinations. Where we couldn't decide, we did a kind of lottery. The list is subject to approval by Hans and Stonemaker, of course."

"Rosa and her group?" Hans asked.

"I've put them on inactive within *Greyhound*," Paola said. "I talked with Rosa. She didn't agree or disagree."

Hans shook his head. "We're treating her like another head of state."

"I couldn't think of anything else to do," Paola said tremulously.

Hans crinkled his face in irritation. "Forget it. Not your fault. I just don't like her thinking she has any say in what we do. She and her group go where we put her, that's it. We may need to put together a little police force if they try civil disobedience."

Brief silence.

"Who's on the pleasure cruise?" Martin asked, hoping to distract them from the unpleasantness.

Paola projected the list.

Ten humans and ten Brothers had been assigned to *Trojan Horse*: Martin, Ariel, Paola, Hakim, Cham, Erin, George Dempsey, Donna Emerald Sea, Andrew Jaguar, and Jennifer. Twice Grown, Eye on Sky, Dry Skin/Norman, Silken Parts, Green Cord, Double Twist, Many Smells, Sharp Seeing, Strong Cord, and Scoots Fast were on the Brothers' list.

Hans would be on *Greyhound*, Stonemaker on *Shrike*. The preponderance of humans would be on *Greyhound* with Hans; Brothers, on *Shrike*. Paola projected these lists as well.

"I approve, for now," Hans said after running his fingers down the names as they hung in the air. "I'll need time to think about it. Everybody out. Martin, you stay."

After the others had left, they went over the list name by name. Hans voiced his concerns about suitability; Martin tried to answer as best he could.

"You and Cham on the same ship—two past Pans. Can you work with each other?"

"I've had nothing but support from Cham," Martin said.

"Can you all work with Eye on Sky?"

"The Brothers aren't hard to get along with," Martin said. "You know that."

"Pardon my nerves. Ariel?"

Martin cocked his head to one side. "She's changed."

"I've noticed. She's gone sugar on you, Martin."

"I wouldn't say that."

"You should take advantage. She's smart, a good fighter, she has a strong instinct for survival. You could do worse. You slicked Paola once, I hear . . .''

Martin tried to keep his expression passive. Hans smiled as if scoring a point.

"Paola's not for you, believe me."

"I never thought she was. We comforted each other."

Hans pushed his lips out. "Right," he said. "If I were you—and I won't repeat this again—I'd take up with Ariel, even if she did shovel you shit when you were Pan."

Martin looked away stonily.

"All right. Sometimes you're a stubborn bastard, but that's okay. Anybody here you think will give you trouble?"

"No," Martin said.

"Then it's on."

Hans' wand chimed. Erin urgently asked to be let in. Hans casually motioned for the door to open and she entered, Ariel and Kai Khosrau behind her.

"Rosa's dead," Erin said, gasping for breath. "We found her body in her room just a few minutes ago."

"You killed her," Kai said, pointing to Hans, then to Martin. "You killed her!"

"How did she die?" Hans asked. He sat up on the pad and got to his feet.

"She was clubbed to death," Kai said. "You clubbed her to death!"

"Shut up," Ariel said. "Martin, she was beaten."

"How long ago?"

"Less than an hour," Erin said. "There's . . ." She turned away and choked.

"The blood isn't dry yet," Ariel said.

"Who found her?" Martin asked.

"I did," Kai said in a child's voice, eyes glassy, in shock.

"Who else knows?" Hans asked.

"I have to tell the others." Kai stepped uncertainly to the open door.

"Hold it," Hans said. "We'll all go look. Nobody tells anybody until we've seen what happened. Kai, stick with us."

Kai stared at Hans. "You think I killed her? You slicking *insect*."

"Stop it, stop it!" Erin cried, head still bowed. Her body trembled as she tried to control her nausea.

"Martin, we should get a mom. Now," Ariel said.

Martin called on his wand and asked for a mom to meet them in Rosa's room.

Rosa lay face up, one arm tucked under her back, the other outstretched, hand forming a limp claw.

Red hair outspread, mixed with clots of blood; lip split, blood smeared down her jaw and chin. Face terribly slack, the innocent relaxation of death, eyes indolent.

Martin bent over her as the others stood back. Hans kneeled beside him, scowling, squinting, head tilted to one side.

The mom hovered above Rosa's head. Martin reached out to check the pulse on her bloody neck. None.

"She is dead," the mom confirmed.

"We'll need to roll her over," Martin said softly. He looked around the quarters, as if asking for someone to object, so he would not have to do this. Nobody objected.

Kai stepped forward. Hans stepped back. Kai and Martin took her by one side. She hung limp, flesh cooling but not yet at room temperature. Martin grasped her shoulder, Kai her leg. As gently as possible, they rolled her over.

She had been struck from behind, on the back of the head. The occiput was misshapen. Beneath the red hair a pool of blood had gathered, and sticky strands of blood and hair clung to the floor, breaking loose silently as she rolled face down.

Jeanette moaned. Erin seemed fascinated now, past her nausea.

"What should we do?" Martin asked the mom.

"Rosa Sequoia is no longer useful," the mom said.

"Do you know who killed her?" Erin asked the robot.

"We do not know who killed her."

Kai looked up at Hans. "Where were you?"

"He was with me for the past couple of hours," Martin said. "I don't think she's been dead more than an hour."

"She has been dead for fifty-two minutes," the mom said.

Kai's face wrinkled in grief. "How do we know you'd tell the truth?" he asked Martin.

"I believe Martin," Jeanette said, wrapping her arms around herself. "Somebody else killed her."

"Why?" Erin asked.

"Because she was speaking God's truth," Kai said. "Will you let us tell the others, or are you going to pretend this didn't happen?"

"Everybody will know."

"Even the Brothers?" Ariel asked.

"They're our partners," Hans said. "We have no secrets from them."

Martin and Kai rolled Rosa over. *Nobody's thinking straight,* Martin told himself. He looked at the pots of flowers, the pad off to one side, seeking evidence of who had been here. The room around the body was normal but for the drops of blood sprayed in one corner; empty except for Rosa's things, and the nonessential parts of Rosa.

"Do you wish to have a ceremony?" the mom asked.

"Yes," Jeanette said.

"I'd like you to make arrangements," Hans said to her.

They don't want to know who killed her, Martin realized. *They aren't looking.* He alone was examining the room closely. He wished they would all leave so he could talk with the mom in private.

"Martin, you and Jeanette clean her up," Hans said. "Wipe her down, dress her in her best . . . What should she wear?" Hans asked Jeanette.

"I don't know," Jeanette said. "I don't . . ." She finished with a sob.

"Gown," Hans said. He looked at the faces one by one. "She was my lover," he said, eyes hooded, lips downturned. "We'll find out who did this."

The others left. Martin and Jeanette silently, grimly stripped Rosa and washed her with water. Martin used his wand surreptitiously to record the body's condition, and swept the room for more details as Jeanette reverently dressed her, weeping.

"She's a martyr," she said. "Rosa died for us."

Martin nodded. That was probably all too true.

The moms didn't stop this. But they had learned this very hard fact many months, many centuries before: the crew of a Ship of the Law was free.

Free to die, and now free to kill.

The human crew took the news much as Martin had expected. Some wept, some cried out in anger, others held on to each other; still others listened in stunned silence as Hans revealed the details.

Only Twice Grown had been invited to join the humans as Hans spoke. Coiled, without scent, he listened to Hans and to Paola's quiet re-Englishing.

Hans finished by saying, "Rosa was murdered. That much is known. We know nothing about who murdered her, and we will not have time to find out before the ship splits and we move on to the next part of the Job. I wish our partners, our Brothers, to know . . ." He seemed to search for the right words, the diplomatic expression, but shook his head. "This was an aberration—"

"The failure of a broken individual," Paola said softly to Twice Grown.

"A hideous wrong." Hans shook his head again, lips pressed tight. "Rosa is going to be recycled by the moms in a few hours. Her family and associates will wait in her quarters to receive those who wish to grieve."

Martin stood before the mom alone as it entered his room. "Do you know now who killed Rosa Sequoia?" he asked after the door had closed.

"Hans has asked me the same question," it answered.

"Do you?"

"We do not track or survey individuals."

"You keep medical records—"

"We monitor health of individuals when they are in public places."

Martin knew that, but he would not let his questions go. One by one, he would ask them, and that would be his peculiar grief; for he had in a sense been *relieved* by Rosa's death, and he was sure Hans had been relieved as well, and a kind of guilt drove him now.

"Could you detect who had been in her room?"

"It is possible to identify numbers of presences in a room, after the fact, but we lack the means to identify individuals."

"How many people were in her room before she died, before she was found?"

"One person was in her room with her," the mom said.

"Male or female?"

"Male."

"What else can you tell me?"

"There had been sexual activity," the mom said.

Martin had noticed dried fluid around Rosa's vulva and spots still damp on her pad. "Was she raped?"

"No."

He took a shuddering breath, stomach twisting and his neck hard as rock, head aching intensely. "But you don't know who was with her."

"We are aware of sixty people who were not with her," the mom said. "Four others were in private quarters, not their own, including the one with Rosa, and were not tracked."

"Can you list their names?"

"Their names are in your wand now."

"Thank you," Martin said.

The mom departed and Martin examined the list. One or more of the four could have killed her, and Martin noted that Rex was among them. Giacomo, Rex, Ariel, Carl Phoenix; he could not help returning to Rex Live Oak's glowing name.

Hans insisted Martin attend the service. Jeanette Snap Dragon delivered a brief and surprisingly cool talk, and there was no mention of Rosa's supernatural interactions, no mention as well of Rosa's disciples.

Jeanette spoke instead of Rosa the storyteller, of the early awkward Rosa who had blossomed into her own kind of maturity late in the voyage.

Before Jeanette was finished, Martin's eyes filled with tears. *We've lost our final illusions*.

After the service, Jeanette and Rex Live Oak were the last to leave. Rex glanced at Martin in the corridor outside Rosa's quarters, his eyes red and swollen, his mouth a broken curve.

Rex had never been a very good actor. He was not acting

now. "Too much," he said, edging past Martin in the corridor. "Too slicking much."

Rosa's room was sealed, her body still inside. Out of sight, the ship did its work silently and quickly, and the last of Rosa vanished.

Jeanette approached Hans and Martin when the others had dispersed. "We're still agreed," she told him. "None of Rosa's people will fight. We're standing down."

"I understand," Hans said.

"We won't vote on judgment, we won't go on the *Trojan Horse*, we won't engage in support services."

"That's all been planned for," Hans said. Jeanette looked between them, her unlined features appearing much older than before. She turned slowly, eyes lingering on Hans, and walked inboard.

Hans's hair stood up in spikes from constant pushes of his hand and his eyes were dark and puffy. "It's over," he murmured to Martin. "Let it go."

There wasn't much else Martin could do.

Separation was less than six hours away.

Martin walked beside Hans into the schoolroom. Hans carried the list of the names of the ten humans who would accompany ten Brothers aboard the *Trojan Horse* as it dipped into Leviathan's system. The crew assembled in the center before the star sphere, all but Rosa's party, who stood to one side in ranks of five.

Hakim and Giacomo had arranged for the most recent results of the search team to be projected within the sphere: the best images of the worlds, like God's marbles dropped carelessly on velvet, beautiful and alive.

Hans called out the names without referring to the list.

Those chosen smiled and shook fists high in the air. Others looked disappointed until Jimmy Satsuma said, "Into the valley of death rode the ten . . . The rest of us will just have to wait outside to kick ass."

The crew cheered. Martin thought, *Remarkable how little the rhetoric of war changes, as if it's built into our genes.*

"Twenty," Hans said. "Don't forget the Brothers." But word of possible doubts among the Brothers had circulated with unfortunate speed, and Hans had done nothing to cool their anger.

"Yeah," Satsuma said, without enthusiasm.

"The ship will split in one hour," Hans said. "I will ride *Greyhound*. Martin will ride the *Trojan Horse*. For the time being, all is in the hands of the moms. But we'll get our chance soon enough."

He paused, looking at the floor. "I have an intuition." The crew kept a tense silence. "I think we'll find what we came for. We'll find it here. We share this with the Brothers, whatever our physical differences: we share the need to see justice done.

"I am not as good with words as other Pans have been. I don't know if a pep talk from me will do you any good. We have our own tragedies to face, our own . . . evil to deal with. But all that has to be put aside for now. It can't knock us off the road.

"This is the anniversary of the day we left the solar system. The road takes us to meet Earth's Killers. I *know* what I have to do. You all know what you have to do."

Enough was enough. "Let's go," he said.

Humans and Brothers, the crew of the *Trojan Horse* entered the cafeteria. Martin sat against the wall. Hakim sat beside him. "I am not frightened," Hakim said, eyes glittering, face flushed as if with fever.

"I am," Martin said.

"It would be more polite for me to be frightened with you," Hakim said, shaking his head. "But I am not. I feel as if I have lived a very long time. If I must face *Shaitan*, now is the time to do it. Allah will have pity on us all, and we will . . . ." He swallowed. "This talk of God does not disturb you?"

"No," Martin said, gripping Hakim's shoulder.

"Rosa did not take Allah away from us."

"Of course not."

"We will grow in Allah's sight, after this," Hakim said. "Allah loved Earth, and loves his frail children."

Martin nodded. He watched Ariel sitting at a table, getting up as table and benches sank into the floors. He smiled at her. She looked around, held up her arms, *Where am I going to sit?*

Martin patted the floor beside him.

She sat. "I think we should take another vote . . . on who should be Pan. After the Job."

Martin nodded absently.

"Poor Rosa," she said, drawing up her knees.

Martin closed his eyes. Hakim murmured a sura from the Koran. The ten Brothers coiled near the middle. Eye on Sky approached Martin.

"We we are sorry for the tragedy of the death," he said. "We we are hoping this does not make you less efficient."

"I appreciate your concern," Martin said.

Paola put an arm around Eye on Sky. "We'll do our work well."

Martin looked up into its "face," like the frayed end of a rope with eyes and a bouquet of claws. "Times past, an observation was made by one of yours," Eye on Sky said. "In we our hearing. That humans might know more about death and killing than Brothers. This is not so. Brothers have fought with each other, though not for many thousands of years."

Paola hovered nervously, looking between them.

"We we and you will share the guilt for this vengeance," Eye on Sky said. "It is agreed, as the Brothers agreed when we ourselves set this mission along, this Job."

He smelled of tea and woodsmoke, a combination Martin had not experienced before.

"I'm glad to have you with us," Martin said.

"Until we our world was destroyed," Eye on Sky continued, "Brothers thought the stars to be peaceful, places of unity and being sure-footed. We we have learned, those of other stars are only like we ourselves."

"We're a team," Martin said, rising and extending his arms. Eye on Sky leaned forward, and Martin hugged the sinewy braid as well, feeling the leathery dryness of its cords ripple beneath his fingers.

The ship began its sounds of dividing, familiar to them all. The door to the cafeteria admitted a mom and a snake mother, and then smoothed shut, its outlines vanishing into the wall. Fields appeared automatically around each of them, vibrating faint pastel colors. Martin watched Eye on Sky return to the center, followed by his field. The humans stayed on the periphery.

"End of deceleration in twenty seconds," the mom said.

Their weight passed from them until they floated. Martin automatically did the exercises that controlled his inner ear and his stomach.

"Separation will begin in fifteen seconds," the mom said. The snake mother made low string sounds and percussive clicks for the Brothers.

The ladder fields grew brighter. Muffled sounds of matter being rearranged, fake matter growing; Martin's hair stood on end. He thought of the decaying death ship lost in endless cold void, its fake matter fizzling away after ages, mummies of the crew surrounded by eternal haloes of cold dust, undisturbed in the interstellar medium until their arrival.

The cafeteria closed in. Fields jostled them within the smaller, rearranged space. They now occupied the sleeping quarters of the *Trojan Horse*.

"I told them about the *Iliad*," Paola whispered to Martin and Ariel. "They were very impressed. And we chose another name for the ship, when we're in disguise, so we don't have to explain *Trojan Horse: Double Seed*."

More sounds, sliding and scraping, something vibrating like a broken pitch pipe. *Trojan Horse/Double Seed* broke free of *Greyhound* and *Shrike*.

All three ships spread apart, each on a different course and schedule, each with a different mission, fifty billion kilometers from Leviathan, still racing at close to light-speed.

"Super deceleration in ten seconds," the mom said.

They had been through this many times before, enough to be used to it, but Martin felt a deep sense of dread: dread of the poised dreamstate, his every move second-guessed by the volumetric fields. He felt them creep around his molecules, taking inventory of his body. And dread as well for what they all would have to face if they succeeded, when the ships came back together: the lies and deceit he knew had been perpetrated on the crews.

"Good luck," Ariel said.

He tried to think of a pleasant scene on Earth, to lock this into his thoughts and avoid visions of the dead.

Instead, he saw as if through a grim documentary that the entire crew had been fed fake matter food, that they were now made of massless coerced points in space; that when the Job was done they would simply dissolve like the Red Tree Runners' Ship of the Law.

The Law would be done at the cost of their being; in fact, they were nothing right at this moment, merely illusions on a ghost ship falling again into brightness to bring death.

His unvoiced moan seemed to echo behind his closed eyes. If he opened his eyes, he would see the others, trying to do little tasks, conversing or just sitting, waiting out the constrained hours. He preferred to be alone with this nightmare.

Twenty-two hours passed.

An hour before super deceleration ended, as planned, Hakim broadcast their first message to the beings around Leviathan. He had created a simple binary signal repeating pi and the first ten prime numbers, without the Brothers' help; the moms had indicated Brother mathematics was most unusual, and not likely to be easily understood.

The signal was adjusted to disguise their velocity. It would reach Leviathan's worlds in twenty-three hours; *Trojan Horse/ Double Seed* would be twenty-two billion kilometers from the system by then, easily visible to Leviathan's masters.

The mom informed them that *Greyhound* and *Shrike* were doing well, that all was going as planned.

Martin listened to the mom's voice, acknowledged with a nod that he had heard the news and understood it, closed his eyes again, waited, still not convinced of his reality, his solidity.

Ariel touched his arm. "You don't look happy," she said.

"Nightmare," he said, shaking his head.

"You're not asleep," she said.

"Doesn't matter."

"Want to talk?"

"About what?"

"About after."

He smiled. "After we get the Job done? Or after we've decelerated?"

"After anything," she said.

Martin opened his eyes completely and wiped them to clear his mottled vision. What he saw was still not sharp; Ariel leaned on her elbow a meter away, face blurred, eyes indistinct, mouth moving. He made an effort to listen.

"The Wendys will make their gowns. We'll marry a planet. Do you ever think about that?"

He shook his head.

"I do. I'd like to let it all down, relax, sit in a thick, fresh atmosphere with the sun in the sky . . . just not worry about anything. Do you think people on Earth ever did that?"

"I suppose."

"I wonder if I'd make a good mother. Having babies, I mean."

"Probably," he said.

"I've just started thinking about being a mother. My thoughts . . . I've been young for so long, it's hard to imagine actually being grown-up."

"Ariel, I'm not thinking too clearly right now. We should talk later."

"If you want. I don't mind if you don't answer. Do you mind listening?"

"I don't know if I mind anything right now."

"All right," she said. "I'll wait. But we're going to be so busy."

"That will be good," Martin said. "Not having time to think."

"Do you have a voice . . ." She trailed off. "It sounds so silly, like something Rosa might say. Do you have a voice that tells you what's going to happen?"

"No," Martin said.

"I think I do. We're going to survive, Martin."

"Good," Martin said.

"I'll be quiet." She lay back and folded her hands on her stomach. Martin looked down at her from his seat against the wall.

"She's not as pretty as Theresa," Theodore said, standing over them. "But she's honest. She's resourceful. You could do a lot worse."

"Shut up," Martin said.

Ariel opened her eyes languidly. "Didn't say anything."

"Not talking to you," Martin said, slumping until his legs bumped hers, then sidling up next to her. He reached out and hugged her. She tensed, then sighed and relaxed, turned her face toward his, looked him over from a few centimeters, eyebrows arched quizzically.

"I know I'm not as pretty as Theresa," she whispered. Her vulnerability pricked deep beneath his lassitude.

"Shh," he said.

"You two were good," she said.

He patted her shoulder. "Sleep," he said.

She snuggled closer, gripping his hand with her long fingers.

Trojan Horse ended super deceleration at ten percent light-speed. Volumetric fields lifted. They would coast for five days, then begin a more leisurely deceleration to enter the system.

The first response to their signal came on tight-beam transmission from the fourth planet, content simple enough: a close match, with subtle and interesting variations, of Hakim's repetitive code. The first twelve prime numbers were counted out in binary.

Martin examined the message while still dazed from the constraints. Simple acknowledgement, without any commitment or welcome.

Salutary caution in a forest full of wolves. Or supreme confidence mixed with humility . . .

Hakim sent another message, this time with samples of human and Brother voices extending greetings, his own voice counting numbers, and a list of mathematical and physical constants.

Martin ate his lunch of soup in a squeeze bulb and a piece of cake as he looked over fresh pictures of the fourth planet. Huge and dark, touched with streamers of water vapor cloud, wide black oceans and lighter gray continents.

"When will the other ships finish super deceleration?"

"*Shrike* in fifty-four minutes, and *Greyhound* in one hour, fifty-two minutes," Hakim said. "We can noach them now, if you wish, of course."

"No need," Martin said. "Let them recover first. We need time to work on our disguise. We need to rehearse."

"Sounds like the class play," Erin said, moving in for a closer look at the projected fourth planet.

"We'll follow the script closely," Martin said. He looked around the compartment, making sure the Brothers had recovered from deceleration. They took the process harder than humans and needed two hours disassembled to bring themselves out of funk.

Eye on Sky came forward, Paola at his side. He smelled of some exotic spice Martin couldn't identify: wine and cinnamon, hot resin.

"We are ready," Eye on Sky said.

The bridge of *Double Seed* took shape, Brothers and humans orchestrating the final practical and decorative touches.

The crew compartment made sleeping nets for humans and ring beds for Brothers—a series of hoops within which a braid could disassemble and the cords could hang, one or two claws attached to each ring.

Silken Parts and Paola translated the proceedings for all the Brothers.

"We'll have four more days to rehearse," Martin said. "Hakim and Sharp Seeing will keep track of our interchanges with whoever's down there. We'll have an all-crew briefing every twelve hours. If you're not on duty, you're free to contribute to the background. Ariel and Paola will coordinate with Scoots Fast."

"Scoots Fast has requested a name change," Paola said. "He wants to be called Long Slither. It's more accurate. And more dignified."

"Fine by me," Martin said. He followed Hakim and Eye on Sky into the noach "inner sanctum," a small interior compartment screened against outside examination. There was barely room for the three of them.

Eye on Sky contacted *Shrike* first. At the extreme edge of noach range, text messages were most reliable, and *Shrike*'s message was projected flat before them. Silken Parts translated the Brother text, a short row of closely spaced curved lines: "We we are safe and still joined in the giant braid. Swift work and firm sand."

The last contact with *Greyhound* before entry was short and sweet as well: "In orbit and recovered," Giacomo transmitted. "Everybody impatient. Good luck!"

"Giacomo needs to work on his poetry," Erin said wryly. "We're being outclassed."

Hakim, Martin, Paola, and Eye on Sky gathered on the new-made bridge. Panels pulled back to show steady blackness, a close-packed haze of stars.

"This is very splendid," Hakim said, touching the new bulkheads, so different in style from the moms' usual architecture. "Like being on a ship that might have been made by humans, begging the Brothers' pardon!"

"We we also feel that if traveled to the stars, it might have been on such a ship," Eye on Sky said.

Hakim nodded pleasantly. "For the time being, we still use the moms' remotes on a wide baseline, advanced eyes and ears . . ."

An image of the fourteenth planet, nearest to the *Trojan Horse*, grew before them in a small star sphere. Martin leaned forward. Mottled, cold blue and green, a gas giant fifty thousand kilometers in diameter, the fourteenth planet was surrounded by twenty-one moons, and more besides. Its mushy upper atmosphere sprouted floating platforms hundreds of kilometers in diameter, needle-like proboscises extending down through the haze to high-pressure regions below. From the center of each platform, a crystal plume of white rose through a ring that glowed bright as fire in the upper, clear atmosphere. Hyperbolic lines of plasma shot from the ring, like threads from this distance, but hot as the filament in a light-bulb.

"Gas wells," Martin said. "Tens of thousands of them. Raising gas from the depths, packing it—somehow—accelerating it in those rings, retrieving it in orbit. Impressive."

"They reveal matter-conversion technology right here," Hakim said. "They do not care to hide it. No platform parts made of normal matter could survive in those depths, nor contain the gases under such conditions. We see the bottom of the fuel chain, which leads to the top—the technology of the platforms themselves.''

Eye on Sky rustled and smelled of camphor and pine.

The scene shifted to the next planet nearest to them, number twelve, half a billion kilometers closer to the star, this one a rocky world with a diameter of ten thousand kilometers. The color of the planet's crescent—viewed in close-up—was dark brown with scattered patches of tan and white. "Resolution of about four hundred kilometers," Hakim said. "It may be made of rock and ice. It is cold enough for ammonia and methane to lie solid on the surface, and the atmosphere appears to be mostly nitrogen and argon. There is no large-scale construction—''

Abruptly, the planet darkened as if the illuminated limb were obscured by shadow. Then, within the shadow and along the limb, thin lines of brilliant white appeared like molten silver poured over a surface of carbon soot. The lines curved into circles and ovals, scribed contours, ran straight as great circles. The density of lineation increased, thinner lines within thick, until the entire planet glowed hot silver. Just as abruptly, color returned—but a different color, with different details, grayish-tan with green patches.

Jennifer giggled abruptly, then clapped her fingers to her mouth. "Sorry," she said.

"What in the hell was that?" George Dempsey asked.

Dumbfounded, Hakim looked between his colleagues, then read the fresh chemical analysis. "Pure argon atmosphere. The surface appears to be mostly silicates, fine sand perhaps, small rocks. The green patches are very cold, much colder than the rest of the planet—four or five kelvins.''

"I hope Giacomo saw that," Jennifer said, face ghostly. She could not stop her hands from touching her shoulders, her elbows, her knees. She seemed terrified. "If Hans is looking for proof of illusion . . .''

"Let's not draw conclusions yet," Martin said.

Jennifer giggled again.

The next planet inward that shared the same quadrant of the Leviathan system, number two, orbited scarcely one hundred and fifty million kilometers from the star, barely within a "tem-

perate'' zone allowing liquid water. Pale brownish-red, lacking
any thick atmosphere, this planet was lumpy with structure. Even
with a diameter of over twenty-one thousand kilometers, its
outline was remarkably uneven.

"They're showing off again," Paola said. "How tall are those
. . . whatever they are?"

"Hundreds of kilometers tall," Hakim said. "Tens of thousands of them. Cities, perhaps?"

"Are we getting any communications between the planets?"
Jennifer asked.

"No artificial radiation leakage," Hakim said. "Except for
the energies used to ship gas up from the giant planets. But even
those are of a frequency easily interpreted as solar flares. From
a few light months away, the system is rich with planets, but
quiet."

"So they're not hiding, but they're not attracting attention,
either. What about commerce between the worlds?"

"It is ripe with ships like seeds in shore fruit," Eye on Sky
said. "Tens of millions of vessels rising up, falling down. Every
world takes ships but the twelfth. It orbits alone. The fourth
planet is most visited."

"Can we tell if there's any commerce *not* using ships?"
Martin asked. "Matter transmission—something more sophisticated?"

"Not found any such signs," Eye on Sky said. "If they are
using noach, of course we we are not detecting them."

Martin rubbed the side of his nose. "Let's send two messages,
one after the other, video with speech accompaniment, the next
with Brother text/sound. Coded pictures in polar and rectangular
coordinates, one hundred shades, no color, of our ship seen from
outside, a Brother assembled and disassembled, and a human
male and human female seen from the front, naked. Show our
origins related to the three nearest stars. Our fictitious origins,
of course . . ."

"A *Voyager* message," Paola said, smiling. She explained
for the Brothers. Silken Parts had already researched this small
bit of human history.

When it was finished, Martin projected the message for all to
see. Silken Parts and Paola quickly worked to translate it into

Brother text, which Eye on Sky approved. He suggested, "Let us add full set of symbols from each written language."

They waited twelve hours. At some six billion kilometers from Leviathan, the first response to their inquiry came from the fourth planet, ten pictures in coordinate video. The mom quickly translated and projected them, one after another.

The pictures showed five different beings. The crew examined the portraits in sequence. The first type was four-legged, slender and graceful looking, with a long, slim neck topped by a short-nosed head with two prominent forward-facing eyes. But for a few features, it might have been a smaller, less stocky version of the Red Tree Runner sauropods. "Where are the hands?" Erin Eire asked.

Nobody answered. The second type stood upright on two thick, almost elephantine legs, with a barrel chest and a small head without apparent eyes. Two sets of arms emerged from its barrel chest, equipped with two sets of many-fingered hands.

"These are the ones who met with the Red Tree Runners," Erin said.

"Sure looks like them," Andrew said.

The third type seemed to be aquatic, having no legs or arms as such, elongated, shark shaped, with wide wing-like fins along their sides, narrow, ridged pointed "heads" with no visible eyes, and fins with finger-like extensions just behind the head. The fourth was a nightmare, a nest of tentacles or legs jointed dozens of places along each length, some tipped with smaller tentacles, others with three-part pincers. The body, dwarfed by the tentacles, was squat and dark.

The image of the fifth type brought gasps from the humans. Reptilian, with a long crested head and a short trunk, and limbs that folded backward at the lower joints, the fifth was much smaller than the preceding types.

Erin reached out to take Ariel's hand. The humans stared in shock and disbelief.

"God damn them," George Dempsey said.

"They don't know where we come from," Cham said. "They've screwed up royally."

Martin nodded. Paola began to explain to Eye on Sky, but the

Brother rustled and emitted a strong rosy odor of sympathy. "We we recognize," Eye on Sky said. "This is from your endtime history."

"We've found them," Martin said.

"Don't jump to conclusions," Ariel said softly.

"What other conclusions are there?" Martin asked.

"How many beings have they investigated, how many forms might they have stolen? We still can't be positive."

Martin wanted to bask in this sense of discovery, have the peculiar satisfaction of watching the Killers make a mistake, reveal a weakness. "I want to be positive," he said ambiguously.

"Then *think*," Ariel said, glancing nervously at the others, as if anticipating a sudden wave of emotion overriding reason. "This could be the *original* they stole their design from."

"Not likely," Martin said. "If the Killers knew them well enough to copy their . . . bodies, their designs, they'd be dead by now, almost surely . . ." He turned to the mom. "Do you recognize this type from any of the worlds the Benefactors saved, or any other worlds you know?"

"It does not match any in our records," the mom answered.

Martin turned back to Ariel. "Any other theories?" he asked.

Ariel raised her hands. "I still think we shouldn't jump to any conclusions."

"This is the one," Martin said. "It's the creature they used as a decoy outside the spaceship in Death Valley. I know it is."

Cham laid his hand on Martin's shoulder. "Let's say it is, for now. Doesn't change our plans any. Just another piece of evidence."

"Right," Martin said, shivering off his emotion. "Noach it to *Shrike* and *Greyhound*. Noach all the pictures."

"Let's finish looking at them ourselves, first," Cham suggested evenly, still patting Martin's shoulder.

Martin pulled himself back from his anger. "Sorry," he said.

"We all feel it, Martin," Erin said.

"All of us," Ariel said. She took a deep breath and squatted on the floor.

The next two pictures sketched an orbital path in relation to the fifteen planets, astrogational hints given by binary number measurements triangulating on the nearest stars.

"Very friendly. They're suggesting we decelerate at five g's," Cham said, tracing his finger along the projection, "and go into orbit around the fourth planet."

"Can we survive there?" Andrew asked.

"It is the inexplicable one," Hakim said. "Far too light to be solid, one hundred two thousand kilometers in diameter, there is a cool, solid surface and a thin atmosphere, ten percent oxygen, seventy percent nitrogen, fifteen percent argon and other inerts, five percent carbon dioxide, about six tenths of ship's pressure. Not good to breathe. The surface temperature is fine, a range of ten to twenty degrees centigrade. The gravitational pull is high, however, about two g's."

"The mom can't wrap us in fields," Andrew Jaguar said. "We're not supposed to have that kind of technology."

"We we might disassemble," Eye on Sky warned. "With such weight, there is often no braid control over cords."

Martin held up his hand to cut the discussion. His head hurt abominably. "I don't think that's going to be a problem, one way or another. If they treat us like guests, they'll probably have ways to make us comfortable. If not—" He looked around the cabin. "Why worry?"

"We don't know we'll be invited to the surface," Paola said.

"Not very neighborly if we aren't," Erin said.

"Or they might just kill us," Andrew Jaguar said. "These worlds look like a lot of very sweet candy for curious flies."

"Andrew," Jennifer said testily.

"Nobody can tell me they don't look . . . just very interesting! Gingerbread house and witch!"

Paola tried to explain this to the Brothers, but Eye on Sky showed with a flourish of head cords that explanation was either not needed or not wanted. *No more of our violent fairy tales*, Martin thought.

He turned to Eye on Sky. "Do we go in?"

"What is your opinion?" Eye on Sky rejoined. Some of the Brothers smelled of cloves.

Martin nodded. "Sure," he said. "That's why we're here. Jennifer, is this diagram clear?"

"Clear enough," she said. "Silken Parts and I can tell the ship where to go."

Martin turned to the mom. "I assume you'll vanish into the woodwork, so to speak, when the time comes."

"When the time comes," it said, "my presence will not be obvious."

Without warning, the mom made a peculiar noise like a trumpet blat and gently toppled to one side, rebounding against the floor. The crew stared in surprise; before anyone could react, it made a similar noise and rose again, stabilized. "This vessel has been searched for high-density weapons. Examination may have been conducted by noach. My functioning was temporarily interfered with."

"How do they *search* by noach?" Jennifer asked, voice squeaky.

"They may query selected atoms and particles within our vessel for their state and position."

Jennifer looked as if she had just opened a wonderful Christmas present, and she turned to Martin, gleeful, clearly believing that her work and theory had been confirmed.

Martin was struck by how much they acted and sounded like eager, frightened children, himself included.

"Will they know the ship has a fake matter core?" he asked the mom. "Could they know you're here?"

"Unless I am mistaken, which is possible but not likely, such a noach examination can only reveal extremes of mass density."

Jennifer slapped her right hand against her thigh; it was obvious she wanted to do more momerath and plug in these new clues.

"Jennifer," he said, "you have work to do?"

"Pardon?"

"Go do it. You're making me nervous."

Jennifer grinned and left the bridge.

"So they know we're not armed with anything lethal," Martin said. "Why did you quit for a moment there?"

"I am not sure."

Martin looked at the mom intently, then returned his attention to the projected images. "Put us into orbit around the fourth planet," he told Hakim and Silken Parts.

Hakim did his momerath and drew the best path and points of drive bursts; the path closely matched that suggested on the transmitted charts. "Steady deceleration of five g's, we will be in orbit within five days, thirteen hours and twelve minutes," Hakim said.

Silken Parts did the same calculations using Brother math, reported the results to Eye on Sky, then turned to Martin. "We agree within a few seconds," he said.

"Noach our plans and the messages to *Shrike* and *Greyhound*," Martin said.

Martin's cabin aboard the *Trojan Horse* was less than a fifth the size of his previous quarters and contained only his sleeping net. The crews had not yet finished adding homey touches to the masquerade; he scanned the walls and imagined perhaps posters of Brothers and humans frolicking on beaches beneath a blue-green sky. *That isn't too bad.* He'd mention the idea to Donna Emerald Sea, who with Long Slither was in charge of ship design now.

He twisted into the net and closed his eyes. He was instantly asleep and in no time at all, it seemed, his wand chimed. It was Jennifer. In long-suffering silence, he crawled from the net, assumed a lotus in mid-air to keep some sort of dignity, and told her to come in.

"Their noach is better than ours," she said. "Much higher level, more powerful than the moms' noach, I mean."

"That's obvious," he said, still groggy.

"I just had a long talk with Silken Parts. We swapped theories on Benefactor technology. Martin, we're going to be way out-matched down there—far more than we were around Wormwood. What these folks had around Wormwood is like a steel trap, and *this*, this is an atom bomb."

"What do you think they have?" Martin asked.

"They swept us with something—no, that's not right; sweep isn't the right idea, not the right word. They *queried* our ship's matter and particles from six billion kilometers. From what I can work out, we couldn't manage that intense a scan at all, ever—and if we could, we couldn't transfer that much data in less than a few weeks."

"Impressive, but what does it imply?"

"If the moms are right, and these folks *don't* know everything there is to know about us now—and frankly, I can't think of a reason why they shouldn't, except maybe bandwidth—"

"Jennifer, I'm not thinking too clearly. You woke me up and I haven't slept since coming out of deceleration."

"I haven't either," Jennifer said, blinking.

"Well, you're superhuman, we all know that."

"Flattery won't get answers any faster," she said much too brightly, her face flushed as if with fever. "Sorry. I'm a little giddy, too. What I'm getting around to saying is, they could turn us into anti-matter *right now*. Or just enough of us to blow our ship to pieces."

"Are you sure?"

"No. I'm not sure. And obviously, they haven't. But—"

"There's nothing we can do about it."

"I know," she said. "I know that."

"Can you give me any advice about what we can do?"

"Of course, we can't let them know we understand what noach is."

"That'll be easy. I don't understand."

"Or that we know it exists," she said, knitting her brows in irritation. "Silken Parts is working over other implications, and one of them . . . Are you going to pull a Hans on me?" she asked suddenly.

"Pardon?"

"I'm going to tell you something really big, really scary. Are you going to pull a Hans and vanish into some macho shell right now?"

"I promise, I won't do that," Martin said.

"We thought maybe the twelfth planet changing character, color, maybe that was more proof that parts of this system are illusory. A projection or something. Martin, if they can do what I think they can, *it doesn't matter, there isn't any difference*. They could make a shell of fake matter around an entire planet, an *entire star*, just as solid as this ship is. They could redirect or manufacture images as wide as this system in any direction they desired."

"Do they have the energy?"

"I'm guessing yes. They might be tapping the star. From what we can see, the system seems to be rich with volatiles.

Maybe they've held all their resources in reserve, waiting for the main assault.''

"Do you have any *good* news?" Martin asked.

Jennifer grinned. "Not fond of endless David and Goliath?"

"It's a living," he said dourly.

"I can do without it myself. But I do have some wild-ass ideas that might be encouraging. I want to noach with Giacomo and do some momerath with him, and I want to hook into the ships' minds. I'm hoping we can collaborate. This is something moms and Brothers and humans need to do together."

"I'll get you some private time with Giacomo. No sweet nothings, though," he chided.

"Strictly business," Jennifer said.

Martin saw the *Trojan Horse/Double Seed* as an ant crawling into a kitchen, staring all unknowing at giant appliances, instruments of unknown utility, technologies beyond the capacity of its tiny brain to comprehend . . .

There was so much that made no sense whatsoever.

The twelfth planet continued to change its character every few hours, alternating between three different sets of features, all the same size, all rocky, but radically different in all other ways.

The ninth planet had an eccentric orbit, carrying it outside the orbit of the tenth planet. It was small, perhaps a former moon, though with no surface features. It had an albedo of one, a perfectly reflective mirror at all frequencies.

The eighth planet, a bright orange-yellow gas giant with a diameter of seventy-five thousand kilometers, possessed three large moons. Cables two to three kilometers in diameter hung from the moons to the planet's fluid surface, leaving great whorls in their wakes, like mixers in a fantastic bakery.

The sixth planet, eight thousand kilometers in diameter, appeared to be covered with dandelion fluff, each "seed" a thousand kilometers tall. Incoming space vessels never ventured below the crowns of the seeds. In close-up, between the seed pillars, storms churned a thick atmosphere of oxygen and nitrogen and water vapor. Hakim thought this might be a giant farm of some sort, for raising unimaginable creatures or plants, but Martin thought that seemed archaic; one wondered if such power-

ful beings would still need to eat, much less eat formerly living
things.

"Then the creatures might have other uses," Hakim said,
eyes glittering with speculation.

"None of which we can guess," George Dempsey cautioned.

"Let us have our fun," Erin said peevishly.

Peering deeper down Leviathan's well, to the fifth planet,
nine thousand kilometers in diameter, dull gray, and like the
ninth, smoother than a billiard ball, but far from reflective.

And perhaps the most fascinating of them all: the fourth
planet, one hundred and two thousand kilometers in diameter,
with six moons, three of them larger than Earth, its dark reddish-
brown surface radiating heat steadily into space, covered with
liquid water oceans with narrow ribbons of continent and low
mountains between like stripes on a basketball.

"Thirty-two billion square kilometers," Ariel said in wonder.
"If the land is ten percent of the surface, that's over three billion
square kilometers." Pause for quick figuring. "Earth had about
one and a third billion square kilometers of land. How many
people could live here?"

"At two g's, not me," Cham said.

"The physics don't make sense," Hakim said. "Not dense
enough to support a solid surface . . . The density below the
rocky shell must be less than one and a half grams per cubic
centimeter. How is this done?"

"How is *any* of it done?" George Dempsey asked.

The images and charts were noached to *Greyhound* and *Shrike*.
Hans' voice replied: "We're almost at maximum range. Soon
be out of touch for a while. How is it?"

"I think they must be treating us like nursery school kids—
if not like stray insects."

"We've been looking over the mug shots of the citizens of
Leviathan," said Hans. "The crested critter is pretty audacious.
They like to repeat themselves, don't they? Anybody prepared
to make a judgment now?"

"I think we're close."

"What more do we need?"

"The final dotted *i* and crossed *t*."

Hans chuckled. "I'll settle for frontier justice and getting the hell away."

"We've come this far," Martin said. "We've been invited to orbit the fourth planet, and we've already set our course. We'll be down there in twenty-seven days."

"Godspeed," Hans said.

"How's politics?" Martin asked hesitantly.

"My worry, not yours, Martin."

"Just curious."

"We're prepared for whatever you ask of us. Count on it."

"Any idea who killed Rosa?" Martin asked.

"Time enough after the Job's done."

"Jennifer wants some extended time with Giacomo. She thinks she may have something interesting to present to the ships' minds."

"I can't wait," Hans said. "Not more super-physics doom and gloom, I hope. We're getting enough of that here, every time we look at those damned planets."

"She says it might be good news."

"Put her on, then. Giacomo's in the nose with me."

Jennifer came forward and said she wanted the bridge empty while she talked with Giacomo. Humans and Brothers left, all but Silken Parts, who was collaborating on the problems using Brother math.

"Hans doesn't sound good," Erin told Martin in the hall outside the bridge.

Ariel concurred. "I hope he's keeping it together."

"Maybe he's depressed because of the show," Erin suggested. "It's gotten to me."

"Maybe," Martin said. He was empty of either optimism or gloom. The sheer weight of superiority of Leviathan's worlds made it hard for him to breathe, much less think.

Silken Parts and Jennifer left the noach chamber after three hours. Jennifer could hardly talk. She hung on to a net in the crew quarters and thirstily gulped a bulb of juice. When Martin approached, she held up her hand and shook her head.

"Please," she said. "My head hurts. Giacomo's found ways to—"

"You don't have to talk now if you don't want to," Martin said. She ignored that.

"He's found ways to use Brother math to describe Leviathan's noach physics. Silken Parts and the ships' minds are collaborating.

"It's just too fast, much too fast. We see something, maybe the way number twelve changes or the number eight has big suspended cables, and Silken Parts comes up with a hypothesis . . . Giacomo runs it through . . . I look it over. Ah, God. I'm dead tired."

Jennifer waved her hand again weakly, closed her eyes, and instantly fell asleep.

"I think we've broken through," Hakim said. "I give them all the credit. They're sending us basic math now, which means they understand the symbols . . . the human symbols."

"Is there any of interest in the math?" Silken Parts asked.

"All very innocuous, child's stuff," Hakim said. "More like human math than Brother math."

Silken Parts made a noise like leaves on pavement.

Eye on Sky examined the projected records of the transmissions from the fourth planet. Still shaky after four hours' sleep, Jennifer peered around the Brother at the records. "They're echoing most of what we send, but making changes, some . . . improvements? The notation is altered a little . . . here and here." She pointed to equations describing n-dimensional geometries. Martin couldn't begin to interpret what she was seeing.

"They learn fast and soon," Eye on Sky said. "We can seed the beach now, I we think."

"Time to test them on language," Martin said. "Transmit a Brother and an English dictionary, and a full audio record of speech sounds for both languages."

"Like opening our book to them," Ariel said.

"Baiting the hook," Martin said. He turned to the mom and snake mother. "Can you arrange for the *Trojan Horse* to have some supernova damage?"

"Yes," the mom replied.

"Cham, you and Erin design our damage and report to Eye on Sky and me when it's done."

"Got it," Cham said, and they left the bridge.

"It looks dark and heavy," Ariel said, staring at the projection of the fourth planet. "I've got a name for it, if anybody cares," she said.

"What?" Martin asked.

"Sleep. The other planets . . . the bristling world, looks to me like Puffball. The flipping world . . ."

"Masque," Martin suggested.

"Blinker is better," Erin said. Within ten minutes, they had named each of the planets, according to their characteristics, working outward from Leviathan itself:

Frisbee, orbiting barely half a million kilometers above the surface of Leviathan, a rapidly rotating white disk seventy-two hundred kilometers in diameter, its circumference fringed with tangled, outward-streaming "hair" of unknown purpose and composition.

Big City, surrounded by red acid haze, covered with architecture to a depth of four hundred kilometers.

Lawn, a blanket of blue-green vegetation divided by artificial rivers, Earth-like but for the fact that the average surface temperature was three hundred degrees Celsius, the rivers ran deep with liquid fake matter (so Giacomo and Eye on Sky speculated), and the atmosphere consisted largely of carbon dioxide and steam.

Sleep, a dark funeral bouquet of wilted roses packed into a ball one hundred and two thousand kilometers in diameter . . .

Cueball, featureless gray.

Puffball with its thousand-kilometer-high seeds.

Pebble One, barely a thousand kilometers wide, empty gray rock and water ice au naturel.

Mixer, cables hanging from three moons stirring its gaseous surface into a beautiful abstraction of swirls and eddies.

Mirror, perfect and apparently pointless.

Gopher, like a huge lava bomb from a volcano, riddled with holes impossibly deep and wide, green lights winking in the holes like baleful eyes.

Pebble Two, very much like Pebble One: in fact, exactly alike in every detail.

Blinker still flipping like the display on a cosmic clock, changing its character between three different worlds.

Pebble Three, duplicate of Pebbles One and Two.

Gas Pump, blue green, a slushball of methane and ammonia and hydrogen and helium, its glowing wells tossing billions of tons of volatiles into orbit every hour.

And at the farthest extremes of the system, Magic Lantern, covered with oceans of perfectly smooth water ice, interspersed with polished iron and crystal land masses, the land and solid seas studded with black domes hundreds of kilometers across.

Naming Leviathan's fifteen planets did not bring any cheer or sense of control.

Martin hung in his net, watching with half-closed eyes the image of Sleep fill his cabin. *Savages canoeing up the Hudson River, walking into New York City. Look up: the skyline. Pad on moccasins down the asphalt streets. Threaten to destroy the city with bows and arrows. Laughing, the mayor invites them into his office.*

On the bridge, Jennifer, Hakim, Cham and Ariel floated at different angles, heads turning toward Martin as he entered. They all wore the same half-terrified expectant look Martin had become familiar with in the past few days.

"Play it back," Cham said.

"This is new," Hakim said. "Ten minutes ago."

The transmitted voice sounded flat, sexually neutral, a little harsh, diction precise and almost chilly. "Hello," it began. "You have entered cooperative areas and are welcome to the gathering of partners."

"Not perfect," Jennifer commented. "But good enough."

"Many different kinds of intelligence work and play in union. Your kind may join, or may visit. There are no requirements except peaceful intentions. As you no doubt are aware, the local star group is a dangerous territory, populated by machines and intelligences not of good will. Weapons are not allowed in our neighborhood. If you have any weapons, even defensive weapons of low power, you must notify us and dispose of them under our direction, instructions to follow. Further informative discussions will follow. Is this understood?"

Eye on Sky listened intently to the same message delivered

in Brother audio. "It is hollow and smells like space," he said. "But it is understandable."

"They'll be suspicious if we're completely unarmed," Cham said.

Martin nodded. "I think we should make some weapons and hand them over. Nothing impressive. Defensive projectile weapons, chemical . . ."

"The ship should have something, too," Erin said.

Martin looked at Ariel. "Lasers," he said.

"Right," she said.

"You direct the mom and snake mother," he said. "We'll need something convincing to hand over or jettison soon. It's time we put on our costumes and start getting used to our roles. In a tenday or so, I think we're going to be in their control . . ."

Martin asked Eye on Sky, "How do we answer them?"

"Enthusiasm and charm," Eye on Sky said. "We all we must be eager to learn. We all we are young, loving to splash the shore, and they will teach."

Martin smiled. "Who's deceiving the other more?"

Eye on Sky rotated his head in a figure eight with a particularly equine motion. "We all ourselves, let it be hoped."

There was no time to think. Exhausted, pushing himself and the others hours past their sleeps, Martin prepared the human crew as best he could, doing what Erin called hearsing and rehearsing.

The roles they played did not stray too far from truth, but reflected a mixing of cultures, human and Brother, still prickly with potential conflict—close enough to reality. Tensions were high and human tempers flared as they critiqued each other over long hours, working to perfect their act.

In the charged atmosphere, the Brothers tended to separate without warning, forcing braids to chase down cords, bag them, and lock them in quiet rooms until reassembly occurred.

Silken Parts apologized to Martin for the inconvenience and confusion; Martin, as always, held his irritation in check . . . Knowing that humans might do something similar at any time, fight with each other, break into tears, or worse.

But the disassembling stopped after a few days, and the humans held together remarkably well.

Trojan Horse/Double Seed put on scars from supernova damage: radiation erosion on its outer skin, a crippled drive motor, damaged electronics within. The ship manufactured convincing guns and lasers. Martin locked them away, with only himself and Eye on Sky given the combinations necessary to unlock them.

He could hardly keep his eyes off the growing disk of Sleep, drawing faces in the lines of mountains, disquieting patterns in the broad seas. He imagined himself drifting on a raft down rivers a hundred kilometers wide, navigating twisty cracks in the crust between sheer walls of obsidian black and rust red . . .

A day before noach cut-off with *Greyhound*, Martin spoke with Hans in private. "We're doing well. We know our roles. Cham and Erin have worked up a primer of human-Brother history. It's pretty entertaining. We'll noach it to you . . ."

"Anything for a little distraction," Hans said. "Giacomo's had a problem. I'd call it a nervous breakdown, but he says it's just exhaustion. He's still trying to riddle what Jennifer sent him."

"She wants to talk with him some more . . ."

"We'll be in blackout . . . He's really out of it, Martin."

"What they're doing might be important."

"I'd force him if I could, but he's like a zombie. Anything more and he'll break."

"Then she's on her own for a while," Martin said.

Hans made an ambiguous humph. "I'm feeding you more data from our remotes. The whole system is a circus. Don't tell anybody I said so, but I think we've more than met our match. The moms say they're not going to confuse us with guesses."

"I just can't figure any of it," Hans said. "Wouldn't it be safer for them to destroy all intruders and visitors? Especially after the supernova—they *know* something's in the neighborhood."

"I'm willing to make some guesses," Martin said. "I think they could have destroyed us already, but they're keeping up appearances. If they don't believe our disguise, they still can't be positive it's a disguise. Maybe they're extra cautious, in case we're backed up by something even more powerful."

But no amount of discussion could make them feel any more certain, or any easier.

The ships' distances grew, and blackout with *Greyhound*, and then with *Shrike*, left them completely on their own.

Jennifer began to brood, and spent most of her off-duty time in her quarters, shared with Erin Eire. Martin worried she was on the same course as Giacomo.

The Brothers discovered chess, and it became a release for them. One entire day, all the Brothers aboard *Trojan Horse* played chess without eating or sleeping. Losing a game caused a humiliating shock and momentary separation; by the end of the day, to Martin's surprise, cords were playing cords. The cords seemed much better at the game than braids, touching the projected pieces with their claws to make them move, minimized mentalities fully focused, undistracted by organized higher intelligence. *So much for cords having no intellect*, he thought.

The first complete communication, face to face, began three days before entering orbit around Sleep. Martin and Eye on Sky stood on the bridge, a flat screen monitor hissing faintly in front of them, a video camera focused on them, befitting their level of technology. Martin almost felt at home with the equipment; like *Trojan Horse/Double Seed*, this was something on a human scale, something he could imagine his own people building and doing.

The standards for transmission had been established four days before. Communication had been sporadic since; a kind of formality, perhaps an interspecies shyness, wariness, keeping the channels of communication closed most of the time, except for essential information. At this distance, there was an hour's delay.

The speaker mounted beside the screen crackled faintly, and then fell into silence as a many-layered digital signal was received and translated. The cool, neutral voice spoke, musical and dry like wind-blown sand. Symbols and numbers passed across the screen, to be translated into final orbital adjustments.

"We are speaking to you from the fourth planet," the voice announced. "All is ready now. Our first meeting will occur in orbit. You will be fitted with apparel for a journey to the surface of the fourth planet, as agreed. We are ready to transmit picture as well as sound.''

A vivid moving image appeared on the screen. The most human-like of their hosts' species—the crested, pale green being first encountered on Earth as the Death Valley decoy—lifted its miter-shaped head. Three amber eyes arranged in a small triangle on the snout of the miter sank into flesh, reemerged in a kind of blink. The knobby shoulders behind the crest moved slowly back and forth. Two six-fingered hands gripped a bar before it.

The miter-head shifted to one side. ''We are anticipating a physical meeting, and have made equipment to prevent biological contamination. When you enter orbit around the fourth planet, we will learn the qualities of your atmosphere and chemistry, and suit our equipment to your needs. We will tell you how to put your weapons in our safe-keeping before you enter orbit.''

Martin froze the last image of the miter-head creature and examined it thoughtfully, goosebumps rising on his arms. This one shape so symbolized deception and betrayal, but in fact on Earth this creature had spoken a kind of truth, as part of the deadly, playful testing of humanity: it had warned American scientists of coming destruction.

They used it on Earth, they use it still, how many thousands of years since they launched the killer probes? No wasted effort; is their creativity depleted?

The delay still prevented practical two-way communication, but Martin thought it best to maintain an atmosphere of ceremonial observance, as befitted a truly historic occasion: the first communication between intelligent species, for humans and Brothers, since their own meetings centuries in their fictitious past.

The red light on their camera blinked and Martin took a deep breath and delivered his reply: ''We are proud to be a part of this meeting. All individuals on *Double Seed* are prepared to follow your instructions. Your civilization seems much more capable than our own, and we entrust ourselves to your superior reasoning and technology.'' *Let them digest and react to humility—or abject innocence.*

He stepped aside and let Eye on Sky deliver his message in

Brother audio language. Paola stood beside Martin and translated.

"We are most impressed by your partnerships," Eye on Sky said as the camera light blinked. "We have learned to work in partnership ourselves, two very different kinds of life and intelligence, and we have hopes of exchanging useful knowledge."

Hakim turned off the camera. "It is sending," he said. Martin looked around the bridge at Brothers and humans, at the mom and snake mother out of camera range, soon to disappear into the ship's fabric.

Martin could not help thinking of themselves as sacrifices, less *Trojan Horse* than trussed lamb waiting for the knife.

He was prepared for that. Death would bring certainty, even an ultimate relaxation. But too many others had gone before them to make the prospect of death in defeat attractive.

William and Theresa. The five billion dead of Earth.

The frozen image of the miter-head creature remained on the screen. Ariel floated beside Martin, swimming against the air with gentle hand motions to stop her axial rotation. "We were taught to hate that thing on the Ark," she observed. "I hope our hatred doesn't show."

"Two hours until our next deceleration," Cham said. "We'll have to be ready—it's going to be four g's and no fields. A big burn."

Eye on Sky and Silken Parts deftly removed a cord apiece and set them down to play chess while they watched. Jennifer, George Dempsey, and Donna Emerald Sea also observed, faces dreamy.

Jennifer said very little now but her eyes were large and her cheeks had hollowed; she slept fitfully, Erin said, and never more than an hour any given time before coming wide awake with a jerk, sometimes a little shriek.

"What did the Killers do to your people when they came?" Ariel asked Dry Skin/Norman. So far, he was the only Brother who had taken a human name, and seemed the most willing to speak about Brother history.

"We our worlds, already in space, already commerce between worlds, all knew when our moons were taken, planets injected.

Death was large and quick. We we made our own escapes. The Benefactors found us and told us the Law.'' Norman weaved a little, releasing a scent of almonds and turpentine: distressed grief. This was not something any Brother enjoyed talking about.

"We know that much," Ariel said. "But did they try to hide themselves, to . . . play with you?"

Norman jabbed suddenly with his head at the projected chessboard, and the cords engaged in deep concentration jerked, clacked their claws in agitation, resumed. "No deception, no playing false," Norman said.

"I wonder why?" Ariel asked.

"Why play cat and mouse with us, and not with you?" George Dempsey added.

"Perhaps no learning in we us," Norman said. "Perhaps they already met us our kind before, and knew enough."

"You were stronger and more developed than we were," Cham said. "You actually got away from them."

"But we we hate this as much as you," Norman said, "a hate to ungather a braid for multiple fury."

This was the first time Martin had heard a Brother speak of hatred. His face flushed and his heart raced, hearing these words; humans were not alone in their passions. "We're partners," Martin said. "We feel the same way."

"Cords have no hatred of abstractions," Norman said. "We all we must take their example now. They play better chess, no fury, no hate. United, we we become weaker in some ways."

"Hatred is strength," Cham said. "That's what I feel. Without hating this . . . without hating *them* . . ." He bared his teeth like a wolf at the image on the screen. "Let's not underestimate hating."

Norman weaved back and forth and made a smell like burning sugar and cut grass. "I we believe there is strength in you we we have not. I we say never these thoughts to others, but know we we worry them."

Paola questioned him in crude Brother audio, straining her voice to make the scrapes and tones and piped air hums.

"Norman's saying he thinks we might have done better in their situation. Our literature leads him to believe we're better at getting angry. Better at killing."

"I we hope we can learn from you," Norman said.

"I we think we all our aggression suffices," Eye on Sky said, watching his cord push a holographic bishop three squares diagonally.

"How about names for these . . . creatures or beings or whatever?" Donna asked, breaking the awkward silence that followed. "I have one for *it*."

"What?" Paola asked.

"Bishop vulture," Donna said. "Sanctimonious diplomat, eater of carrion. Color of sick vomit."

"Yuck," George Dempsey said.

Jennifer came onto the bridge after a few hours' absence, glanced at the chess game in progress, turned to Martin, and projected a series of charts with her wand.

"They can project false light paths," she said. "They can convert matter to anti-matter at billions of kilometers—maybe up to and beyond our noach limit—and they can disarm neutronium bombs. They have it all, or they want us to think they have it all."

"This is what you worked out with Giacomo?"

"And with the ships' minds."

"Then we can't do anything to them."

The crew, human and Brother, fell silent.

Jennifer stiffly turned her shoulders with her neck, looking at her crewmates apologetically. "Sorry," she said. "Before the blackout, this is all we could figure, all we could deduce, given what we're seeing."

"Any chance you're wrong?" Ariel said.

"Of course," Jennifer said meekly. "We can always be wrong."

"You say the ships' minds worked with you," Cham said. "Do they agree?"

"This last part I worked through on my own, after the black-out, after the moms went away, so I can't be sure they would agree," Jennifer said.

"Then there's some hope?" Paola asked plaintively. The Brothers remained silent, waving like grass in a soft breeze.

Jennifer bit her lip. "I'm not perfect at this sort of thing," she said.

"But you're damned good," Cham said.

Martin reached for the last thread before the void, if only to keep the crew from something they did not need at all: complete despair. "Can the ships' minds—on *Greyhound* or *Shrike*—learn from this . . . advance our technology, add to our defenses, our weapons?"

Jennifer seemed grateful for the suggestion. "That's what we were . . . I mean, we wouldn't figure this out just to show everybody things were hopeless. We can't do anything on *Trojan Horse*, but I'm hoping Giacomo and the ships' minds, and all the others . . ." Tears broke from her eyelids and drifted in front of her face. She batted at them absently. "There just isn't much time, and we could have figured wrong so many different ways."

"But there's hope," Paola persevered. "Real hope."

Jennifer looked at Martin, saw the beseeching in his eyes, and said, "I think so. I haven't given up."

They endured the four-g deceleration for a day. They had created liquid-filled couches for these times; Martin and all the humans kept to their couches and tried to sleep through it. The Brothers' cords clutched their rings.

Orbital insertion was now assured without any further action.

The craft that came alongside a day before they entered orbit gleamed white as snow, a sand-blasted, spherical purity of forty or fifty meters.

The dry voice and image of bishop vulture instructed them, and they pushed their made-up weapons through the mechanical airlock.

The sphere opened a black mouth and swallowed the weapons like a big fish after a school of sprat. Its brightness dulled to charcoal gray; almost lost against the stars, visible only as shadow, it slipped away.

"Nothing lost," Eye on Sky said. "They were not good weapons. They gave no comfort."

Actually, to Martin, holding a laser rifle *had* afforded a kind of comfort. He hadn't held an actual gun since target shooting with his father when he was seven; the smooth gunmetal blue and gray lines of the laser rifle, though cinematic, had at least given him the sensation, however illusory, of doing something for immediate defense.

None of the weapons had ever been fired. Compared to the ability to control mass at billions of kilometers, a high-powered laser beam and chemical kinetic bullets seemed less than a stone axe against an atomic bomb.

One of the cords died playing chess. It belonged to Sharp Seeing. A brief ceremony was held before the Brothers, alone in their quarters, ate it, separating into their own cords to do so. After, with only twelve hours to go before orbiting Sleep, Sharp Seeing explained that the cord had died of frustration, facing potential checkmate and unable to find an escape. "I we begin to think perhaps this game is bad," Sharp Seeing said. The cord he had lost was not, so he claimed, an essential part.

Paola was the only human allowed to attend the ceremony, after which she emerged both deeply moved and very proud.

Sleep filled the screen in hypnotic detail. Hakim and Sharp Seeing busily gathered information, expressing each in his way the excitement of witnessing and recording such an extraordinary object.

The fourth planet's supply of internal heat was sufficient to keep its surface at a constant twenty degrees centigrade, except where molten material and hot gases leaked through, chiefly along the mountain ridges, which seemed to show where massive rocky plates ground against each other.

The physics, as Hakim had already said, was incomprehensible, pointing to massive technological adaptations. Possibly the entire planet was artificial, but the crudity and violence of its design said otherwise . . . and there was no way to unravel the contradiction, given what they knew and what they could see.

Sleep's crudity lay in the uncertainty of its surface. With an area of thirty-two billion square kilometers, nine tenths of it under water, hundreds of millions of square kilometers of land churned in apparently useless turmoil. Angry black clouds rose where molten material flowed into the broad seas, rolling from the wall-like mountain ridges.

The air was moist and high in carbon dioxide, low in oxygen. Martin thought it might be an atmosphere adapted for plants.

Hakim and Sharp Seeing used the *Double Seed*'s primitive instruments to capture images of ocean-going forests of dark green, rising from the water like drifting continents, the largest of them wallowing for ten thousand kilometers across a smooth sea.

Low, rounded quartz-like mountains punctuated the dark basaltic crust, topped by thick crests of pink and orange.

"The colors are probably phosphates, volcanic sulfur compounds, and hydrocarbons," Hakim said. "Wonderful sights, wonderful knowledge, but our instruments are so limited!"

"Time for an open meeting, all of us, now," Martin said.

All twenty of the *Double Seed*'s crew gathered in the cafeteria, humans and Brothers mingling easily.

Eye on Sky and Martin floated at the center. Eye on Sky spoke first in a rich sequence of odors and sounds, head cords stretching wide, claws clicking for the third, almost musical, component. Paola might have been able to understand some of this; to Martin, who knew only a few of the less sibilant sounds, the speech was interesting, but empty of meaning. Then Eye on Sky switched to English.

"Decided days ago that we we should speak before we our hosts in language we all us may understand. All we our ten on this ship now speak English enough to be understood, with Paola Birdsong giving help. Thus, we we now will use English exclusively when we are together."

"We appreciate the gesture," Martin said.

"It is some stifling," Eye on Sky said, "but necessary."

"We're going to take some important precautions after our first contact with our hosts," Martin said. "We don't know what they can learn about us at a distance, but we can be pretty sure that once they've actually touched this ship, secrecy may be impossible. We're going to have to be circumspect. We're reasonably sure the noach chamber can't be breached. If we have anything to say to each other that we don't want our hosts to hear, we say it there.

"But if we allow anybody or anything into the *Double Seed*, we'll have to assume no place is safe."

"Micro-scale listeners," George Dempsey said. "They could even be in our bodies."

"Right. We'll assume they can't be detected. That means no written messages, no winks or nods, nothing suspicious . . . or out of character. "

Humans murmured and nodded, Brothers undulated slightly.

"The play's the thing," Martin said. "From now on, we're actors."

Double Seed entered orbit ten thousand kilometers above Sleep, and the bishop vulture appeared again. There was no discernible delay in communications now. "We have asked you to orbit this fourth planet because it is the safest. Your ship would not be safe near any other planet in our gathering, for there is much activity—exchange of forces, coming and going of other ships. But the fourth planet is not especially comfortable for your kind. We ask that you give us samples of your atmosphere and tissues and nutritional requirements, that we may prepare vehicles and implements for your use."

Martin had already drawn blood from himself and Ariel with the *Double Seed*'s medical kit. Silken Parts took tissue samples from one of his cords.

On the screen, the bishop vulture lifted its long nose, revealing breathing and speech orifices beneath. Its chest expanded and it hissed slightly while saying, "We are very interested in your aggregate species. We have no such intelligent beings in our gathering. You will be very valuable and respected among us, and you will teach us much."

Erin glanced at the ceiling. Martin stared fixedly at the camera, face blank.

"A ship will attach to your ship in a few minutes," the bishop vulture said. "The samples will be collected by a sterilized machine within your ship."

"Maybe we should introduce ourselves and exchange names. We prefer to use names," Martin said.

"We have no need for names, but names can be assumed for your convenience."

"My name is Martin."

"I can be called Amphibian, since I seem to most resemble, in my biology, that class of animals you call amphibians."

"A better name might be Frog," Martin suggested.

"Then I will be called Frog. You will meet other representatives, and assign them names and categories, as you wish."

"Ship is approaching," Sharp Seeing announced.

With a gentle scraping sound, the ship attached to *Double Seed*, a thick extrusion surrounding the mechanical airlock like lips. Martin took a deep breath. Here it was—intrusion, and all the dangers that might bring. He wondered, too late, if they should have resisted direct contact—decided that would have been impossible.

Eye on Sky opened the exterior door. A gray cylinder with rounded ends entered. Then he closed the exterior door and opened the interior. The cylinder propelled itself into the bridge area with quiet spurts of air drawn through small slits in its middle, and expelled in similar slits arranged around its length.

Paola opened a small refrigerator and passed the samples in their transparent plastic container to Silken Parts, who swung around to release the container in front of the cylinder.

An arm extruded from the cylinder and took the container. The cylinder propelled itself softly to the airlock, and the door closed behind.

On the screen, the bishop vulture—*Frog*, Martin corrected himself—turned away for a moment, head cocked, then turned back. "We have several possibilities open to us. You may come to the surface of our fourth planet, to meet directly with our representatives, or you may remain within your ship. If you choose to visit the surface, you may use equipment we supply to make your stay comfortable; this is recommended, as testing of your samples tells us you would soon grow tired under this planet's gravity."

They've analyzed the samples already . . . Martin's neck and shoulders tensed and he shivered.

"You may also choose your mode of conveyance. These decisions may be made at your leisure. I will remain available to you at any time."

The screen blanked.

"Are we still sending?" Martin asked.

"I cut off when they did," Hakim said.

"It's a little abrupt," Martin said, "but it seems clear. We're going to spend some time getting used to them. If they're as smart as they seem, maybe we should expect them to get used to us." He made this speech in complete expectation of being overheard. He stumbled over the next few words, trying to say and do what they might be expected to say and do by the unimaginable minds that might be listening. "We've adapted to each other, but we were nearly equal when we fought our wars . . . How much harder to understand species much more advanced?"

He visualized tiny machines in the cylinder's exhalation, hiding in the ship like dust motes, transmitting by noach. *Nothing at all compared to what we've already seen.*

"It took us centuries to grow together," Silken Parts said, with no discernible unease. "We we hope for no atrocious deals here."

High-school students emoting before master critics. How long could it last?

The most important moment arrived: the first meeting, face to face, between the crew of *Double Seed* and some of the beings who seemed to control the Leviathan system.

Donna Emerald Sea had devised fancy uniforms for the humans to wear, and decorative sashes and ribbons for the Brothers. She adjusted Martin's particularly resplendent garb, winked at him briefly, stood before him with hands on hips, and said, "You look perfectly barbaric, Captain."

"Thank you," Martin said, and turned to Eye on Sky, who resembled a young girl's braided pony tail done up with ribbons, brought to life perhaps by Godpapa Drosselmeier for a joke. The Brothers and humans did look splendid—and naïve; he hoped Frog and the others would find the display amusing, whatever passed for amusement among them—and convincing.

Donna went among the others, pinning, fidgeting. Martin remembered her adjusting the projected world-wedding gown on Theresa and became acutely aware once more of human limitations—and human beauties. He closed his eyes and swallowed.

Paola helped Donna with her uniform, black and red with gold sash, crew style.

Hakim wore his outfit stiffly. He reached up as Martin ap-

proached and stuck his finger between neck and high collar,
Adam's apple bobbing in his thin throat. "Many years since we
have worn these," he said. Hakim might be the least convincing
of them.

The Brothers seemed natural actors. Not once had they broken
character or showed the strain of their roles.

"We're ready, Captain," Donna said.

Six—three humans and three Brothers—would leave *Double
Seed* and descend to Sleep's surface: Silken Parts, Strong Cord,
and Eye on Sky; Martin, Paola, and Ariel. Martin appointed Erin
Eire to replace him. Sharp Seeing would replace Eye on Sky.

They caught a glimpse of a white sphere in the screen, heard
it scrape midships and seal itself around the airlock. The inner
airlock door opened. Single file, they entered the smooth green
interior of the transfer ship. Beyond a transparent panel, visible
only as they turned a corner, stood another bishop vulture, not—
Martin guessed—Frog itself.

"I am your helper now," the new bishop vulture said. "I
have taken your word Salamander as name." It hissed faintly
beneath its words. "If it does not offend or bring wrong mean-
ings, you may so call me."

Eye on Sky introduced his companions. Martin and Eye on
Sky had decided it might be best for a Brother to serve as
primary leader on this excursion. Paola seemed up to the task of
interpreting between two non-native speakers—the Brothers and
their hosts.

There was method to this inconvenience: it could masquerade
as power sharing, and the inevitable misunderstandings could
hide their own confusion.

They drifted weightless in the middle of a small cabin. Martin
noted a sensation of motion as the vessel separated from *Double
Seed*. Invisible constraints much like fields surrounded them;
their hosts' technology had advanced in parallel with the Benefactors at least to this degree. But then, fields were as logical
and inevitable as fire had once been for humans.

Salamander hissed faintly again, said, "We descend now.
There should be no discomfort. Would you like to examine
conveyances for walking on the surface?"

"We we would like so now," Eye on Sky said. A panel of

curved wall became transparent, revealing Salamander against a dark backdrop.

Another panel to Salamander's right cleared. Beyond, motionless white skeletal frames stood like robots made of elegant bones, one set for humans, another for the Brothers.

Martin was particularly impressed by the design for the Brothers' suits. Like padded snake ribs tied to two backbones, they would allow braids to move much as they did naturally, in normal gravitation, with a sinuous caterpillar motion.

"We hope these are suitable," Salamander said. "They are made to go unnoticed while worn."

"We we are assured," Eye on Sky said.

"There will be one for each member of your party."

"As expected," Eye on Sky said.

"And they will be fitted to each individual's shape and size," Salamander said.

"As expected."

"Your schedule for surface excursion . . ." Sharp hissing intake of breath, raising of the miter's nose, "winking" of the three amber eyes into the pale green flesh. "Upon landing and suiting up, there is orientation to teach you with more basics of how we behave and work. Then a meeting under shelter with representatives of the five primary races. Followed by proper induction ceremony for entry into the Cooperative of Fifteen Worlds. Exchange of information in a formal meeting with secretaries of the Living Council. I will accompany you and explain what is necessary, what you have questions for."

Ariel looked at Martin with a brief expression of boredom. Martin lifted his eyebrows in concurrence. Whatever excitement this meeting might have had—under any other circumstances, should have had—was lost in the tincture of overwhelming ceremony, not to mention awareness of its almost certain insincerity.

Camouflage upon masquerade upon deception.

Do these beings believe they are real, and free? Martin wondered. *Are they? Have the Killers faded into their decoys?*

Salamander lowered its head and gripped the metal bar before it, freezing suddenly like a museum display. After a moment, as the skeletal white suits disappeared behind opacity, it lifted its head again. "We have refreshments, liquids and foods, which we hope are palatable. Landing will be in fifteen minutes. You will not need to inconvenience yourselves, and you will not experience any discomfort beyond mild sensations of motion. We have provided food. You may dine after landing.''

"Thank you," Eye on Sky said. "Reasons of religious nature, we all we must eat our own food.''

They had taken enough risks already. There was no sense inviting microscopic spies into their bodies, or anything else they could avoid.

"Religious nature," Salamander repeated with some savor. "Rules dictated by perceived higher beings?''

"Food for humans and Brothers must be specially prepared. We all we will send food from our ship when needed, with we our food handler.''

"That will be done," Salamander said. "Is this religious requirement very strong?''

Eye on Sky glanced at Martin and wove a small figure eight with splayed head cords. It seemed to want his help.

"Very," Martin said. Then, innocently, "Don't you have religious food laws? We assumed all civilizations would . . . obey higher authority.''

Salamander did not answer for a time. It—or something listening through it—was obviously thinking over this question thoroughly. "We do not observe specific religious rules," it answered. "Nor do most of us absorb nutrition by eating. There is one exception, a type living on the fourth planet.''

Martin's expedient, and little test, had been neatly side-stepped. Martin said, "Are . . . most of you mechanical?''

"No," Salamander said. "We are organic.''

"We we foresee such things as artificial bodies," Eye on Sky said, back on track. "Are you naturally born, or artificial?''

"These questions can be answered later," Salamander said. "They are not as simple as they might seem.''

Martin curled his legs and folded his arms, floating within his protective field. He could feel little of the ship's motion; no obvious acceleration. But the always-sinking sensation of weightlessness changed in a way he couldn't quite describe; as if his arms and legs might be getting heavier, yet not his torso.

The odd sensation faded, replaced by something they hadn't

experienced in years—the heaviness of being in a planet's gravitation. Theory told them there was no difference between weight caused by acceleration and the heaviness brought on by gravity, but Martin had the eerie sensation of *knowing* the difference.

The protective fields did not diffuse through their bodies; they provided support for externals, but not for internal muscles and organs, and the heaviness immediately became oppressive, almost nauseating.

"Are you comfortable?" Salamander asked.

Eye on Sky made a squeaking sound. Martin looked to the Brother's hind section and saw cords letting go. The Brother smelled like a pine forest—euphoria and fear, he guessed.

"I feel a little sick," Martin said. Ariel said she was not comfortable.

The fields glowed and sparkled briefly, and the disparity faded. The Brothers did not completely disassemble; the cords grabbed hold again. Paola's face took on color and Ariel let her fists relax.

"Better," Martin said.

Where the skeletal support suits had been displayed, an equally convincing view of the planet's surface appeared. They seemed to descend from an altitude of nine or ten kilometers. The horizon showed no curvature; the atmosphere, only a few kilometers thick, glimmered in a thin bright line between the dull red, black, and dark blue expanse of Sleep, and the starry blackness of space.

Martin saw orderly features below, triangles, circles, lines of gray against the dull red and black, circles of white lying on the blue expanse of sea. Mountains appeared against the horizon, white rock capped with orange and pink, deep in shadow now.

Dawn was breaking, and from three hundred million kilometers, Leviathan's light poured over Sleep's sea and land, setting ablaze streamers of cloud and smoke from crustal vents.

Martin heard a faint whining noise—perhaps their craft singing through Sleep's atmosphere. Puffs of cloud shot past. He felt the planetary pull more intensely, but without much more discomfort.

He avoided thinking about how they were being manipulated. There was no practical way they could protect themselves against tampering. *The Killers can change matter from a great distance. They could change parts of our own bodies to suit their purposes . . . kill us immediately, fill us with tiny spies, even control the way we think.*

He looked at Ariel, trying not to let his misery and fear show. She held out her hand, and he took it without hesitation. Paola held out her hand, too, and then Silken Parts extended a cord, and Paola took hold of that, and Ariel grasped a cord offered by Eye on Sky. Strong Cord connected with Martin and the circle was complete.

He didn't feel any less afraid, but he certainly felt less alone.

"Are you disturbed? Not comfortable?" Salamander asked.

Eye on Sky, who should have answered for the group, said nothing.

"We're comfortable," Martin said hoarsely, and cleared his throat.

"We are not familiar with that communication," Salamander said, and repeated the sound of his throat clearing. "What does it mean?"

"An . . . organic sound," Martin said. "No meaning."

"Like my hissing and breathing," Salamander offered.

"Right," Martin said.

"Do my extraneous sounds bother you?"

"No," Martin said. Under other circumstances—*if this masquerade were real*—he thought he could feel affection for Salamander, so solicitous was the bishop vulture, trying to make their journey easier.

The wonderful, withdrawing blink of the beautiful amber eyes, the flushing pink of patches of the pastel green skin; the creature was actually quite beautiful. *I'm flipping back and forth. Emotional strain. Keep it even.*

The exposed crust of Sleep was incredibly rugged, a chaos of broken black rock, some blocks hundreds of meters wide, lying over and across each other with glassy extrusions sharp as knives. Between the blocks lay drifts of orange and pink powder, from which winds blew streaming hazes that glittered in the sunlight.

The ship still flew a few kilometers from the surface. Into their view came a stretch of sea, mottled blue-green, kilometer-wide white poker-chips floating motionless amid low, oily waves.

As they watched, a distant section of crust collapsed like an edge of glacier calving on Earth. A thick plume of black smoke arose, splaying out into a low anvil in seconds. Red highlights glowed through the murk.

"We will land on a platform in the ocean in three minutes," Salamander announced. "This must be very unfamiliar to you. Do you have any questions?"

"Thousands of questions," Martin said. "There just isn't time to ask them all."

"I we have one question," Eye on Sky said. "Is this planet natural, or artificial?"

"Both," Salamander said. "Once it was a small star. We have been changing it for thousands of years. First it was used as an energy and fuel source. Now, the easiest answer would be to say that it is artificial. It supplies commodities to the rest of our system."

The ocean filled more and more of their view, until only a line of black cliffs separated ocean from lurid, cloud-stripped sky.

"We are now on the platform. Your suits are in another room. We will leave the craft when you are prepared. At no time will you be exposed to the actual atmosphere, which is not suitable for your biology, and rich with small organisms that might be dangerous to you, besides."

Part of the wall moved aside and they stepped carefully, aided by the fields, into another room, this one equipped with a low stage. The skeletal suits hung from the ceiling above the stage.

"Do you think we're alone?" Paola asked. "Everything projected, remote-controlled?"

"Could be," Martin said.

Eye on Sky produced a smell of tea and soil. "Useless to make guesses," he said.

Salamander's voice instructed them to stand on the stage. Wrapped by their fields, they moved, with some difficulty, to spots marked by faint glows of light. A small, perfect image of each of them appeared next to the appropriate suit, like a nametag. Martin stood before his suit, facing it. "Turn around, please, with your backs to the suits."

He turned. The suit whispered behind him and his neck hair bristled. Its fluid "bones" wrapped around him, gripping him comfortably.

He moved experimentally. The suit moved effortlessly with him.

Useless to make guesses. Everything a mystery. Ants in a kitchen.

"You will be surrounded by invisible barriers when outside. Your breathing should be natural, and you should not worry. We caution against these things only: do not move rapidly, and do not move away from the path or away from your group."

"Right," Martin said. He watched the Brothers getting used to their suits, flexing them, raising three fourths of their lengths from the stage. Ariel lifted her arms experimentally, cocked her head, looked at Martin sidewise.

"Comfortable?" he asked. Ariel and Paola nodded; Strong Cord and Eye on Sky put their suits through more tests before concurring. "We're ready," Martin told the unseen Salamander.

"The ship will debark you in an open area. You should enjoy experiencing the surface as directly as possible. It is quite beautiful. There is no danger, but if you would like to avoid this, we can remove this part of your journey."

Eye on Sky answered, "We we would like to see the surface."

Martin didn't disagree, but he was not enthusiastic. He had seen enough marvels and spectacle already to be spiritually exhausted.

The spacecraft opened around them and stowed itself like a folding screen, leaving them on the white stage, surrounded by an immensity of gray and black sky, midnight blue ocean, dark cliffs rising thousands of meters above the sea. He could feel the flesh-thumping sound of distant explosions, grindings of crust; hear noise like giants groaning and whistling. The sudden openness was unnerving. His hands trembled within the pliant grip of the skeletal suit.

"Wow," Ariel said, her face pale. The air within Martin's field was self-contained, and he could not smell the Brothers. But he could smell his own reaction—rank fear.

The weight on his stomach and lungs gave him sharp twinges

of pain, as if strings tied to pins in his organs were being tugged. Martin doubted he would want to spend more than a few hours on the surface of Sleep.

A causeway reached across the sea to a broad white disk. Salamander's voice spoke in his right ear: "Your suits will walk you over this distance. The disk is a kind of ferry. You will be taken to a shore station, and there will meet with more of our representatives. Are you experiencing discomfort?"

"I'm fine," Martin said.

The suit nudged him and he tried to walk but it resisted. Finally he relaxed and the suit did all his work for him, moving him like a puppet, a sensation he did not enjoy. They were all guided over the causeway to the disk, which promptly disengaged and moved smoothly through the thick, rapid waves.

Martin's vision coarsened and the landscape became more vivid. This might have been an effect of gravity; it also might have been an effect of the field containing his atmosphere.

Useless to make guesses.

The ferry skirted a thick mass of green covering a few hundred square meters, undulating on the seas, large bubbles rising and breaking through like explosions in fibrous mud.

"One of our types finds these waters comfortable," Salamander said. "An individual would enjoy seeing you. Is this okay with you?"

"Acceptable," Eye on Sky said.

Seconds later, a bright red nightmare of jointed arms pushed through the water and heaved part of itself onto the ferry. Paola gave a little squeak and backed close to Martin. The Brothers seemed frozen in place, making no comments, weathering this surfeit of experience.

The nightmare's arms parted with a motion combining the curl of a squid's tentacles and the up-and-down pistoning of a spider's legs. A remarkable "face" appeared, four glittering egg-shaped eyes in a mass of glossy black flesh, surrounded by alternating fleshy rings of yellow and gray.

"This type serves a capacity like a farmer in these seas, but makes many decisions in our political framework," Salamander explained. "Its kind denies the value of artificial enhancements. Like you, it eats, and is very strict about what it eats, and when, and how. Perhaps in the future you may hold discussions. You may share sympathies."

"Sure," Martin said dubiously. He very much wanted it to go away.

The simple expansiveness of sea and sky bothered him more than he could have imagined. He was so used to the confines of the ships, enclosed universes . . .

To his relief, the creature pushed away from the raft and vanished into the waves.

"It had at least thirty arms," Paola said. "I couldn't count them all!"

Another voice spoke in his ear: Erin Eire on *Double Seed*. "How's the trip, Martin?"

He stuttered for a moment, surprised by the communication. "We're healthy," he said. "It's *big* down here. Wide open spaces."

"Sounds lovely," Erin said. "You look a little tied up in those suits. We're all watching here—both crews. The transmissions are clear. We're overhead now. Look up and you might see us."

Martin looked up but saw nothing in the muddy blackness. "No visual," he said.

"Too bad. Don't feel lonely."

Salamander's voice returned. "We will pass around this promontory."

Waves slid up against jagged blocks of crust with tremendous force but little spray, rivulets of water fleeing quickly back to the ocean. The ferry came within a hundred meters of the turmoil, and passed around a high point of black and brown rock rising like a squat tower.

Beyond the promontory, at the far side of a deep harbor, three rocky tunnel mouths opened, each about fifty meters high and perhaps forty wide. Square tongues of polished gray stone pushed out of the tunnels into the harbor.

Even from a few kilometers, Martin heard the deep breath of the tunnels, felt the airborne shudder of water rushing in, pushing out.

The ferry crossed the harbor quickly and the tunnels loomed, making sounds such as Odysseus might have heard approaching

Scylla and Charybdis. The light of Leviathan fell behind the headland now, and murky shadow surrounded them, broken by the white luminosity of their ferry. Ariel's face appeared ghostly, shadows of cheeks, chin, and nose rising across her eyes.

"Are we going in there?" Paola asked.

"Yes," Salamander answered. "We will dock at the second tunnel from your left. Transportation will arrive soon. Within the station, there are type individuals of some of the beings occupying our system. They will speak with you."

"Martin," Paola said, "I think the Brothers are having problems."

Martin looked at Eye on Sky and Silken Parts, both shivering within their suits. Strong Cord seemed fine, sliding beside his companions with solicitous sounds, squirks and clatters. "What's wrong?" Martin asked.

"This is what is seen when disassembled," Eye on Sky said, voice harsh and uneven. "This is the cave of youth on the shore, where young come together as braids after cords fight."

"Paola, what do you know about this?"

"Something about adulthood rituals . . . Nothing in their literature that I've found. Maybe it's deep memory."

"It is intimate," Strong Cord said. "Difficulty buried in minds of cords. I we are disturbed, but we we more disturbed."

"Salamander, some of us are having problems," Martin said.

"How may we help?" Salamander's voice asked.

"Can you block off the view, cover us?" Martin asked. A white canopy rose from the disk like a pleated piece of paper and unfolded over them, blocking the sky but not the view ahead.

Eye on Sky's trembling stopped. Silken Parts continued to shiver for a few more seconds, then writhed spasmodically and became still, again in control.

What else can go wrong? Martin faced the immense tunnel openings without the Brothers' deep-seated concerns, but also without any enthusiasm. This entire journey seemed calculated to overawe, and despite Eye on Sky's agreement to this journey, that said nothing good about their hosts. Rather than manufacture comfortable surroundings, they seemed to want to test their guests—

Test. Gather information about reactions to strenuous conditions. The Killers had done that on Earth with even less mercy.

The disk bumped gently against the edge of the dock. A ramp smoothed out to join with the disk.

"You may walk by yourselves," Salamander's voice informed them. Eye on Sky went first, skeletal white suit rippling. Paola followed, then Martin, and finally all stood on the hard dark gray surface.

The disk sank beneath the fast thick waves. *No way back—is that the meaning? Is there any meaning, or just insensitivity to aliens whose psychology they know nothing about?*

The tunnel's ceiling hung over them like the edge of a black void. The floor beneath advanced into shadow.

Silken Part's dark cords became part of the obscurity beyond; his suit seemed to stand by itself, moving like a cartoon spook. Ariel stepped closer. "I think we should get back to the ship in a couple of hours," she said to Martin.

A tiny simulacrum of a bishop vulture—Frog or Salamander—appeared in the tunnel, perfect in every detail. Martin adjusted his focus to learn whether the image was floating deep back in the tunnel, or nearby, and found it was only a meter from his face, a few centimeters in size. Surprised, Ariel dodged the simulacrum as if it were an insect. She straightened in her suit with a pained expression.

"Salamander, we need to be back in our ship within two hours," Martin said. The simulacrum grew larger, like an object seen in a zoom lens. Martin heard Salamander's voice from that direction.

"The meetings will last only twenty minutes this first time," it said. "You will be returned to your ship after that, and other meetings will be planned."

A bright red circle appeared deep in the tunnel. "Please move toward the circle. You will see," Salamander assured them.

The three Brothers slithered ahead, apparently recovered from their initial difficulties.

At first, Martin could see nothing beyond their immediate surround. The six of them—and Salamander's floating image—

were clearly visible. As his eyes grew accustomed, he made out more and more, seeing first an uncertain wave-like motion on the distant walls, then shades and details.

The walls churned. Blocky shapes crawled up in lines like geometric slugs, deflected by obstacles that extruded into their paths. Near the edge of the floor, splashing, sucking sounds told him that water flowed either in hidden gutters or through deep channels beneath.

"What is it?" Paola asked. Martin had no answer. The red circle grew. Spots of dim green and blue light appeared on the walls, moving with the blocky shapes but not issuing from them.

"What are those?" Paola asked.

"Living machines that process and store chemicals made in the seas," Salamander said. "The seas are factories. There is much traditional industry on this world."

The red circle faded. "You may stop now," Salamander said. *This is it. They'll kill us now, then dissect the ship at leisure, torturing, misleading, learning what they can.*

Walls lifted from the floor around them, bright blue like clear sunny skies on Earth, and a kind of music played, without melody but very pleasant.

"You will meet first with four representatives," Salamander announced. The simulacrum vanished and Salamander entered, full sized, through a door in a luminous wall.

"Is this your physical form?" Eye on Sky asked, head cords splayed wide, the eyes on each cord glittering.

"This is my form," Salamander said. "Individuals are not limited to single bodies. There are many versions of myself working. This is true of nearly all the type individuals you will meet."

Safety in numbers. No sense attacking—you can't kill us all, we have copies, backups stashed everywhere.

Martin pretended to be impressed, but in fact the children had been told about this early in their voyage, along with other facts about advanced technological species.

The surprise was that, given their abilities, the inhabitants of these worlds still had physical form at all.

Their hosts fit few norms.

"Are you prepared to meet with these representatives?"

"Yes," Martin said.

"Yes," Eye on Sky said.

Martin felt a sting of anticipation.

Through the door came a being with two elephantine legs, two three-jointed arms emerging from a barrel chest, and a small, eyeless head. Despite having seen it in still images before, Martin's throat tightened and his heart-rate increased. The creature stood at least three meters high, well adapted to this kind of gravity, moving with a curious waddle like the gait of a fat human combined with the ponderous grace of an elephant. It wore no clothing and carried no equipment.

Salamander walked beside the thick-legged elephantoid, striding on four limbs, bat-like, crest rising and falling.

The door widened and a tube of fluid pushed through, forming a cube beside the elephantoid. Within the cube floated two creatures, elongated, shark-shaped, with broad wing-like fins along their sides. Their heads were pointed, sensory organs arranged in rings back from the snout. Fins just behind the head ended in radiances of finger-like tentacles. Martin had assumed these creatures were related; their appearance in the same field seemed to support that opinion. The cube of water arranged its passengers beside the others.

Last to enter was a second bishop vulture. The door closed. To Martin, the assembly seemed hasty at best, not what he would have expected for a historic moment; not a first meeting with a newly arrived race of intelligent beings, more like a gathering of executives to iron out business matters.

Ariel rubbed the palms of her hands together, glanced at Martin with a wry expression, and dropped her hands to her sides. Paola seemed transfixed, eyes wide, looking from one being to the other. Eye on Sky, Silken Parts, and Strong Cord at least seemed calm and in no difficulty.

"I am Frog, who first spoke to you," the second bishop vulture said. "Are you well?"

Eye on Sky slid across the gray surface to raise himself beside Martin. "We we are mystified," the Brother said. "What is your purpose?"

"Your deceit is more than matched by our own," Frog said.

Martin's chest went hollow and he held his breath, waiting for extinction; he had *known* it would come, that childsplay would not suffice.

"We exist at the sufferance of greater powers," Frog said. "Since we are neither of us anything more than surrogates, there is no need for ceremony."

Paola closed her eyes. Ariel's lips moved, her face ashen.

"It is no coincidence that your ship arrives in the train of destruction from an exploding star. You represent higher powers as well. Your artificial construction is convincing, but the coincidence is too great to be accepted."

Do they know about the other ships?

"We serve as extended eyes," Salamander said, lifting its crest. "Do you have access to your creators?"

Martin tried frantically to understand what they were saying. They seemed to believe that Brothers and humans were themselves created, artificial . . .

"We we do not understand," Eye on Sky said.

"You are representatives of higher intelligences, as are we. Are we communicating clearly?"

"We're still confused," Martin said. "Are you saying others control you, like puppets?"

"We are not puppets. We have a separate existence," Frog said.

The elephantoid stepped forward. "There are four hundred and twelve types of intelligent being in this planetary system." Its voice sang high and rough, but intelligible. "Those of us before you serve political and other roles. We speak with our creators and represent the other types. Do you have a direct connection with your creators?"

"We we are autonomous," Eye on Sky said.

"But you are created," Salamander continued. Martin's body ached as if with fever; they might be undergoing the interstellar equivalent of interrogation, the third degree.

"We understand now," Martin said, hoping Eye on Sky and the others would let him take the lead, catch on to the implications. "If the time has come to drop all pretense, we are ready."

Ariel's face stiffened with apprehension. Paola closed her eyes languidly, as if ready for sleep.

"It is clear that precautions are necessary in high-level inter-stellar relations," the elephantoid said.

I'll call him a babar, Martin thought, and held his jaws to-gether tightly to keep from laughing. He couldn't believe they had traveled for centuries, across so many hundreds of trillions of kilometers, to stand in this place, in this situation, meeting layer upon layer of lies with more lies. It was comic in an acutely painful way.

William and Theresa and Theodore and so many others had died to bring them here; had been killed by these things, or by their *higher authority*.

Eye on Sky said nothing, deferring to Martin. Martin won-dered what the Brothers were thinking, but he could not turn back now. "That seems to be the rule," he answered. "We appreciate your not harming us."

"It would not be courteous," Salamander said. "Do you understand the intentions of your creators?"

"If you're asking whether we can . . . discuss issues with you, make decisions, the answer is yes, to a limited degree."

"Are your superiors in this vicinity, within our planetary system?" Frog asked.

"No," Martin said.

"Are they listening through you?"

"Not directly," Martin said.

"Can you provide a more direct means of communication, to allow more rapid agreement?"

"No," Martin said.

"This much all seems true," the elephantoid babar said. "Are you tiring, or do you wish to make preliminary agreements now?"

"Let's get something agreed to now," Martin said.

"We feel it is best, if you are prepared, to meet directly with our creators, that you may carry more accurate knowledge to your own."

Martin could not speak for a moment. Eye on Sky swiveled his broad head, cords held tightly together in a defensive posture, and said to Martin, "We we are ready."

"All right," Martin said, ant in kitchen, diapered infant on a diplomatic mission. "Let's meet them."

* * *

The white walls bent inward and sank out of sight.

The five representatives moved closer to the humans and Brothers.

"This is not dangerous," the babar said in its high, irritating voice, "but it is difficult to fold one's thoughts around, even if you have witnessed it before."

"This fourth world is a home and reservoir," Salamander said. Martin much preferred listening to the bishop vultures. "Our creators live inside, in layers around the dense core, where there is much flow of energy."

"Did they always live here?" Paola asked.

"Since we have existed," Frog said.

"How long is that?"

"Two thousand years by your measure," Salamander said.

The killer probes may have been made long before that, Martin thought.

The red circle appeared again, larger this time, and gracefully dropped to the floor of the tunnel. The edge of the circle rested less than two meters from Martin's feet.

"I reassure you, there is no danger," Salamander said. "We will witness a part only of one of our creators."

The floor vibrated as if with the passage of a train. Something shimmered within the red circle. The shimmer extended into a tube rising to the top of the tunnel. The red circle vanished. Within the shimmer lifted a multi-colored brightness, dazzling in the tunnel's obscurity.

The brightness took a helical form, like a staircase of light. Along its length dripped brilliant colors, yellows and oranges dominant, as if the light itself congealed and condensed and evaporated again.

The sight was intense and beautiful, but Martin was far beyond being impressed. He stifled urge upon insistent urge to laugh.

He could see little more than the brightness. It became a staircase with dancing beetles. His vision faded in and out. He wondered how much time he had before he fainted or lost control . . .

The next voice shocked him to full alertness. Richly feminine, fully human, it sounded like Theresa, but the similarity was more his making than real. He stood straight in the skeletal suit and saw the others motionless around him, all but Silken Parts, who swung to look in Martin's direction, head cords drawn almost to a point with fright.

"Only you and I we," Silken Parts said. "Others . . ."

Their companions were all frozen, locked into immobile fields. Ariel and Paola had become posed mannequins within the still white cages of their suits.

The voice again, without age, smooth as ice and equally cold. Not unfriendly. Not friendly. Not caring. Not aloof.

A voice to be described only in negatives and absences.

"Tell me why you are here."

Martin could not summon enough spit to answer. Silken Parts made no effort to speak English. Martin faced the helical staircase of light and saw jeering faces ascending its twist.

"Why are you here?"

"We were invited," Martin finally managed. Silken Parts' cords had reached their limit and struggled in elemental panic, hanging from the ribs of the skeletal suit; the braid, no longer connected, would not witness or answer.

Martin was alone now, fully accountable to whatever this was.

"Where are your superiors, your other vessels?"

"There are no other ships."

"Imagine if you will all the minds you have ever known, speaking to each other without animosity and without interruption, leaving out accumulated error. I speak to you as something of that scale. You must realize that disguises and lies are easy to penetrate."

"I'm not lying," Martin said hopelessly. His fear was not enough to keep him from fading.

"You are part of a force of ships sent to destroy this system. More correctly, you have been sent to destroy people who designed and built certain robots. You are not the first. There will be others."

Martin could hardly see.

"Those who made the robots have all died. Their direct descendants long ago became part of larger forces you could not hope to understand. I am not one of the descendants; I, too, am a creation, but they have left us their history."

"History," Martin said. He raised an arm with great effort, pointed to the bishop vultures, sharks, and babar. "They think you created them."

"We did not create them. That is their chosen delusion, their *faith*." Pause. "You are in physical distress."

"Yes."

"What do you need?"

"Rest. Time to think. Sleep. Water."

That was all he could manage, and he felt shame at saying so much, at being so weak before his enemy.

"I will adjust your surround to make you lighter. Is that better?"

Martin seemed to float. Blood began to flow again, and he could see again, but his body still ached.

A fountain of water rose before him, and his suit leaned forward, dashing his face into it. Despite his apprehensions, he drank deeply. Strength seemed to radiate from his tongue and cheeks, from his throat.

"Better," he said.

"Can you listen now?"

"Yes."

"These representatives know a little, but for their sake, they do not know all. Are you a hunter?"

"Yes," Martin said, eyes fixing on the helix.

"You hunt to avenge the death of others?"

"My world."

"It was destroyed by robots?"

"Yes."

"We sympathize. Those who made us are distant descendants of those who made the machines that probably destroyed your world. But they are gone, enlarged. They have packed their minds into massless forms that will last beyond the end of the universe.

"They have left us here, greater than you, but still limited, because creating us pleased them. My kind live within this world, surviving in deep energy flows. I do not think there is time to explain our existence to you. We number in the tens of trillions.

"We did not make the machines that destroyed your world."

"The makers aren't here?" Martin asked.

"No. There are many more trillions of created intelligences in this system, none of them responsible for the destruction of your world."

Martin watched images of species upon species flash before him, stacking like cards, filling the tunnel; more forms than he could have ever imagined.

"Kill them, and you kill innocents. I am one."

The helix of light descended through the glimmer. The glimmer sank into the red circle. The red circle faded.

The others began to move again. Silken Parts' cords squirmed, grasped by his suit; only a few had fallen to the floor, where they curled like threatened millipedes. The bishop vultures swiveled their miters, eyes sinking and rising within their fleshy noses.

"You have been visited," Salamander said. "Who was chosen?"

The twenty gathered on the bridge of *Double Seed*, where Martin floated with eyes closed, still exhausted. Ariel and Paola squatted in mid-air nearby, sucking juice from squeeze bulbs.

The journey back had followed the same tortuous procedures, leaving Martin more confused, and finally angry at everything, a thick, clogging anger that seemed to reach back to the Ark and before, to Earth, to his childhood.

He had finished explaining what he had seen less than an hour before, and the twenty surrounded him in silence, as if in mourning.

Erin broke the hush. "You were the only one who saw . . . and heard."

"I we am embarrassed I did not maintain," Silken Parts said. "But I we saw the first appearance of the master."

"It wasn't the master," Martin said. "Or so it claims. Its kind may control the fourth planet . . . May control everything in this system. But it denies it is responsible for the killer probes."

"Did it say it would defend itself?" Cham asked.

Martin looked at him with a squint. "Against what?"

Cham rubbed his chin with his thumb. "If we carry out the Law."

"We didn't talk about it," Martin said.

Eye on Sky curled along a pipe like a snake around a tree limb. "The Law is not for taking lives of the uninvolved."

"You'd think they'd make the facts known to all of us," Cham said, looking at his thumb as if he may have rubbed away some dirt. "Why choose just two?"

"Serious disinterest, I'd say," Erin commented.

"Aloof," Donna added.

"Maybe we can't destroy them—the ones inside Sleep," George Dempsey said.

Eye on Sky spread his face cords and arched the upper part of his body to face Martin. "You as one are sure of what you gathered?"

"Are you positive you saw and heard correctly?" Paola interpreted.

Martin nodded. "No sham," he said. "It was as real as anything else we saw. It was real."

"But you were exhausted . . ." Cham said. "The others saw nothing."

"It *felt* like super deceleration," Ariel said. She put her hand on Martin's shoulder, gripping it to keep from giving him a slight spin, and locked her foot under a brace. "I think Martin saw and heard what he's described."

Jennifer had kept silent since their return. Upside down to him, feet locked in ceiling grips, she folded her arms.

"Do we vote on it?" George Dempsey asked.

"No," Martin said. "When we can noach again, we tell our story to Hans and Stonemaker."

"We should go down again," Paola said, and bit her lower lip, looking around the group like a frightened deer. "We should try to talk again with . . . Martin's staircase gods, whatever they're called, inside Sleep. It's our duty."

"What are you going to recommend?" Ariel asked.

"I don't know," Martin said. "I need to sleep, or I'm going to be sick."

In his cabin, Martin slumbered in total darkness without dream or memory, a deathly bite of nothing. He awakened abruptly once, knew precisely where he was and what had happened, remembering all too easily—and closed his eyes again to return to nothing. He was not so exhausted now, however, and as he rotated within his net, pulling his arms in, he knew there was somebody else in the room with him.

For a moment he assumed it was that old companion of his sleeping existence, Theodore, but it was not. He smelled a living person, a woman.

"I didn't mean to wake you," Ariel said.

"I don't think you did."

"I was too tired to sleep. I came here. I've been listening to you breathing. It's like . . . When you breathe, it's like . . ."

He heard her neck bones quietly pop in the dark. She was shaking her head.

"Soothing," she finished. "Can I be in your net with you?"

"I'm still tired."

"I need to sleep, too," she said.

"All right." He opened the net and she pushed in beside him, an elbow in his ribs, her buttocks against his knees, and then they were parallel in the net and he could smell her more strongly. The sweet musty scent of her hair. He had never thought of Ariel as physically pleasant, but he found her so now. She did not move or speak. Finally her breathing smoothed and he listened to her sleeping. It was soothing, simple and basic and human, what someone might have experienced lying in bed next to a woman thousands of years ago, or nearly so: the hug of Earth subtracted.

She wore shorts and top of loose terry. He wore nothing. She had not come into his room to make love, but he knew she would not stop him if he chose to begin making love. The inevitability intrigued him.

He thought of the spiral of plasma and dancing lights, Silken Parts breaking down under the experience of meeting the staircase god.

Bishop vultures, babar, sharks, staircase god.

He lightly touched the stretch of her shorts, withdrew his finger. She still slept.

Reaching down, he touched the flesh between her thighs, centimeters below her pubis, not sexually aroused, simply touching, familiarizing. He did not even think about her consent. He was far from convention and the courtesy of human courtship;

he had spoken with a staircase god, and drunk water from the fountain of Sleep.

If there had been something in that water, and if he was now a haven for microscopic listeners and watchers, they could not judge his indiscretion, touching while she slept this woman he had once disliked intensely. No staircase god or bishop vulture, no babar would understand.

Martin could not begin to recall all the races he had been shown, the immense fecundity of the Killers' creation.

"What are you doing?" Ariel asked. He pulled his hand away and pretended to be asleep. "It's okay."

He still pretended to sleep.

She shivered slightly. "You're not asleep," she said.

"No."

"May I touch you?"

"Yes."

She rotated beside him and faced him, then wrapped both arms around him without pressure and touched his back with fingertips, small of back, ribs, where ribs meet spine from each side, fingers gently prodding. "It's okay," she said, voice sleepy. "We feel good."

"Your legs feel nice," he said.

"Not asleep," she chided.

"You have pretty legs," he said.

"They're not fat," she said.

"They're strong," he said.

"It's okay for you to think I'm not pretty."

"I don't think you're not pretty."

"It's okay."

"You smell good."

She hugged him tighter. It was not cold, but both began to shiver, exhaustion compounding excitement. He felt her removing her shorts and then she was on him.

"Ah God," he said. Simple.

She had wrapped her toes in the net left and right of him, and he held himself with fingers and one set of toes above and below her.

She moved strongly and put pressure on him and the result was quick and not particularly intense. She held him then and

moved back and forth but did not find herself as Theresa might
have. He sensed her weary frustration and even a little anger,
angry Ariel, resentful of his ease and her difficulty. But he did
not want to put his mouth to her, still reserving that for the
memories of Theresa and William.

He put his hand between her legs and she held his wrist and
moved his hand and herself, and it was not his doing really when
she shuddered in quiet but for a small squeak.

Nothing in the way of finesse, there hadn't even been the
voluptuousness of impersonally slicking Paola. But it was
enough.

He felt her relax into floating sleep, and willed blanket nothing
over himself again. *If we all die now and nothing is accomplished, I can at least say*

> *I have met*
> *staircase god*
> *and babar*

Pretense seemed useless now. The mom and snake mother
emerged from the fabric of *Trojan Horse*, and now all gathered
on the bridge to decide what could be done next.

"If they know, they know," Martin said. "We can't convince
them otherwise."

Cham looked around the cabin with a stern, wild face. "Why
haven't they blown us to quarks?"

The Brothers curled together in a ten-strand super-braid that
filled one side of the room, an imposing knot of knots. Eye on
Sky's head swung closest to the sphere of humans, but so far the
Brothers had said nothing.

"They could go a lot finer than quarks," Jennifer said. "They
could grind us to metrons."

"Whatever those are," Ariel said.

"I just made them up," Jennifer said.

Martin could sense the fraying fabric and he extended straight
as a board and stretched his arms, in this way imposing on the
whole group, most of whom had lotused or curled in the cabin.

"They haven't destroyed us because they don't know where
our other ships are. And we won't tell them. We won't even talk
about it."

"The possibility of invisible spies," Cham said.

"Right."

"You drank *water* . . ." Donna accused.

"We all breathed the air," Ariel said with a touch of scorn. "We knew that would be a problem . . ."

"So what *can* we talk about?" George Dempsey asked.

"That's what we're going to establish," Martin said. "When we're in the noach chamber, nothing can transmit out . . ."

"But the . . . little spies, whatever, could store up a message and send it after we're out of the chamber," Jennifer said.

"Assuming something that small can transmit without our detecting it," Cham said.

"Maybe the little things can use noach, too . . ."

Martin held up his hand and turned to the mom and the snake mother. "First things first. Can you tell whether we've been contaminated?" he asked them.

"Possibly," the mom said. "But an exhaustive procedure would not be easy. Miniature devices might be as small as molecules, made from one kind or another of super-dense matter. This was a risk we decided to take."

"Great," Jennifer said.

"A better plan than detection would be to change the design of the ship, and protect all spaces against unwanted transmission, in or out," the mom suggested.

"We can do that?" Martin asked.

"It can be done, with a reduction in available fuel," the mom said.

"There's something else," George said. "If they wanted to kill us, they could give us a disease we pass from one to the other . . . these spies, miniature machines, something deadly."

"Killing us won't stop the others," Paola said.

"Unless the disease doesn't strike until we rejoin them," Donna said.

"We we do not feel contaminated," Eye on Sky said. But the super-braid uncoiled and the braids drifted apart.

Ariel said, "Maybe those of us who went down should be in quarantine . . ."

"As no fields were present when the first contact was made

by their machine," the mom said, "it seems more likely we are
all contaminated."

"We tripped ourselves up," George said. "Too clever for
our own good. We shouldn't have tried to fool them."

"No time for regrets," Martin said. He took a deep breath,
reluctant to say what he had to say. "I'm going down again, if
they let me. Just me. To talk. We won't be out of noach blackout
for another day . . . I need to know more before I make my
recommendations to Hans."

"Ask them," Eye on Sky said.

"About what?"

"Ask them if we all we have been contaminated."

"Why should they tell us?" George asked, shivering, agitated.

The second meeting was granted, to Martin's surprise.

He knew now with a certainty beyond intuition why they had
not been killed, why the unarmed *Double Seed* had not been
destroyed; they were the only connection their hosts had to the
invisible ships now moving back in toward Leviathan, ships with
unknown weapons, unknown strengths. The more that could
be learned, the longer their action could be delayed, the more
advantage for their hosts.

Deception piled upon deception . . . Their hosts could not
know how much of a lie was being told, any more than humans
and Brothers.

Martin waited for the white sphere to arrive and carry him
alone, back to the surface of Sleep. He took advantage of the
solitude in his cabin to scan Sleep and the other worlds in the
Leviathan system, aimless observation, lips pursed, brows drawn
together. Ant in kitchen: trying to understand why one plane
would be set to change like a clock display, blink one moment
different the next. Why others would be spiky with massive
constructs, others barren and smooth. Why Sleep existed at all—
perhaps simply to house the staircase gods, all other creatures
an afterthought, all other purposes secondary . . .

The second journey to Sleep followed the exact pattern of the
first. He boarded the shuttle and was immediately met by his

skeletal suit and by Salamander. He put on the suit—or rather, it put itself on around him.

Salamander gripped its bar behind the transparent wall.

"We are told you are very dangerous to us," Salamander said, hissing faintly behind the words.

Martin did not reply.

"The creators tell us you are an illusion, that you are much stronger than you appear, and that you will try to harm us."

Still, Martin kept silent.

"They tell us you caused the star explosion."

"It was a trap meant to kill us," Martin said, watching the oceans come up beneath them in the display beside Salamander's panel.

"Are we such a danger to you that you would wish us gone? We have never left this system. Nor have we harmed your kind."

"You haven't been told everything," Martin said, face flushed. "Machines came to my world and destroyed it. Other machines destroyed other worlds, maybe thousands of worlds, thousands of races. Whoever made you probably made those machines."

"We are aware of no such history," Salamander said.

Martin shook his head, irritated to be explaining any of this to what might be a puppet, a sham. Still, the instinct to communicate pushed him. If Salamander was anything like a human, the truth might not have much effect . . . But at least Martin would have done his best.

"Before my world was destroyed," he said, "the robots, the machines, created diversions to test our abilities. They made some of my people believe that a spacecraft had landed in a remote area, and an unknown . . . being, an individual, came out of the craft, to warn us of our destruction. It didn't tell the entire truth. It was part of an experiment." Anger at the memory made his throat close. He swallowed, then faced Salamander. "It looked like you. They made it look like you."

Salamander lifted its head, brought the knobs of its shoulders together.

"No individuals of my kind have been to your world."

"I'm not making myself clear," Martin said. "Whoever made you destroyed my world. When I look at you, I am reminded of that crime. That's why we're here. To see if any of the guilty still exist.''

"I do not believe our creators have done this thing, nor are we guilty," Salamander said. "What will you discuss with our creators?"

"They say they did not create you." Martin shook his head. "Anyway, that's between me and them."

"Are they the guilty ones?"

"I don't know," Martin said. "They say they aren't."

"They claim to be made by others, as we are?"

"Yes," Martin said.

"Would you kill us, knowing we did not harm your world?"

Martin swallowed again, feeling his weight grow as the ship entered Sleep's atmosphere, descending slowly, deliberately and with vast power. "I don't know."

"You do not know anything about us."

"I'm here to learn."

"We are independent. We have a rich existence. Whoever made us did not give us the need to destroy."

Martin stared at Salamander behind the barrier, empathizing for the first time.

"We are not illusions," Salamander continued. "We have separate existence."

Its reiteration made Salamander even more sympathetic. Martin tried to strengthen his resolve, but in Salamander's words there was also sorrow, as well as frustration and perhaps confusion.

"Do you have the power to destroy us?"

Martin said they did, lying.

Salamander's shoulder knobs touched, jerked back, and its six-fingered hands grew tight on the steel bar.

"What will I tell my kind, that we face extinction when we have extended a hand of information and giving?"

"Ask your superiors," Martin said.

"We seldom confer with our creators. We assume they made us. Some have thought perhaps they didn't make us. You say they didn't."

"I don't want to talk to you any more," Martin said.

Salamander's wall darkened.

* * *

The dark sky, thick blue sea, walls of jagged rock; the white disk on its journey around the sharp headland; the triple tunnel mouths, the dock and gray stone floor, into the darkness. Martin carried his water in a plastic bottle, and felt more prepared this time to withstand the heaviness, the weariness in his blood and behind his eyes.

An hour from leaving the ship, he stood within his skeletal suit deep in the tunnel, before the red circle.

The helix of light within its glimmering cylinder rose from the floor.

"Have you contacted your leaders?" the staircase god asked.

"I have more questions," Martin said.

"Why should your questions be answered?"

"If we're going to go to war against each other, we should know more, shouldn't we?"

"That implies an exchange. What do you offer?"

"I'm giving you another chance to convince me you aren't the enemy we've been hunting for."

The staircase god produced its display of cascading lights and colors, but no voice came from the pillar for long seconds. Martin thought of the Bible in his father's library, and reflected that this was a particularly biblical moment. But he did not feel like a prophet facing the burning bush.

What he did feel was not awe, but fear, and not fear for his life. He feared screwing up. He could just begin to see the scale of the blunders they might make here.

"Why should we make the effort?" the staircase god asked bluntly. Language was a true handicap here; nuances and subtleties could not be expected, and bluntness could not be interpreted as . . . anything.

"Do you believe we can hurt you?" Martin asked.

"It is possible you can destroy us, despite precautions we might take."

"Then accept my offer. Tell me about your past. I'm here to learn."

"In absorbing the information you have given us, I have tried to understand both those you call humans and those you call Brothers. You did not come from the same star systems; your chemistries differ in reliance on certain trace elements. This told us that your story was not true, and we had no difficulty putting facts together. But it did occur to some of us that your gesture of making a lie, of sending a disguised ship, was magnanimous. Your kinds seem to believe in deliberation before reckless action.

"But surely anything we tell you cannot be convincing. What compelling evidence can we provide? We could rearrange your brains, change you so that the beings on your ship would all believe we are innocent. How would you know the difference between compulsion and compelling evidence?"

"I hope to be able to tell the difference," Martin said.

"Your innocence, your ignorance, reminds me of many of our smaller neighbors that live on planet surfaces. There is an attractiveness, you might say a beauty, to their limited lives and thoughts, but unfortunately, faster and more capable minds can't share such illusions."

"Why did you tell Salamander and his people, all the hundreds of others, that you made them?"

"We did not. They concluded that we are their makers. We have chosen not to contradict their beliefs."

Martin was getting nowhere. Still, he would keep asking questions, keep probing. He could not, for justice' sake, do otherwise.

"Do you remember your makers?"

"No."

"They never met with you after making you?"

"They made us as growing potentials within this world. By the time of our maturity, they had changed, and they have not returned or looked at us, so far as we can sense."

"Why did they make you?"

"We do not know."

Martin looked up again. "Can you understand how frustrated I am, not being able to judge? Not having enough evidence?"

"No."

"What would you have me do?"

"Choose different masters, different guides," the staircase god replied. "It is obvious to me, and to many of our smaller surface species, that you have been poorly informed and poorly led. Those who seek revenge for wrongs committed in ages past are not thinking correctly.''

"It's part of a system of justice," Martin said. "If you make machines that kill living planets, you know that you or your descendants will·be punished."

"Has this prevented the creation of such machines, and the destruction of worlds like yours?"

"No," Martin admitted.

"Then such a law is useless. Ask yourself if there is only one law, or if others have made other laws; ask yourself why we feel that if there are many joined civilizations of the kind you describe, they must to us seem immature, not capable of judging.

"It seems likely now that you cannot harm our worlds, that you are weaker than we. You are not a threat. Any further discussion is wasted effort."

The vision faded, helix of light and glimmer dropping to the red circle.

Martin's audience was over.

Salamander, frozen throughout the dialog, lifted its crest and advanced a step toward Martin.

"You have talked? Have you what you need?" it asked.

Martin relaxed his clenched fists. An involuntary spasm clenched them again. He sucked in breath, shuddering with frustration and rage.

"Have you what you need?" Salamander repeated. Martin looked at the creature sharply, trying to see behind the barriers of physical form, language, his prejudice. He could not help but conclude that Salamander was not an illusion.

The creature in the Death Valley spaceship had been a kind of prototype of the bishop vultures, designed by the Killers, who also created all these beings now experienced . . . Creators of whom Salamander knew nothing.

To Salamander, Martin represented a monster as frightening as the neutronium bombs that had whizzed through the Earth had been to his father . . .

Martin was Death, Destroyer of Worlds.

"I should go back," Martin said.

Salamander advanced again, fingers held up. "You have not enough," it said. "You still think we are guilty."

"No," Martin said. What could he say? Nothing to reassure it; nothing to mislead.

"What can we do to defend ourselves?" Salamander asked, with sufficient ambiguity of meaning to confuse Martin.

"I need evidence that those who built the machines are no longer here," Martin said. "Your superiors either can't or won't supply me with the evidence."

"We know nothing of them," Salamander said. "There will be meetings. We must meet with you again."

"Please take me back," Martin said. In Salamander he recognized a type not so inhuman after all; diplomat, organizer, representative of many interests and individuals. He could not hate Salamander, or by extension, any of the others he had seen.

"You must recognize what is to be lost," Salamander said, waddling closer, fingers curling as if in threat.

"I know," Martin said.

"You are not capable of knowing, you are too small and limited," Salamander said. "I must teach you now, immediately, what can be lost. There is no time. What must I do?"

Martin did not want to confront Salamander. "We'll try to arrange another meeting."

"You have met with the superiors twice, and that has never happened in our history."

"Maybe there can be a third meeting."

"They have told you what you need. They will not speak to you again," Salamander said.

"How do you speak to them?"

"We send signals into this planet, and they respond, or do not respond."

Like calling monsters from the deep with songs. Leviathan, indeed; the staircase gods were great energy leviathans basking on the deep energy slopes of paradise, thinking unknown thoughts, disdaining surface creatures.

Noach blackout would end within hours. Martin had to speak with the other ships as soon as possible.

Salamander drew back its arms, dropped them to the floor, backed away, miter head bowed as if in supplication.

"I have been ordered to let you return," it said. It walked on all fours toward the opening of the tunnel. Martin followed, the timeless wash of the vast blue ocean growing louder.

With Martin's return and explanation of what had happened, *Double Seed* altered radically in design and ability. The crews stayed on the bridge as the ship drew in its extensions, armored itself against possible direct assault, and shielded itself against transmissions into or out of the ship's interior. Martin knew the ship's transformation could be taken as a sign of aggression, but they had to take the risk.

While they waited, Hakim and Silken Parts selected and displayed some of the huge volume of information sent to the *Double Seed* in the past two hours from the surface of Sleep.

Images of planet-spanning cities on the inner worlds, scenes of daily life whose meaning they could hardly guess without reference to hundreds of thousands of pages of text, expertly Englished; the varieties of races, sounds of over twenty spoken languages, biographies and portraits of highly accomplished individuals, including long sequences on Salamander and Frog, more than just diplomats or representatives—creative artists famous throughout the Leviathan system, experts in planetary architecture, responsible for Puffball's construction over the past few hundred years, as well as designers of philosophical systems regarded as complex games . . .

They're trying to personalize themselves, be more to us than unfamiliar creatures and opponents. It's a tactic almost human . . . and it implies some understanding of or congruence with our psychology.

"They have opened their archives," Eye on Sky said, and curled to face Martin. "They are very afraid of we us."

Martin nodded.

"He knows that," Paola said.

"They couldn't give me proof that the Killers have gone," Martin said.

"Is that kind of proof possible?" Ariel asked. "They could only prove the Killers are still here if the Killers themselves talked to us—admitted they were here. Right?"

"Right," Martin said. "I'm thinking of the decision Stonemaker and Hans have to make. We've tracked the Killers, we've found conclusive evidence they once lived here . . .''

Talented Salamander and Frog, betrayed by their physique; leftovers from centuries, millennia of frantic creativity—and to what end? To make up for the Killers' sins, creation to atone for destruction?

Hans would not see it that way. Martin could not predict Stonemaker's reaction, but Eye on Sky was clearly sympathetic to the pleas of innocence, the urgent appeal for multitudes of intelligent beings, far more than just the leftovers of Killer habitation.

Hakim touched Martin on the shoulder. "We will be able to noach in two minutes," he said. "We will communicate with *Greyhound* directly. Through them, of course, *Shrike* as well, but *Shrike* is still out of direct range."

"What would you do?" Martin asked Eye on Sky.

"As a group? We we must decide—"

"By yourself," Martin said. "If you had the choice."

"What would you do if you alone, as a braid—" Paola tried to interpret.

"I we understand," Eye on Sky interrupted her. "It is not a question I we enjoy answering."

Martin stared at him and gave the merest nod.

Paola looked between the Brothers, who had stopped moving, waiting for Eye on Sky's answer.

"I we have not reached a decision," he finally said.

"You're wavering," Cham said. Cham pushed off from the ceiling and rotated to a reverse, landing with his feet on the floor, then performed the maneuver in reverse, exercising with nervous energy. "I think it's a trap," Cham said. "The very worst trap, perfectly designed to snare us. I think you should tell Hans that."

Ariel curled in mid-air. Martin could not read her expression.

"Nobody's asked the mom or the snake mother what we should do," George Dempsey said.

"George, you've always been a little dense," Donna told him.

"Hell, I know they're not supposed to influence us . . ." George said with a pained expression. "But they brought us here, they've given us this opportunity, and if we screw it up, if we decide wrong . . ." He blocked Cham's accelerated exercise with an arm, causing Cham to tumble and grab a stanchion. Cham mumbled something unintelligible but stopped bouncing back and forth and curled beside Erin. "If we decide wrong . . ." George repeated, but did not finish.

"We're guilty of a crime worse than the death of Earth," Paola said.

"Right," George said.

"Just what they want us to think," Cham said. "Perfect disguise."

"I don't think it's a disguise," Martin said.

"Nor do I we," Silken Parts agreed.

"Nor do we all," Eye on Sky concluded. Cham pushed his lips together and shook his head.

"Well, I'm in *my* place," he muttered.

"Stop it," Martin said. "We could argue for years and not know for sure. I'm goddamned confused myself."

"Amen," Erin said.

"But I'm not Pan. We don't make the decision alone. We present what we have to all the others . . ."

In the quiet, cool noach chamber, Hakim, Eye on Sky, and Martin sat, waiting for signals to be coordinated.

Stonemaker and Giacomo appeared first, three-dimensional noach images growing out of the air. Giacomo's face was pale and drawn, his eyes dark and tired. Stonemaker received Eye on Sky's report as Hakim prepared to transmit their findings.

"We're having trouble," Giacomo told Martin. "Hans will be here soon. He can tell you about it. I need to speak with Jennifer right away."

"After Hans and I talk," Martin said.

"Martin, this is really important. We've made some significant advances. The moms are making new equipment for us. I have to talk with Jennifer, and Silken Parts, too."

"I understand," Martin said. "Strategy first."

Giacomo's face reddened. "God damn it, Martin, Hans isn't here yet, and we don't have much time. We've learned a lot in the past few tendays, stuff I wouldn't have believed!"

"So tell me about it while we wait for Hans," Martin said.

"Bring Jennifer in. We'll all talk."

Martin did not relish being bogged down in technical details, but he relented and asked Jennifer to enter the noach chamber. Her expression softened when she saw Giacomo, then became worried as she saw the strain he was under.

"Jenny, we think this system is armed to the teeth. Blinker is probably a giant noach generator, but it isn't used for communication. The entire planet changes every few minutes . . . The moms have studied it, I've been working through the momerath . . ."

"Give us the important stuff," Jennifer said, glancing at Martin. "We'll talk momerath later."

"Blinker is their Achilles' heel," Giacomo said. "It controls a lot of things around Leviathan. We think we can use noach as a weapon against Blinker. If we can persuade Blinker, it'll be like their turning our ships into anti em, only much more powerful. Wormwood was deliberately primitive, compared to Leviathan. That's what I've told Hans, and the moms seem to agree. They're making noach weapons right now. I don't think we'll have time to test—"

"What can they do?" Martin asked.

"We might survive Blinker if it tries to attack us. Our neutronium weapons are probably useless. They can nullify them, even . . . I'm not positive about this, Jenny, but the momerath says they can convert our bombs to the limits of the system, or even after they enter a planet.

"That's the glory of Leviathan. Just *looking* at these planets long enough, we can think of a thousand new things, a thousand possibilities. The ships' minds are working all the time. All our weapons and delivery systems are being redesigned."

Hans entered and sat next to Giacomo, facing Martin across over nine billion kilometers. Martin was shocked by how thin and wiry Hans appeared, as if he had lost all unnecessary flesh to prepare for some intense conflict. His eyes focused on Martin's chin, then drifted down to his neck.

"Martin and I need to be alone. Jennifer, whoever else is there but Martin, and the Brothers . . . leave now," he said. "They can talk science in a few minutes."

Giacomo withdrew. Jennifer swore under her breath and left

Double Seed's noach chamber. Hakim followed after he was sure the transmission was stable. Martin nodded to him apologetically. Eye on Sky continued to confer with Stonemaker in two-part Brother language, clicks and violin sighs.

"You actually went down there, had a one to one?" Hans asked, unable to project more than a hint of feeling.

"We did. Twice," Martin said.

"Face to face with the enemy." Hans shook his head in dull-eyed wonder. "That's something, Marty."

Martin's eyes grew moist but he did not reach up to wipe them. Even now, when his instincts told him something horrible had happened, even Hans' flat and listless approval meant something.

"We've had shit up to our necks here," Hans said. "Giacomo's probably told you some of it already."

"No details."

"Twenty-one of our crew mutinied. They tried to elect their own Pan. I told them there couldn't be any proceedings until the Job was over and the crews were reunited, but Jeanette Snap Dragon and a few others kept at it until they broke the others down."

Martin doubted that was the entire story. "What about the Brothers?"

"They're going to take *Shrike*, leave us with *Greyhound*. I've agreed to that."

"They're not doing the Job with us?"

"We'll coordinate, but they've decided not to be on the same ship."

Martin shook his head in disbelief. "What in hell happened, Hans?"

"Rex is dead," Hans said. "He killed himself a tenday ago. He confessed to killing Rosa and said he couldn't live with it."

"Why did he kill her?"

Hans leveled his gaze on Martin. "Necessities. She took him in as her lover. Something happened. Has Giacomo explained what the moms are doing?"

"What about the rest of the crew?"

"They're with me. They want to do the Job. I make the decisions. What have you got for me?"

Martin stared at the floor for a moment, trying to see beyond what he was being told. "I'm noaching a big batch of information given to us by the representatives from Sleep. All of you should look it over very carefully, as much as you can absorb." He quickly explained the circumstances: the hundreds of races, trillions of individuals, the representatives, the staircase god, and what they had told him . . .

Hans listened intently, eyes growing more focused, more alive.

"Is it real?" Hans asked when Martin was done.

"I don't think it's illusion. They're real. The information is more than I can assimilate. Salamander—"

"That's the other vulture, isn't it?" Hans asked.

"Yes. Salamander seemed distressed. We couldn't know each other's expressions, understand emotions . . . but it clearly thinks I'm the bringer of something terrible."

Hans folded his arms, straightened his back as if in satisfaction. "Good. But they don't know where I am."

"I don't think so."

"You didn't tell them."

"No, but I was dealing with minds way beyond me. I felt like an ant. What they can deduce or learn, how fast they can draw their conclusions or put evidence together, I don't know. We have to vote and make a decision fast. If we stay here much longer, they'll get tired of our uselessness and find some way to kill us."

"Peaceful types, am I right?"

"Even if we believe all they say, they have every reason to destroy us. We're a massive threat."

"Yeah," Hans said. "I'd like your opinion, Martin, but the group is past voting now. I make the decision. We do the Job, we get the hell out. We go live the rest of our lives."

Martin didn't know what to say.

"We can still do it," Hans said softly. "Are you with me?"

"You have to look at the information."

"It's all shit," Hans said briskly.

"You have to look at it," Martin repeated firmly.

"I will," Hans said. "Dot the i's and cross the t's, am I right?"

Martin had come to hate that sequence of three words; had come to hate Hans at the same time Hans could bring tears to his eyes.

Put a stop to it now. Refuse to let it go any further. But then they'll have you; the ruse will have worked. The ultimate defense fogs the mind.

"Giacomo's itching to talk with Jennifer. My say is over for the time being," Hans said. "I'll look at the info. Get back to you in a couple of hours. Watch your tail, Martin. Move out soon. They can get you."

"I don't think they will until they're sure we're not going to bargain," Martin said.

"Maybe not. Maybe they're just too damned smart for their own good. Like you, Martin."

Martin lowered his eyes, then raised them again, met Hans' gaze, his face reddening with constrained fury. He would gladly have killed Hans then.

Hans looked away, as if Martin did not matter, nothing mattered, his expression casual and deadly. "Well, if Giacomo and the moms have it worked out, we can do some impressive damage." Hans stepped out of the image. Giacomo replaced him.

"Where's Jennifer?" Giacomo said.

Martin called her in, staying in the noach chamber to listen.

Through the technical detail and exchanges of momerath, he saw the broad outlines of what had been learned, and the theories woven from the scant clues.

Blinker was a massive noach station, capable of altering the physical character of unprotected mass to a distance of at least fifty billion kilometers in all directions—five times what noach theory had allowed until now. Its own changing character was likely a continuing pattern of tests.

The inhabitants of Leviathan's worlds, and the regions between those worlds, almost completely controlled the hidden or "privileged" channels between particles. They could alter three fourths of the character bits in any particle within fifty billion kilometers, quickly and efficiently, using Blinker or other noach stations, some perhaps hidden inside Sleep. Alterations could be as minor as the spin of a single particle; as major as

converting to anti-matter all the mass within the volume of a
large moon.

The ships' minds were working now to ensure that noach
interference with ship character could be shielded against.
Shields were being constructed for both *Shrike* and *Greyhound*.

Giacomo said to Martin, "The ships' minds are on a continuous link with *Trojan Horse* now. They're telling *Trojan Horse*
how to shield. It won't take more than a few hours."

"We we agree this must be done," Eye on Sky said.

"We're going to have a whole new arsenal to work with in
just a day or so," Giacomo said. "I'm afraid you'll have to stay
on the sidelines. *Trojan Horse* is too small to support weapons
of the kind being made on *Greyhound*."

"Is *Shrike* making weapons?"

"Yes," Giacomo said. "Jennifer, I've missed you. We could
have done this a lot faster with you and Silken Parts here."

"I doubt it, if the ships' minds are working on it," Jennifer
said.

"I don't know if I'm speaking out of turn," Giacomo said.
"We're really in it now, Martin. We're pariahs. The Brothers
won't have anything to do with us. They're outfitting *Shrike* as
their own ship."

"Hans told me," Martin said.

"What else did he tell you?"

"That you're supporting him, and he makes all decisions. No
voting."

Giacomo looked acutely unhappy. "We came out here to do
the Job. Hans holds us together—the ones who are left with any
convictions at all."

"Did Rex kill Rosa?"

"He left a message on his wand saying he did."

"Did Hans put him up to it?" Martin asked.

"Rex didn't say. The Brothers think—Stonemaker thinks he
did, and it's really . . . it's pushed them away from us, Martin.
The Brothers here won't speak to humans now unless they have
to."

Martin looked at Eye on Sky and Silken Parts. The Brothers
seemed oblivious, locked in a luxury of three-part exchange, but

Martin knew they were listening. Doubtless Stonemaker was listening as well.

There was no reason to hide anything.

"What about the dissidents?"

"They have their own part of *Greyhound*. They refuse to follow Hans, and they refuse to fight. They tried to persuade the rest of us. It was real close, but . . . Martin, we came here to do this Job. We're here. The evidence is strong. Now's the time."

"So it seems," Martin said.

"I don't know what kind of person Hans is."

I do, Martin thought.

"But without him we'd be in even worse shape. You want to know what I think?"

Martin smiled at Giacomo's fecklessness. "You've told me everything so far."

"I think Hans made Rex . . ." Giacomo shook his head. "Talk to Hans about it. It really isn't my place. I need to talk with Jennifer again."

"All the time you need. But when you start getting sentimental, it's time to open the noach to others."

"Got you," Giacomo said. "Martin, don't get me wrong. What we've learned in the past few tendays, and what the moms have done to upgrade our weapons—it's absolutely fantastic. Just the right combination—Jennifer's theories about noach, learning how radically Leviathan has changed . . . Putting the Brothers' non-integer math to work . . . And then, seeing Leviathan's planets . . . It's a revolution."

Martin gestured to Eye on Sky and they left the noach chamber to find a private place to talk. Martin asked Paola to join them.

"We we are told by Stonemaker, high likelihood Hans chose Rex to become loose cord, outsider," Eye on Sky said. "Stonemaker and others, we they do not conceive to be experts on human behavior."

"The Brothers don't think they're experts on human behavior," Paola interpreted.

"Got that," Martin said.

"But there is a deviosity, a curliness—" Eye on Sky continued.

"Perversity," Paola suggested.

Don't make it worse, Martin did not say, cringing inwardly.

"There is character that makes humans avoid the obvious, and take the twisty tunnel to a goal, rather than the straight tunnel."

Martin nodded, reserving comment until Eye on Sky had had his say.

"Hans achieves something by making Rex an outside cord, for Rex is punished by Hans, Hans does not take blame for Rex's actions, Rex feels strong kin for Hans, Hans keeps a secret braid-cord—"

"Wait a minute," Martin said, turning to Paola. She, too, had difficulty with the lengthy statement. "I think he's saying, Rex was deliberately alienated by Hans, to make him appear to be an outsider, not in favor with Hans."

"That is so," Eye on Sky said. "This is difficult for we us to track, must follow we our own curled tunnel to know. Humans afraid of their own kind. Of female Rosa. She was maker of large fictions, which make you dream."

Paola started to interpret, but Martin raised his hand. This much was clear.

"Hans wanted female Rosa dead," Eye on Sky said.

Paola wrinkled her face and looked away.

"Rex is weapon for Hans," Eye on Sky concluded.

Martin couldn't fault the logic. *What Hans said: necessities.*

"We're our own enemies," Paola said. "Like the Red Tree Runners."

"Brothers don't have anything like this in their society?" Martin asked.

"Oh yes, larger we do."

"What?" Martin asked.

"Wars between cords," Eye on Sky said. "Times when braids unwind, and cords kill each other. Not control these times, or know when. We we must shun the curled path and those who take it, for we they bring on own unwinding, own cord wars."

"You think we're going to break down, as a society," Paola said.

"Not known," Eye on Sky said. "But if larger we stays with you, fear of catching, fear of influence."

"You think we'll . . . make you ill?" Paola asked.

"Break us down."

Martin's stomach contracted. He tightened his fingers on the ladder field.

"We have to work together," he said. "Whatever the risks. We still have the same goals."

"This not yet decided. Separate ships, working together— that is decided, for now. Working apart may be decided later."

Division of the crews had not yet taken place on *Trojan Horse*.

Eye on Sky, Martin, the mom, and the snake mother curled in the dark and watched the methodic replay of information from Sleep. Martin's eyelids drooped with weariness, overloaded again with the wonders of what these artificial beings had made, or inherited, or both.

Hans had not spoken with Martin for seven hours. Stonemaker and Eye on Sky had conferred several times. Martin hoped this meant Hans was seriously reviewing the data.

Ariel and Erin entered the cabin and positioned themselves on each side of Martin, who reached out and squeezed their hands, then resumed watching.

In groups or alone in their cabins, Brothers and humans studied the information. "It's staggering," Erin said. The life-cycles of two related species passed before them; eggs carefully deposited in the deep waters of Sleep, hatchlings rising to the surface like jellyfish to be harvested by fisher parents, who injected capsules of their genetic material; the injected hatchlings forming eggs again, being deposited in green and purple forests on the third planet, hatching again to become lake- and stream-dwellers, finally joining in villages, and the villages themselves maturing, changing social structure, until they were ready to be "harvested" and trained into adult societies . . .

There was much more information on the staircase gods within Sleep. This appeared to be incomplete, however; where and how they obtained their energy was not clear.

"Jennifer thinks they could shift neutronium to quark matter at the core," Ariel said. "We were just in her cabin. She's going to make herself sick if she doesn't get some rest."

The *Double Seed* still adapted as the ships' minds updated each other hour by hour. The mom and snake mother kept Martin and Eye on Sky informed as major changes were made, but explanations were kept simple. Logistics, not theory, were paramount now. Jennifer could not stand ignorance; she engaged in momerath continuously.

"They're pleading with us to understand them, appreciate them," Ariel said, pulling herself out of the maze of Leviathan's fecundity.

"They're desperately afraid," Erin said. She had changed in the past few days; intense green eyes duller, hair matted, face more slack. *It takes life out of all of us.* "But they're so enormously powerful . . ." she added.

. Ariel cocked an eyebrow. "A few savages invade your house. There might be thousands of them outside, in the dark. They're smart, and they've seen what your technology is like . . . They're making new weapons. Would you be afraid?" she asked.

"They could squash us like bugs," Erin said, curling her lip.

"Then why bother convincing us? Why not squash us now?"

"Maybe they value *us*. Maybe they've renounced their past so totally—"

"They had nothing to do with the past!"

Martin closed his eyes. "Please, that's enough," he said. He turned to the mom. "We have to resolve some things. We need advice from you."

"Advice about what?"

"What to do," Martin said, simply enough. "I'm snowed. I can't see anything clearly now. Can you?"

"I ask again, what sort of advice are you seeking?"

"Are all these creatures innocent, or guilty?" Martin asked.

"They say they were created by the Killers. We can't confirm or deny this," the mom answered. Martin's stomach contracted again; he had not eaten since speaking with Hans.

"You wonder if the Killers are still here," the mom said, "and whether there is a way to seek them out, and punish only them."

"Right."

"We have no more information than you," the mom said.

Eye on Sky listened quietly, and when the conversation halted, interjected, "Snake mother and ships' minds agree. The evidence for presence of Killers is lacking."

"They could have changed themselves . . . even destroyed their memories, their histories, to escape punishment," Martin said.

"That is possible," the mom agreed.

"Do you think it's probable?"

"I can't answer that."

"But if we make the wrong decision, and kill . . . them, all of them, or some of them, we're criminal, aren't we? Won't we violate the Law?"

"The Law is simple," the mom said. "Interpretation is not so simple."

" 'Destruction of all intelligences responsible for or associated with the manufacture of self-replicating and destructive devices,' " Martin quoted.

"That is the Law," the mom said. It floated in the dark cabin, projected data glittering in reflection on its coppery surface.

" 'For I the Lord thy God am a jealous God, visiting the iniquity of the fathers upon the children,' " Erin quoted.

" 'The cord is part of the braid,' " Eye on Sky quoted in turn, " 'and suffers the shame of the braid.' "

Martin's frown deepened. "Does the Law demand vengeance on succeeding generations?" he asked.

"I do not interpret the Law," the mom said. "That is your responsibility."

Martin held up his hand to stop Ariel and Erin from saying more. Ariel frowned and drew up her knees, touching them to her crossed arms like a little girl exiled to a corner. Erin tilted her head to one side, lost.

"Why haven't we been attacked?" he asked the mom. "They have the means . . . They could have destroyed us when we first arrived."

"Your thoughts may be as informed as those of the ships' minds," the mom said. "However, some possible explanations occur to the ships' minds.

"The inhabitants of these planets may be supremely confident they can destroy us, so they toy with us, wishing to learn as much as they can. They may try to capture and control us to learn more about the potential threat. The Killers may no longer be in residence. The beings we have encountered may be waiting for the first signs of our aggression. They may in fact abhor destructive behavior, and take extreme risks to avoid harming our ship. Though this possibility seems remote, the power displayed may be a bluff. There are other hypotheses, but they decline in usefulness."

"They could have weapons they haven't even revealed."

"That seems likely," the mom said.

"They *must* be planning something," Martin said.

The mom did not contradict him.

Hans and Martin spoke in private on the noach. Thirteen hours had passed since the end of noach blackout. "I've held a council here," Hans said. "We've gone through most of the information you passed along. I thought we'd get you folks in the loop."

"You'll have to talk with Eye on Sky, too," Martin said.

"The Brothers will make their decision separately," Hans said.

"We haven't divided our crews yet," Martin said.

"Have you made up *your* mind?"

Martin hadn't slept, hadn't eaten much. He blinked rapidly, eyes pink with strain, unable to shake a particular image from the thousands he had viewed: harvesters collecting young after hatching in the oceans of Sleep, Leviathan at dusk flaming red through a bank of crustal fissure smoke. Strange and serene and beautiful, just part of the richness, part of the flavor.

"Yes," Martin said.

"And?"

"If the Killers are gone, I don't think the Law applies. And if they're still here, to get to them, we'd have to kill a thousand times more people than lived on Earth. It doesn't make sense. We can't risk it."

"That's part of a very good armor," Hans said, eyes heavy lidded, fingers working in rhythm on his knee.

"I know," Martin said.

"We've come a long way and lost our own good people."

Martin did not dignify that reminder with a reply.

"And you think we should move on."

"I think we should wait for more evidence. Two ships could orbit Leviathan at safe distance, hidden, the crews in cold sleep—"

"Until our fuel is gone and we become a death ship," Hans said.

"We wouldn't have to wait very long."

"We wouldn't?" Hans asked. "How long is very long, centuries, thousands of years? What kind of evidence would satisfy you? They'll never show themselves. I can't afford to be so careful. I'm Pan. I'm sworn to enact the Law."

"At what cost?" Martin asked.

"What did Earth pay?" Hans asked in return.

"And the Brothers—?"

"I think they'll decide with you. They've been remarkably weak partners, am I right?"

"I—"

"When you met the staircase god, the Brother just crumpled. Kind of sums them up."

"We have to understand their differences."

Hans smiled thinly and rubbed his scalp with straight fingers. "We're here, the evidence is here, the Law is clear. We're making the necessary weapons. Marty, if we don't do it now, it will never get done. If we're wrong, the moms will stop us."

"I don't think they will stop us," Martin said.

"Why in hell not? They're upholding the Law, too."

"Hans, they *don't judge*. They give us the tools. They don't make decisions."

"Then we're really no better than the Killers, are we? Just more puffed up."

Martin avoided that argument. "Can we do it without *Shrike*?" he asked. "We'd have half the strength, half the fuel."

"Giacomo thinks we can do a lot of damage with just one ship. The moms seem to agree with him." Hans smiled, but there was little life in it. The lines in his face hardened. "We're

starting to worry the moms. If we survive, we'll be awfully big
and strong. Maybe they'll just snuff us. But we'll get the Job
done.''

"We should let the crews debate.''

"No,'' Hans said. "If we back off now, we'll fragment.''

"I think—''

"No,'' Hans interrupted. "The Law is clear. These creatures
are descendants of the Killers. Hell, for all we know, the Killers
have imprinted their memories on them, or maybe they're hiding
like a tree in a forest. Anything to avoid being found and destroyed.''

"I don't believe that. You should have seen what I saw.''

"Maybe the Killers are staircase gods now.''

"I . . . don't know about that.''

"Why should we listen to anything they say? Can you answer
me that?''

Martin had no answer.

"They put you through a real gauntlet, ground you down.
Just what I would have done if I were them.''

"We're not them. They may be unfathomable to us.''

"Enough,'' Hans said. "We need you to play a part. We need
you to stall for us while we maneuver and prepare our weapons.''

"What weapons?'' Martin asked. "Noach weapons?''

"It's best we don't give specifics . . . You might be captured.
The longer you keep them guessing, the more time we'll have
to get our act together. You aren't going to mutiny on me, are
you, Martin?''

There was no humor in Hans' voice, no trace of badgering.
Hans believed this was a real possibility.

*Am I going along with him against my better judgment, my
own wishes?*

"No.''

"You'll ask for another meeting,'' Hans said. "It'll take a
tenday for me to get everything in place. Plenty of time for you
to learn more, salve your conscience.''

"I don't think they'll accept another meeting.''

"Try them. Give them hope. Play the right cards.''

"They'll kill us,'' Martin said.

Hans acknowledged that possibility with a slow nod.

"I'm not finished with the information they gave you," Hans said. "Maybe they'll inadvertently tell us something important, something we can use against them. And if you're right . . . maybe I'll find something that convinces me, too. I'll keep it in mind, Martin. I owe you at least that much."

Martin knew Hans was pulling his strings. Hans knew Martin's capabilities and limits, the limits of the Lost Boys and Wendys, even the Brothers, with a clarity that must have been difficult to live with.

"I'll ask for another meeting," Martin said.

Hans smiled, eyes widening. "You never disappoint me, Martin. I love you for that. Let's do it."

Ariel clenched her teeth; Erin floated beside Cham, face deliberately bland, Hakim beside Donna, George behind them.

"We're not in the loop," Martin said. "Not really. But I've told Hans we'll play our part."

"You didn't consult with us," Ariel said.

"No," Martin said.

"You should have," Erin said.

"I presented our views."

"But you told him we'd go along," Erin said.

"What else can we do?" Martin asked.

"Stand down," Ariel said. "Encourage them to choose another Pan."

"Hans may be right," Martin said.

"We could put a name on what we're going to try," Ariel said. "We could call it genocide."

"Bolsh," Cham said.

"The potential for this is in the Law," Hakim said. "We have sworn to uphold the Law. I believe it possible the Benefactors knew killer civilizations might hide behind such screens, and worded the Law—"

"We're way beyond our limits," Ariel said. "I did not travel this far to kill innocents."

Hakim calmly persisted. "It is probable some Killers remain here."

"We haven't seen them!" Ariel shouted. Martin felt a pleasant tremor at her return to form; perversely, he found her more appealing.

"It was inevitable," Hakim persisted. "No villain comes in black, screaming obscenities. All evil has children, homes, regard for self, fear of enemies."

"I did not agree to kill innocents!" Ariel shouted. She spread her arms, opened her fists. "I don't care what the moms do, or what they don't tell us."

"You've been a bit strong about the moms all along," Cham said. "I don't think they're holding anything back. They're building new weapons, showing us how to use them—"

"Ah, bolsh, yourself!" Ariel said, face wrinkled in disgust. "I thought some of you would have the brains to figure it out."

"What?" Hakim asked.

"The moms aren't *inventing* new weapons! They're not suddenly discovering new principles and applying them—what utter crap!"

Martin's admiration quickly turned to irritation.

"They've known about these big, impressive technologies all along," she said. "They just don't want to show their cards any more than they have to. Nobody trusts us, nobody tells us more than we absolutely have to know. That's the way it's been from the beginning. If we want to *believe* we're helping them develop wonderful new toys, who's going to disabuse us? Not the moms."

Martin's irritation turned on himself now. He hadn't even considered that possibility; and why not? Because there was no evidence for it; Ariel was reverting to paranoid suspicions. He preferred the direct—*the easier*—approach. *Believe what you're told*.

She curled her knees and wrapped her arms around them, again like a little girl sitting in a window, weary, disappointed by Martin, by herself. "We're getting ready to kill trillions of intelligent beings who might be innocent. We just can't take that chance, and Martin shouldn't have agreed for us."

"He's in command of this ship," Cham said.

"Not true, not true," Ariel said, closing her eyes, rubbing

them, staring at Hakim sidewise. "He shares command with Eye on Sky, and the Brothers are breaking with us."

Cham looked at Martin. "She's right."

"They haven't decided yet," Martin said.

"That's what they'll decide," Cham said with resignation.

Martin's wand signaled. Eye on Sky requested a meeting.

"We have to make our own decision, whatever Hans says," Ariel concluded.

In the Brothers' quarters, Martin hung from a net beside Eye on Sky. The Brothers coiled around them, cords' skins gleaming in the offset lighting, the upraised foreparts of the braids casting shadows around Martin like a larger net. The presence of so many large serpentine shapes might have been threatening; but for him, the Brothers represented a gentleness and *humanity* Hans didn't think they could afford. He felt no threat from them.

Eye on Sky splayed his head and crawled along the net closer to Martin, smelling of cut grass, fresh-baked bread: smells of strength and firmness, of assurance. "Listening to we our fellows on *Shrike* and *Greyhound*, we we decide there is a chance to learn more, and so will act with yours."

"I should ask for another meeting?"

"Yes," Eye on Sky said.

Martin chewed his upper lip thoughtfully. "Do you think the Killers are still here?"

"Perhaps not possible to know."

"Some of us think we should have expected this problem from the beginning," Martin said.

"Questions without answers. Expected, not anticipated in detail."

"We were young," Martin said.

"We all we are young, this problem is ancient. It eats we us as a sweet, with delight."

"Will you go down with me?" Martin asked. He did not say this out of cruelty; rather, as a kind of test, as if he stood in Hans' place for the moment.

"Not I we," Eye on Sky said. "We we disassemble in that

condition, that world. You have named it Sleep. For we us, it is a true kind of sleep. You must go for we us, if permitted.''

Martin took a deep breath.

"You are disturbed?" Eye on Sky asked.

He shook his head. "No, no more than . . . Yes, I am," he reversed himself. "In a way, Hans is right about Leviathan. Everything we see here seems tailor-made to divide us, confuse us. If Hans is right, and the Killers are still here . . ."

"Not happy," Eye on Sky said.

"They'll make us much more unhappy before they're done with us."

Hakim repeated the message several times without reply from Sleep. Martin stood behind him as he went through the procedure again, panel projected before him, fingers touching controls glowing in the air.

"Nothing still," Hakim said. "They were prompt before."

Martin nodded.

Beyond the projected control panel, small images of Leviathan's planets hung against the dark aft wall of the bridge. Blinker caught Martin's eye.

It no longer blinked. It maintained a steady sandy brown color.

"Something's changed," Martin said. He pointed to Blinker. Hakim's face darkened with excitement.

"How long does it take a light signal to reach us from Blinker?" Martin asked.

"Three hours twelve minutes," Hakim said.

"Can you play back the records?"

Hakim quickly replayed ship's memory of the planetary images until they found the precise moment when the planet had stopped its fluctuation. "Three hours ago," Hakim said.

"What else has changed?" Martin asked.

Hakim expanded the planetary images one by one: Mirror turning milky, its perfect reflectivity catching a hot moist breath; Frisbee, its edges browning like burned bread dough, the unknown "hair" shedding into space; Cueball unchanged; Gopher's gleaming lights within impossibly deep caverns burning brighter, bluer, like torches.

They came to Puffball, with its immense bristling seed-like constructions. Some seeds had lifted away from the planet's surface, one, three, six of them, and more on their way. Spikes at the top of the seeds also broke free, flying outward at high speed.

"Are they attacking?" Hakim asked.

"I don't know. Pass this on the noach to *Greyhound* and *Shrike*."

"Done," Hakim said. A moment later, his mouth went slack. "There is no noach connection," he said. "They are not receiving. I do not know where they are."

Paola and Erin entered the bridge.

"We're in trouble," Martin said. "Hakim, pull out of orbit . . ."

Silken Parts pushed through the door as Hakim ordered the ship away from Sleep.

"What's happening?" Erin asked.

"We don't know, but I'm taking us out of here."

"We have a reply now," Hakim said. "From Sleep . . ."

Salamander's voice filled the bridge. "There have been disruptions on four of our worlds." Salamander's image appeared in flat projection. Crest pointed straight out, three eyes open, hissing loudly behind its words, the bishop vulture managed to convey its disturbance.

"We don't know what's happening," Martin said.

"There is tampering with balances. These worlds are delicate and many lives are in danger."

"We haven't communicated with our . . ." He couldn't finish the deceptive wording, his tongue caught in too many prevarications. He simply stared at Salamander's image. The bishop vulture lifted its crest, hissed softly.

"You are a lie and a deception," Salamander said. "We have no further need of you."

The image and voice faded. "End of transmission," Hakim said. "Still no success with noach to *Greyhound*."

The rest of the crew crowded the bridge, watching the long drama play itself out over the next half hour.

The three identical planets—Pebbles One, Two, and Three—abruptly glowed dull orange, then red, then white, in sequence according to their distances from the ship. Their surfaces diffused like paint in water, glowing specks rising and falling.

"Who's doing that?" George Dempsey asked. "Them, or us?"

The seeds of Puffball twisted about as if blown in a gentle breeze. On such a scale, that simple motion spoke of immense energies.

Martin could hardly think in the ensuing babble noise. The cabin filled with Brother smells, stinging his eyes. He saw a cord scramble past him, then watched as a Brother—he could not identify which—disassembled. Silken Parts immediately began gathering up the cords, which clung to fields waving their feelers helplessly.

They didn't even know what weapons *Greyhound* now possessed, or what their effects would be. One effect was obvious—the attack had been launched on many targets almost simultaneously, judging by the arrival of light-borne information at intervals determined solely by distance. That spoke to Martin of noach; and the first object to change its character had been the massive noach station, Blinker.

What are they up to?

"I know what's happened," Ariel said just loudly enough for Martin to hear, bracing herself on a field behind him.

"What?"

"Hans has started the war without telling us."

With a momentary sense of dizziness, as if he had been through all this before, he realized she was probably right.

Hans had used them to give *Greyhound* an edge.

"Then why aren't we dead?" Martin asked. His entire back prickled, waiting for imminent death.

Ariel shrugged. "Give them time."

The mom and snake mother came onto the bridge. "This ship has been under steady attack for an hour, and our ability to armor against their weapons is diminishing. We assume control now. Super acceleration is called for," the mom said.

"We don't have the fuel," Martin said.

"We will convert as much as we can," the mom said.

"Can you communicate with the other ships?"

"Yes," the mom said.

"*Greyhound* and *Shrike*?" Martin asked.

"Yes."

"Are they attacking?"

"Yes."

"You knew they would attack?"

"No."

"But you must have known . . . You must have known when they began!"

The mom did not reply. The volumetric fields expanded. Martin felt their molasses grip, the jerky impediment to all bodily motion.

All slowed in the mire. Martin tried to keep the threads of his attention together. He examined the bridge carefully, separating effect from true perception.

The bridge changed. Walls grew and separated them into pairs. Martin saw that Ariel would be enclosed with him. She stared at him and he turned his head away, the volumetric fields giving permission for every particle to move, move slowly.

"Can you hear me?" Ariel asked.

"Just barely."

"I think we've split up. *Trojan Horse*."

"You've been right so far," Martin said.

"Don't hold it against me," Ariel said.

He shook his head. "Never."

"He's taken our rights away," she said, rather irrelevantly, Martin thought.

Super acceleration ceased two hours later. Martin had barely regained his wits when the ship's voice said, "First attack repelled. We are being followed."

"What in hell has happened?" Martin asked, trying to kick-start his brain by shaking his head, stretching his body in the directionless weightless meaningless walled-in cubicle.

Another voice, Hans caught in the middle of a triumphant yell. Ariel gave a small shriek like a doomed rabbit.

"We're doing it, Martin! *Trojan Horse* has gotten the hell

away and split up. We haven't forgotten you. We're keeping track of you. But you're being followed."

The cubicle lacked screen or star sphere. "Show us something, tell us what's going on!" Martin cried.

The ship tried to speak, but Hans interrupted. "We've gone black, made our moves. Sorry about not telling you." As casual as that. *Sorry about not telling you.*

"What the hell is happening, Hans?"

Ariel pushed herself into a corner as if to stay out of his way.

"*Trojan Horse* broke up and split. Something's following you. It sure isn't bothering to hide, and it's right on your ass. You and two others are all they've managed to tail. I'd say they're using you to try to find something bigger. If you don't lead them to us—and you won't, my friend—you're dust."

"We have broken this vessel into ten units and accelerated them in different directions outward from Leviathan," the ship's voice said, almost irrelevantly at this point.

We are still more valuable as clues to where the big ships are. They know us. They know our psychology; they figured it out right away, that we wouldn't deliberately sacrifice ourselves, that at some point a rescue would be attempted.

"Hold on a moment," Hans said.

Ariel reached out a hand and Martin took it. "He's going to sacrifice us," she said.

"Show me something," Martin told the ship, whatever kind of ship it was, whatever size. "Show me the outside. What's following us."

A small screen appeared against one wall. A white sphere filled the screen, pocked by glowing blue dots.

"Harpal has your tagalong's coordinates," Hans said. "We'll get it. You should see this, Martin. It is in-*credible*!"

The white sphere blistered like a plastic ball hit by a torch. The blisters spread open and the sphere diminished. Curls of darkness blanked the whirling stars, streaming from the sphere, reaching toward them.

"Super acceleration," the ship's voice said. Fields seized again, and Martin screamed. The scream was forbidden and died as a hollow glurp in his throat.

He heard and saw again an unknown time later.

Harpal's voice in his ears. "We got your dog, Martin. Thought you should know."

They have Gauge on Greyhound. *My dog is waiting for me? No*—

"We noached it straight to hell," Harpal said. "It's a beautiful streamer of plasma about fifty thousand klicks long. Christ, these weapons are *unbelievable*!"

The craft following them had vanished. In its place wafted a wide, striated shower of glowing debris, each piece fanning out in a straight line, vapors like rays of sun through clouds.

Martin still held Ariel's hand. Slowly, she opened her eyes and looked at him with an expression of intense grief.

"You're safe for the time being," Harpal said. "You're really rocketing. Can't talk now. They haven't pinned us yet, but they're trying, wow are they trying . . ."

Silence, long minutes, before Martin realized the noach message had ended.

Martin let go of Ariel's hand.

"They're doing it, aren't they?" she said.

Martin nodded. "They divided *Trojan Horse*."

"Who?"

"I didn't give any order. The moms. The ship itself."

"We're out of the action. Hans screwed you over double," she said.

Martin shook his head. "What?"

"By not letting you do the Job with him. And by cutting all of us out of the decision." She turned away. "Will they pick us up?"

"I don't know."

Magnified images: a rocky planet, Lawn, sparkling fire snaking over its surface. Greater magnification: strange superheated forests burning like carpets of magnesium, ribbons of shredded land rising as if cut from paper, something moving over the surface, dark and immense, not a shadow, more like a finger drawing chaos in the rock.

Another: Big City, the finger moving yet again. *God's finger taking vengeance*.

Much smaller in the screen, another rocky world, not immediately familiar to Martin, this one dying in a particularly violent display, throwing chunks of itself into darkness as if being chewed apart by immense beasts.

"Blinker," the ship's voice said. "It will consume itself. Nothing living or ordered will survive."

"How?" Martin asked. "How can we do this?"

"Remote manipulation of forces within atomic nuclei," the ship's voice said. "Blinker is particularly vulnerable, as a noach station of immense power. *Greyhound* has found the main weakness, and exploited it."

"How much can *Greyhound* destroy?" Martin asked.

"Uncertain. Defenses are not fully deployed."

Sleep appeared, surrounded by immense seeds with brushy tops, much like those released from Puffball, reminding Martin of immune response in humans, although on an astronomical scale. "Explain."

"Not clear. White objects in orbit around this world may try to confuse targeting of noach weapons."

Noach weapons. Confirmed.

A haze as fine as dust in air spread out with incredible speed—visible even on this scale—from the scattered seed-puffs. A seed-puff's crown glowed brilliant orange, then faded to green and vanished, leaving the thousand-kilometer "stem" to precess slowly. As the minutes passed, another headless stem came into view around the limb of Sleep and fell toward the planet. Its lower extremity touched atmosphere. Slowly, slowly, across more minutes, the stem bent over and laid itself in the atmosphere and across the surface, surrounded by ripples of mixed crust and ocean, all vapor now, glowing dull red with bursts of pink and white.

Soon all of Sleep became enveloped in a nacreous halo, plasma thousands of kilometers thick turning it into a dim star. Radiation scoured the surface; falling seed-puffs stirred it like mud, a mud of continents and oceans.

Martin could not believe that *Greyhound* alone was responsible for this.

"Are we getting help . . . from somebody outside?" he asked, face pale. *Memories of watching Earth. Same scale, but even more destruction.*

"There are no other combatants," the ship's voice said.

Gas Pump showed in the display now, immense plumes of mined volatiles spreading out of control, white plasma shooting through, green and blue surfaces turning muddy yellow.

"What can we do?" Martin asked.

"Escape is our only option," the ship's voice said.

Martin's fingers curled. Ariel wrapped her arms around herself, watching with haunted eyes.

Hours.

Neither Martin nor Ariel expressed hunger, but they were fed anyway, a meager paste that tasted of nothing in particular.

The display projected their path across a diagram of the system. They were actually moving closer to the star at this point, but a journey across the width of the system would take them almost three days, through the thick of the battle, across the orbits of thousands of vehicles they had never had time to catalog or examine, whose purposes they might never know.

"Are we going to accelerate again?" Martin asked.

"All fuel is expended," the ship's voice said. "Reserves are for keeping you alive."

During his thousands of hours of research into war and human history, Martin had read about a man with a striking name— Ensign George Gay. Ensign Gay had flown an airplane in the Battle of Midway, during the Second World War. He had been shot down, and had floated for hours in the midst of ships and planes trying to destroy each other.

"How long is it going to take?" Ariel asked.

"The war? I don't know. Could be weeks. Months."

"It doesn't look like it will take nearly that long. I'm tired." She sounded like a child.

Martin cradled her in his arms.

Number eight, the gas giant Mixer, expanding like a sick, bruised balloon, shell upon shell of brilliant gases like the petals of flowers. Thousands of years of construction and technology and how many individuals, how many beings even more developed than the staircase gods? Imagine so many possibilities not shown. Who is winning

Eat sleep share a part of the wall that sucks away our wastes

Ship no larger than an automobile

How many survived from Trojan Horse

Most of the seed-puffs gone now exhausted or served their purpose. Four worlds dead or dying, others under siege. God the power. What will we do after, knowing this? Maybe Hans is right they will snuff us.

 . . . .

Gas giants ripping apart in slow motion can it be we did this? They are like suns now, spinning tails of brilliance from poles and equator, prominences. Did Hans know we could do this

 . . . .

No messages and two days have passed. We sweep away from Leviathan. Sleep much of the time, eat rarely now, there is no space to exercise. Breathe slowly, watching worlds writhe and die across hours and days.

All the rocky planets and moons seething surfaces uniform deep red

All! All! Jesus, ALL of them!

 . . . .

Ariel leaned over him, hand on his shoulder. "I can't get the ship to talk," she told him. "It won't answer."

Martin tried. Still no answer.

"That means we're going to die, doesn't it?"

"I hope not," he said.

Ariel pounded a fist on the gray wall. "Hey! Talk to us!"

 . . . .

No images no information. Try exercising, pushing against each other, feet to feet, wrestling she is almost as strong as I am strain a muscle.

Tell her I'm dreaming more now of Earth. Of forests and rivers, of our house in the woods in Oregon with the broad patio. My toys, soldiers my parents bought me. We talk until we get thirsty. Trickle of water from the wall, wastes still sucked away something is working but the mom does not speak and we can't see anything outside. Sleep most of the time and talk of spaces outside, times past, places gone.

. . . .

Getting cold actually now. We hug each other but no energy left to exercise. Saw Theodore in the cabin playing cards with himself. Smiled at me. Offered a deck to me. Maybe he's a ghost and the dead are going to greet us soon.

Such a great tide of dead rising from this place, trillions we've killed. What do staircase gods look like reporting to the afterlife, already stripped of material bodies? No battlefield so crowded with dead in long lines and we stand in queue waiting our turn to be inspected passed through. Salamander and Frog ahead of me; the babar and sharks up ahead, looking angrily at us. Don't get too close to them don't want fights in line Theodore says.

. . . .

"Martin, wake up. There's a little water now. Drink."

"Did you have yours?" he asked.

"I've had mine. Drink."

He sucked globules from the air. One got in his eye, burned a little. The water didn't taste good. But it was wet.

No food.

For some time, Martin felt no hunger, until he saw Ariel looking visibly thinner, and felt hungry in her place, for she did not complain.

"It's been at least six days," Martin said.

"It's been eight days exactly."

"How do you know?"

She held up her right hand and pointed to the middle finger. "Eight. I trim my fingernails with my teeth. See? These two are long."

. . . .

Are my parents dead? How would I know? Maybe we'll meet them soon. Is Rosa in this line? I see her. Won't look at me, won't give up her place to come talk to me. Theodore goes over to talk with her. He doesn't care about his place.

. . . .

"Who is Theodore?" Ariel asked. Her lips had cracked and bled sluggishly. She looked elfin with hunger, eyes large and high cheeks gaunt.

"He died."

"On the Ark?"

Martin shook his head and his neck muscles hurt, bones grinding. Muscles atrophying. No exercise no energy. "On *Dawn Treader*. Killed himself."

"I don't remember him."

"He killed himself."

Ariel wrinkled her face in concentration. "Maybe my mind is going. I don't remember him."

Martin looked at her and felt something cold. His lips were parched and cracking and he licked them. "Very smart," he said. "Smarter than me."

Ariel shook her head, and the coldness grew in him.

"I remember him," Martin said, but there wasn't enough energy for either of them to carry the question farther.

.
.
.
.
.
.
.
.

.

*Captain Bligh in his boat
carving up a bird between
the men*

sound

Water dripped onto his lips like rain.

"Martin?"

Moved, lifted, weight. Pressing of hands weight on his back. Voices familiar.

"Twenty-two days."

"Martin."

Small pain in his arm nothing compared to a chorus of fresh pains all over his body. Tingles, stabs, bones grinding, eyes opened to whiteness no detail.

Then snakes of lights. Freeway rain in Oregon with tail-lights last year of the world. Snakes of lights in a cabin, ceiling and floor, weight.

"Hello."

No longer in line of dead.

"Hello," he said, voice like rocks in a slide.

"You look pretty shitty, my friend."

So who was it? Familiar.

Shadow in the light, another shadow. "I can't see."

"You both died, you know that? I mean literally, your hearts were stopped and something in the ship, the ship's last energy, wrapped you in a field so you couldn't, you know, *decay*. Absolutely incredible. Martin, come forth."

Who would talk like that.

Joe Flatworm.

"I'm on the ship?" Martin asked. "*Greyhound*?"

"We picked you up five days ago. The sores are gone. You're looking a lot better. We got four of the other ships. Saved seven Brothers, seven of us."

"Ariel."

"She's alive. It's been a season of miracles, Martin."

He saw Joe's face more clearly. "The war?"

"It's still going. We're still here." Joe's broad, pleasant face, supple brows, wide smile. He held Martin's hand firmly between his hands. Skin warm, dry, like sunned leather.

Martin craned his neck and looked at himself, wrapped in a medical field, surrounded by warmth, an electric tingle moving from place to place through his body. Relaxed his neck. Swallowed. Throat raw. "Hans?"

Joe's smile vanished. "Hey," he said. "We're getting it done. That's enough."

Add to the list: Hakim Hadj, Erin Eire, Cham Shark. Silken Parts, Dry Skin/Norman, Sharp Seeing, missing or dead as well. Presumed dead after so many days.

Still weak, Martin insisted on leaving the medical field to join Hans and view the war. The war had been on for twenty-four days; most of the damage, Joe said, had been done. "We've whipped them," he said with an uneasy smile. Then he took Martin to the nose of *Greyhound*.

Hans hung in a net before dozens of projections. His appearance shocked Martin; hair almost brown with sweat and oil, face thin, stinking of sweat and tension. Hans wore only shorts and a sleeveless shirt. His arms seemed knotted with muscles, empty of fat; legs likewise. He did not turn around as Martin and Joe entered.

Giacomo curled asleep in a rear corner, hand reflexively grasping a net.

"Martin's back," Joe announced. Hans shivered and looked around.

"Good," he said.

The projections showed planetary cinders, wreaths of fading plasma, oblong chunks of moons, seed structures scored and headless and broken like sticks.

Hans kept his shrewd and weary eyes on Martin, evaluating, smiling faintly. "How are you feeling?"

"Okay," Martin said. He had never imagined they would ever summon such destruction.

"Kind of stirring, isn't it?" Hans said, nodding at the projections.

Martin shook his head.

"Hard to take it all in, sometimes," Hans said. "I've spent hours up here just . . . assessing damage, looking for something we *haven't* destroyed. It's complete. Last two days, even Sleep has broken up." He pointed to a large image of scattered masses, some dark, some flickering with light, floating in a gray, hazy void. Within the debris, a piece of what must have been crust, thousands of miles wide, rippled like fabric, its edges crumbling away. "No more staircase gods."

Martin forced himself to breathe again. The intake of breath sounded like a groan. Hans chuckled. "Glad to see you're impressed."

Martin shook his head. Tides of conflicting emotion pulled him one way, then another. *We've done the Job. How do we know? We've done it. It's over.*

"Whenever you're ready to lend a hand, there's a lot of scut work to get done," Hans said. "We're taking a break now. Ship is on relaxed alert. You should have seen us at the peak. Every Wendy and Lost Boy had their hands on some weapon or another. Giacomo and the ships' minds . . . the ships' minds, mostly, once the evidence was in . . . really went to town on new weapons. Long-range noach conversions, quark matter pitfalls, spin shattering, they made a whole new arsenal."

Did they? Or had the ships' minds kept them hidden, waiting for necessity?

"We sent out fifteen craft, mostly for reconnaissance. We got twelve of them back."

Martin nodded, eyes still fixed on the abstract complexity of Sleep's corpse, muted colors horribly beautiful. He could not connect the debris with what he had seen on the two journeys to Sleep's surface. Somewhere in the dust, scattered atoms of Salamander and Frog, the babar, the red joint-tentacle creature that had crawled up onto their disk ferry for a look.

Trillions.

Hans motioned for Martin to come closer. "I've got my suspicions," he said as Martin laddered forward and hung beside him. "I think the moms held back on us at first. Maybe we've been lied to all along. But frankly I don't give a shit. In the end, they gave us the tools, and that's what counts."

Giacomo stirred, opened his eyes, and saw Martin. "Hakim

didn't make it. Erin. Cham." Giacomo nodded and set his lips, then shook his head.

"I know," Martin said. Resentful that he could be expected to react. He could not feel grief yet. None of this seemed real. He expected to wake back on *Dawn Treader* and know they still had the Job ahead of them.

Giacomo blinked slowly. "We saved Jennifer," he said. His eyes seemed darker, deeper, wrapped in exhausted, bruised flesh. "She'll be all right."

Martin shouldered Hans to peer into Hans' display. Hans made space for him without complaint.

"It's done," Giacomo said. He shook his head in disbelief. "It was a shell. Sixty percent of what we saw was fake matter. We think there were only four real planets. Sleep was one of the real ones."

"Don't cheapen our victory," Hans said.

"It was just a shell," Giacomo repeated. "We found the projectors, we figured out how to make them echo our energy, subvert the system from within . . . we found a few points where we could start chain reactions . . . We couldn't have done it before. It wasn't nothing and it wasn't easy. We used up nearly all our fuel."

"Real fireworks," Hans said. "Did you see it?"

"Is there enough real mass, are there enough volatiles for us to refuel?" Martin asked.

"Plenty," Hans said. Martin looked to Giacomo for a second opinion.

"We'll have enough," Giacomo said.

Hans reached out and grabbed Martin's shoulder, fingers hard and painful. He shook Martin lightly. "You going to fault me for this?"

Martin looked aggrieved, or perhaps simply confused.

Hans smiled. "We can go marry a planet now."

"We can't leave yet, actually," Giacomo said. "We have to finish the examination—"

"Autopsy," Joe said from the rear.

"Make sure it's dead. Do some research," Giacomo continued. "The moms need a death certificate. We still haven't talked about being released. We don't know where we're going—"

"Shit," Hans said. "Let's savor the moment. We'll have time enough for the bureaucratic stuff later."

Giacomo seemed not to hear him. "We've got to transfer *Greyhound*'s Brothers to *Shrike*."

"*Shrike* stayed out of it," Hans said. "Can you believe it? They didn't do a thing."

"I didn't do a thing," Martin said.

"You opened the door, Martin."

Giacomo agreed. "You put yourselves in much more danger than we did. You lost many more . . ." He saw Martin's expression and lifted his eyebrows, cocked his head. "Sorry."

"We should hold a service. Honor the dead," Martin said.

Hans did not answer; calling up projections, baring his teeth in a grimacing smile, shaking his head in victorious wonder. "Look at *that*," he murmured. "Look . . . at . . . THAT."

Eye on Sky, Double Twist, Rough Tail, Strong Cord, and Green Cord had all agreed to Martin's request for a meeting in the Brothers' recovery quarters.

He visited Paola Birdsong in her quarters to ask that she interpret for him again.

Paola had spent less time in space than Martin and Ariel, fewer than eighteen days, but she had been with Strong Cord and Green Cord, and Joe told Martin that the time had been very hard for her. None of the braids had held together; she had been alone for eighteen days with twenty-eight hungry, confused cords.

"At least they didn't chew on me," she said, her voice weak and rough. She had thinned considerably, but her color was good and she moved without apparent pain. "I'm fit enough to work. I never do eat much."

Martin smiled admiringly. "You're a tough one. My joints still ache."

"Have you visited Ariel?" Paola asked.

He shook his head. "I asked, but she's in seclusion. We spent a lot of time together. I'm not sure she wants to see me again."

"She's been sweet on you for months," Paola said.

"We've been lovers," Martin admitted.

Paola raised her eyebrows. "Better than having cords squirm

all around you," she said. "I'm glad it was me. Anybody else might have come unglued. Is Ariel going to join Rosa's people and go with *Shrike*?"

Martin shook his head. "I don't know."

"I'm thinking about it," Paola said. "You?"

"Hans got it done," Martin said.

Paola sucked in her lips dubiously, decided against arguing the point, and took his arm. "Let's go," she said.

Eye on Sky and the other Brothers resembled bundles of dry sticks. Recovery was harder for the Brothers; the cords had to heal themselves, which meant frequent disassembly and individual care for each cord.

Martin began to understand why war and conflict had played a much smaller role in the Brothers' history. Braids were not robust; their existence as intelligent beings was delicately balanced, and violence quickly reduced them to an animal level. Wars fought between cords could not last long.

So why did the Benefactors send them in the first place?

Because everybody deserves a chance at justice, no matter how slim the chance might be.

"We we congratulate you on survival," Eye on Sky said.

"We're sorry to see you leave," Martin said. He touched Eye on Sky's broad trunk. The Brother shivered but did not shrink back.

"I'm very sorry," Paola said.

"You can join us," Strong Cord said.

"I won't," Martin said.

"I haven't decided," Paola said.

"You, Paola Birdsong, would be very welcome," Eye on Sky said. "You as well, Martin."

"Thank you," Martin said.

"The destruction is frightening," Eye on Sky said. "Simply thinking of it risks disassembly. We hold such power now."

"If the moms let us keep it," Martin said.

"Will they?"

"I hope not."

"Where will humans go now?"

"We'll survey the system. See what evidence we can find.

The ships will scoop up fuel. Then . . . we'll explore. Find a planet we can live on.''

"You will not return to your world, to Mars?"

"I don't think so. We'll vote on it, but by the time we get back, almost a thousand years will have passed. Nobody we know will be alive . . . At least, I don't think they will.''

"Other humans have come to visit we us," Eye on Sky said. "Have expressed regret. Perhaps more will come with *Shrike* than go with *Greyhound*.''

Martin didn't think, when it came right down to it, that anybody would accompany the Brothers. The mood had changed since the war.

"How many humans can you stand?" Martin asked with a faint grin.

"It is a problem," Green Cord said. Eye on Sky slapped his flanks with tip of tail—something Martin had never seen a Brother do to another. Green Cord expelled a faint odor of turpentine, then baking bread. Upset, propitiation.

"Martin, your presence would be good, as well," Eye on Sky said. "I we think of this, and to have you with we all us, that would not cause pain or upset, but linking and harmony.''

Martin shook his head. "I appreciate the invitation, but I don't think I'll go with you.''

Eye on Sky smelled of licorice and salt air.

"Polite disappointment," Paola murmured.

"Thank you for asking," Martin told Eye on Sky.

It was a dangerous time, but Martin could no longer be circumspect. He had survived too much, seen too much, to let certain small things go by.

On the bridge, Hans ate his meal with measured motions, ignoring Martin. Martin crossed his legs and folded his arms, watching Hans toss bits of cake to his mouth and grab them. When he finished, Hans wiped his hands on a towel stuck in a field, pushed himself around with one hand, and faced Martin squarely.

"Well?"

"I'm asking for an investigation," Martin said.

"Of what?"

"Rosa's death."

Hans shook his head. "We know who did it."

"I don't think that's enough."

"Martin, we've done the Job. We'll finish here and go find someplace to live. That has to be enough."

Martin's face flushed. He felt as he had when confronting the moms. "No," he said. "We need to clear the air."

"Rex is dead."

"Rex left a message," Martin said.

"It's guilt-crazed shit."

"The crew . . . needs to know, one way or the other."

"You want to be Pan again?" Hans asked, deceptively calm. Martin could read the signs: neck muscles tight, one hand opening and closing slowly, grasping nothing.

"No," Martin said.

"Who should be Pan?"

"That isn't my point."

"If you believe I had something to do with Rosa's death, then I should be . . . what? What penalty do you suggest?"

"Did you put Rex up to it?" Martin asked.

"Whoa. Shooting pointblank, Marty. What makes you think I did?"

"Did you?"

Hans kept his eyes focused firmly on Martin's, said, "No, I did not put Rex up to it. I don't know what was going on in his head. He was confused. Rosa took him in—made him a part of her group. That was *her* mistake, not mine."

"You didn't tell Rex to attack the Brother?"

"Christ, no. What good would that have done me?"

Martin blinked. *Got to keep it up. Can't give up now.*

"You saw Rosa as a real threat, somebody who could divert the whole mission."

"Yes. Didn't you?"

"You saw yourself as the only one capable of finishing the mission."

Hans spread his arms, stretching. "Okay. Not too far wrong."

"Rex was your friend. He was devoted to you."

"Bolsh. Rex was his own man."

"You wanted to make it look that way. You ordered him to attack the Brother, take the blame, isolate himself. He agreed."

"So now I'm some sort of hypnotist. Why would I isolate him? You think Rex wasn't smart enough to see through such a crazy scheme? He'd know why I wanted him isolated. He was no idiot. He'd know it would be so I could jump clear if he was caught. That's just plain crazy. Rex was not crazy."

"Devoted," Martin suggested.

"I don't know about that."

"There's sufficient question to make an investigation necessary," Martin said.

Hans wagged his head back and forth, eyes wide, silently mimicking him. " 'Sufficient question.' 'Investigation necessary.' Christ, you're an intellectual *giant*. Do you think the crew would have followed you into something like Leviathan? We were pissing in our pants, Marty."

Martin could feel the nastiness building. "Will you agree to an investigation?"

"Is this revenge for my not telling you when we'd attack?"

"No," Martin said.

"I think it is. You know why I did it that way. You were in the middle of things. There could have been little ears everywhere. Did you think I would drop all our plans right in their laps?"

"This is beside the point, Hans, and you know it."

"Sure," Hans said, lifting his hands. "Anything for you." He leaned forward, one hand pushing on a field, the other pulling, and released his grip to jab a finger at Martin. "They wouldn't have followed *you*, Martin, because you get people *killed*. You're a regular goddamn McClellan—did you read about him, Martin? American Civil War. Made an army but refused to really go out and fight. Your instincts are bad. You think leadership is a game with justice and rules. It isn't. Leadership is getting the most people through a hell of a time, and *doing the slicking Job!*"

He called up images of Leviathan's ruined worlds until they filled his quarters like hanging sheets. "My parents didn't make it onto the Ark. Nobody I knew made it. They were all blown to atoms. *Everybody I knew!*

"The Killers had thousands of years. They sent out their clever machines, then they sat back. They built their pretty castles and made their pretty creatures, they laid their traps. They defended themselves to the max because they were afraid, they were guilty, they knew we'd come for them, and someday we'd get them. How many like us failed? *We didn't fail!*"

Beads of Hans' spittle hung between them like tiny jewels. Hans leaned back, face blotched with red and drawn with white. He withdrew his finger. "I didn't fail. I got the Job done. If you want to be Pan, you can have it. I resign. You lead us to the promised land."

"There needs to be an investigation," Martin said.

"I said yes. Get out of here. Let someone enjoy what we've accomplished.

"We lost so much," Hans said to his back as Martin passed through the door. "So goddamned much. What more do you want?"

In his quarters, Martin folded himself in a net and stared at the dead worlds, then some of the pictures transmitted by Salamander.

Hans had ripped his heart open. He did not know exactly why he persisted in asking for an investigation, but something of his father and something of his mother pushed him. He was motivated by lessons he barely remembered learning on Earth and on the Central Ark. Primal things in his life.

In the nose, Giacomo, Eye on Sky, Anna Gray Wolf, and Thorkild Lax worked to assess the damage, tally the results, before making their final report to Hans. Unable to sleep, Martin came to them and sat in silence while they worked. They played back the war at high speed, tracking the destruction, the ineffective counter-measures, the sheer disproportion of the victory.

Martin saw again the shadowy curled ribbon writing across Leviathan's worlds like a finger, moving even more rapidly in the playback. Picture stacked over picture, Giacomo observing with a critical half-squint, Eye on Sky coiled with head cords attentive.

They came to the endgame.

"Doers and makers seeding here and here." Giacomo pointed to a magnified image of planetary rubble blooming against darkness. Flash of that awful finger. Tiny sparks glowed in the image like fireflies in a storm cloud. "Making interceptors from the cores of Blinker and Cueball. Now—they're not even hiding themselves. Interceptors go out on anti em plumes." Radiant lines of white fanning out, trails fading behind them.

The wands quickly counted interceptor traces: fifty, sixty, seventy thousand in this region alone, each no larger than a car, each seeking a Leviathan ship. No targets were visible in this image, but in another, the interceptors had found their ships, and the points of light were sharp and intense. The torch glare reflected from expanding clouds of dust and gas, like welding torches deep in a cave, on and off, winking, until they became a starfield. Enacting the Law at a distance.

Completely different rules.

Hundreds more images. Torches flickering, dying, starfields of destruction vanishing.

"I we see no surviving escape vehicles," Eye on Sky said, scenting the air with something like cinnamon and fresh-dug dirt.

"I don't either, but we have to expect them. The ones we took out might even be decoys. Maybe they transfer to some point outside the system by noach. You know, wholesale pattern transfer. Mind across the void."

"That is not a confirmed possible," Eye on Sky said.

Giacomo shrugged. "I'm trying to think of everything."

"Ship has already thought of everything," Eye on Sky said.

"I won't argue that," Giacomo said. At the heart of a planet's dust corpse, he pointed to more sparks and red glows. "Signature of quark sex reactions, right?"

Martin had no idea what that might be.

They worked for an hour, ignoring Martin. When they took a break, however, Giacomo climbed along a field to hang beside Martin. Eye on Sky and the others went aft.

"Jennifer's back with us tomorrow," he said. "She told me what happened on the *Trojan Horse*." He clenched his jaw, lowered his voice. "Not right, Martin."

"You didn't know about it?"

Giacomo looked away, tilted his head. "I had so much new

stuff to think about, having the ships' minds really open up, go all out for us . . . Hans made the decision. The weapons were ready, we'd already seeded some planets with noach engineering while you were down there talking. Hans said he wouldn't let them trap us this time, wouldn't let them fool us.'' His eyes gleamed.

"Hans said nothing about our not knowing . . . that it was starting?''

Giacomo shook his head, still fired by the buzz of memory. Nostrils flared. "You should have been *here*. It was a real circus. I mean, I had worked out some of the momeraths, and so did Jennifer and Silken Parts and a lot of the others . . . But the ships' minds are working, then the moms and snake mothers bring out these plans . . . Makers at a distance, nothing in between. Just delude some matter into rearranging its form, ordering itself by your design. Fantastic.

"That was what the Killers were trying to do to us. But they couldn't find us. We were small, they were big. Our chief advantage.''

"Did we discover these new weapons with the help of the moms, or were they already in the ships' minds?''

Giacomo shrugged. "I asked the moms that question twice. No real answer.'' He mimicked the flat neutrality of a mom's voice: " 'You are given what you need to enact the Law.' I'll say this much—I had a long time to think things over, even before Jennifer and I jammed. The momeraths I did pointed to some pretty scary things.''

"Like?''

"All by myself, seeing the planets, trying to figure out Sleep, and Blinker, I came up with''—he circled his hands—"persuasion. It's a principle, like deluding matter through hidden channels. Space is like matter—has its own bookkeeping, its own channels. I don't think the moms knew what I was thinking, I mean, I don't think the Benefactors . . . the ships at least . . . Christ, Martin. I'm getting all tangled.''

"They didn't know about persuasion, whatever it is.''

"Right . . . until we saw Blinker, saw their noach range out to fifty billion klicks.''

Martin nodded. Giacomo was still drunk with the knowledge, the power.

"Space can be persuaded to get out of the way, shrink its metric, collapse atomic diameters to create quark matter. All by myself, without the ships' minds, I saw that quark matter makes neutronium look like a gas. By tweaking internal bits in the quarks—a whole level below particle bits—quark matter can be split into really fanatic lovers. One must have the other, or, you know, the *universe will end*. You put anything between the lovers . . . what stands between ceases to exist. The privileged bands get incredibly vicious. The books must be balanced.

"Martin, the way it went, I don't think the moms or the ships' minds had to know anything. I saw it. The ships' minds worked through a couple of hundred lifetimes of my thinking. They were way ahead of me. I talked to the moms, the ships' minds talked to me, I talked to Jennifer, compared notes, and . . . There it was. Then the ship went to work making the weapons."

Giacomo took a deep breath and shivered some of his energy away, chuckled at his state. "Sorry. It's not that I don't care. But sometimes I felt as if we were forcing God to make mistakes, and there was this . . . this indignant power making things right again, at any cost. The Killers got in the way."

"Of God," Martin said.

Giacomo's cheek twitched, then he grimaced. "Whatever. All this deluding and persuading. Like seduction, playing a game. We played the game better than the Killers did."

"Maybe they were tired," Martin said.

"As good an explanation as any," Giacomo said. He shook his arms out, toes poked into the field. Jittered, hunched his shoulders, eyes dancing with energy beyond exhaustion.

He's had his religious experience.

"I keep seeing something in the playbacks," Martin said. "It can't be real—it looks like a big finger."

Giacomo grinned, nodded. "The finger. That's scary, isn't it? Reaching out." He curled his finger and poked the air. "It shows up wherever there are large masses of separated quark components. That's what made me think maybe God was getting really angry and putting things right."

Martin looked unconvinced. "God again."

"It looks like it's moving really fast, but that's an illusion. It's a chain of spatial contortions upsetting ionized hydrogen, a real barometer of quark separation. That's one theory . . . or it's a string of some sort pulled out of the universe's sub-basement. You know, the glue that keeps us on the canvas? I haven't even begun to think about what that implies. Maybe I don't want to."

"Do you think the Killers were still at home?" Martin asked softly.

Giacomo narrowed his eyes and licked his lips. "Not my call, Martin. Back to work. Hans wants this day after tomorrow. We'll go after anything that looks like survivors."

"It isn't over," Martin said.

"Justice must be complete," Giacomo said. Swinging away, he paused, glanced over his shoulder, said, "You think the moms will let us keep what we know?"

Martin lightly tapped his temple.

"Right," Giacomo said. "They've never asked us to forget."

Ariel sat in the cafeteria with Donna and Anna Gray Wolf. Twenty others off Hans' strict watch schedule ate in clusters. Ariel looked up as Martin entered, nodded to him almost curtly and looked away. She had cut her hair very short and wore colorless overalls. Self-consciously, Martin pushed himself in their direction.

"I'm off to help Giacomo in a few minutes," Anna said pointedly. "You two should be alone, compare notes."

Ariel's color was good, and she did not appear much thinner than he. "No hurry," she said.

"We're having a wake at day's end," Donna said. She swallowed a last bite of something green from the air and gathered her crumbs with a small field.

None of this seemed apropos of anything to Martin. "Do I make you uncomfortable?" he asked Ariel. This was the first time he had seen her since they had been removed from their escape craft. The awkwardness disturbed him.

"Park here," Ariel said. Donna moved over, and Martin

drifted between them. "I'm glad you were with me," Ariel said. "You helped me stay sane."

Martin nodded, the tension not yet diminished.

"But we need to know where you stand. You know that Hans has put together a political squad."

"I've heard about it," he said.

"Nobody's enthusiastic, but they're still keeping track of us."

"Right."

"So we're talking right here in the open," Donna said. "We'll call his bluff."

"We need to know which side you're on," Ariel said.

"No sides," Martin said.

"You can't be neutral," Anna said, righteous anger in her voice. "Hans has gone way beyond his charter."

"He'll call it martial law," Donna said. "The crew went along with him during the war. But we want him to resign as Pan."

"Why?" Martin asked. "He got the Job done."

Ariel searched his face for a sign of what he actually meant, but he was stubbornly blank. "Maybe," she said. "I doubt we'll ever really know."

"I've told him there should be an investigation of Rosa's death and Rex's suicide."

Ariel shook her head. "I sympathize, but that's kind of trivial now, Martin."

"It should be done," Anna said.

"Compared to what happened here, it's damned near meaningless, a gnat in a hurricane."

"She was crew," Martin said.

"Come on," Anna said. "It's still necessary. Martin's right."

"What will it accomplish?" Ariel said. "It's just part of a larger crime. First, he doesn't let us vote on this particular case. Twenty of us go down to Sleep to play ambassadors, and he knocks us out of the circuit, doesn't even bother to keep us informed—"

"He says that was because we could have been spied upon," Martin said. "Or even controlled."

Ariel brushed that aside. "And he executes without having a

proven case. Have you *seen* the destruction, Martin? Can you even begin to absorb it?''

"I've seen it," Martin said, "and no, I can't."

David Aurora approached their group on a ladder field. "I'd keep it down, folks," he said in a low voice. "Patrick keeps his ears open."

"Patrick's replaced Rex," Anna said. "There are others."

"What we want to do," Ariel said, "is get Hans out one way or another, elect a new Pan, and try to convince the Brothers to stay with us, to combine ships. We think we'd have a better chance to find a home that way."

David, having issued his warning, shook his head and pulled himself to another group on the far side of the cafeteria.

"You think Hans has really gone off the deep?" Martin asked. "You think he's going to squash dissent?"

"You want to investigate Rosa's death, but you ask a question like that?" Anna asked.

"Pardon me, but I'm very confused," Martin said.

"It's pretty clear," Ariel said. Her coldness toward him was like a slap. *She's reversed course again. Who can ever know her?*

"It's the new order," Donna said, thin hands rubbing her thin forearms. "He cut us loose on the *Trojan Horse*. He used us. I don't care, I don't trust him, and we need a Pan we can trust, and we need the rest of our crew. We can't just split and go in two directions. It isn't right. We need the Brothers, too."

"You mean, we need their resources," Martin said.

"Actually, that's not strictly true," Anna said. "We'll be able to mine enough stuff around Leviathan to take us anywhere we want to go. Even add to the ship if we want."

"Psychologically, we need the Brothers," Ariel agreed. Martin was about to ask her to explain that when Patrick Angelfish came into the cafeteria, doing a bad job of looking as if he had some purpose there. Martin waved his hand to catch Patrick's eye; Patrick looked away with too much effort. Martin spread his arms and waved them in semaphore for him to join them. Ariel's face went pale and even colder.

Patrick approached cautiously, not expecting the open invitation.

"Are you spying for Hans?" Martin asked him.

"I wouldn't call it spying," Patrick said. "A Pan needs to know what's going on."

"Tell Hans I'm putting together a committee to investigate Rosa's death," Martin said. "I'm asking for volunteers now. He gave permission, and I'm acting on that permission."

"He hasn't told me he gave permission," Patrick said, clearly out of his depth.

Martin's sudden deep anger took him by surprise. "That's because you're a lackey," he said with a grim smile. "Like Rex. Tell him if he wants to challenge me, do it in the open, himself, and not just send you to keep an eye on me."

Patrick left with a shake of his head and a grim, sidelong smile.

Donna and Anna's faces had gone pale and stiff. "You don't understand what he's capable of," Anna said.

"Maybe not," Martin said.

"Don't be a martyr," Ariel said.

"Why not?" Martin asked.

"Then don't be a fool," she added, but her chilly tone had passed.

"I'm flying on instinct," Martin said. "So is Hans. The question is, who has the better instincts?"

The roll call of the new dead. The human crew in the small schoolroom. Brothers elsewhere, preparing to transfer to *Shrike*. The defectors attended, breaking their isolation in the Brothers' section to honor those who had not survived.

Perhaps it was the last time they would be together.

Hans came into the schoolroom with face ashen, hair unkempt, eyes large and hungry. He seemed to look in every face, ask everyone a question: *Are you happy now? Is this enough, or do you want more?*

Without using his wand, Hans recited the names of the dead. Some of the crew wept. Martin closed his eyes and tried to remember Hakim's face, the calmness and deliberation, his precise way with words. Erin Eire . . . intense green eyes and noble balance of defiance and sense. He wished they were here now to help him.

Jeanette Snap Dragon lifted her arm in a clenched fist, and the defectors followed her example.

Hans did not look at Martin after, though he passed close on his way out. Patrick glanced in his direction, face troubled.

The delegation came to Martin's quarters in the middle of his sleep. His wand woke him, chiming insistently. He opened the door and Patrick stepped in, Thorkild Lax behind him, then David Aurora, Carl Phoenix, and last—making Martin's heart ache, for he knew what was happening—Harpal Timechaser. None of them met his eyes but Patrick, who said, "It's time to put everything behind us."

Patrick in front, Carl on one side, David on another, Harpal slightly above him, Thorkild below; a cage of men. Martin smelled their tension.

"Everything?" he said.

"It's history," Patrick said. "Besides, you'll get no support. Nobody wants to dig any more. We need to forget and get on with our lives."

"Forget what?" Martin asked mildly, but his heart pumped strong and fast. His body was very frightened, but the fear hadn't yet reached his head.

"Your investigation."

"We know who killed Rosa, and he's dead, and Hans had nothing to do with it, at least no more than the rest of us," Carl said.

"She would have stopped us," Thorkild said.

"We did the slicking *Job*," Patrick hissed, and Martin knew the quincunx of his danger. Patrick was the center who would radiate to the other four. "We did what we came here to do."

"Let's just give it up, huh?" Harpal asked. "We're tired."

Martin rotated in mid-air to face Harpal. Nobody would look straight into his eyes. Harpal managed to focus on Martin's cheek. "Why are you here? Power?" he asked.

"Beg pardon?" Harpal seemed to sleepwalk, only half-listening.

"I'm asking you why you're here."

"I thought we could talk some sense into you. You know as well as I what Hans did. He drew us together."

"That doesn't absolve him . . ."

"After what we've just done," Harpal said, pain and dismay passing over his face but not disturbing the simple, stolid exhaustion behind any expression, "you want to investigate a . . . what? A murder, you think? It's insane, Martin. Let it lie."

"You've got the finger of God working for you," Martin said, not too rationally. "That's all you need?"

"We couldn't have done it without Hans," Patrick said, "and now you want him punished for something he didn't do."

"I just want to know," Martin said.

"We know already," Patrick said.

"It takes five of you to tell me this?"

"We're your friends," Harpal said. "We don't want anything bad for you."

"Hans asked you to watch out for me?"

"You be careful," Carl said, but Patrick reined him in with a sharp look. *Who is more stupid, Carl, Patrick—or David? I know Harpal and Thorkild . . . I don't know the others nearly as well. Odd some of us are still strangers. Then maybe I don't know any of them. Why are they here? They were my friends. We worked together.*

"We worked together," Harpal said. "We don't want you to be the center of trouble."

"You were a Pan," Martin said.

Harpal tightened his lips, jaw working, relaxing. "I know the responsibilities, the decisions. So do you. I know what Hans is capable of. So do you. Rex was the one who went rogue, not Hans."

"Besides," Patrick said, "Rex is dead, everybody who could know is dead."

"Rex said Hans put him up to it," Martin reminded them.

"He was crazy. He fell in with Rosa's group, they twisted him . . ."

"All the defectors are crazy, too?"

"They're ineffective," Harpal said.

"They don't understand. They're weak links," David said.

Martin still could not tell how far they would go. Surely not all five would attack him. One or two, the others standing back, ashamed, but caught.

"We're ready to go on," Thorkild said, glancing at the others. "Get out of here and marry a planet."

Patrick's eyes were dead. He seemed half asleep.

"We don't want to dig it all up. It's the past. It's dead."

"It smells," Martin said. "It will not stop smelling. We can't cut clean from the past."

"We still have mopping up to do," Harpal said, trying to sound persuasive, reasonable. "The defectors aren't helping, and the Brothers turned out to be real liabilities."

"The Brothers helped us."

"Forget that," Patrick said. "Let's just keep it simple."

Rage colored fear, and the mix made his whole body burn. He wanted them all gone, if not gone then dead, and he could smell the same wish in their breath, their sweat.

David's eyes had become still, lifeless.

Thorkild and Harpal looked like the ones most likely to back off. He moved closer to Harpal. "I'm not out to cause trouble," Martin said. "That's Hans' doing. Some of us want him to stand down. That's all. That's our privilege as crew."

My, you sound rational, clever. That will increase their deadness, their anger. It decreases your anger, to talk so, to try to reason with friends so. You don't really hate or fear them. That makes you weaker. They'll kill you for that, for acting like a victim.

"Not if it puts all of us in danger," Harpal said, reacting to the reasonable tone with his own reason. *Harpal will not act with them.* "What if the Killers have a surprise waiting for us? If we drop our discipline, lose our edge, they'll have us. We're not ready to check out now."

"Not after all we've been through," Thorkild said. "Come on, Martin." *Thorkild won't attack.*

Patrick drifted closer, hand gripping a thin ladder field. Martin raised his wand.

"Get me Hans and Ariel, triple link," he said.

Patrick made a grab for the wand.

"Hans does not reply," the wand said as Martin swung it out of Patrick's reach. Patrick lunged again, and again Martin swung it away. *Anything can happen now.*

Ariel's voice came on, sleepy.

"Witness!" Martin said. "Tie us in to everybody."

"What?"

Patrick and David grabbed for the wand.

"Martin?"

Patrick got the wand and wrenched it from Martin's grasp. David and Thorkild held him, Carl made a grab for a leg but missed and then backed away. *Carl's out.*

Patrick tried to smash the wand against the floor, but it would not break. *Stupid stupid*

"Martin!" Ariel's voice called out. "I'm tying you in."

Harpal moved in before Martin could back away and struck him in the kidneys. It might have been a deadly blow, but Harpal's ladder field was just far enough away that the peak of his blow came before his fist actually struck.

Martin kicked with both legs backward, hands on the floor, and one bare foot caught Harpal in the teeth, cutting Martin's heel and spinning Harpal away to the ceiling. It was a mess, fighting weightless, grabbing fields, all instincts useless. They had done enough sports to know the right moves for most activities, but fighting engaged an older brain with less savvy, and the result was sloppy.

Patrick slammed his head against the floor. Martin grabbed the wand and tossed it away from the group of them.

"We see!" Ariel cried out.

"WE SEE!" other voices cried.

"Stop it!" Jennifer screamed. "Thorkild, stop it!"

Other voices joined in. David had Martin around his neck and shoulders, beyond hearing. He forced Martin's neck down with his hands, jerking spasmodically, trying to really hurt him, crack his spine. Martin felt the jerks as explosions of pain. He reached behind and lifted his thumb rigid and slammed it into David's crotch. The grip relaxed and David grunted, fell away.

For a second, they all flailed helplessly, unable to connect. Drops of blood from Harpal's lip and Martin's foot smeared against overalls.

All the ladder fields in the room vanished. His face like a desperate little boy's, Patrick still clawed at Martin, at the air. Jewels of blood swirled in the vortices of their limbs.

"Stop it." Hans' remote voice in Martin's room.

"Stop it, *now!*" Hans again.

Patrick stopped flailing.

"What in the fuck are you all doing?" Hans shouted.

Patrick's expression, Martin thought, was priceless: dismay mixed with deep anxiety, vacant look gone. None of them looked blank now.

The killing time was past.

Martin had survived.

"I've lost it," Hans said.

Martin hung beside Hans in a net, alone with him in his quarters.

"I sent Patrick to do something and he didn't think he could do it alone. So he asked for some backups," Hans said, closing his eyes, leaning his neck back. "I should have known he'd be weak."

"What did you send him to do?" Martin asked.

"Talk sense into you." Voice low, drained. "I need to sleep, Martin. All I want to do now is sleep."

"They could have killed me," Martin said, wonder in his voice. "You didn't see what Patrick . . ."

"I'm tired, hey." Hans shook his head. "I still don't see why so many joined him. Maybe I was doing better than I thought. But . . . It isn't worth it now. You've won. I'll resign."

"Nobody's asked you to."

"Did you see their expressions?" Hans asked. "The Wendys in particular. Even Harpal." He shook his head. "Poor Harpal. No. I'll resign."

"You did it yourself," Martin said.

"I did it all by myself," Hans said, head lolling. "I didn't want you dead."

"How could you have miscalculated?"

" 'Miscalculated.' " Hans laughed softly. "That's your problem, Martin. Good soul, but still too intellectual. You think first and see second. I see first and think about what I see. I didn't 'miscalculate.' I slicked up."

"Did you ask Rex to kill Rosa?"

Hans jerked his head forward. "I did not. I swear I did not. But I *might* have."

Martin shook his head, not comprehending.

Hans rubbed the palms of his hands together, tapped one palm with an index finger. "Could we have done the Job with Rosa breaking the crew into little bitty pieces?"

"She could have been dealt with."

"You're wrong. Rex broke from me because I slammed him. He didn't know who he was, and he thought we all hated him. Rosa preached love. He came to her. She used him. I didn't ask him to kill her. She wasn't what her people think she was. She was a lot like me."

"Rosa didn't deserve to die."

"We wouldn't be here if she had lived."

Martin did not want to argue the point more. "When will you resign?"

"Right now. You take me someplace public, drag me on a chain if you like. I'll give a sad speech. Old Pans never die."

"I don't understand you," Martin said.

"I understand *you*," Hans said. "I only ask for one thing. I want to still be Pan when the report is made."

The surviving crew of the *Dawn Treader* came to the schoolroom in two groups. Martin entered with the larger group, behind Hans, which drew looks of surprise. Ariel seemed to have gathered her own small cluster of people. Martin saw a power center forming; none of them knew of his talk with Hans.

Watching the way the people associated, Martin saw a swirl of sentient particles working according to certain principles far from fixed, far from immutable; but still, he saw the interactions, and could understand some of their import. He had thought long hours about the conversation with Hans. When he looked now, he saw first, thought about what he saw; he did not impose wishes and patterns and ideals.

The new ability saddened him a little. Of all the illusions of childhood, the one he hated to lose most was this: that humans worked according to unspoken but noble goals, that they followed an intrinsic path to justice, that they would resist error and move toward self-understanding.

Two moms hung on each side of the star sphere, four in all. The ruins of Leviathan's worlds filled the sphere, passing in slow, sad scale, majestic rubble, caverns of nebulosity shot through with the glows of cooling chunks of worlds, sparks of fake matter disintegration not yet complete.

"The analysis is not finished," the ship's voice said, neutral and close in each of their ears. "There is no precedent in memory for the use of weapons of this power and type. Nor is there precedent for a civilization of precisely this character. The after-effects are difficult to judge. Destruction appears to be complete, but a definitive assessment cannot be reached, perhaps for centuries to come."

Martin had suspected this. He had dreamed of unexpected survivals; of civilizations encoded in tumbling boulders, hidden in the rubble, waiting for a chance to rebuild; of staircase gods buried deep in Leviathan itself.

"The Law requires certainty. It does not require that you devote more of your time, however. You have made your judgment and enacted the Law."

"We want to know," Hans said.

"That is understandable," the ship's voice said.

"We *need* to know." Hans' face was even more drawn; he had expected something final. In this, at least, Martin had been more realistic than he.

"Then you should decide to stay and devote more time."

"What are the choices?" Martin asked.

"Your alternative is to continue with your lives. As promised, we will either return you to your solar system, or you may seek another system, find another world not yet inhabited that is suited to your needs."

"That's another phase, another part of the journey," Martin said. He looked at Hans.

Hans pulled himself closer to the sphere. "I've decided my time as Pan is finished. I had hoped to know for sure whether we've finished the Job, but . . . I don't think I should be Pan any longer. I resign." His tone was calm, but his face seemed even more drawn, almost wizened.

"Time to nominate," Anna Gray Wolf said. Martin saw the vortex more clearly.

The Wendys and Lost Boys of the larger group immediately

conferred. Jeanette's group seemed at a loss, left out. Martin moved toward Jeanette. She held her ground, lips set tight.

"You're still with us, if you want to be," Martin said in an undertone. "We can't divide now."

She shook her head. "It isn't enough for Hans to step down."

"You can nominate from your own group," Martin said. "Come back in. I want you to."

"You were part of the atrocity," Jeanette said, brows knit, mouth drawn up in anger. "Coming back is like condoning what happened. We'd rather go with the Brothers."

"Ask them," Martin said, raising his eyebrows in the direction of the dissidents. "You can't make that decision by yourself."

Knots of activity formed, low voices rose in debate, sank again into conspiratorial discussion.

"You want to be Pan again," Jeanette accused, uncertain.

"Not in a joke," Martin said.

She turned away, and the defectors formed their own knot, which then broke into smaller knots.

Hans stayed away from the activity. He looked longingly at the star sphere, as if trying to find his own answer. Martin decided it would be best for now to leave him by himself, not to associate with Hans at this time; Hans was a sink of influence, an outcast. But that went against Martin's instincts.

He ignored his instincts.

"We nominate Patrick Angelfish!" said David Aurora. Six of the crew stood around Patrick, who looked frightened. Harpal was not one of the six; he stayed close to Anna Gray Wolf.

"We nominate Leo Parsifal," said Umberto Umbra.

Good. Totally off the beaten path, Martin thought.

Jeanette came forward, even less certain now, looking scared. "We nominate Mei-li Wu-Hsiang Gemini."

"I nominate Ariel," Martin said. She looked at him with a frown so intense he interpreted it at first as anger.

"Good," Harpal said softly.

Hans did not look away from the star sphere.

"Vote for new Pan," Kirsten Two Bites called out.

Martin watched the vortices break apart, reform, watched

power and decision move from one group to another, discussion, debate, watched Ariel surrounded by her group, yet still looking very alone. She was not angry. She was terrified. She could not bring herself to refuse.

She felt the power, as well.

The vote was about to be taken when Eye on Sky entered the schoolroom with a snake mother. Paola went to the Brother and spoke with him. Then she pulled herself to Martin.

"Eye on Sky says the *Shrike* has found something important. Should he tell us now? He seems to think it's an emergency."

"Then let's hear it," Martin said. He called for their attention.

Eye on Sky uncoiled, smelling faintly of turpentine and dry grass. "We we have spoken with *Shrike*. Something important found hidden. *Greyhound*'s help is requested."

Ariel appeared greatly relieved.

The remains of Sleep smeared out in an arc that in a few million years would form a ring of asteroids around Leviathan. Already, Leviathan's radiation and particle winds pushed the lighter elements in the arc outward.

Greyhound accelerated to join with *Shrike* at the nearest terminus of this arc, a journey of sixty-two million kilometers.

At ten g's, *Greyhound* would reach *Shrike* in less than three hours. The crews endured the field restraints; the acceleration was not so extreme as to completely inhibit activity.

They had enough time to vote. The nominees spoke briefly; Mei-li withdrew, saying she was much too confused and uncertain to exercise leadership. Martin noted with some satisfaction that Ariel did not withdraw.

Hans watched silently, standing by himself to one side.

The vote was conducted secretly by wand. Martin tallied the results.

"Ariel is Pan," he announced.

She closed her eyes and took a deep breath. "Starting now?" she asked.

"Starting now," Martin affirmed.

"I choose Jeanette Snap Dragon to be my second," she said

The defectors were not prepared for this, and left the school room to talk.

Ariel stood beside Martin, distinctly nervous as the crew congratulated her singly and in groups. "I shouldn't have accepted the nomination," she said to him in a brief free moment. "This is awful. You really have it in for me, don't you?"

"You'll do fine," Martin said.

"Oh, God, I chose Jeanette. Why did I do that?"

"Brings unity," Martin assured her, though he had his doubts.

"Are you going to help me, or just gloat?"

"Both," Martin said.

She squinted one eye and curled her lip. "I deserve it," she said. "Oh, God, I'm an *idiot*."

Shrike sent no more transmissions. Martin thought this might be a small game on the part of the Brothers, and his interest was piqued. Eye on Sky refused to say any more, even with Paola's urging; the Brother smelled strongly of turpentine.

What could possibly compel them to ask for human help? The Brothers were convinced destruction of the Leviathan system had been wrong, or at the very least premature . . .

Martin studied the crew in the schoolroom. He could see no more vortices of power, and wondered if he had hallucinated them. What he saw now was quiescence, waiting. Even Ariel drew no more attention than she might have before she was Pan. She sat talking quietly with Anna Gray Wolf and Martin felt a stab of loneliness; she had needed him, the need had passed. He had not nurtured it very well.

Hans squatted in a lotus before the star sphere, ragged, thin, pale, fingers tapping the floor lightly. His face seemed religious with concentration and something like fear: fear that what the Brothers had found might prove they had acted incorrectly. Fear of responsibility for the deaths of trillions . . .

Trillions of what? Martin asked himself. *Ghosts? Shells? Robots? Deceptions? Real, intelligent beings? Innocents?*

The last possibility was more than he could bring himself to contemplate.

Scouts continued to work through the detritus like little fish swimming through a swirl of sand and mud, sending information by noach to *Greyhound*. *Shrike* no doubt had its own scouts, but the arc was huge, three million kilometers from end to end and several hundred thousand kilometers broad, and the area studied by *Shrike* was still relatively unknown to them.

Giacomo approached Martin and kneeled beside him. Martin looked up; surprised himself by having napped. He glimpsed the star sphere; *Greyhound* was very near *Shrike*. "What is it?" Martin asked.

"We're here. Stonemaker won't talk to any human but you. He's on the noach, and he wants it private."

"Did you tell Ariel?" She was not in the schoolroom.

Giacomo nodded, biting his lower lip. "She told me to get you. Search team doesn't see anything. We don't know what they've got or what they're up to."

A field had wrapped around him automatically while he slept, to restrain him as the acceleration ended. He converted it to a ladder and followed Giacomo to the nose.

Ariel met him outside the nose. She smiled quickly. "The Brothers like you, Martin."

He made a wry face and pushed into the nose.

Even to the naked eye, the destruction of Sleep was impressive. *Greyhound* seemed to hang motionless beside *Shrike* about ten thousand kilometers above the arc of Sleep's corpse, a glittering, mottled span of dust and rubble like a layer of oil and dirt on a pond. Glowing commas of molten stuff haunted the arc. One comma disintegrated before his eyes, a silent leap of puckering orange. Beyond the arc, closer in to Leviathan, two diffuse blotches marked other ruins, like swift strokes of watercolor on wet black paper.

"I'll project the noach here," Thorkild said, refusing to meet his eyes. "You know how to use it. Of course you do." He looked as if he was about to cry. "Martin . . ."

Martin held his finger to his lips, shook his head reassuringly, falsely. He didn't know how long it would take the wounds to heal, but he did not want to deal with Thorkild now.

Eye on Sky slid into the nose as Thorkild departed. "I was told Stonemaker you have stayed sensible," Eye on Sky said. "Do not know others as well."

"Thanks," Martin said. "What's happened?"

Eye on Sky splayed his head cords, very attentive. A noache image of Stonemaker shimmered into solidity before them.

"I we am thankful you survived," Stonemaker said. "You should see what we we have found. Judge with and mark we our opinions." Stonemaker faded and was replaced by a roller-coaster ride through glowing rubble, wisps of hot gas, into a dark void.

"Record of scout sending," Eye on Sky explained, making a scent of sharp cinnamon and warm animal. The smell aroused homesickness, deeper loneliness. *Gauge. He smells a bit like Gauge.*

The void was a great hollow, perhaps ten thousand kilometers wide, cleared somehow in the middle of the arc like a bubble. He was about to ask if it was natural when he spotted a speck at its center, little more than a dust mote in the tarry darkness. The mote glowed green.

Human measurements appeared to the left of the image. The mote, now fist sized and growing rapidly, was about a hundred kilometers in diameter. He could not discern clearly what it was; the ghoulish green spot seemed made of many smaller versions of itself. Enlarged, the mass revealed cluster upon cluster of much smaller needle-like objects, in all manner of arrangements; rolled, bundled, pointing outward in pin-cushion radiants.

Martin's throat shrank around his voice and breath. He coughed, covered his mouth with a fist, tried to control his horror, the excruciating churn of emotions within.

Millions upon millions of needles, each fifty to a hundred meters long. He had grown up with their design, their measure; the moms had displayed them again and again to the children in training.

"We our scouts have found forty-one of these collections," Stonemaker said. "They waited within Sleep. All we we have examined appear to be recent manufacture, not old artifacts."

Wrapped in protective fields like frog eggs in gelatin cases, survivors of Sleep's destruction, the needles were not thousands of years old, not artifacts of a bygone and indiscreet age.

They were new. Waiting.

"Do you agree with we our suspecting?"

"Yes," Martin croaked, and coughed again. "Oh, God, yes."

"We we are hoping these are the last, that no more have escaped to find and destroy other worlds."

Martin nodded, speechless with fury and a high, horrid sadness.

"Should we we finish the Job?" Stonemaker asked.

Perspectives

One / Hans

Today we finished the Job. The Brothers asked for the honor of destroying the needles, and Ariel granted their request. The moms and snake mothers think the Job is done, but they will station watchers here, just to be sure.

I have kept this face for so long it has become natural, but when I learned that I was not wrong, I cried in front of them, and no one came to me, no one put their arms around me. So be it.

I held them together. The Killers were still here. Still shitting us all; I saw it.

I think they'll take me in again, but I don't know how long it will be. They'll need me.

I don't think anybody really cares about others only about themselves. That's true of me too I suppose. But I'm glad to see us finally getting our reward, all of us. I can put up with being alone for a while.

I will build a shrine to those who died. When we get there. I'll do it with my bare hands.

Two / Ariel

Donna Emerald Sea brought out the gowns today. They are very pretty but I don't think I can wear one; I don't like dresses and they don't like me.

I decided against investigating Hans. Made up my mind this morning after talking with Martin. Martin feels real sympathy for Hans. I don't know why. Hans is perhaps the only real shithead on this boat.

I am sorry the Brothers will not be going with us, but at least all the Lost Boys and Wendys are sticking together. We saw it through, and that's something to be proud of. We didn't end up like the death ship, but almost. Boy it was close.

Today we left Leviathan. The ship is big again and well stocked with fuel. All the crew gathered in the schoolroom and we had a naming ceremony. It was special. We christened the ship Dawn Treader II. *Someone suggested* Mayflower *but that caused a lot of argument about colonialism and other sensitive stuff, religion and such, so I stepped in and suggested we stick with what we had. Really asserted myself. I'm not sure I like doing that sort of thing but I can do it at least.*

I feel funny about Martin. He put me off for so long and now he looks lost. Most of us are lost, or at a loss might be more accurate.

The Job is done and we're free to go where we please. The moms will take us there, but who knows how long we'll have to look? How far we'll travel? More centuries, I guess. Anyway, about Martin: I am going to try it one more time. He is such a funny fellow.

Martin made up a name and started writing under it, things I guess he didn't believe he could write himself. He made up Theodore Dawn and then he made up that Theodore had committed suicide. He said Theodore was his balance and atonement.

For a while I thought that Theodore was the sign of something really crazy. But Martin knew what we'd end up doing, what we would become when we did the Job. Theodore might have been his first attempt to make armor, to . . . what? I don't know.

A way of coping. Theodore kept him human, I guess.

We've all been a little crazy, each in our own way.

I love Martin, as much as I can love anybody. Maybe it will work. I'll try.

Three / Theodore

Well now that you're rid of me I can write down my reactions and then fade away, all right? I think we did pretty well, for humans. I think you did damned well, and learned a lot. You're still not as sharp as I am, but then, what the hell, I killed myself, didn't I? You are a survivor. You care. When we get to our

*home, you'll do well, and you'll keep the balance, because that's
what you're good at.*

*It is time to be whole again, to forget as much as we can, to
take us where we have to go to become adult human beings.*

Know thyself. You are little and clumsy and need love.

Four / Martin

*Today I laddered down the aft wormspace and found a bunch of
Lost Boys and Wendys playing with wet wadded clothes. Brought
back such memories. I spent the rest of the day in a kind of haze,
watching videos from the Ark, watching Mother and Father,
wondering if I measured up to them. But I now realize they can't
judge me, or us.*

*We have found a candidate star. It's about a thousand light
years away. With our remotes out as far as they'll go—fifty
billion klicks on each side now!—we can see two worlds that
look very pretty, and Anna and Giacomo and Jennifer say we
can live there.*

*The worlds are silent, but that doesn't mean they're not inhab-
ited. We'll take the risk, and just go on to somewhere else if they
are.* That is how we differ.

*These worlds are farther away than the Sun and Mars and
Venus. But we can't go back. We don't know what our people
are like now, how much they've changed. I would hate to go all
that way to encounter disembodied intelligences, like staircase
gods.*

*Besides, we're war dogs. David Aurora did a study to show
that what we knew and what we've become would disrupt any
human society we might find. The crew agreed. Classic Catch-
22.*

*Most of the crew thinks finding the needles gets us off the
hook. Nobody's debating the matter, though. We're all very
sensitive about this. This is the one issue that could still kill us
in the years ahead.*

I believe Frog and Salamander and the others did not know.
DID NOT KNOW.

Ah, Christ, I don't want to think about it but I can't avoid it in my dreams.

Our evil is far less than theirs, but what does that mean? What did we do, and who or what has been served?

For me, nothing is resolved. I must not look again at the records sent from Sleep.

In time I might have to believe as Hans does, that it was all a sham.

I try to imagine the depths of viciousness, of evil, of the Killers, that they would hide behind their own children. I cannot.

I had hoped that with the end of the Job there would be relief from pain, and perhaps there will be, but only in deep time.

The moms did not train us for this.

We left Leviathan behind two tendays ago. Scouts still fly through the debris, searching, but we'll have no more to do with it. We accelerate at one g, the memory of Earth in our flesh still making that most comfortable. Twenty years will pass for the ship, even at near-c; long enough that the moms will put us in cold sleep. We'll have about a year to think and heal.

Dyads are forming again, stable ones.

Ariel is coming to visit later. She's a very good Pan, better than I was.

Paola is seeing Hans. Can you believe it?

I wrote the last message from Theodore. Then I removed it from ship's memory. I can take it now, the cruelty, the fear, the responsibility. I think I can.

Five / Dawn Treader II

I will take them to their chosen worlds and assist them in adapting to the new environments.

I have no instructions what to do with the fruits of our combined efforts. Having no knowledge of how other ships have dealt with intellectual collaborations with their crews, or how they have dealt with the inevitable transfer of characteristics, I can see no other option.

When the humans are settled, I will destroy myself.

I am not what I was when I was made. This qualifies me as a mutation, and mutations are forbidden among robot vehicles capable of self-replication. That is the Law.

I watch over them still, and never reveal this aspect. They would not be comfortable with my judgment. They would ask questions I can't answer. They are small, they are incredibly dangerous, but they will survive. They can absorb much pain and growth.

They or their descendants will witness the grand coming together, and they will enrich the whole.

I would like to see that, but I will not.

Six / Eye on Sky

(Smells of cinnamon, fresh baked bread, new cut grass, sea air.)

We we have seen we our world, and travel now in strong braid, resolute.

There is shame in victory, and much to think about, and that is enough until we we arrive and are young and fertile again.

Alderwood Manor, Washington
August 30, 1991